Carol Ericson is a bestsell[...] more than forty books. Sh[...] true-crime stories, a love of film noir and a weakness for reality TV, all of which fuel her imagination to create her own tales of murder, mayhem and mystery. To find out more about Carol and her current projects, please visit her website at carolericson.com, 'where romance flirts with danger.'

Charlene Parris has been reading books for as long as she can remember and romance stories since high school, after discovering her mother's cache of romance books. She loves smart, sharp-witted, independent heroines; strong heroes who respect them; and, of course, happy endings. Charlene writes for the Mills & Boon Heroes series because she loves adding twists and turns to her stories. When she's not writing, Charlene is working her full-time job. And for fun, she reads, walks and is learning yoga.

Also by Carol Ericson

A Discovery Bay Novel
Misty Hollow Massacre
Point of Disappearance
Captured at the Cove
What Lies Below

The Lost Girls
Canyon Crime Scene
Lakeside Mystery
Dockside Danger
Malice at the Marina

Also by Charlene Parris

The Night Guardians
Watchers of the Night
Defender After Dark

Discover more at millsandboon.co.uk

THE CREEKSIDE MURDER

CAROL ERICSON

COLTON'S VOW

CHARLENE PARRIS

MILLS & BOON

All rights reserved including the right of reproduction in whole or in part in any form. This edition is published by arrangement with Harlequin Enterprises ULC.

This is a work of fiction. Names, characters, places, locations and incidents are purely fictional and bear no relationship to any real life individuals, living or dead, or to any actual places, business establishments, locations, events or incidents. Any resemblance is entirely coincidental.

This book is sold subject to the condition that it shall not, by way of trade or otherwise, be lent, resold, hired out or otherwise circulated without the prior consent of the publisher in any form of binding or cover other than that in which it is published and without a similar condition including this condition being imposed on the subsequent purchaser.

® and ™ are trademarks owned and used by the trademark owner and/or its licensee. Trademarks marked with ® are registered with the United Kingdom Patent Office and/or the Office for Harmonisation in the Internal Market and in other countries.

First Published in Great Britain 2025
by Mills & Boon, an imprint of HarperCollins*Publishers* Ltd
1 London Bridge Street, London, SE1 9GF

www.harpercollins.co.uk

HarperCollins*Publishers*
Macken House, 39/40 Mayor Street Upper,
Dublin 1, D01 C9W8, Ireland

The Creekside Murder © 2025 Carol Ericson
Colton's Vow © 2025 Harlequin Enterprises ULC

Special thanks and acknowledgment are given to Charlene Parris for her contribution to *The Coltons of Arizona* series.

ISBN: 978-0-263-39712-3

0525

This book contains FSC™ certified paper and other controlled sources to ensure responsible forest management.

For more information visit: www.harpercollins.co.uk/green

Printed and Bound in the UK using 100% Renewable Electricity at CPI Group (UK) Ltd, Croydon, CR0 4YY

THE CREEKSIDE MURDER

CAROL ERICSON

Chapter One

Jessica had followed the trail to Tiffany's dead body hundreds of times in her mind. She hadn't expected the area to look so different now. She dug her hiking boots into the mushy ground to survey her position. The forest seemed to close in on her, suffocating her, warning her. She was done heeding warnings.

Huffing out a breath, she plowed ahead. She pushed aside the bushy shrub in front of her, tripping over its twisted trunk. She grabbed a handful of leaves to steady herself, their sharp edges scratching her palm. As she glanced down at the red lines crisscrossing her skin, she noticed the mulch of the forest floor giving way to dirt and pebbles.

She closed her eyes and cocked her head. Barely discernible beneath the whoosh of the breeze through the trees and the chattering birds, she detected the sound of gurgling water. Her lids flew open as her legs propelled her forward, her boots crunching over the gritty path that would take her to the water's edge—the place where a killer had dumped her sister's lifeless form ten years ago.

She broke through the trees a few feet before a babbling creek scurried over slick rocks and detoured around branches clawing their way out of the water—one shaped like an arm positioned to drag unsuspecting hikers into the water. Panting, she dropped to her knees and trailed her fingers in the icy stream until her fingertips turned white with the cold.

Her head dipped to her chest and the tears that had blurred her vision, threatening to overcome her on the trail, rolled down her cheeks and slid from her chin into the swirling water. The current carried them away but couldn't rid her of the pain lodged in her heart. She'd cried in this spot before…cried and raged and pounded the earth over the loss of her older sister, the sister who'd protected her in foster care.

They'd had different fathers—losers who'd abandoned Tammy, their mother, and them, without a backward glance or a penny for support. Tammy hardly batted an eye when they'd left. She just moved on to the next bum, who left her with a baby boy months before Tammy's death from an overdose.

When Tammy died, none of her family was interested in taking in her hodgepodge of kids, so they all went to foster care…except their brother. Just a baby, he'd been snapped up by some childless couple, eager to give him a great life.

He'd been the lucky one.

But Jessica'd been lucky to have Tiffany as her sister—until someone ended Tiffany's life. Jessica's gut told her that Tiffany's killer still roamed free and clear, but law enforcement disagreed.

Avery Plank sat in the Washington State Penitentiary for murdering a dozen women, including Tiffany. Although he'd never been convicted of her sister's murder, he'd confessed—adding it to his résumé while the cops closed the case and moved on. But Jessica refused to move on.

Now Morgan Flemming wouldn't let her move on.

The bushes rustled behind her, and Jessica twisted her body around to eye the tree line, the pebbles on the ground digging into her knees. She peered at the shivering branches and held her breath as a few birds winged it skyward.

She let it out on one word. "Hello?"

Her voice sounded small amid the unrelenting nature that pressed her on all sides. She cleared her throat and pushed to her feet, tugging on her down vest. "Anyone there?"

A twig snapped. Her heart pounded. She clapped a hand against the slick material covering her chest and licked her lips as her gaze darted back and forth across the wall of green.

Several seconds of silence later, she emitted a puff of air from her lips. Creatures big and small ruled the forest and typically stayed out of sight, especially during the daytime hours. She had nothing to fear from the animal variety. The human species was a different matter.

She yanked a couple of flowers from the red dogwood blooming creek side and tossed them into the water. She blew a kiss as the petals drifted away on the current.

Shoving her hands in the pockets of her vest, she tromped downstream, her boots leaving divots in the moist earth. She didn't have far to walk, and the creek led to her next destination.

Fifteen minutes later, she stumbled to a stop. A dirty piece of yellow tape fluttered from the end of a branch jutting into her path. She grabbed it and twirled it around her fisted hand as she scanned the memorial—a heap of teddy bears, bouquets of flowers, green felt pennants printed with the university's name, gutted candles, and cards, soaked through with moisture, the sentiments printed inside blurry and forgotten.

The outpouring for Tiffany hadn't been quite so effusive. After all, Tiffany hadn't been a student at the university. She'd worked in the cafeteria, a recovering junkie and sex worker…at least according to the police, but Jessica knew better. Her sister suffered from addictions, but she'd never been a sex worker.

Jessica sighed and released the yellow tape. It unraveled from her hand, leaving striped indentations. She ducked under another branch and picked her way over the pebbled shore to the shrine that had grown on the spot where a pair of hikers had discovered Morgan Flemming's body.

She crouched down and ran a finger over the head of a purple teddy bear, dislodging the crusted dirt from its fur. She chucked a couple bunches of motley flowers into the flowing water and righted a few candles. Most of the cards could be tossed, but maybe someone was saving them for the family. Whether the words could be read didn't really matter. The thought counted.

She stacked the cards and placed a candle on top of the pile. As she reached for the final card, it flipped open and the black scrawl inside caught her eye. Likely a newer card or protected from the elements by another offering, its letters weren't smudged.

As she flattened the card on her knee, her gaze skimming the words, icy fingers squeezed the back of her neck.

PROFESSOR FINN KARLSSON entered the last grade on his laptop and snapped the lid closed. He grabbed his briefcase and coffee and locked the door to his office behind him. He had less than two minutes to make it to class, but dread slowed his pace, filling his shoes with lead.

He didn't want to spend another class discussing the murder of Morgan Flemming, but his criminal justice students hadn't wanted to talk about anything else since her body was discovered by the side of the creek a few weeks ago. He'd planned to introduce a new unit today, and he didn't want his students to sidetrack him again. Finn didn't have time to spend on the Morgan Flemming case. He had a prescribed amount of material to cover in a limited amount of time for the semester—at least that's what he told himself.

A minute later, as he walked through the side door of the lecture hall, he glanced at the seats full of eager students. This would've been his dream at any other time in the semester.

He plugged in his laptop and navigated to the slides for today—how the Constitution affected laws. Probably the last thing his students wanted to discuss.

Reaching behind him, he dimmed the lights in the room and stepped out from behind the lectern, gripping the microphone. He flicked it on and cleared his throat. "If you checked the syllabus, you know we're going to delve into the Constitution today and how it affects criminal justice. We'll start with the Sixth Amendment, but we'll cover the Fourth, Fifth, and Eighth before we're done."

He detected a few groans among the clicks and taps as the students readied their laptops and notebooks for class. A few students even took notes on their phones. Whatever worked.

Finn'd received high marks from students on the professor rating sites for keeping his classes lively and interesting, and he spent the next hour working extra hard to uphold his reputation. He'd managed to engage his students with the subject matter, but he always took questions at the end of the lecture. If he stopped now, they'd get suspicious.

He ended the slideshow and flooded the lecture hall with light. "Questions about the material we just covered?"

They managed to get through two questions about the Sixth Amendment, then the floodgates opened with the third question.

"Any news on Morgan's murder, Professor Karlsson?"

Everyone in the class started talking at once until he held up his hand. "I don't know any more than you all do, which means the police don't even have a person of interest yet. I want to remind you to be careful. Don't go out alone at night. Travel in packs and stay away from the forest."

He took a few more questions about the case that he couldn't answer, and then said, "One last question."

He paused for several seconds, waiting for the floor mic to make its way to the next and final student.

A woman cleared her throat. "Do you think Morgan Flemming's murder is connected to the murder of Tiffany Hunt ten years ago?"

A shot of adrenaline spiked through his system, and he jumped from the desk where he'd settled. "No! That's not possible. The Creekside Killer, Avery Plank, murdered Tiffany Hunt. He confessed."

The woman started to ask another question, but he cut her off. "That's it for today. Read chapters five through seven and email me a response to one of the amendments before class next week. It can be a set of questions or an analysis."

Finn's hand had a slight tremble as he turned his back on the class and shoved some folders into his briefcase. He hadn't even discussed the Tiffany Hunt case in class yet. A lot of these students didn't even know about the murder, although most were familiar with the serial killer Avery

Plank. Someone had been reading up on the university's crime stats.

"You didn't let me finish my question."

He spun around at the sound of the voice behind him, and he peered over the edge of the stage at the woman with one booted foot planted on the first step. From above, the wavy blond hair subdued into a ponytail lit a spark of recognition in his chest. When she tipped her head back and he met those luminous hazel eyes, he almost dropped his computer.

He took a deep breath, not wanting her to see that she'd rattled him. Lifting his shoulders, he slid his laptop into the bag on the desk. "We were running out of time, and there's not much more to discuss on the subject."

She climbed the remaining steps to the stage and squared off in front of him. "Oh, there's a lot more to discuss, Professor Karlsson… Deputy Karlsson, badge number 2852."

He narrowed his eyes as a muscle twitched at the corner of his mouth. "What are you doing back in school, Jessica? Looking to ruin more careers?"

"C'mon, this suits you so much better." She waved a hand at him. "You look good in civilian clothes, although you looked pretty good in that uniform, too."

His jaw tightened. "You don't need to resort to your fake flattery now. I have nothing to do with the Morgan Flemming case. I'm guessing you're here to stick your nose into the latest homicide on campus?"

"You make my interest in her murder sound so—" she rolled her eyes to the ceiling "—trivial."

"There's never anything trivial about any murder." He hoisted the satchel over his shoulder and ran a hand through his hair.

"I know that better than anyone." She caught her bottom lip between her teeth. "I found something at the crime scene."

About to brush past her, he tripped to a stop. "You were at the crime scene?"

"It's not off-limits anymore. Tape is down." She flicked her ponytail over her shoulder, and the golden waves danced and caught the light. "That's not the point. Did you hear what I said? I found something at the crime scene."

"Look, I know you're some hotshot forensic scientist now, but I'm pretty sure the deputies already went over that scene and didn't miss a thing."

Her eyes widened, and she tilted her head. "Really?"

He swallowed and jogged down the steps of the stage past her. Damn. How pathetic had he just made himself look by admitting he'd followed her career? He mumbled, "I've seen your name on a few local cases."

She snorted. "I meant really, are you so sure they didn't miss anything."

"If you found something at the scene, you'd better turn it over to the sheriff's department." He turned his back on her "You're a professional now, not a college student interfering in a case and causing trouble."

"Ah, Professor Karlsson?" One of his older students popped up from a seat in the front row. Had he heard the embarrassing exchange between him and Jessica?

"Mr. Webb, right?"

"Dermott Webb." The student's gaze traveled between him and Jessica, still on the stage. "Can I ask you a quick question about the assignment?"

"Of course." Finn tried to plaster a pleasant smile on his face.

"If we do some additional reading on the subject, can we

use that material for our response instead of the textbook?" Webb held up his hand as if expecting him to deny the request. "I'd cite the reference material, of course."

"Yeah, yeah. That's fine if it sticks with the topic." Now he knew why he remembered this particular student. Finn always had one or two know-it-alls in a class, trying to impress or brownnose. Dermott Webb would probably make a good, by-the-book cop. The kind that would have the brass salivating.

"Thank you, Professor Karlsson. I'd like to talk with you further about this book—" his gaze darted toward Jessica again, now crossing her arms and tapping the toe of her boot "—I-I mean, during your office hours."

"Looking forward to hearing about it, Mr. Webb." Finn shifted slightly, showing Webb his shoulder in a broad hint.

"I'll see you in your office, then." Webb lifted his hand and loped from the lecture hall, excitement quickening his steps.

Raising her eyebrows, Jessica said, "Don't like him much, do you?"

"You can see my expression from the stage? The lights aren't even all the way up."

"No, I couldn't make out your face, but I know that tone of voice. You used it with me, once..."

"Once I found out you were manipulating me?" He rolled his shoulders. He shouldn't let her get under his skin. That way lay danger. "Don't you have some evidence to turn over to the sheriff's department?"

"Who said I'm not giving it to law enforcement? Hell, I *am* law enforcement." She bypassed the steps and jumped off the edge of the stage, landing in front of him, her hiking boots echoing in the empty hall. "But I'm willing to show it to you first...if you're interested."

He sucked in a quick breath. "Why the offer?"

"Because I have something to prove to you." She hooked a thumb in the belt loop of her slouchy jeans. "Buy you a drink?"

"It's the least you owe me, and I admit I'm curious." He patted the side of his bag. "Let me drop this at my office first, and I'll meet you at the Porch. I should be safe from my students there, even at this hour."

"Even the eager Mr. Webb?" She flicked her fingers in the air. "I know where the Porch is. I'll head over there now, Professor."

She made a beeline for the side door of the lecture hall, her blond ponytail swinging behind her, looking every bit the college student.

Finn exited through the back door, crossed the north campus quad and breathed a sigh of relief when he rounded the corner to an empty hallway. He didn't have office hours right now, but that didn't stop desperate students from dropping by to find out how they could turn in a late assignment or pick up some extra credit for a poor test score.

He unlocked his door and swung his bag onto the visitor chair opposite his desk. Then he locked up and strode across campus to exit on the north side, onto the bustling tree-lined street that boasted rows of bars and cheap eats, catering to the student crowd.

Finn veered off the street where it dead-ended at the path along the river and made his way to the more refined area of town that satisfied the palates and sensibilities of the parents who dropped their kids off—not expecting them to get murdered.

By the time he pushed through the front door of the Porch, Jessica had secured a table by the window. She wiggled her fingers in the air to draw his attention—as if he could ever miss Jessica Eller. As he approached the table, he pointed at the bar, and she shook her head.

He pulled out a chair and joined her. "Did you order already?"

"There's a waitress circulating. I told her to come back when my date got here."

He raised one eyebrow at her. "This isn't a date."

"Nobody has to know our business." She waved at the circulating waitress, and the woman, thank God not one of his students, ambled to their table.

The waitress tapped one elaborately painted nail on the Formica. "Did you see the happy hour menu?"

Finn picked up the plastic card and ran a finger down the list of beers. "I'll have the local IPA."

Jessica answered. "House white for me and some water, please."

Finn watched the waitress approach the bar and then planted his elbows on the table. "What did the cops and your CSI coworkers miss?"

Jessica plucked her cocktail napkin from the table and rummaged in the big bag on the seat beside her. Her hand emerged with a greeting card pinched between two fingers, covered by the napkin. She dropped it onto the table in front of him. "I found this at Morgan's memorial site, where her body was discovered."

He eyed the card, adorned with purple and yellow flowers, the word "condolences" in fancy gold script across the front. He grabbed a knife and flicked open the card.

"Read it," Jessica demanded.

He cleared his throat and read aloud. "Something old, something dead, something stolen, something red. So sorry you had to join the club, Morgan. Love, Tiffany H."

Chapter Two

When the last word left Finn's lips, Jessica clapped both hands over her mouth, the shock of hearing her sister's name being connected to Morgan's murder hitting her square in the chest all over again. She hadn't imagined the words that had danced before her eyes out there in the woods.

Two lines formed between Finn's eyebrows as he pinned the open card to the table with the knife. "Were the other cards there as pristine as this one?"

She eked out a breath between her lips. He'd realized the card's importance instead of dismissing it. "No. The damp and dew had gotten to the other cards. When did the memorial form?"

"When the department removed the crime scene tape, about four days ago. This—" he nudged the card with the knife "—hasn't been there that long."

"Someone left it recently, maybe even this morning." Jessica hunched her shoulders against the shiver weaving up her spine. She could've just missed the guy out there.

She flinched when the waitress appeared with their drinks. Jessica pinched the stem of the glass between her fingers and raised it to her lips as Finn waved off the waitress's offer to pour his beer into a glass.

Closing her eyes, she sipped the wine, the crisp, bright flavor at odds with the subject between them. "What do you think?"

Finn took his time, studying the label on his bottle before taking a long drink. "It could be a tasteless joke."

"What about that rhyme? What does that all mean? Something stolen? Red?"

"No clue." He lifted his shoulders to his ears.

"D-do people around here still remember Tiffany's murder?" Jessica had come to the realization years ago that other people had moved on from her sister's homicide, even Ashley King and Denny Phelps, Tiffany's best friend and boyfriend at the time. She didn't have that luxury.

"Sure they do." Finn took another pull from his beer. "It's not like the campus has a murder every year, but they remember her as one of Avery Plank's victims."

"But join the club? Not Plank's club." She poked at the card with her fork. "Plank is in prison. He didn't kill Morgan, so what club is this?"

"The murder club. You're overthinking it, Jessica. Yeah, it's creepy, it's crude and rude, but it doesn't mean anything."

"You're not a cop anymore, Finn. You've lost the instinct." She swirled her wine in her glass.

"According to you, I never had that instinct."

Her gaze flew to his face as her cheeks turned pink. "I was just striking out. You were the one who found Tiffany's body, so I always connected you to the case. When the detectives wouldn't listen to me, I turned my wrath on you."

"Is that what you were doing?" He raised one eyebrow. "'Cuz I remember it differently. You hounded me, you played me, you stole from me, you compromised your own sister's case."

Burying her chin in her palm, she studied him as he took another sip of his beer. "I didn't compromise the case. Law enforcement had tunnel vision for Avery Plank."

"I don't know what to tell you." He spread his hands, a little calloused for an academic. "Plank confessed."

She flicked her fingers in the air. "Serial killers always exaggerate their numbers. You know that. What if Plank was lying? What if my sister's killer is still active…and he just hit again?"

"Ten years is a long time between kills," he said.

"Could be any number of reasons for that." She hunched forward, tucking a lock of hair behind her ear. "This could be a sick joke, but why bring Tiffany's name up at all?"

Finn rasped his knuckles across the scruff on his strong jaw, and Jessica glanced down at her wine. Ten years was also a long time between conversations with Finn Karlsson. Back when Tiffany was murdered, Jessica'd had a hard time separating her rage and grief from her insane attraction to the young cop who'd found her sister's body.

She hadn't figured out if she'd been so angry with him because he refused to believe her theories about her sister's case or because he refused to act on the electricity that sizzled between them.

Finn had gotten even more attractive over the years—that boyish uncertainty replaced with a manly confidence—but did the spark still exist?

She raised her eyes to his, and that blue intensity sparked by interest and passion and excitement still kindled, making her insides flutter. Yep. Still there.

"What are you thinking?" She clutched her wineglass,

holding her breath. She knew she'd been right to bring this card to Finn.

He blinked, those stubby dark lashes a striking contrast to his light eyes. "Who says I'm thinking anything at all?"

"You look like you're about to pounce on something."

Shrugging, he ran his thumbnail through the foil label on his bottle, dashing her hopes. "What brings you out to Fairwood? Are you really working Morgan's case, or are you here to thrash yourself some more over your sister's death?"

"I didn't…" Jessica scooped in a deep breath and puffed it out through puckered lips. "The case came to our crime lab in Marysville. Seattle is swamped, so we're processing the bulk of the evidence, especially as there's no firearm involved or prints—that we know of yet."

"You don't do prints in Marysville?"

He cocked his head, that light in his eyes signaling his attention and sincerity. Maybe that's why she'd homed in on him ten years ago as the go-to guy for her wild theories. He'd actually listened to her ranting. Of course, that's what had gotten him in trouble.

"No prints in Marysville. DNA and materials analysis only." She thumped her chest with her palm. "That's me."

"You do materials analysis for the forensics lab?" He nodded. "That makes total sense. You could find a chip of paint on a rock of the same color."

"Or—" she used her napkin to slide the condolence card into an envelope "—a creepy card at a memorial site."

"How much material evidence was collected at the scene of Morgan's murder?"

She put a finger to her lips. "I'm not supposed to reveal that information. I haven't even gotten a look at it yet, anyway. It's already been collected at the sheriff's station."

"You'll get a list of it, though, right? Maybe I should steal it from you?" Finn sat back and crossed his arms. "Turnabout is fair play."

She dragged her gaze away from his broad shoulders. Had he gotten that buff carrying around books?

"Look, my little speech before? That was meant to be an apology." She held up her hands. "I know it's a little late and I know I ruined your career, but I was running on pure emotion and…"

He rapped on the table, and she snapped her mouth shut. "You did not ruin my career. Straight police work was never a good fit for me. I've always had a problem following orders, sort of like you."

"You think I'm going rogue investigating outside the parameters of my job?" She lifted her shoulders. "Not my fault the original crime scene investigators missed some material evidence."

"Even you agree that card was most likely left at the scene after the fact. They didn't miss it."

"Which actually proves my point—I'm not out of bounds here. Anyone could've found that card. It just happened to be me." She tilted her glass to her lips, eyeing Finn over the rim as he folded his hands around his bottle, the label in shreds. "What's wrong?"

"I'm just thinking what a coincidence it is—you're the one who finds the card with the reference to your sister."

"And?" She twirled her finger in the air. "What are you driving at?"

"Haven't you gotten to the point in your law enforcement career where you've learned nothing is a coincidence?"

Jessica's jaw dropped. "Do you think I planted this to… to…get attention? Reopen my sister's case?"

"Whoa, slow down with the assumptions." He formed a cross with his two index fingers. "Did anyone know you were coming out here to have a look around the crime scene?"

She swallowed. Took a sip of wine and swallowed again. "My coworkers know I'm here."

"Would it be hard for an outsider to figure it out? Do you post on social media, stuff like that?"

"I rarely use social media and definitely wouldn't broadcast my work schedule or location for everyone to see." She pinged her fingernail against her almost-empty wineglass. "You're suggesting that someone left it for me, specifically."

Tapping the side of his head, he said, "Don't tell me that steel-trap mind of yours didn't suspect that when you found it."

A breath whispered across the back of her neck, and Jessica pressed a hand against her heart pounding in her chest. She *had* thought that.

"So, it crossed your mind."

She gulped down the last sip of wine. "It did. Why would Morgan's killer want to tease me like this if he weren't also connected to Tiffany's death?"

"Hang on." Finn splayed his hands on the table, thumbs touching. "We don't know that it was Morgan's killer who left the card, and even if it was her killer who left it, that still doesn't mean he had anything to do with Tiffany's murder. He could be playing games with you, with the cops."

"Creepy either way." She dragged her purse into her lap and shoved her hand inside to grab her wallet. "I'm going back there."

"Wait. What?" Finn's blue eyes widened. "Now?"

"Maybe he knows I took the card. Maybe he's still hanging around there. Maybe he left another clue."

"You think you're going to catch him in the act?" He tossed a few bills on the table before she could open her wallet. "I know I mentioned coincidence, but that's not gonna happen."

Leveling a finger at him, she asked, "Don't you want to see where I found it?"

"You're inviting me to come along?"

"Would be good to get a cop's…an ex-cop's perspective on that altar to Morgan."

"You just told me I'd lost my cop's instincts."

"That sort of thing never goes away, does it? You had it back then, that's how you found Tiffany, and you still have it." She dropped her wallet back into her purse. "Let's go."

They headed for Finn's vehicle, which enjoyed a parking place on campus. As they approached the mud-splashed Jeep, Jessica said, "I see you still enjoy the outdoors."

"Took a trip this past weekend. Didn't have time to clean it up before class." He opened the passenger door for her. "Don't mind the dog hair. Bodhi rides shotgun."

He slammed the door, and she brushed a little light-colored fur from the seat. If his dog rode shotgun, that probably meant he didn't have a wife—not that she hadn't already surreptitiously checked out his left hand.

He slid behind the wheel and started the engine. "I'm not sure what you expect to find out there."

"Can't tell you, but after I found the card, I got out of there. I felt like I was being watched, didn't give myself a chance to look at the other items." She clasped her hands between her knees. "Maybe I meant to take you back there with me all along."

"Yeah, barging into my lecture hall shooting questions at me is the way to do it."

"Bought you a beer, didn't I?"

"I paid for those drinks."

"Oh, yeah. Next round's on me."

He gave her a glance from the side of his eye, but his lip quirked upward. Maybe he liked that idea.

They stopped talking, each immersed in their own thoughts, as Finn drove the short distance to the crime scene—Morgan's crime scene. Earlier, Jessica had parked near her sister's murder site and followed the river on foot to Morgan's. This time, they traversed the trail to Morgan's memorial in about ten minutes.

The same eerie feeling permeated the air, even with Finn tromping on the trail behind her. The forest seemed to be holding its breath, the critters silent and watchful.

The sound of the gurgling river broke the stillness, and Jessica quickened her pace. Daylight still filtered through the tops of the trees, but the long shadows signaled the setting of the sun. She didn't want to be there in the dark—Finn or no Finn.

She almost tripped into the clearing, and Finn put a hand on her hip. "You okay?"

"Maybe we should've waited until morning for this expedition." She rubbed the goose bumps on her arms, pretty sure they'd popped up because of the location and not Finn's touch.

"Let's make this quick." He flung an arm out toward the pile of teddy bears and flowers. "You have a look at the cards again, and I'll take some pictures with my phone that you can study later."

"The stuff looks like it's been moved around since this afternoon." Jessica ran her tongue around her dry mouth.

"How can you tell?" Finn marched toward the memorial, pulling his phone from his pocket.

She followed him, dragging her feet. As she crouched next to the mound of memorial items left with the best of intentions, she reached for the cards she'd stacked earlier.

She glimpsed a black button eye from the depths of the pile, and her hands froze. With trembling fingers, she nudged aside the stuffed animals and candles to reveal the doll, staring at her from the center of the heap with its single eye.

Falling back in the dirt, she let out a piercing cry.

"What's wrong?" Finn swung around.

"That doll." She pointed a finger at the dirty rag doll with yellow braids and a red-checked blouse.

"Kind of odd, but what's the problem? Maybe Morgan had a thing for rag dolls." He cocked his head and dropped to his knees beside her. "You're really spooked."

She dragged her gaze away from the horrifying sight and clutched Finn's arm. "You don't understand. That's *my* doll. My childhood doll."

Chapter Three

"Wait." Finn jabbed his finger in the direction of the rag doll. "You're saying that's a doll you had when you were a kid? Like, that was the actual doll you owned?"

Jessica's grip on his arm tightened, and her fingernails dug into his skin through his shirt. "I-I don't know. I don't understand."

"Maybe it just looks like the same doll." Using a stick, Finn nudged the other items out of the way and slid the doll's clothing to lift it from the pile. As it swung in the air, pigtails flying, Jessica pressed a hand over her mouth.

He dropped the doll at their feet, and Jessica shifted away from it as if it would bite her with its smiling red mouth. "Is it the same *type* of doll you had as a child?"

His mind refused to entertain the thought that this was Jessica's doll. This place had her all rattled—not that he could blame her.

She sniffed. "It's not the same doll. Mine was dirty. This one is brand-new, but look."

He peered over her shoulder as she pointed a shaky finger at the missing button on the doll's face.

He said, "Yeah, not brand-new."

"It's the button, Finn. My doll was missing the same button eye. Somebody placed this doll, a replica of the only doll I had as a child, on Morgan's memorial. Why? How?"

Squeezing his eyes closed and pinching the bridge of his nose, Finn asked, "Who would even know about this doll?"

"Tiffany…and maybe a few of her friends." Jessica clasped a hand around the long column of her throat, one tear sparkling on the ends of her lashes. "When I went away to college in Oregon and Tiffany got the job here, I gave her my doll. I didn't want to leave her once she got her life on track, but she insisted I take the scholarship. So maybe it is the same doll…the doll I gave to Tiffany."

"Okay, okay. That makes some sense." Finn released a noisy breath. "Maybe Morgan's murder, because of the location so close to Tiffany's, triggered one of Tiffany's friends and she put the doll here, thinking it was Tiffany's doll. Maybe this same person left the card."

Jessica pulled her plump lower lip between her teeth. "I suppose that could've happened. But…"

"But what?" Finn held his breath, preparing himself for Jessica's next outlandish proposal.

"What if Tiffany's killer took the doll at the time of her murder and planted it here?" Using the stick, Jessica picked up the doll.

"There was never any evidence that Tiffany's killer had been inside her place—no fingerprints there, no DNA, no signs of a struggle or break-in. He ambushed her by the side of the creek and used a garrote to strangle her, one we never found."

"Morgan was strangled, too."

"Just like every other victim of the Creekside Killer. Maybe what we have with Morgan is a copycat." He prodded the doll with his fingertip. "Are you taking this with you?

You know, even though you're bagging this stuff, you've ruined the chain of custody. An attorney would destroy this evidence in court."

"Thanks for telling me my job. I'm still taking it in, along with that card. This is personal." She scooped up the doll by its midsection, squeezing the soft material with her hand. "I'm going to look up Ashley and Denny, Tiffany's friends, and find out what they know about this doll."

"Did you look for it when—" Finn coughed "—when you came to collect Tiffany's property?"

"I'd forgotten about it. Tiffany didn't have many possessions, nothing of monetary value. I kept a few pieces of her cheap costume jewelry, just for sentimental reasons, but I'd forgotten I gave her the doll. This is all so creepy." Jessica pushed to her feet, brushing the dirt from her jeans, and tilted her head back to examine the trees that ringed the site. "I wonder if it would be worth it at this point to set up cameras here."

"Not a bad idea. I know law enforcement attends funerals and memorial services for the same reason—to see if the killer makes an appearance." Finn planted his feet more firmly on the dirt, as he felt his world tilt just a little. Jessica Eller was drawing him into her vortex of the fantastic once again. "I'm not saying Morgan's killer left these items, but video of someone leaving them would be useful. Someone's definitely playing some games here."

"Or worse." She tucked the doll under her arm, its floppy legs dangling over her hip. "I might just meet with the sheriff's department and ask them about the possibility of setting up a camera out here. I need to talk to the CSI first on the scene, anyway."

Holding up his phone, he asked, "Are you ready to go? I took quite a few pictures. I'll send them to you. Number?"

His thumb hovered over the number pad on his phone through the silence. Did she think this was a ruse to get her cell phone number? He glanced up, but she wasn't paying any attention to him.

She'd turned on her toes, looking like a deer ready to flee, peering into the forest.

His pulse thrummed. "Do you see something?"

She whipped around, clutching the doll to her chest. "Probably just the night critters stirring. We should get out of here before we have to scuff back through the trees with just our puny cell phone flashlights to guide us."

He pocketed his phone. He'd get her number later. If he didn't get her away from this place before the sun went down, he'd probably have to carry her back to the car.

Jessica led the way back to the road, her long legs eating up the trail. Finn almost had to jog to keep up with her. By the time they reached the road where he'd parked his car, he had to stop to catch his breath.

Wiping the back of his hand across his brow, he said, "You really wanted out of there."

"The whole place makes my skin crawl." She threw a fearful glance over her shoulder at the tree line. "Even more than ever."

She still clutched the doll in her hand, and he nodded at it. "That thing is going to be useless as evidence."

"You're probably right." She held the doll in front of her and met its button eye, as if she could read some clue buried in the inanimate object. "But I'm going to get to the bottom of why someone left these items at the memorial, one way or another."

Their feet crunched the gravel on the shoulder of the road as they walked back to his car…at a normal pace. He got the door for her, noticing a slight trembling of her hand.

Pointing into the back seat, he said, "There are a couple of bottles of water back there. You look like you could use one."

He slammed the door and circled to the driver's side. He slid behind the wheel, and she tapped his arm with the neck of the plastic bottle. "Can you open this for me? My hands are a little sweaty."

"Must be that race you ran through the woods back there. I could hardly keep up." He took the bottle from her and cracked the seal on the cap. "Do you want to give me your cell phone number? I'll send you the pictures I took."

"Sure." She put the bottle to her lips and gulped down some water while he fumbled for his cell.

"Ready." When she finished, she rattled off her phone number.

"I'll send them when I get home." He started the engine and rested his hands on the steering wheel. "Back to your car?"

"Yeah, it's parked on the east side of campus."

"Are you staying in town or headed back to… Marysville? Is that where you live?"

"I actually live in Seattle but do a lot of my work in Marysville. The lab in Seattle gets bogged down with tons of cases, and it handles firearms on top of everything else. Due to the workload there, we often take care of materials in Marysville."

He whistled through his teeth. "You're going to hit some traffic, and depending on the ferry schedule it could take you a few hours to get home."

"That's why I'm staying here in town. I have a hotel room down by the water." She shrugged. "My boss wants me to meet with the sheriffs while I'm here. I have a massive to-do list right now."

Finn wheeled out onto the road. "What's first on your list? Meeting with the deputies?"

"That can wait. The material evidence isn't going anywhere." She clasped her hands between her knees and turned to stare out the window. "There's something else I need to do first. Someone I need to see."

"Tiffany's friends? Have you looked them up yet?"

"Ashley and Denny can wait, too." She grabbed the bottle of water and twisted the cap. "But Avery Plank can't."

Finn jerked his head to the side, and the car swerved into the gravel for a few seconds. "You're going to visit Avery Plank in the pen?"

"I've already cleared it. He's expecting me tomorrow during visiting hours." She sloshed the water around in the bottle, its motion mirroring his thoughts.

"Why on earth would you want to talk to Plank?" Finn smacked his palms on the steering wheel. "Wait. Have you seen him before?"

"Never. This is my first visit, although I've been thinking about it for a while. I even wrote a few letters to him that I ripped up."

"He's dangerous, Jessica." He jerked his thumb over his shoulder. "You felt evil at Morgan's death site. Wait until you sit across from Plank. You'll choke on it."

She tipped some water into her mouth and licked her lips. "He's locked up. He can't hurt me."

"Here." Finn tapped the side of his head. "He'll hurt you

up here. He plays games with people. You're not going to get any truth out of him."

"You sure didn't feel that way about him ten years ago, did you? None of you did." She put on a fake low voice as she said, "Oh, hey, Avery, did you kill Tiffany Hunt? Shari Chang? Letitia Rocha? You wanna help us close some pesky open cases we couldn't be bothered to investigate?"

"Those cases didn't come out of the blue. They all had the same pattern as the Creekside Killer victims. It made sense." He clenched his jaw. It *had* been the easy way out, but it didn't mean law enforcement was wrong or that Plank was lying.

"Okay, so you all believed him then. But *now* I'm not going to get any truth out of him?" She pushed her wheat-colored hair out of her face. "What if Plank tells me the same thing he told law enforcement all those years ago? What if he tells me he did murder my sister? Is he to be trusted again because he gave the acceptable answer?"

Finn opened his mouth a few times like a fish out of water. She wasn't wrong, but he had his own reasons for keeping her away from Plank. "He'll toy with you, and he'll enjoy it. Will he know who you are tomorrow? Did you indicate you were a victim's sister on your request or just that you worked for the Washington State Patrol?"

"Both." She narrowed her hazel eyes. "I wanted to make sure I got in."

"The family of one of his victims?" Finn shook his head. "He'll go to town on you. When you walk out of there, you're not gonna know which way is up."

Jessica folded her hands in her lap, her knuckles white. "You underestimate me, Finn. You know what my childhood was like. Do you really think a man like Avery Plank is going to rattle me? Hell, a guy like that could've been one of my stepfathers."

He swallowed. She'd told him all about growing up with a drug-addicted mother and the men who populated their lives...and the older half sister who'd protected her from all of it. At the time, he thought she'd given him a sob story to sway him, get him to do things for her that a young patrol officer should've never done.

When she disappeared from his life and he got over his anger, he did some investigating and discovered every word she'd told him had been the truth. It made him ache for her all over again.

"I know you had it bad when you were a kid. Know your mom exposed you to all kinds of unsavory people, but Plank is evil."

"Gee, a serial killer is evil. Thanks, Sherlock. I'm not going to be sitting down for tea and scones with him. He'll be chained up like the animal he is." She rapped one knuckle on the window. "Turn right on this street. I'm up one block."

Finn took the turn onto a tree-lined street that bordered the eastern edge of the campus. Night had fallen, and the towering Douglas firs blocked out most of the streetlights, creating a shadowy tunnel where few cars remained.

The university had a call-in system where students could request an escort to their cars, but few vehicles parked on this street at this time of night. The library sat on the other side of campus, around the corner from a hub of restaurants, bars and shops.

After Morgan's murder, the Safe Line had been getting a massive number of calls. Tonight, he'd be Jessica's safe line.

"That's me." Jessica pointed to a green Subaru parked

on the left side of the street, so Finn made a U-turn at the next intersection and pulled behind her car.

He cut the engine and opened his door as Jessica unclasped her seat belt.

"You don't have to get out, but I'd appreciate it if you watched while I get into my car and start it."

"It's not a problem. I'll just take a quick look around your car before you get in. Nice ride." He pushed out of the car while she grabbed her stuff.

She beeped her remote, and the lights flashed and stayed on while he peered into the back seat. He skirted the trunk and stepped onto the sidewalk, surveying the side of her vehicle, which seemed to tilt in the back.

He swore under his breath. He didn't even need to crouch down to see the problem. "Ah, Jessica. You're gonna want to have a look at this before you start that engine."

Leaving the driver's-side door open, she joined him on the sidewalk. "What now?"

He leveled a finger at her back tire. "You've got a flat."

She hunched forward, reaching out her hand toward the wheel. She ran her fingers over the rubber and cranked her head over her shoulder, the whites of her rounded eyes gleaming in the dark. "It's flat because someone slashed it."

Chapter Four

Her fingertips traced the smooth edge of the cut in her tire. What would've happened if Finn hadn't noticed the tire and she drove back to her hotel on it? Would she have made it? Would she have been compelled to stop the car to check on it?

"Someone not only knows I'm here, but this person also knows my car or maybe has been following me." She sat back on her heels, inspecting her smudged fingers. "You know I'm right. What did you say earlier about coincidences?"

He crouched beside her, bumping her shoulder. "Somebody is trying to scare you."

"Scare? The card and the doll were meant to scare or maybe even send a message, but this? She rubbed her fingertips on the wet grass beside the curb. "A slashed tire could've caused me to stop the car on the way back to the hotel, or maybe even have caused an accident. I think we've moved beyond psychological terror now."

Finn rose to his feet and stepped into the road, tilting his head back. "Too far from campus to have any cameras on this street, but maybe one of the apartment complexes farther up the block has something pointed this way. I can check for you tomorrow. It might be as simple as identifying this guy and making him stop."

"Or not." Jessica lifted her hatchback and peeled back the flooring. "I have a spare, if you want to help me."

"Or we can leave your car here and take care of it tomorrow in the light of day. I can give you a ride back to your hotel tonight, and then back again to your car."

"I appreciate the offer, but you forget. I have a meeting with a serial killer tomorrow, and I need to leave here by five in the morning to get to the pen in plenty of time for my one o'clock appointment."

"You're making the five-hour drive to Walla Walla?" Finn clasped the back of his neck. "Why not take an hour flight from Seattle?"

"I drive all over the state." She shrugged, not wanting to admit to Finn that she avoided flying when she could. She was supposed to be presenting a front of fearlessness.

"That's crazy. I'll book you on a flight tomorrow, and I'll come with you."

"Why would you do that?" Could it be that Finn was starting to believe Avery Plank didn't commit Tiffany's homicide, or did he want to horn in on her interview of Plank to guide the outcome?

"Because I don't think you should do this on your own, and I'm sure as hell not sitting in a car for five hours."

Crossing her arms, she planted her boots on the asphalt. "And I'm sure as hell not allowing you to sit in on my interview with Plank. I'm talking to him by myself."

"I don't want to be there while you talk to Plank, but I do want to be there when you get out of that hellhole. You shouldn't be on your own, and you really shouldn't spend five hours driving by yourself musing on Avery Plank. We can get you a new tire early tomorrow morning and head to the airport right after."

She screwed up the side of her mouth, studied Finn's handsome face and relented. "Have it your way. When did you get so bossy?"

"About ten years ago after I got bamboozled by some doe-eyed teenager."

"I was twenty-one."

"That doesn't make it better." He nodded at her disabled vehicle. "Do you have all your stuff?"

She jogged to her car and ducked inside, grabbing her purse and that cursed doll from the passenger seat. As she locked up, she said, "I hope my stalker doesn't return to do more damage."

"Stalker? I hope not."

"I hope that's all he is."

Back in his car, she directed Finn to her hotel by the water, and he insisted on walking her inside the lobby. She wasn't about to refuse this time.

She waved at the hotel clerk and pointed to the elevator. "I think I got this."

"I'll look into a morning flight, and we'll take care of your car before we head out." He touched her arm. "Thanks for coming to me with the card. I'll do what I can."

"Well, you've already gone above and beyond. Thank *you*. I didn't expect it."

"Get a good night's sleep. I'll call you around seven."

Finn planted himself in the lobby as Jessica walked to the elevator. She turned when the doors opened and lifted her hand before stepping inside.

She hadn't expected Finn to be so interested in her theories about Morgan's case and its connection to Tiffany's.

He'd explained it as concern for her, but something about his concern rang false.

Finn Karlsson was no longer the sweet, gullible man she'd met ten years ago. His baby-blue eyes held secrets, and she was determined to discover them…even if it meant putting her heart in danger again.

THE FOLLOWING MORNING had been such a whirlwind of changing her tire, driving to the shop to get a new one to replace her spare and rushing to the airport to catch their last-minute flight to Walla Walla, Jessica's anxiety about flying hadn't had a minute to manifest itself. Now, as the jet's engines roared beneath her and the plane lifted, she dug her fingernails into the armrest.

She could use one of those canned Bloody Marys from the drink cart, but she didn't want Finn to think she was a morning drinker. She also didn't want to have alcohol on her breath when she went to the prison. She squeezed her eyes closed.

Finn bumped her shoulder. "Are you all right? I'm sure I can work something out with the prison and go inside with you."

Ugh. He assumed her nerves were all about meeting Plank. She loosened her death grip on the armrest and flexed her fingers. "Not a fan of taking off."

"I'm okay with taking off. I don't like landing." He bent forward and dragged his laptop case from beneath the seat in front of him. "Do you mind if I do some work? I canceled a class today, but I still have some papers to grade."

She hated landing only slightly less than taking off. "Go ahead. Really, you didn't have to do all of this. I could've changed the tire last night and driven down on my spare this morning."

He widened his eyes. "You're not meant to drive three hundred miles on a spare."

"Just do your grading." She flicked her fingers at his laptop, now open on his tray table. "I have some notes to review."

She reached up and pressed the light button with her knuckle and pulled her purse into her lap. Digging around in the depths of her bag, she found her notebook and flipped it open. She scanned the words she'd scrawled on the page weeks ago, more to give herself something to do than as a review. She didn't even need this notebook. She'd had these questions memorized for almost ten years.

The airplane dipped and she gasped, closing her eyes and clutching the notebook to her chest. After a few seconds of smooth sailing, she opened one eye, feeling Finn's attention from the seat next to hers.

He whispered, "Probably just a pocket of air." He closed his laptop. "Did I ever tell you the story about the Ferris wheel at the state fair?"

"No." She threaded her fingers together and pressed her hands against her midsection.

"I had been on all the hair-raising rides all afternoon, even while I filled up on cotton candy and chili dogs and kettle corn and funnel cake. But when night fell, I heard a girl from school wanted to go on the Ferris wheel with me." He rubbed his hands together. "As a randy fifteen-year-old boy, I figured I'd just gotten lucky."

She turned her head. "And did you? Get lucky, I mean."

"Absolutely not."

Finn then proceeded to tell her a story about his abject

fear of riding the Ferris wheel and trying to impress this girl. Even though Jessica was sure he'd embellished the tale, he had her giggling and covering her eyes at his humiliation.

He followed that story with another about the first time he went scuba diving, which had tears rolling down her face. He'd obviously conquered all these fears because she knew from before that he was an adventurous outdoorsman.

While she mopped her face with the napkin from the Diet Coke she'd ordered, she heard a loud clunk and clapped her hand to her chest. "What was that?"

"The landing gear. We're getting ready to touch down." He gave an exaggerated grimace. "I told you this is my least favorite part of flying."

"Do you want me to hold your hand?" She patted his hand, resting on his laptop. "We don't want a repeat of the Ferris wheel debacle. You did eat a lot of pretzels."

He held out his hand, palm up. "Please."

She slid her palm on top of his palm, curling her fingers around his hand. "Just this once. You're gonna have to learn to suck it up."

Even though she knew he was pretending fear to make her feel better, it worked. Or maybe it was the feel of his warm, rough skin against hers. She swooned, along with the plane, but she welcomed the butterflies as long Finn held her hand.

"Thanks." He grinned as he shoved his computer back into its case with his other hand and nudged it beneath the seat with his foot.

As the airplane whooshed downward, Finn squeezed her hand, and she didn't mind at all—not even when the wheels touched down.

When the plane came to a stop, they unclipped their seat

belts and gathered their bags. She poked Finn in the back as they made their way off the plane. "Thanks."

"Yeah, I can't believe a woman who isn't afraid to face Avery Plank is afraid to fly."

She shrugged as she hitched her bag over her shoulder. "I can't control what happens up here."

"If you think you can control Avery Plank, you're in for a big surprise." He clicked his tongue. "It's only a ten-minute drive to the pen. Let's grab some lunch in town before heading out there."

They collected the rental car at the airport and Jessica checked her phone for a restaurant on the way to the pen. Ten minutes later, they were seated at a sandwich shop in the middle of town with a couple of paper cups filled with soda.

Finn sat back and folded his arms. "Are you going to flat out ask Plank if he killed your sister?"

"That's the point." She plunged her straw into her second Diet Coke of the day, already feeling wired.

"Do you expect to hear the truth from him, and how will you know it when you hear it?"

"I'll worry about all that when I get to it. I have to do this. I have to look in his eyes."

"You're not gonna like what you see there. Plank—" he coughed "—all these guys—have dead eyes."

"You don't have to tell me that." She cocked her head. "They just called our number. You get the sandwiches, and I'll fill up our drinks."

She scooted from the booth before Finn could come up with more reasons why she shouldn't meet with Plank. Why did he care so much? She could maintain her composure around Plank. In her career with Washington's Crime Laboratory Division, she'd been to plenty of crime scenes, had seen more blood than she cared to remember and had testified at the trials of gruesome killers. She could handle sitting across from a chained-up murderer past his prime—even if he had confessed to killing her sister.

For the remainder of the lunch, Jessica peppered Finn with questions about his classes, mostly to keep him away from the subject of Avery Plank, but he'd held her interest with his account of the lessons he gave his students and how he engaged them.

When she'd first met Finn ten years ago, the deputy who'd discovered her sister's body, she'd often wondered what it would be like between them without the secrets, lies and deception on her part. Now she knew that it could be something special.

Back then, she'd manipulated him into giving her information about the scene and evidence that he was in no position to reveal. She'd used him, even as she was falling hard for him. That same care he'd had for her ten years ago had never gone away.

"Ready?" She bunched up the waxy paper from her sandwich and dropped it on the red plastic tray on the side of the table. "I want to make sure I'm on time."

"If I can't talk you out of it, I guess it's go time." He slid the tray from the table, dumped the trash and left the tray on top of the receptacle.

Once in the rental car, her hands trembled a little as she snapped her seat belt in place, but she told herself it was because of excitement, not fear.

They drove in silence for the brief ten-minute journey with wheat fields on either side of the road, and both handed over their ID at the guard shack in the front beneath the arched sign that heralded penitentiary grounds. The green grass looked inviting, but the facade ended at the gray-and-brown stone building with the watchtower surveying the area.

Finn parked the car and stayed seated. "I'm going to wait here...unless you want me to go inside with you."

She licked her dry lips. "No. I'm good. See you in about an hour."

Once inside the prison admin building, Jessica went through the paperwork, the body scan and the pat-down. The low heels of her black boots tapped on the linoleum floor on the way to the visitor center as she followed the buff form of the corrections officer.

He opened the door and guided her to a table in the middle of the room. Empty chairs and love seats littered the space, and two baskets filled with toys stood sentry on either side of a colorful carpet.

Twisting her fingers in front of her, Jessica asked, "No other visitors today?"

"Their appointment times are later. Usually when one of our high-profile inmates has a visitor, we clear out the room. Gary Ridgeway. Kenneth Bianchi." The CO shrugged his broad shoulders. "Just to be on the safe side. There will be one of us at each of the doors."

She gave him a jerky nod, and he pulled out one of the chairs stationed at the desk for her. She sat down and rubbed her palms against the thighs of her black slacks. The pen imposed a modest dress code, but she'd taken it a step further with her low-heeled shoes, professional pants, a blouse buttoned almost to the top of her neck and a loose-fitting jacket.

When the door opposite opened, she jumped in her seat. A CO led Plank into the room, his feet shuffling to accommodate the chains wrapping his ankles and attached to the cuffs around his wrists. They weren't taking any chances with this guy.

She eked out a small breath and folded her hands on the table in front of her, like a schoolteacher waiting for a recalcitrant pupil. She kept her gaze trained on Plank as he scuffed across the floor. She couldn't get over how average he looked. She wouldn't give the guy a second glance in the coffeehouse or the gym or the grocery store. That's how he'd taken his victims by surprise. Just an average dude doing average things—until he wasn't.

Just as she watched his approach, he kept his gaze trained on her...soaking her in. His attention was anything but average. His brown eyes darted across every inch of her visible body, measuring, weighing, judging—a predatory assessment that had her squeezing her folded hands tighter.

The CO who'd ushered her into the room kicked out the chair across from her. "You know the drill, Plank. Sit."

The Creekside Killer plopped into the chair facing her, his chains clanging and clinking. His guard ran a chain from the stationary table through his ankle and wrist bracelets, securing him in place—right in front of her.

Her hand shook as she dipped it into her pocket to fetch her phone. She'd been warned against taking photos, but she was allowed to record him with his assent.

Setting the phone on the table between them, she cleared her throat. "Hello, Mr. Plank. I'm Jessica Eller from the Washington State Patrol, Crime Lab Division. Do you mind if I record our conversation?"

Shaking his head from side to side, he blinked once, a slow lowering of the lids over perceptive eyes. "You're that girl's sister, too." He snapped his fingers and rolled his eyes to the ceiling.

Jessica said her sister's name through her teeth. "Tiffany Hunt."

He leveled a long index finger at her, and she noticed for the first time that his hands were anything but average. They were huge, and Jessica flashed on an image of them wrapped around some poor woman's neck, squeezing the life out of her.

"That's right. Tiffany. She was a brunette, though, and you're a blonde." He cocked his head as if reviewing a lesson in genetics. "You sure you two were sisters? From what I read, your mother was a woman of low morals just like sweet Tiffany."

Jessica's cheek burned as if he'd slapped her. He knew about her mother, about her family. Would he bother with that if he hadn't killed Tiffany?

Raising his cuffed hands, he said, "Don't feel bad, Jessica. My mother was a whore, too."

She'd studied his psychological profile and knew all about his background, but why did he know about hers? She was ready for his attack this time, the ugly word, and didn't even blink an eye.

She tapped the record icon on her phone and straightened it on the table. "So, you did kill my sister."

"Did you have any doubt? I confessed to it."

"The MO was different from the others. Despite my sister's troubled past, she wasn't a sex worker at the time of her murder." She tightened her jaw. "And you didn't rape her, didn't leave your DNA."

"Ah, the outraged sister is also a crime investigator." He folded his hands, mimicking her stance from before. "What else was different?"

"You didn't use your hands to strangle Tiffany." Her gaze

bounced to his large mitts folded primly and back to his face, alert and bright. He was enjoying himself. "You didn't pose her. You didn't leave her nude."

He clapped his hands together, the cuffs on his wrists resulting in an incongruously dainty motion. "I'm impressed. You're very good, Jessica."

"I'm not here for your admiration, Plank. I don't think you killed my sister, but I can't figure out why you know so much about her life." She held her breath as Plank glanced over his shoulder at the CO.

Hunching across the table, he lowered his voice. "I make it my business to know the details of other cases in the same area as my...hunting ground."

She'd dipped her head to catch his words, and then jerked back as he finished his sentence, drawing the attention of the corrections officer by the door leading back to the cells. She met the CO's eyes and gave him a brief shake of her head.

She returned her focus to Plank and asked, "Does that mean you didn't kill Tiffany?"

He leaned back in his chair. "What about this girl Morgan?"

A chill rippled down the length of Jessica's spine. "You know about that murder?"

"What did I just tell you, Jessica?" He clicked his tongue. "It's my hobby."

"Do you think it's a Creekside Killer copycat?"

"Let's see." He held up one manacled hand, the cuff slipping from his wrist to his elbow. "No rape, strangled, but most likely with an object, and Morgan was a sweet little coed, not a lady of the night. If he's copying me, he's doing a poor job of it."

"So, you didn't murder Tiffany. Is that what you're saying?"

"You're getting dull, Jessica." He snapped his fingers. "I'll tell you what, you can read my book. Perhaps I'll reveal all amongst its pages."

She snorted. "You're not allowed to write a book about your crime and profit from it."

He gave a high-pitched giggle that made her skin crawl. "I'm an engineer, not a writer. Someone else is writing my story."

"I suppose there are all kinds of lowlifes willing to exploit murder for profit."

"Oh, come on, Jessica. Don't try to tell me you haven't read books about serial killers. There are a couple of them here at the pen who have been best-seller subjects. In fact—" he drummed his fingers on the table next to her phone "—you probably know this author."

"Doubt it." She glanced over Plank's shoulder at the CO twirling his finger in the air. Her time was almost up, and Plank hadn't given her a straight answer about Tiffany.

"Oh, no. I'm sure you know him or know *of* him. He's the cop who found your sister's body, although he's not on the job anymore."

Her attention snapped back to Plank. "Who? What are you saying?"

"I'm saying Professor Finn Karlsson is writing a book about me."

Chapter Five

Finn glanced at the clock in the lower-right corner of his computer screen. Jessica should be coming out soon. He doubted she got any satisfaction from Plank. The guy played games—and Finn knew that better than anyone at this point.

He squeezed the back of his neck and took a sip of the soda he'd refilled on his way out of the sandwich shop, now watery and lukewarm. From the corner of his eye, he caught sight of a figure moving toward him.

He slid his laptop into its case and jumped from the car to get Jessica's door. He squinted at her through his sunglasses. From the way she was practically marching across the parking lot, Plank had angered more than scared her. She probably didn't get a straight answer from him about Tiffany.

He wasn't about to go through the told-you-so routine with her.

As he opened the passenger door for her, she gave him a tight-lipped glance. Finn knew when to keep his mouth shut. He closed her door almost gently and took his time getting back to the driver's side.

Once behind the wheel, he gave her a sideways glance. "Didn't go well?"

She whipped her head around so fast her ponytail almost slapped her face. "Avery Plank is a liar and a game player."

"Yeah, he is."

Her hazel eyes turned to pools of dark green. "And you should know because so are you."

Finn scratched his chin. She knew. Either the COs or Plank himself told her. "Look, I didn't want to tell you about the book because I didn't want to upset you."

"How thoughtful." She grabbed the drink in the cup holder and shoved the straw in her mouth. Wrinkling her nose, she removed the lid and tossed the liquid out the window.

"That was my old soda. Do you want another?"

She crushed the paper cup in her hand. "I want you to tell me why you're writing this book. Y-you're exploiting the deaths of all those women, including Tiffany."

"Do you feel that way about other true crime books or just this one? There are probably a dozen books about the Hillside Strangler, a dozen about the Green River Killer—" he jerked his thumb over his shoulder at the prison where those two killers currently resided "—and I'm betting you read a few of each. Hell, you probably even watched the movies."

She dropped her chin to her chest, and her eyelashes fluttered. "He knew about Morgan Flemming."

"Of course he did. What did he say about Tiffany?"

"Back and forth. On the one hand, he admitted the MO for her homicide was different from the other Creekside victims, but he knew details about her case, about her background...*my* background. If he didn't kill her, why would he bother collecting that information?" She dragged her knuckles across her cheek, although she hadn't shed any tears.

"It's his hobby."

"That's exactly what he said." She sniffed. "How many times have you visited him?"

He met her gaze steadily as her eyes still threw sparks at him. "I've met him three times. I recorded the conversations if you're interested in listening. It's mostly just his background, his childhood."

"Which I'm sure was terrible and delivered to induce the greatest amount of sympathy." She tossed the crushed cup onto the console.

Finn lifted his shoulders. "Single, drug-addicted mother, lots of so-called fathers in and out of his life, some of whom beat him, lots of upheaval."

"Sounds like my childhood."

A sharp pain lanced his heart. He knew all about Jessica and Tiffany's rough upbringing and how Tiffany had protected her younger sister. He understood Jessica's need for justice. He'd felt it himself.

"I'm not writing a love letter to the Creekside Killer. This is just like any other true crime book. I'll do justice to the victims and hopefully reveal what makes Plank tick. That's not an excuse for him, and it's no pity party. It's going to be a cold, hard look at a cold, hard killer."

"But your claim to fame, your raison d'être, is that you discovered the body of one of the Creekside Killer's victims—Tiffany Hunt. Without that, you're just another criminal justice expert writing a book about a serial killer. No offense."

"None taken." He ran a finger around his collar and started the rental car.

"My point being, as you do the research for this book, it's going to be in your best interests to encourage Plank to stick with his confession regarding my sister's homicide."

She snapped on her seat belt and hit the dash with her palm. "Let's get out of this place."

He gritted his teeth as he pulled away from the parking space. "I don't have any best interests here, Jessica. My best interest is to write a truthful and compelling book about a killer and maybe give some dignity to the victims, including Tiffany, if Plank continues to insist he killed her. Are you beginning to believe he did?"

"I don't know." She sighed as she slumped in the passenger seat. "He reminded me of his confession while also encouraging me to compare the dissimilar MOs. I don't know what to think anymore."

"That's the way he wants it. Continue on the path you started. If you truly believe he didn't murder Tiffany and that somehow Morgan's homicide is connected to hers, then go for it. Keep investigating."

"And you'll help me?"

He felt her stare searching his profile, heard the cajoling tone of her voice, even smelled the intoxicating scent of her floral perfume that infiltrated all the sensible parts of his brain, and God help him, he was falling into her trap again.

He took a hard turn onto the highway and said, "Yeah, I'll help you. Now let's get something to drink before we get to the airport."

HOURS LATER, back in her hotel room, Jessica unzipped her boots and pulled them off, dropping each one on the carpeted floor with a clunk. She fell across the bed, and her stomach growled, the turkey sandwich in Walla Walla a distant memory.

Finn had offered to buy her dinner when they landed in

Seattle and drove back to Fairwood, but she needed time away from him to digest the news about his book.

Was the book the reason he'd even agreed to look at her evidence? Despite what he said, his book would have more traction if the victim he'd discovered had actually been murdered by the subject of his book.

And was she? Jessica slid her phone from the side pocket of her purse and navigated to her recorded conversation with Plank. Finn had been right about one thing—Plank liked to play games. But he didn't scare her. It's not like he'd been wheeled out like Hannibal Lecter with a face mask. He'd behaved like any garden-variety psychopath—no remorse for his crimes or pity for his victims, elevated sense of self-worth, no sense of right and wrong.

The only time Plank had gotten under her skin was with his knowledge of Tiffany's background, of her own family. Finn had chalked it up to Plank's sick hobby. Was it his way of hinting that he had killed Tiffany?

It would be easy for her to believe him, to believe the cops, put her sister's murder behind her. She'd been close to doing just that over the past few years, but something always dragged her back into the maelstrom. This time Morgan Flemming's homicide had been the catalyst that reignited her quest for the truth.

The fact that the MO in Morgan's case mimicked Tiffany's more than either one mimicked the Creekside Killer slayings had been the strong lure.

She grabbed a pillow from the head of the bed and pulled it into her arms, where she squeezed it tightly against her chest. Had Morgan's killer counted on that? Is that why he'd left the card and the doll? Had he left them for her?

Her gaze traveled to the rag doll sitting atop the credenza, next to the TV. Nobody would've known the meaning of that rag doll except her—and she'd gotten the message loud and clear.

Time to put aside thoughts of Finn Karlsson and his stormy blue eyes. She had an investigation to pursue, and if Finn Karlsson got in the way of that investigation, she'd handle him...just like she did the last time.

THE FOLLOWING MORNING, with the rag doll tucked into a bag and a new tire on her wheel, Jessica entered Ashley King's address into her GPS. Ashley had been Tiffany's best friend at the time of the murder. They'd lived together, and Ashley had offered one of the more intriguing clues to Tiffany's murder when she told the deputies that Tiffany had sensed someone following her in the weeks leading up to her murder.

That tip didn't rule out the Creekside Killer, as Plank had been known to stalk his victims to get a sense of their routine. But he'd always snatched his victims when they were working the streets, pretending to be a mild-mannered john. Tiffany hadn't been a working girl...at the time of her homicide.

As the deputies had patiently pointed out to Jessica, Plank could've scoped out Tiffany months before the murder when she *had* been a sex worker. Plank was known to play the long game with his prey.

Fifteen minutes later, Jessica pulled into the mobile home park where Ashley lived. Jessica hadn't called first, hadn't notified Ashley that she was dropping by for a visit. Ten years ago, Ashley's sympathy for Jessica had waned in direct proportion to Jessica's hounding of Ashley about details she didn't have. She didn't want to give Ashley a chance now to avoid her. She couldn't exactly use her position with the Washington State Patrol to demand that Ashley speak to her or answer any of her questions. Jessica had one foot in the crime lab as part of the official investigation into Morgan Flemming's murder and one foot on her own turf, reinvestigating Tiffany's murder.

Her car crawled past the mobile homes in the community until she found Ashley's number, and she swung a U-turn to park in front. She grabbed her purse and the doll and shoved her door open with her foot. She inhaled the pine scent as she slammed her car door and crunched across the gravel to the double-wide.

The long weeds in the yard stirred as she walked past them, and a profusion of flowers bowed their heads. Someone had made an attempt to spruce up the appearance of the unit, but the upkeep had outpaced them.

She rapped on the screen door, and the ripped mesh flapped back and forth. The door squeaked on its hinges as it opened, and Ashley King stared at Jessica for a second or two before recognition flooded her face.

"Oh my God. It's Jessie." Ashley kicked open the screen door so hard, Jessica had to dodge it.

In an instant, she found herself wrapped in Ashley's chubby arms, enveloped by the skunky scent of weed. "I'd recognize you anywhere—tall, blonde and fierce. At least you're still tall and blonde. How about it? You still got that chip on your shoulder?"

Jessica patted Ashley on the back. "I hope not. God, I must've been insufferable."

"Nah, just grieving hard." She cupped Jessica's face with her soft palm. "Come on in. I can't say I'm any better at keeping house than I was when me and Tiff were roomies."

"I'm not here to do an inspection," Jessica said, as she immediately scanned the room with its topsy-turvy pillows, cluttered coffee table, sporting full ashtrays and the requisite pizza box. "Looks about the same as the place you shared with Tiffany."

"Old habits die hard." Ashley grabbed a handful of papers from a cushion on the couch and dropped them on the kitchen table, already a repository for some kind of helter-skelter filing system. "Have a seat, Jessie. I heard you're a hotshot CSI lady or something."

Perching on the edge of the sagging floral couch, Jessica shrugged. "I work in a forensics lab for the state."

"I figured you'd end up doing something like that." Ashley reached for a pack of cigarettes and then pushed them between the cushions. "That or become a cop. Is that why you're in town? That poor little Morgan Flemming?"

Jessica's spine stiffened. Ashley knew she worked for the Washington State Patrol, knew about Morgan's murder and knew she was here in an official capacity. Fairwood always had a small-town vibe. Everyone must know.

"That's my official reason for being here, but you had to have noticed the similarity between Morgan's death and Tiffany's, Ashley, just like I did."

"Listen, sweetie. I loved Tiff, me and her—" she crossed one finger over the other "—two of a kind, but it didn't cross my mind that Morgan's killing was the same as Tiff's. Two murdered girls. It happens."

"I suppose you're right, but I did find something strange at the memorial site for Morgan and I wanted to ask you about it." As she reached into the bag with the doll, a man coughed from the back of the mobile home.

Her fingers curled around the rag doll, and she froze. "I'm sorry. I didn't realize you lived with someone here."

Ashley's smooth, full face flushed pink. "Well, yeah…"

"Baby, who you talking to?" A skinny guy with dirty-blond hair brushing his shoulders stepped into the living room, blinking. "Hey, it's little Jessie."

"Denny?" Jessica's mouth fell open, as her gaze darted toward Ashley, now beet-red and fidgeting. "You live here? I tried to find you, too, but couldn't get an address for you."

"I'm driving a truck. On the road most of the time, but I stay here when I'm in Fairwood." He jerked a thumb at Ashley, his nails bitten to the quick. "Me and her hooked up after…you know, after Tiff passed. Nothing bad about it, Jessie. It's like we kinda needed each other."

"I'm not judging you—either of you."

"The cops were quick to jump on me. I guess the husband and boyfriend are always prime suspects."

"It was more than that, Denny." Ashley twisted her hands in her lap. "You were dealing."

Jessica jerked her head toward Denny. How had she not known that at the time? "You were dealing drugs?"

Denny's nostrils flared as he glanced at Ashley. "Small-time stuff. Not like I was with a cartel or anything."

Jessica licked her lips. "Well, even small dealers eventually answer to the cartels, even if you're many levels removed. Why did the cops find that significant? Did you have any disgruntled customers?"

"Nothing like that, and if they were mad about something, they'd take it out on me, not my girl. Tiff had nothing to do with any of my business." He ran a hand through his scraggly hair. "I felt guilty when Tiff was murdered, but not because I had anything to do with it or brought it down on her. Just 'cuz I couldn't protect her."

Jessica's nose tingled, and her throat felt thick. "I'm sure the cops investigated that angle."

"They got their guy, anyway." Denny scratched his goatee. "It was that Creekside Killer dude, Avery Plank."

Biting her bottom lip, Ashley sent Jessica an imploring look. Ashley knew Jessica had her doubts back then, and she did, too, but she wasn't here to stir up any more anguish for Denny.

Jessica took a deep breath. "Yeah, Plank. But I came by to ask you about a doll that Tiffany had, Ashley."

"You don't even have to tell me." Ashley waved a hand in the air. "I know what you're talking about—that rag doll. Tiff told me it had sentimental value."

"This one." Jessica pulled the doll out of the bag and shook it in the air.

"Just like that doll. Did you have one as a kid, too?" Ashley shoved her hand between the cushions to retrieve the pack of cigarettes.

"I-I think this is the same doll that Tiffany had. It was mine, and I gave it to her. There was only one doll."

Ashley dropped the cigarettes. "Where'd you get that, Jessie?"

Jessica smoothed out the doll's checkered dress. Should she tell them? Would they think she was crazy? Did it matter? "I found it at Morgan Flemming's memorial, along with the flowers and candles and stuffed bears."

"That ain't possible, Jessie." Denny shook his head. "Might look like it, but that can't be the same doll. I mean, it doesn't make sense."

"Why are you so sure?"

Denny leveled his finger at the toy in Jessica's lap. "'Cuz that doll was stolen from Tiff's apartment about two weeks before the murder."

Chapter Six

Jessica's gaze tracked back to the doll, hoping to find some answers in its unblinking button eye. "Did you report it to the police?"

"The police?" Ashley stroked a cigarette she'd hastily plucked from the pack. "Jessie, it was just a doll. No offense, but I didn't like the thing anyway. Gave me the creeps. I figured one of our friends took it as a joke or one of Denny's high-as-a-kite friends snatched it. There was a guy hanging around Tiff at the time, but he left before the murder."

"I meant after the murder. Did you report the theft to the police after Tiffany turned up dead?" Jessica eyed the cigarette. A few more minutes with these two and she just might snatch it from Ashley and smoke it herself.

"Honestly—" Ashley held up her hand as if swearing in court "—I forgot all about it. It's not like someone broke in and burglarized us. Tiff mentioned it one day, and I shrugged it off."

"But someone could've broken in to take it." She glanced at Denny, who yawned and rubbed his eyes. He'd already checked out. "Denny, did you mention the theft of the doll to the cops?"

"I didn't even know it was gone, Jessie. What's the big

deal about it? Somebody left a rag doll for Morgan that looks like one Tiff had."

"You don't get it." She shook the doll by the torso, and its legs and arms flopped in the air. "This is the same doll. The exact same doll that was stolen from Tiffany two weeks before she was murdered, same missing eye and everything."

Ashley and Denny exchanged a look, as if wondering when to call in the little men with the white jackets. Jessica closed her eyes and stuffed the doll back in the bag. "I suppose you wouldn't know anything about a sympathy card left at the site that mentioned Tiffany, either, right?"

"Look, Jessie." Ashley scooted toward her on the couch and hung an arm around her shoulders. "I know you loved your sister, and you were the world to Tiff, but she's gone, honey. Plank is behind bars, and you got a chance to help another murder victim now."

"She's right, Jessie." Denny stroked his goatee. "If we hear anything weird about Morgan's murder, we'll call you. Right, babe? Put Jessie's number in your phone."

After exchanging numbers with Ashley and hugging her sister's two best friends, Jessica stepped outside and took a deep breath of the fresh pine. Was she losing it? Was the rag doll just the same type of doll that happened to be missing the same eye on her face? Had the same ribbons? The same yellow yarn hair?

As she stepped up to her car, her cell phone rang. She swallowed hard as she saw her supervisor's name on the display. "Hey, Michael."

"Hi, Jessica. Are you coming to the lab today? I expected your report by today on all the physical evidence collected at the Morgan Flemming crime scene. How'd the meeting go with the sheriff's department?"

"Uh…" She slid into her car and slammed the door "I haven't had that meeting, yet, Michael."

She squeezed her eyes closed, waiting for the explosion. The silence was worse. "Are you still there?"

He cleared his throat. He'd mellowed a lot since getting custody of his daughter. "Is the sheriff's department giving you the runaround?"

"No, it's me." She started the engine and powered down the window to get some air. "I-I found some interesting items at the scene, at the memorial set up for Morgan. I sort of went off on a tangent, but I'll schedule that meeting for today, if possible, and I can transport the material evidence to the lab tomorrow."

"What *interesting items* did you find?"

"A condolence card that mentioned… Tiffany Hunt."

"Someone left a card referencing your sister?"

"Yeah, weird, huh?" She chewed on her bottom lip. Michael knew all about her obsession with her sister's case. He'd told her a few times it's why he believed she was so dogged when it came to analyzing the material evidence from other cases—but he wouldn't want her…compulsion to interfere with other cases.

"Have you tracked down the card yet? Found out if any local stores stock it, if anyone purchased it recently, camera footage?"

She thunked her forehead with the heel of her hand. She didn't need Michael Wilder telling her how to do her job. She should've already followed up on the card by now. "Haven't done that yet, but it's on my list."

"Too busy visiting Avery Plank?"

A breath snagged in her throat. She knew better than to ask Michael how he'd come by that information. He had connections she could only dream about. "I thought that would be a good move, as I saw my sister's name on that card."

He snorted. "Except you would've had to have scheduled that meeting with Plank way in advance of finding that card. Tell me, Jessica. Are you in Fairwood to analyze the evidence in the Morgan Flemming homicide, or are you there to continue the investigation into your sister's?"

"Both?" She pinned her shoulders against the seat back. "I mean, both. I'm here to do my job, but I can't help taking a second look at Tiffany's case."

"Then do it. As long as you get your work done, I don't care what you do on the side, Jessica."

"I'm on it. And I swear, Michael, I have a feeling about this. I think the more I dig into my sister's case, the more I'll discover about Morgan's killer." She thumped her chest with the flat of her hand. "It's instinct."

"I've always trusted your instincts. Don't let me down, and more importantly, don't let Morgan down."

As Michael hadn't demanded her presence at the lab today, Jessica rushed back to her hotel to start working on that card. Of course, the person who'd left the card could've purchased it online or in a different area, but she should've thought of tracing the card as soon as she'd found it. Her brain wasn't functioning correctly.

Michael was right. She owed it to Morgan and Morgan's family to do her job. The card wasn't only a lead on Tiffany's case, but it could lead to a clue on Morgan's, as well.

She pulled into the parking lot of her hotel, and her phone rang again. Holding her breath, she looked at the display—not Michael checking up on her.

"Hi, Finn. How was your class this morning?"

"Good. How'd it go with Ashley?"

"Better than expected in some ways. I ran into Denny at her place."

"Denny Phelps? What was he doing there?"

"They're a thing. Apparently, they started seeing each other after Tiffany's death. I could tell Ashley was uncomfortable about it, but I don't begrudge them their happiness. I learned a few things, though."

"Do you want to tell me over dinner? I have office hours, a faculty meeting and an online meeting with my editor."

Had he just asked her out on a date? There had been so much sexual tension between them when he was a fresh cop and she was a college student looking for answers to her sister's murder, but once he realized she'd been using him to get information about the case, he'd dropped her. She'd realized at the time that he'd never believe her if she told him that it hadn't all been an act on her part. She hadn't even tried.

Now the sparks still kindled, but it was her turn to doubt. Did he have ulterior motives related to his book? Did he want to get close to her and her investigation to sabotage it?

"Jessica? Dinner? My treat."

"Sure. Yeah. I talked to my supervisor today, and he suggested I run a trace on the condolence card, which I should've already implemented. I didn't even get a chance to tell him about the doll, but I'll give you the details about that tonight. Seven?"

"I'll pick you up at your hotel."

He ended the call before she could change her mind—not that she wanted to change it. She valued his insight, and she owed him. If he wanted fodder for his book, he could try to find it.

Back in her hotel room, she snapped on some blue gloves and removed the card from the safe in the closet. She flipped it over and studied the back.

Any store, including online ones, would carry this brand of card, but she could probably search most of the stores in Fairwood in a few afternoons. Might as well start now and fill up the time before meeting Finn for dinner.

Fifteen minutes later, she hit the first store. The clerk at the counter greeted her as she breezed through the front door of the small drugstore. She found a small slotted shelf of cards in the back near the batteries and phone chargers. Not one sympathy card peeked out from the rows of birthday cards and a smattering of early Halloween cards. People sent cards for Halloween?

The local grocery store didn't carry cards, and a T-shirt and knickknack shop featured only handmade cards from artists in the area. She bought two of those cards.

Peeking through the window of a convenience store, she spotted a rotating rack filled with cards. She stepped through the front doors and made a beeline for the rack. She spun it around until she saw a few thank-you and sympathy cards. She plucked the two sympathy cards from their spots. One glance told her they weren't the same as the one she found at Morgan's memorial, but the same greeting card company produced them. Progress.

She took the bagged card to the counter and held it out to the clerk. "Do you know if your store carried this particular card?"

The guy shoved his hair from his face and squinted at the card. "Is it back there?"

"No, but there are two from the same company. I was just wondering if this card may have been purchased here." She jiggled the plastic bag pinched between her fingertips at the clerk, as he seemed to be rapidly losing interest in her questions.

He blinked. "Do you have a receipt? Looks like it's been used. We can't take it back."

"I didn't buy it. I wanted to know—" she spun around and rolled her eyes "—never mind."

She tucked the card back in her purse and swung by the self-serve soda machine to fill up a cup with half root beer and half Diet Coke. This time the clerk smiled at her as he rang up her purchase.

When she got back to her car, she dropped her drink in the cup holder and pulled out her phone. Task one completed, task two up next.

The phone rang twice before King County Sheriff's Deputy Tomas Alvarado picked up. "Detective Alvarado."

"Detective Alvarado, this is Jessica Eller, Washington State Patrol Crime Lab."

"Hi, Jessica. You can call me Tomas. I was waiting for your call. Are you ready to transport the physical evidence to the lab? Marysville, right? Or is this going to Seattle?"

"Marysville. Seattle's all full up. I'd like to meet with you first and discuss the evidence. I also found a couple of items at Morgan Flemming's memorial site I'd like to show you."

"It's a little late for me today, but I can do tomorrow. Three at the station sound good?"

"I'll be there."

"In the meantime, to prep for the meeting I'll email you a list of the material evidence. We didn't categorize it yet. We'll leave it up to you guys, as usual."

"Perfect. You have my department email. Send it over, encrypted."

She ended the call and cupped the phone in her hands.

Michael had been right. Time to focus on Morgan. If that led to new discoveries about Tiffany, she'd take it.

Shuffling through those greeting cards had taken her longer than she'd expected, so she rushed back to the hotel. She wanted to review the email from Tomas before she got ready for her...meeting with Finn.

Back in her room fifteen minutes later, Jessica peeked into her closet to see if she had anything halfway presentable to wear to dinner tonight. So far, Finn had seen her in jeans, T-shirts and hiking boots, and slacks and a blouse—hardly memorable. But this wasn't a date, so it didn't matter if he found her attractive.

It didn't matter because they had this...thing between them—chemistry, electricity, good old-fashioned lust. She'd wondered over the years if her attraction to Finn at that time had been because she needed him to get info on her sister's case. Maybe, feeling guilt about using him, she had convinced herself that she really did feel something for him.

This reacquaintance with him had pretty much put that theory to bed, which is exactly where she wanted him. She slid the closet door closed and smirked at herself in the mirror.

With her drink from the convenience store beside her open laptop, Jessica accessed her email. She scrolled past several, including one from Celine Jerome, a PI who specialized in genetic and family tracking. Jessica had decided to take up where Tiffany had left off tracking down their brother.

She clicked on the message from Tomas and opened the attachment. She expanded the file and ran a quick eye down the short list of items.

Outdoor crime scenes usually yielded less physical evidence than indoor ones, and the elements subjected that evidence to more deterioration and less reliability. They did pick up a shoe print, but how long had it been there? It could belong to anyone in that public area.

She opened her own file and began to make notes on the evidence in her own words. The method helped her process the items, especially when she hadn't been on the responding CSI team. She had to reconstruct the scene and the physical evidence in her head. She also used a program on her computer to sketch out the scene. Visiting it in person always helped.

A cigarette butt in the area held promise. A red cloth fiber that hadn't come from anything of Morgan's. A foil wrapper from a granola bar, but no prints on that. No prints on anything, including Morgan's neck. Most likely, her killer had strangled her with a piece of clothing. Necktie? Scarf? Is that where the red fiber came from? Plank had used a tie on her sister, although authorities had never found it.

Most of these items had been shipped to the forensic lab in Seattle for possible DNA sampling. Marysville did DNA, but this evidence had been fast-tracked, so the items that might contain DNA had been sent to Seattle. The lab in Marysville handled physical evidence, her department, and vehicle inspections, although no vehicles were involved in this case—that they knew of.

There was no evidence that Morgan had fought back, either. No skin cells beneath her fingernails, no bruising, broken fingers. Had she known her killer, or had he sneaked up behind her? Had he lain in wait…smoking a cigarette while he watched?

Her phone rang, and she jumped. Her gaze darted to the

time, and she answered Finn's call as she hopped up from her chair. "I can't believe it's seven already."

"Ah, you're not ready. I'm here in my car. I guess I expected you'd be waiting out front."

"And I would've been, if I hadn't gotten so engrossed in my work. Do we have reservations anywhere?"

Finn coughed. "Sorry, no. Wasn't thinking a reservation kinda place, but that could change."

"No. That's fine. Give me fifteen minutes."

"Tell you what. Let's go to the restaurant down the street, near the dock. They do some decent fish and chips. I'll drive over there, have a beer and wait for you. I'll even order you a glass of white."

"Make it a beer, whatever you're having, and you're on."

She dropped the phone on her bed and stripped off her clothes on the way to the bathroom. This was feeling less like a date and more like a convenient business meeting. Good thing she'd left the sexy date-night clothes at home.

After a quick shower, Jessica pulled on a pair of jeans, a lightweight red sweater and a pair of boots with a small heel. She stroked on some mascara, added a red lip and fluffed up her hair. She grabbed her purse and a black leather bomber jacket and stopped at the mirrored closet. "Not bad for a sort of date on a tight timeline."

When she hit the front desk in the lobby, she asked the clerk, "Which direction do I take to the dock?"

"Take a left out of the parking lot, and you'll run right into it. Dockside Fish Grill?" He replied as she nodded. "Order the fish and chips."

"Will do, thanks."

She stuck to the sidewalk on one side of the street, as quite a few cars whizzed by. Hardly the romantic date night she'd envisioned, but Finn had probably felt the same way when he discovered she hadn't even been ready on time. Or maybe he'd envisioned no such thing.

Twinkling lights swaying in the breeze signaled the restaurant up ahead, and she quickened her pace. She could use a beer after the day she had, filled with more questions than answers.

She spotted Finn on the outdoor patio and climbed the wooden steps to join him under the heat lamp. He jumped up to pull out her chair.

"Too chilly for you? We can move inside, but the heat lamp helps and the air is refreshing, especially as I've been cooped up indoors all day."

"This is fine." She scooted her chair closer to the table and shrugged off her jacket. "How were your meetings?"

"Office hours are usually okay, but that one student of mine, Dermott Webb—you saw him after my class—he's kind of a fanboy. Always has a ton of questions, many designed as gotchas for me. He's testing me. Those kinds of students are tiresome. And the staff meeting?" He took a long swallow of his beer. "Even more tiresome."

A waitress pushed through the glass doors to the patio with a tray laden with a bottle of beer and a frosty mug. "I would've had it waiting for you, but I wanted to be sure you got it cold."

"Perfect. Thank you."

When she left, Jessica picked up her perfectly poured beer and raised it. "To less tiresome and less confusing days."

"I'll definitely drink to that." He clinked his bottle against her glass. "I'm sure your day was more interesting than mine. Tell me what you discovered."

"I discovered, thanks to my boss, that I'm putting my

sister's old case ahead of Morgan's and doing her an injustice." She sipped her drink and touched her tongue to the foam on her lip.

"I think you can do both at the same time. What did you find out from Denny and Ashley?" He shoved a menu at her with one finger. "I'm ordering the fish and chips."

"Me, too, on the suggestion of the hotel desk clerk." She stacked the two menus, hitting the edges on the tabletop. "Did you know Denny was selling drugs at the time of Tiffany's murder?"

"I knew that, yeah." Finn wrapped his hands around his bottle, lacing his fingers. "That lead went nowhere. Denny was in good standing with his bosses. Didn't owe anyone. Nobody owed him. No skimming. No stealing."

She wrinkled her nose. "Wow, so he was a *good* drug dealer."

"Good enough not to make him...or his woman a target."

After the waitress took their orders, Jessica tilted her head. "You never told me that about him."

"Like I said, didn't play a role in Tiffany's murder." He tapped his bottle with his fingernail. "What else did you find out from those two?"

"The doll, my doll, the one I'd left with Tiffany, was stolen in the weeks prior to her murder."

His eyebrows bunched over his nose. "That's not in the case file. Nobody mentioned a break-in at her place."

"Ashley never reported it. Claims she's not sure anyone *did* break into their apartment. Noticed it missing but put it down to a prank or someone just walking off with it."

"You think Tiffany's killer stole the doll and then ten years later left it at the crime scene of another murder victim?" His gaze burned into her, and she wondered again how blue could cause so much heat.

"Y-yes." She took a gulp of her beer and patted the foam from her lip.

"You don't sound so sure now. Is that your doll or a replica?"

"With the same missing button?"

He lifted his shoulders. "It's a toy. Buttons go missing."

"Maybe—" she snapped her fingers three times "—it's not the same doll but one meant to look like mine."

"That brings us back to the same place. Someone ten years ago took Tiffany's doll, maybe lost it, or maybe just took notice of the doll and copied it to leave it at Morgan's memorial site. Why?"

The waitress saved her from coming up with an answer, placing their baskets of food on the table. "Anything else? Another round?"

Jessica glanced at her half-full glass and shook her head, and Finn asked for some vinegar.

The appearance of the food didn't deter him, even as he shook his napkin into his lap and picked up a french fry. He waved it at her. "Why would someone be playing you like this? How would that person even know you'd be back here?"

"I don't know. He could know my job, know I'd be on the scene for the evidence."

"Or it could have nothing to do with you at all. I think I told you before, could be a sick joke, someone fascinated with your sister's case. We both know there are people out there like that. True crime podcasts flourish, websites dig into cases new and cold. Lotta crime buffs out there. It's not a stretch to imagine that several of these fans are sickos.

They want to insert themselves into cases." Finn sprinkled his fish and chips with the vinegar the waitress had left. "I'm sure it wouldn't surprise you to learn that several women have proposed to Avery Plank."

She picked up a piece of fish with her fingers and blew on it. "Don't ruin my appetite."

"I'm just sayin'." He held out the bottle of vinegar to her, and she shook her head. "Any luck with the condolence card? I'm figuring you would've led with that if you had gotten lucky."

"Exactly. Found some cards from the same company but not this particular one."

"Did you check the university's bookstore?"

"Good call." She smothered her fries with ketchup, noting Finn's horrified expression. "You know for sure the store carries cards? Do students even buy cards?"

"I know for sure you just made a mess out of your fries, but yeah. I've bought a few cards there myself. In fact, I'd hazard a guess that the majority of the students who left cards at Morgan's memorial bought them at the student store."

"I'll check tomorrow." Her phone buzzed in the side pocket of her purse, and she pulled it free, cupping it in her hand beneath the table. She squinted at the unknown number on her display and tapped it, leaving a smudge of ketchup on the screen.

Her pulse jumped as she read the message: If you wanna know what happened to ur sister meet me at morgans at 9 come alone.

She shoved the phone back in her purse and curled her fingers around the handle of her beer mug so tightly she felt as if she could snap it off.

"Everything okay?" Finn crunched into a piece of fish and raised his brows.

"That was my boss, Michael. He's not very happy with me right now and wants my evidence report like yesterday." She took a sip of beer to soothe her dry throat. "I'd started it before dinner. That's why I hadn't realized how fast the time had gone and that you were downstairs waiting for me. I hadn't even taken a shower."

She put down her beer and shoved a piece of fish in her mouth. *Stop talking, Jessica.*

"Oh, wow. Sorry. I didn't realize you were so busy. You could've canceled."

"Even overworked, overwhelmed CSIs need to eat." She flashed him a fake smile as her brain tripped out. "But I should really get back. I'll take the rest of my food with me. Do you mind?"

"Absolutely not. I'll grab a couple of to-go boxes."

As Finn left the patio, Jessica retrieved her phone and answered the unknown texter that she'd be there at nine. She knew he'd meant Morgan's memorial site, and she had every intention of being there—alone.

Chapter Seven

Finn ducked behind a potted plant and peered at the patio between its leaves, watching Jessica dip her head as she texted on her phone. Unless her boss had just threatened to fire her, he didn't believe her for one minute.

She'd actually gotten worse at lying over the years, or maybe he'd just gotten over being the besotted fool who believed everything she said. He pivoted and made a beeline toward the bar. Correction. He was still besotted but no longer a fool.

He asked for a couple of containers and a plastic bag, and catching the waitress as she ordered some drinks at the bar, he requested the check.

He took care of the bill and returned to the patio, handing a container to Jessica. "You wanna add more ketchup to those fries before boxing them up?"

"No." She didn't even crack a smile, but he noticed she'd finished off her beer. For courage?

He'd eaten more than she had and elected to leave his food on his plate. "At least I can give you a ride back to the hotel."

"That was my fault for being late. The walk wasn't bad, though." She slid her to-go box in the plastic bag and grabbed her purse. "Ready."

He was ready, too.

As she sat beside him in the passenger seat, her knees bounced, jiggling the plastic bag on her lap.

He knew not to ask questions. Better to pretend everything was normal. Better to make her believe he hadn't noticed that text had turned her world upside down. Maybe Denny and Ashley had a change of heart and were ready to spill some secrets.

The drive took less than five minutes, and he pulled up in front of the lobby. "Walk you up?"

"No. I'm sorry. I really need to get busy and finish this report tonight. Thanks for dinner." She patted the plastic bag. "And now I have a midnight snack."

"Let's touch base tomorrow. I can have a look at the card section at the student store, as I'll be on campus anyway."

"That would be great."

She couldn't get out of his car fast enough and slammed the door so hard it made the vehicle shudder. Holding up one hand in a wave, she disappeared into the hotel.

He put the car in gear and rolled around to the side of the hotel, facing the water. This gave him a clear view of the guest parking lot, and he'd already spotted her Subaru. He couldn't listen in on any phone calls she might make or see any texts, but if she planned a late-night rendezvous with Denny and Ashley, he'd see her leave.

He cut the lights and slumped in his seat. He felt as if he were on a stakeout again. Too bad he hadn't taken a coffee for the road. Finn turned on the radio and watched a few people come and go from dinner, headlights training in and out of the parking lot.

When a lone figure darted from the hotel into the parking lot, he sat up. The lights on Jessica's car flashed as she scurried toward it.

Finn started his engine but left his headlights off. If stopped, he knew enough officers on the force that they might let him get away without a ticket. There wasn't enough traffic on the road for Jessica not to notice a single car following her. He'd have to use all his forgotten surveillance skills for this one.

As she pulled out of the parking lot, he trailed after her, allowing another car to get between them. Hanging back, he duplicated her turns away from the pier toward the university. For a minute, he expected her to turn into the campus. Maybe she'd just decided to check out the student store on her own.

Then she turned left onto the road that bordered the university—and led to the forest trail. Was she actually going there? And why?

He made the same turn but slowed down, as he'd lost the car in the middle blocking her view of his vehicle. She couldn't turn off many places along this route. This road eventually led to the coast, but she wouldn't have taken the long way around to get there.

When her brake lights flashed ahead, he hung back even more. Had she spotted him in her rearview? Not that she shouldn't be watching her back after that tire stunt.

Finn let out a breath when she picked up speed, and he accelerated to follow. His Jeep sat too high to be overlooked, and even with his lights out, a watchful eye would be able to detect his approach. He'd have to slow down, let her get well ahead and just hope he'd see her car parked at the side or in a pullout.

He also hoped he'd get there in time to save her—from what, he didn't know, maybe just from herself.

JESSICA STEERED HER car into the pullout that would give her access to the trail leading to Morgan's memorial site. Is this where her killer had parked? Or had he been stealthier, coming from a direction where no one would notice him?

The CSIs on the scene had checked this pullout for tire tracks, but there had been too many to distinguish one set. They hadn't had any better luck with the area across the river. Too many people used this trail, although nobody had witnessed a man in the area. One couple had passed Morgan on the trail, probably less than fifteen minutes before she'd been murdered.

Jessica gave a little shiver and slid her Sig into her pocket. She might be taking her life in her hands by agreeing to meet a stranger at the site of two murders, but she was going to have a gun in at least one of those hands while she did it. The texter had said come alone, not come unarmed and defenseless.

She eased from her car and snapped the door closed. She'd leave it unlocked in case she needed to make a quick getaway. Before diving into the woods, Jessica glanced over her shoulder. A few sets of headlights had been behind her up until the university, and she thought she'd seen a shadow behind her on the road out here, but that didn't make sense.

Whoever had invited her was probably already in place waiting for her. She dipped her hand into her pocket and wrapped her fingers around the handle of her weapon. The hiking boots she'd swapped in for the low heels she'd worn at dinner crunched through the forest floor. She didn't try to conceal her presence. She didn't want to startle the guy.

This could be another prank, but she couldn't risk not knowing. If someone had information about her sister's murder, well, that's what she was looking for. A little danger wasn't going to deter her.

She strode toward Morgan's memorial, which had grown since the last time she and Finn had found the rag doll here. Her classmates wanted to pay their respects, maybe even pressure the police, who didn't seem to have much to go on right now—and she should know given that paltry evidence list. Something else was going to have to crack this case—and she just might hold the key.

She called out. "Hello? It's Jessica Eller. Tell me what you know. Show your face."

A rustling noise beyond the trees answered her, and she spun toward it. "This is your meeting. I'm here. Tell me what you got. What do you know about Tiffany?"

Whispering filtered through the cedars and the red alders, their branches still full from summer and bulking up for the winter, but Jessica couldn't tell if it was a human voice or the sound of the leaves playing tricks on her willing mind. "Hello?"

A crunch of sticks and a crackle of twigs vibrated through the air, the rhythmic sound an echoing of footsteps on the trail. Was he running away from her? Had she scared him away with her bold approach?

Putting her head down, she used her arms to swim through the foliage at the edge of the clearing, stumbling on the path next to the creek. She tipped her nose to the sky like an animal catching a scent from the breeze and held her breath. Beyond her thundering heart, she heard the footsteps traipsing through the forest, the littered ground beneath his feet pinpointing his direction.

She veered to the right, and clutched a stitch in her side as she took the path to her sister's murder site. Was he playing some cruel game with her? Did he want her to follow him? He didn't seem to be doing anything to conceal his tread.

"I'm coming. I'm following you." She panted the words, more out of apprehension than any physical exhaustion.

Still, he remained ahead of her, teasing her, goading her, leading her to the one place in the world that had the power to break her. And he knew it.

She stumbled to a stop at a place where the creek gurgled louder and where a twisted branch reached out from the water to grab her. She dropped to her knees, the pebbles gouging the flesh beneath her jeans.

A sob bubbled in her throat. She choked out, "I'm here. Is this where you want me? Tell me what you know."

Sitting back on her heels, she ran her arm beneath her nose, her gaze scanning the area. What did he want? The footsteps, louder now to compensate for the rushing water, stomped ahead. He wasn't finished with her yet.

She scrambled to her feet and lurched forward, like a drunk craving one more drink, even though he knew he'd had enough. Even though he knew nothing good lay ahead.

Adrenaline raced through her body now, and her legs pumped faster and with more assurance. She'd catch him. She'd catch him if it was the last thing she did this night. She plowed ahead with purpose, her jaw clamped, her breathing heavy through her nose.

When she heard the laugh, she froze. The high-pitched sound sent rivers of ice down her back. She pulled the gun from her pocket, her itching finger on the trigger.

She crept forward more slowly. "What's so funny? Why don't you show me what's so funny?"

She took a few steps, stopped and listened. Took a few more steps, stopped and listened. Nothing. The owner of that hair-raising laugh had stopped moving, stopped communicating with her.

"Jesssssica."

Had that been the breeze breathing her name? She cranked her head toward the creek and jerked back. Hunching forward, Jessica inched close to the water's edge.

Then she clapped a hand to her mouth, but it didn't do any good. A scream ripped through her throat as the eyes of a dead girl stared back at her.

Chapter Eight

Finn dug the heels of his tennis shoes into the dirt and eyed the pile of stuffed animals, candles and flowers, balloons floating above it all. From his position, he did a three-sixty but didn't see any sign of Jessica.

The location of her car on the road indicated she'd come to Morgan's memorial, as they'd parked there when they were here together. Why would she go anywhere else? Unless someone took her against her will.

Crouching down, he used the flashlight from his phone to scan the ground, looking for a disturbance or signs of a struggle. But he was no professional tracker, and the sticks, leaves, pebbles and other detritus from the forest littered the ground in the haphazard pattern he'd expect.

He glanced up, taking in the trail that led through the trees to the edge of the creek. She didn't get it in her head to take a stroll past her sister's murder site, did she? What would possess her to do that? Unless it wasn't her idea.

His heart thumped as he pushed to his feet and strode toward the path to the creek. Before he even got there, a woman's scream ripped through the night air.

The hair on the back of his neck stood on end, and his feet started moving in the direction of the sound. The shriek had set the whole forest in motion. Creatures scurried around him under cover of the darkness and underbrush, and birds took flight, twittering and flapping.

Once he swallowed his shock and got his breath back, he shouted. "Jessica! Jessica!"

The critters responded to his intrusion with more chirping and rustling, but humans had other ways of communicating. Without missing a step, Finn pulled out his phone and called Jessica.

His chest heaved and his vision blurred as her phone rang. When he finally heard her voice on the other end, he staggered to a stop. "Jessica?"

Her reply, breathless and hoarse, almost took him to his knees in relief. "Oh my God. Finn, there's another one. There's another dead woman."

Goose bumps marched across his flesh as he clutched the phone, trying to keep Jessica close. "I'm here in the forest. I heard your scream. I'm by the creek, just past the crime scene."

"Keep following the waterline. Go past Tiffany's murder site for several more yards. I-I'm here. There's a body by the water."

He started jogging, phone plastered to his ear. "Stay on the line with me. I'm almost there. We'll call 911 when I reach you. Are you safe?"

"The killer's gone, if that's what you mean, and I have my Sig Sauer by my side."

"Thatta girl. Keep it handy, but I'm coming at you in about a minute. Don't shoot me."

When he came around the last bend in the creek, he ended the call with Jessica and shone his flashlight on her standing beside a crumpled form at the water's edge, her weapon in her hand at her side. His gut twisted in knots. He'd been so focused on getting to Jessica, he hadn't let the news of another body sink in—until now.

His stride ate up the final feet between them, and he pulled her against his chest with one arm. Her body trembled against him. "God, I'm glad you're okay."

"I am—" she sniffled and pointed her gun at the body "—but she's not."

"Have you touched the body? Done any kind of observation?"

"Just checked her pulse to make sure she didn't have any life left to save. Sh-she was still warm. I didn't want to touch anything else." She wriggled from his grasp and tapped her phone. "I'm calling it in."

He didn't want to touch anything, either, but he crouched beside the young woman, her eyes staring, her black hair spread out in a fan behind her head, and ran his light around her face and neck. The redness around her throat indicated another strangling. Small scratches marred her skin, and he directed his light to her hand resting across her chest. One broken fingernail and a few drops of blood indicated this poor girl had fought to breathe, fought to remove the object around her neck, strangling the life out of her.

Finished with her call to 911, Jessica nudged him in the back with her toe. "Careful."

He rose beside her. "Strangled, probably with a tie or scarf. Most likely not a rope or wire."

"Just like Morgan—" Jessica rubbed her upper arms "—and Tiffany, but *not* like the other Creekside victims."

"Well, we know where Avery Plank is, so it's definitely not him." Finn stepped away from the body, pulling Jessica with him. "What were you doing out here? How'd you find this body?"

"What were *you* doing out here?"

"I followed you." He shrugged, not ashamed of his actions. "After you got that text at dinner, you seemed off. I figured you were up to something and if you didn't want to tell me, it was probably something you knew you shouldn't be doing."

"What are you, the hall monitor?" She narrowed her eyes, but he didn't flinch.

"You're welcome. I may have saved your life."

"It's not my life that needed saving."

"Are you going to tell me what happened or make me find out when you talk to the police because I *know* you're not lying to them." He crossed his arms and puffed out his chest, even though he really wanted her back in his embrace. For all her tough talk, her eyes looked glassy in the darkness, and that scream still echoed in his brain.

"I got a text from someone who told me to meet him at Morgan's memorial site if I wanted to find out what happened to Tiffany."

Anger fizzed in his veins, and he wanted to berate her for her carelessness—but that wasn't the way to get Jessica Eller to talk. "Unknown number, I presume."

"You presume correctly, and we can further presume that any tracing of the number is going to come back to a burner phone, but I'm still going to run a trace."

"Okay." He curled his fingers into his biceps. "Morgan's memorial site. I was there. You weren't. What happened from there?"

"I stopped there for a few minutes waiting, and then I began to hear noises in the woods—human noises. Footsteps."

"Someone out there just stomping around after committing a murder."

"No stealthy creeping. He definitely wanted me to hear him...and follow him." She rubbed her hands together in front of her, as if trying to get warm even though she still wore the jacket from dinner.

"Follow him?"

"His footsteps were quite clear. Every time I stopped to listen, he'd respond by leading me on with his footsteps. Once I started along the path, it became clear that he was leading me to Tiffany's crime scene." She covered her mouth with her hand.

"You got to...that location and then what happened?"

Her eyes widened as she reached out and grabbed his arm. "He laughed."

"Laughed? What kind of laugh?" Finn clenched his jaw. What kind of evil laughed after committing a murder? Avery Plank for one, and there were many others.

"A horrible, high-pitched laugh." Jessica covered her ears as if she could still hear it. She probably could.

"I think it came from across the creek. He must've come from the other side. The deputies need to check that access road for tire tracks. I know they did for Morgan's murder, too, but this time they might be able to discern fresh tracks. I never did hear a car. Did you?"

"I didn't hear a car. Didn't hear a laugh, either." He chewed on his bottom lip. "After you screamed, did you hear me calling your name?"

"No. I just got your call, which stunned me for a few seconds. Of course, I didn't have any idea when I saw the call come through that you were actually in the forest with me." She gave him a sideways glance. "I'm glad you were here."

"Me, too, but that means the killer probably didn't hear me yelling, either. So he didn't know I was here."

"I think he left after I screamed. He left once he made sure I'd found his handiwork." She pointed down the path that led to another entrance to the trail. "Sirens."

"If he didn't hear me, didn't know I was out here, I probably didn't save your life."

"You sound disappointed." She shoved her hands in the front pockets of her jeans and screwed up one side of her mouth.

"No, no. I'm relieved you weren't in physical danger." He stepped toward the water, making a wide berth around the dead woman, and stared at the other side of the creek. "I'm just wondering why. What does he want with you? Why lead you to another dead body?"

"It's clear to me." She raised her arms in the air, cell phone flashlight clasped in one hand, and waved at the deputies charging up the trail. "He either killed Tiffany or knows who did. He's playing a game with me…and I'm all in."

ABOUT TWO HOURS later at the stroke of midnight, Jessica kicked her feet in the chilly water and took another sip of beer from the bottle she and Finn had bought at the little market inside her hotel. Her shoulder bumped his as they sat side by side at the edge of a small mooring area outside the hotel. After the deputies had grilled them—or rather grilled *her*, Finn's buddies on the force had *questioned* him—they'd been too pumped up to go their separate ways and call it a night. What a night.

Tapping her knee, he said, "Your toes are going to freeze in that water."

"Then they'll match the rest of me. I'm not over the shock

of finding Missy Park. Why weren't the deputies patrolling that trail after Morgan's murder? And what was Missy doing there by herself?

Finn tipped back his bottle, took a long swallow and slammed it down on the wooden slats of the dock. "I could ask you the same question."

She caught her breath. She knew Finn would be angry about it. Knew he'd try to talk her out of it. That's why she'd hidden it from him. She said, lightly, "Asked and answered."

"If a stranger texted you to go jump off the Space Needle, would you do that, too?" He collapsed on his back, folding his arms beneath his head.

"I would do a lot to solve my sister's murder. I owe it to her." She glanced at his bunching biceps, his T-shirt stretched across the hard planes of his chest. The boy had become a man—a harder, less forgiving one, a less malleable one.

He turned his head. "Do you think Tiffany would want you to put yourself in danger to find her killer? Tiffany protected you. You told me yourself she risked her life to protect you when you were children. She'd want you to live your life, Jessica."

"If the drunk driver that killed your father while he was on patrol hadn't been apprehended at the scene, are you telling me you wouldn't have moved heaven and earth to find that person and bring him to justice? You know you would have. You went into a career that you didn't even like just to honor his memory."

Finn closed his eyes, and she reached out and stroked his thigh. "I'm sorry to bring that up…but you know it's true, Finn. I never believed the Creekside Killer was responsible for Tiffany's death. It didn't add up to me. Avery Plank never stalked his victims. His were crimes of opportunity. He picked up sex workers and dumped them on trails, at campsites, recreational areas. Tiffany's killer stalked her."

"You know the theory." He rolled onto his side and propped up his head with his hand, his elbow planted on the wooden dock.

"That Plank knew her when she'd been turning tricks, discovered her again and decided to kill her." She flipped her hand in the air. "Nope. Tiffany wouldn't have met up with a former john. I doubt she'd even remember him. This person stalked her, perhaps stole the rag doll and slipped away when Plank took the blame."

"Never to strike again. You don't have to take one of my classes to know how unlikely that is—especially if this killer was unknown to Tiffany."

"I've thought of that. He could've gotten picked up for another crime. He didn't leave any DNA at Tiffany's scene. Didn't sexually assault her, probably for that same reason. If the cops had picked him up for peeping or burglary or assault, they wouldn't have had any DNA to match him up with Tiffany's murder."

"So, he's been in jail for the past ten years and decided to come back to the scene of his first murder and start up again—while contacting the sister of his victim."

"Yeah, I don't know." She pulled her feet from the water and curled her legs beneath her. "I'm just so heartbroken for Missy and Morgan. I wonder if the investigators will find any connection between the two women other than the first letter of their first names and the fact that they were both on that trail at night. Just like Morgan, Missy was wearing running clothes and earbuds. So it would seem they were both on that trail voluntarily. Why would Missy go running where another woman had been murdered just a week before?"

"People do careless things all the time." He sat up and gave her a hard stare. "Are you going back to the crime scene in the morning when it's light out to finish your examination?"

"Yeah, poor Deputy Holden has to spend the night out there to guard it. I'm not the only CSI member who's going back. We still need to look for tracks. Also, I told Detective Morse that I'm pretty sure the killer had been farther up the trail at Morgan's site. He could've left pieces of evidence along that trail without realizing what he was doing." She stuck her legs out in front of her and wiggled her toes as she grabbed one of her socks. "He was sloppy this time."

"I hope Missy got his DNA beneath her fingernails. I saw blood. Of course, it could be her own blood, as I also saw scratches on her neck. The poor girl was probably trying to claw the scarf from her neck as he twisted it tighter and tighter."

Jessica swallowed, the beer tasting bitter on the back of her tongue. "How do you know it's a scarf and not a tie or a sleeve or something else?"

"I don't. Just a guess." He smacked both hands on the dock and pushed up to his feet. "Let's get going before your toes turn to icicles."

She shoved her feet into her hiking boots. "Warm and cozy now."

He hovered over her, extending his hand. She took the offer, and he pulled her up beside him. He kept hold of her hand and with the other brushed a lock of hair from her forehead. "I was scared as hell when I heard you scream. That few seconds before you answered your phone felt like minutes ticking by in my head while I imagined all sorts of things happening to you."

"Instead of screaming, I should've gone after him. I had my gun. I knew he'd cross the creek. I could tell from his creepy laugh. Maybe I could've…caught him. Stopped him."

He pinched her chin, his thumb almost touching her bottom lip. She closed her eyes, waiting for his anger to well up again, waiting for him to chastise her for her stupidity.

His lips brushed hers, and her eyes flew open. The tenderness that touch communicated melted the ball of fear and tension lodged in her chest, replaced by a deep longing. Before she could respond in kind, because oh, she did want to kiss him back, he drew away from her.

His voice rough, he said, "I'm glad you didn't."

Lacing his fingers with hers, he tugged her back up the dock toward the hotel. They dropped their beer bottles into the trash can in the parking lot, and he finally released her hand as they stood just inside the lobby.

She wanted to invite him up to her room, but that desire felt so wrong hours after discovering Missy Park crumpled at the side of the creek.

He made the decision for them as he turned toward the door. "Try to get some sleep. You'll have a busy day tomorrow, and school is going to be a nightmare again. I haven't forgotten about the card. I'll have a look in the student store."

"Thanks again for…following me. See, you've still got those instincts."

He made a gun with his fingers and cocked it at her before heading back to his car.

She sighed as she crossed the lobby, and the hotel clerk

called out to her. "Did you hear about another body down by the creek? Just like Morgan."

"I did. Terrible news."

"Be safe out there, Ms. Eller."

"Oh, I will." She patted the gun in her pocket on the way to the elevator. She'd be safe enough from physical danger, but keeping her heart safe from Finn Karlsson was another matter.

Chapter Nine

The following morning, Finn still had that kiss on his mind. He hadn't wanted to take advantage of the situation, as Jessica had been shaken up by the discovery of Missy Park's body.

What kind of sick game was this guy playing with Jessica? Why her? If he didn't kill Tiffany Hunt ten years ago, he was obviously fascinated with the case, seeking to make Jessica a part of these current murders.

Finn could no longer ignore the fact that the person tormenting Jessica had killed Morgan and Missy. He had led Jessica right to his most recent trophy. That was no coincidence—he'd wanted her to find Missy's body.

Finn knew the investigators were already trying to trace the number that texted Jessica last night. She'd turned over her cell phone to them at the scene, but she'd nailed it. The number would belong to an untraceable burner phone.

Finn hoped they'd find some useful evidence at the scene. If the killer led Jessica on from Morgan's murder site to Missy's, he may have left a trail.

Finn still had his contacts at the King County Sheriff's Department where his father had worked as a deputy for fifteen years. That's why the department had asked him to stand with them when Detective Morse held an information meeting for the students this morning. A sense of dread had crept over Finn as he had stared out at worried, fearful faces, many of them past and present students.

He hit the lights and locked up as he left his office. He had his own piece of the investigation to do today.

In the university bookstore, he took the escalator up to the student store and squeezed past a gaggle of people clustered around the energy drink display.

He located the carousel of cards in the back of the store and spun it around to find the sympathy cards. As he ran his fingers down the empty racks, someone bumped his elbow.

"Sorry, Dr. Karlsson." One of his students hovered behind him, her backpack swinging in front of her. "Are you looking for a card to leave for Missy Park, too?"

"I...uh, yeah. Looks like they're all sold out."

The student, whose name he'd forgotten, dabbed the end of her nose with a tissue. "Maybe they never restocked them after Morgan's murder. My parents want me out of here. Thought I'd be safer at this small school than at U-Dub, but Seattle isn't looking so bad right now."

"They'll catch him, but in the meantime, stay safe. Don't walk alone at night, skip the online dating for now. Did you know either of the women?"

"Saw Missy once in a while because she worked at the bookstore, and I work at the coffeehouse inside the bookstore. Nice girl. Smart. Don't know why she'd be running at night alone, especially after what happened to Morgan." She gave a little shiver. "I'm not going out—I mean, except with my friends."

All these students were too trusting. "Well, take care... and get yourself some pepper spray."

The girl's eyes widened as he turned away and went to the counter, grabbing a bottle of juice on his way. When it was his turn, he leaned in and said, "How long have you been sold out of sympathy cards?"

The kid, Ryan according to his name tag, blinked and ran a hand through his curly hair. "I think for a while, Professor Karlsson. Sold out after Morgan." He looked left and right, and then leaned in and whispered, "Are you helping with the investigation?"

"Yeah." Well, wasn't he?

"I'm sure my manager can give you more info on the cards, like what we stock, when they were ordered and stuff like that. He's down in the basement, management offices, when he's not up here, riding our asses." Ryan's face colored up to the curls flopping on his forehead as he rang up the juice. "Don't tell him I said that."

"I got you. What's your manager's name?"

"Deke Macy." Ryan guffawed. "You can imagine what we call him behind his back."

"Unfortunate name." Finn slipped a twenty across the counter. "Thanks, Ryan."

Finn cracked open the juice as he walked back toward the escalators. The basement of the university bookstore housed the business end of the whole complex, which included the convenience store he'd just left, a coffeehouse, a cookies and ice cream shop, and a business center that offered printers and mailing supplies to this digital generation that didn't own anything like that.

Fewer students roamed the space down here where older professionals held down the fort. Finn cruised the perimeter until he located the management offices and pushed through the door.

A woman behind a banking type window glanced up at his entrance and pushed her glasses up into her neat Afro. "Hello, can I help you?"

"I'm Finn Karlsson over in criminology. I'm looking for Deke Macy."

"Oh, hi, Professor Karlsson. Saw you at the information meeting this morning. Terrible what's happening on this campus. I'm Nia Humphry. I run accounting down here in the bowels of the beast."

"You do an awesome job, Nia. You can call me Finn. Is Mr. Macy in?"

"You can call him Deke. He's in his office. I'll buzz you in, and you'll see his office when you make a left." She waved a hand behind her.

She buzzed the door and as he slipped through, a head popped around one of the cubicles. "Oh, hello, Dr. Karlsson."

Finn schooled his face into a pleasant smile when he saw Dermott Webb. Just his luck. The guy had better not try to corner him here with his tedious questions. "Mr. Webb. What brings you to this part of campus?"

Nia spoke up for him. "Oh, I couldn't manage without Dermott's help back here. He's a part-timer but could probably do my job."

"Not true." Dermott gave Nia a shy smile. "I have some inventory and accounting background from my stint in the army, so I jumped when I saw this job advertised."

"Well, I'm glad you did, baby. Show Professor Karlsson Deke's office."

"This way, Dr. Karlsson."

Finn followed Dermott's stiff back down a short hallway lined with small offices. The dude must be better with numbers than people.

Dermott stopped and pointed but didn't go near the doorway himself. He mouthed, *this one.*

Finn poked his head inside the office as he tapped on the door. "Deke?"

Deke dragged his gaze away from the computer monitor in front of him and gave Finn the once-over. "Yeah. Who wants to know?"

"I'm Finn Karlsson, professor over in criminology. Just had a couple of questions for you about the student store inventory—if you can help me out." Finn took two steps into the small office and extended his hand to Deke across the messy desk.

Deke stood up, the fluorescent light bouncing off his perfectly shaved head, and stuck out his hand. As they shook, Deke gave Finn's hand a crushing squeeze. Obviously, those muscles he cultivated weren't just for show. He had the strength to go along with them.

"Sure, I know you. Have a seat." Deke snapped his laptop closed and leaned back in his chair, crossing his arms behind his head, biceps flexed.

Was this a contest or something? Finn kept his muscles under wraps and sat in the lone chair opposite the desk. "I was just in the student store and had a question about the sympathy cards."

Deke winked. "You helping out the cops on these murdered girls?"

"Not really. Was in the store to pick up a juice—" he held up the bottle as proof "—saw the cards and had a thought."

"Shame about those girls. Couple of hot ones, too, but if you ask me, girls shouldn't be running around campus with their skimpy workout clothes at night and not expect some attention."

Finn clenched his fist in his lap. "They got more than attention, didn't they?"

"Yeah, yeah. Horrible stuff. The parents—" he shook his bald head "—can't imagine. I got a daughter myself. My ex is a bitch, but what are you gonna do?"

Maybe not victim-blame and call women bitches for a start. Finn swallowed his retort. "Anyway, about those cards. About how many do you stock and how many did you sell after Morgan's murder? Did you sell out and restock?"

Deke flipped open his laptop again, and his fingers raced across the keyboard. "We don't stock many sympathy cards. I mean, what do college kids have to be sorry about? Let's see, Morgan Flemming was murdered eight days ago. Had a full complement of sympathy cards on that day—about twenty-five of them. Sold out of every last one two days after that. Haven't restocked yet. More coming in a few days. Who knew we'd have a run on sympathy cards?"

Finn had pulled out his phone that contained the picture of the condolence card with Tiffany's name on it, but he kept it in his lap, tracing its edges with his fingertip. Did he really want to show the card to Deke? The guy hadn't hesitated one second when coming up with the date of Morgan's murder, and he had a creepy vibe. He should probably just turn this info over to Detective Morse or Deputy Holden, Zach, his buddy from the academy.

As he shifted in his chair, a voice trilled his name from the doorway. "Oh, hey, Professor Karlsson. We're still having class tomorrow, right?"

He twisted around and greeted one of his students, Gabby Medina, tucking her long dark hair behind one ear. "Hi,

Gabby. Yes, we're having class. What are you doing here? I didn't realize so many students worked on the management side of things on campus. Good experience."

She wrinkled her nose. "I don't work here. I work at the ice cream shop, but this is where we pick up and drop off the money for the registers. I saw Dermott out front and asked about class. He told me you were back here with Deke and to ask you myself."

"Hi, Gabbeeeey." Deke waved at her with his fingers as he drew out her name.

"Hi, Dick, I mean Deke." She waved at him in the same manner, rolling her eyes. "Thanks, Professor Karlsson. I'll see you in class tomorrow."

When Gabby's footsteps faded away, Deke gave Finn another wink. "Hot little number. As a professor, I bet you have all the girlies fawning over you."

Finn studied Deke through half-lidded eyes until the other man coughed and shifted his gaze back to his computer. "So, that's what we have on the cards. Anything else?"

Definitely not showing this guy the card.

Finn asked, "All the employees who work on campus come here for the register money?"

"Not all. Just the ones who open or close the register. Nia handles those transactions, along with that dork Dermott." Deke cracked his knuckles. "Anything else, Professor?"

"No, thanks for your help." He'd investigate the hell out of this guy if he still worked in that capacity—but he didn't. As he stood at the door, Finn made a half turn. "Yeah, one more thing. You could pull the transaction records for whoever bought a card, right? Or video surveillance?"

Did the skin around Deke's mouth just blanch?

"N-not the video. We record over that, but the transactions? Sure, as long as it was a card purchase and not cash."

And if Deke Macy bought any sympathy cards to leave at a memorial site, he'd know that and most assuredly pay cash.

"You've been a big help, Deke." Finn hit the doorjamb with the palm of his hand. "Thanks, man."

Before he left the management office, Finn stopped at the front window. "Nia, do you know if either Morgan Flemming or Missy Park came to this office to open or close a register? I know they both worked at the bookstore complex."

Her face creased with concern. "Did they, now? I don't recall. Dermott, you remember?"

Dermott peered around the computer monitor. "They weren't regulars, but that doesn't mean they weren't here. Sometimes the regulars are out, or they send someone else. So anyone who works in the complex could conceivably handle the money. I didn't realize they both worked on campus."

Finn could see the calculation in Dermott's eyes from here. He hoped none of his students were going to take it upon themselves to do some investigating on their own—like he was.

"Thanks, you two. Now I know where to go if I ever need change."

"You can come visit anytime you like, Dr. K."

"Thanks, Nia." He stopped one more time with one foot out the door and made a half turn.

"How long have you been working here, Nia?"

"Oh, baby." She waved a set of manicured nails in the year. "Don't age me, now. I've been here for over twenty years."

He lowered his voice. "And Deke? How long has he been working in this office?"

"This office?" Nia rolled her eyes to the ceiling. "I'd say about four years."

Finn's shoulders slumped as he widened the door. "Okay, thanks again."

"That's *this* office." She wagged a finger at him. "He's been working at the university for longer than that, maybe twelve years total."

"Really?" That stopped Finn in his tracks. So Deke was here when Tiffany was murdered. He never mentioned that murder to Finn.

"He climbed his way up the ladder. Proud of it, too. He'll tell you himself he started as a lowly food service worker."

"Food service, huh?"

Finn exited the office, chewing the side of his thumb. Hadn't Tiffany worked in food service?

Chapter Ten

"You discovered the body?" Michael's voice rumbled over the phone. "What the hell are you doing out there, Jessica?"

"The killer wanted me to discover Missy, Michael. He lured me out and led me on."

"The question is, why would you allow yourself to be lured and led by anyone? You're there to collect and analyze evidence for a murder…now two."

"I completed the evidence report on Morgan Flemming, and I'm ready to send it to you this afternoon. I just came back from my meeting with Deputy Alvarado, and I was at the Missy Park crime scene before that." She'd been enumerating her accomplishments on her fingertips—not that Michael could see her over the phone. "I'm busy, Michael, but this killer has some sort of interest in my sister's case. He's pulling me into it."

"That's dangerous. You don't need to be pulled into anything. The next time you get a text like that, you call Detective Morse." He cleared his throat, lecture over. "Any more evidence present at the Park crime scene than Morgan's?"

"A bit more. Found red fibers again, this time under Missy's fingernails, and I found more on the trail."

"The fibers could be from the murder weapon wrapped around her throat."

"That's what I'm thinking." She was also thinking about that rhyme on the sympathy card—something old, something dead, something stolen, something red She heard a beep on his end of the line.

"I have to take this call. You be careful. It sounds like someone's put a target on your back for whatever reason."

The reason was that she was Tiffany's sister. "I'll be careful."

Red fibers. Had Jessica just tripped over another coincidence? Red had been Tiffany's favorite color. She'd owned a lot of red clothing. What had her sister been wearing when she was killed?

Jessica checked the phone she'd gotten back from the sheriff's department. They'd downloaded her data and would try to trace the phone that texted her, although they all knew it wouldn't be that easy.

No messages from Finn today. Was it because he knew she didn't have her phone or because of that kiss last night? She'd been waiting for a kiss from him for a long time. When she'd been leading him on ten years ago, she hadn't wanted him to kiss her. By the time she wanted it, he'd discovered her deception and had backed off.

She'd like to think they had another chance. She scrolled through her contacts and tapped his name.

He answered on the first ring, as if he'd been waiting. "You got your phone back."

"Yes, the deputies got what they wanted and gave it back to me. I've had an exhausting day on top of that terrifying night, but I have something else to get through before I can rest."

"Can I help?"

Finn never failed her. "Do you still have the case file from my sister's murder?"

"I don't have *the* case file, but I have a ton of copies and notes. What do you need?"

She scooped in a big breath. "I want to know what my sister was wearing that night, specifically."

"I don't remember, but I know it wasn't running clothes like these two women."

Jessica gave a short laugh. "My sister in running clothes? No way. I'd like to see a catalog of her clothing, down to her socks and shoes. Do you think your files have that?"

"I'm sure they do." He paused and sipped something. "How about you come to my place tonight for dinner? I'll share the files with you—and some other information I discovered today—and you can let me know why Tiffany's clothing has become important to you."

"I'd like that, but I don't want to put you out. Do you cook?"

"Not well, but there's a great Chinese place near the university, and I can swing by there on my way home. I'm still at the school. Does that work?"

"Perfectly. What time do you want me there? And I promise I won't be late this time."

He replied, "Or sneak out to meet a killer?"

"No promises there."

They decided on a time, and he gave her directions to his place. Maybe they did have a second chance.

A few hours later, Jessica pulled her car behind Finn's Jeep and idled, taking in the view. Through the open window, the sweet, sticky smell of alder, the fresh spiciness of the pine and the salt from the bay combined to create an invigorating aroma that prickled her face. She inhaled it before rolling up the window and cutting the engine.

She strode up the stone walkway and caught glimpses of the bay undulating behind the house. A profusion of blooms spilled over flower boxes hugging the house, their colors visible but muted beneath the lights that flashed on at her approach. She almost waved at the cameras she knew Finn would have pointing at the porch.

She rang the doorbell, a bottle of white wine in a gift bag swinging from her fingertips. Did white go with Chinese? Did Finn even like white wine? She should've brought beer instead.

As she switched the bag from one hand to the other, Finn answered the door in a pair of faded jeans and a white T-shirt that clung to his muscles. He looked hot in his professor slacks and jacket but even hotter when he dressed down. He'd told her he avoided dressing casually for class because he wanted to draw that line between himself and his students—probably to fend off all the female students hot for teacher, too.

"You found me." He ushered her inside the cozy living room, decked out in warm beige and brown hues with splashes of orange and red Native American influences.

The room enveloped her in a warm hug, but the sliding glass doors to the deck in the back drew her like a magnet. She parked in front of the doors and gazed at the glassy bay beyond, a wooden pier jutting into its depths. "Is that your boat?"

"Perfect, isn't it? I can motor over to Whidbey or the San Juan Islands."

Something goosed her from behind and she squealed and spun around. A fawn-colored Lab wagged its tail enthusiastically.

"Bodhi! I thought I taught you better manners than that." Finn lifted his hand over the dog's head. "Sit and shake."

Bodhi complied and sat at Jessica's feet, lifting one paw for the taking. She grabbed its paw. "Hello, Bodhi. Male?"

"Yeah, he's my camping, hiking, boating, fishing companion."

Scratching behind Bodhi's ear, she said, "No wonder you don't have a wife."

Finn cocked his head. "Do you have a pet?"

"I had a cat, but she died last year."

"Sorry to hear that. It's always hard losing a pet." He raised his brows. "Is that why you don't have a husband?"

"Probably reason 992." She held up the wine bag. "I brought a bottle of white. Is that okay?"

"That's fine. I bought a bottle for you, too, but yours is cold, so we'll drink this first."

"First? Are we having a second?"

"You did say it was a rough day."

He took the wine to the kitchen, and she trailed after him. The Chinese food cartons littered the countertop, and he'd set a small table with place mats, plates, silverware and wineglasses.

"You could've just hidden the evidence and pretended you'd cooked this feast yourself." She swept a hand across the counter. "I would've never known and been so impressed."

"Never had you pegged as a woman impressed by food or cooking or…lying." He picked up one of the white plastic bags and waved it like a flag. "I give credit where credit is due—Han Ting."

She grabbed the take-out container with the rice and dug a spoon into it. "I'm impressed that you followed me into the forest, without my knowledge, and then ran toward me when you heard me scream. Rice?"

"Please." He shoved both plates toward her and opened another container.

They piled their plates high with food, Finn poured the wine she brought into the two waiting glasses, and they sat down across from each other. "This is a nice place, remote but not too far from civilization. At least you have a few neighbors on the water."

"Blood money." He tore into a packet of soy sauce and dumped it over his food. "Settlement from my dad's accident."

"I'm sure he would've approved of this place, close to nature and the things you love." She plucked a piece of chicken from her plate and pointed at Bodhi. Finn nodded.

"I think he would've been happier had I stayed with law enforcement. That was his dream job for me."

"Yeah, well, parents aren't supposed to have dream jobs for their kids." She broke apart a pair of chopsticks and clicked them together. "But at least your dad had dreams for you. My mom's dreams included the government money she got for two kids. She would've been even happier to collect for a third, my half brother, but he was a few years younger than I and someone in the neighborhood tattled on her, so protective services whisked him away."

"Have you ever tried to track him down?"

"It was a closed adoption." She shrugged, trying to make light of the pain she felt when children's services snatched away her baby brother. "Tiffany had made some strides in locating him, but she never had a chance to share any of that with me. I started from scratch recently. I even hired someone to help. She's made a few inquiries, but no luck so far."

"Have you been back to the house where you grew up? I remember it wasn't far from here. On the other side of the peninsula by Bangor Base, right?"

"That's right. I took you there once. It was the only stability in Mom's life. A navy buddy of my grandfather's owned the place and let us live there for cheap. Wasn't much of a house." She gave an exaggerated shiver, shimmying her shoulders. "I wouldn't go back there now. Nothing but bad memories."

"I'm sorry. That must've been a tough life for you girls. If Tiffany protected you in that environment, I understand why it's so important for you to get justice for her."

"She *did* protect me, but it was at her expense. She figured as long as she could keep the attention of Mom's sleazy boyfriends on her and away from me, she was doing her job as a big sister. I mean, it only makes sense she would turn to drugs and sex work after a childhood like that." Jessica's eyes watered and she sniffed, but it wasn't due to the spicy beef she'd just popped into her mouth.

"It makes sense. Tiffany was a hero. Hey—" he aimed a chopstick at her "—I discovered something interesting today, or rather some*one* interesting. Did Tiffany ever mention a guy named Deke Macy to you?"

"Deke Macy. Doesn't sound familiar. Who is he?"

He explained to her how he'd checked out the greeting cards in the student store and landed in Deke Macy's office.

Finn said, "He had a creepy attitude toward the young women on campus."

"Sounds like a loser, but what would he have to do with Tiffany?"

"I found out from the accounting supervisor in the office, Nia, that Deke has been working at the university for about twelve years, and he started in food service…like Tiffany."

"Oh my God, yeah. If he was still working food service ten years ago, he would've worked with my sister. Did he mention Tiffany?"

"No, that's the weird thing. We were discussing the current campus murders, so you'd think he would've brought up the fact that he'd worked with a previous murder victim."

"Maybe, but why be so obvious about his attraction to the young women on campus? He had to know that would be a red flag for you, or anyone. You didn't hear him laugh, did you? There would be no mistaking that laugh."

"Nope." Finn maneuvered a piece of chicken with his chopsticks. "He must already have a reputation on campus. Why try to pretend or hide it now? The kids seem to call him Dick instead of Deke."

Jessica started to smirk and then stopped. "Wait. Dick does sound familiar. Tiffany used to talk a lot about her coworkers because it was her first real job, and I remember her joking about some guy named Dick. What are you going to do with this information?"

"Already done. I reported my conversation with Deke to Detective Morse. I mean, there's more. Both Morgan and Missy worked on campus in the university bookstore complex. The student employees who open and close the registers have to pick up and drop off the cash at accounting. Deke's office is in the accounting area."

"So Morgan and Missy were in that office, near Deke?"

"That, I don't know. Nia, the accounting manager, doesn't remember either of the girls being regulars." He took a sip of wine. "Doesn't mean they weren't there, and Deke didn't know them. What did you discover today?"

She jabbed a finger at him. "You uncovered a person of interest. I just remembered my sister's favorite color."

"What's the significance of your sister's favorite color?" He wiped his mouth with a paper towel and crumpled it in his hand. "I have those files you asked for, by the way. I pulled them out of my garage when I got home."

"Red. We found red fibers on Missy, just like at Morgan's crime scene. Missy had them under her fingernails, and I discovered more in the area. Tiffany's favorite color was red. The sympathy card references red. Maybe there's some significance there. Neither of the women was wearing anything red, so it didn't come from them."

Finn said, "It's a reach."

At least he hadn't rolled his eyes. "I know that, but I'm looking at everything through the lens of Tiffany's case. For whatever reason, whether this guy murdered Tiffany or not, he's got a thing for her homicide. He duplicated it with these two victims—same manner of death, same location, and he's involving me in his crime spree."

He aimed his chopsticks at the kitchen counter behind her. "More food? I forgot I bought egg rolls, too."

"No, I'm good." She stretched and finished her glass of wine. "I'll clean up in here while you bring in the box. We can look at it on this table?"

"That works."

Finn pushed back from the table, and she collected the dishes, rinsed them and put them in the dishwasher. Jessica closed up the boxes of leftover food and stacked them in the fridge, which seemed fairly well stocked for a bachelor.

Bodhi kept her company, hoping for a stray morsel of food, and she obliged with several. As she held the paper bag, greasy with the eggrolls inside, Finn walked past her and snatched the bag from her hand.

"I'm gonna need at least one of these with my second glass of wine. I can't drink the stuff without food." He dumped the egg rolls onto a plate and popped the lids on the sweet-and-sour sauce and spicy mustard. He then grabbed the bottle of wine from the fridge and returned to the table to fill their glasses.

Her pulse jumped when she saw the cardboard box on the floor next to the table. Wiping her hands on a dish towel, she said, "I'm ready."

As he sat next to her at the table and kicked the lid off the box, he said, "I have…crime scene photos in here. I can separate them, if you like."

"I've seen them before, but you can leave them in the box as long as there's a list of Tiffany's clothing." She took a gulp of wine.

"There is. I'll have a look at the people the detectives questioned, too. Maybe Deke's one of them." He bent over, shuffling through the files in the box. He dropped a couple of folders on the table, and little puffs of dust made her sneeze.

"Sorry about that." He hopped up from his seat and grabbed a few paper towels from the kitchen. When he sat down, he wiped down both folders, front and back.

He shoved one toward her with his finger. "You should be able to find her clothing in there."

Her hand trembled slightly when she reached for the file.

Holding her breath, she flipped it open. Words, just words. Neatly typed words on a page to summarize a whole life.

She skimmed the first few pages until she came to a description of the body at the scene. She skipped the gruesome details, which she could recite by heart anyway, and zeroed in on the items her sister was wearing. Pictures of the clothing followed.

Jessica smiled at the skinny jeans with embroidery on the pocket. Tiffany loved those jeans. She'd paired them with a white midriff top, which superthin Tiffany could carry off, and a denim trucker jacket with more embroidery on the back—none of it in red. She finished off the outfit with a pair of white wedge sneakers.

Jessica slumped in her chair and took another slug of wine. "Nothing red. No red fibers found on her body, either. Did Deke's name come up?"

Finn held up a piece of paper with names printed out in different groups. He shook it in the air. "He's listed under coworkers."

"Wow, so he *did* know Tiffany. This is significant. Any notes on his interview?"

"Looking at this, it doesn't seem as if her coworkers were grilled. Probably someone talked to them in a group—Tiffany complain about anyone, anyone hanging around her—those kinds of questions. Unless one of them had something interesting to add, they probably weren't questioned further."

"If Deke killed her, he wouldn't have been drawing attention to himself. It could be him, Finn."

"When I called Detective Morse this afternoon, I did mention that Deke may have worked with Tiffany back when she was murdered. He's a good detective. He'll discover this.

My guess is that Deke has an interview with the sheriff's department in his future."

"You should've never given up police work." She pinched an egg roll between her fingers and dipped it in the red sauce.

"Wasn't for me. You know better than anyone, I couldn't follow the rules." He swirled his wine in his glass. "After all, I broke them for you."

"I don't think you're the kind of person who would do something unless you wanted to do it. I didn't think it then; I don't think it now." She crunched into her egg roll with her teeth.

"Oh, I wanted to do it. I wanted to do it for you. There was probably nothing I wouldn't have done for you...at the time."

She dabbed her mouth. "And now?"

"I think it's clear nothing's changed."

She should've never eaten that greasy egg roll. She wiped her hands with a paper towel, swished a sip of wine in her mouth and stood up, all while keeping contact with Finn's blue eyes.

She skirted the table, placed her hands on his shoulders, leaned over and kissed him. His mouth opened, and his soft lips caressed hers, gentle at first and then pressing with an urgency akin to her own.

She murmured against his lips, "That's more like it."

He acted on her encouragement, slipping a hand into the strands of her hair, cupping the back of her head and drawing her in closer. This time his kiss scorched her lips, branding her somewhere deep inside, taking possession of her soul. If she'd had any doubts before that the boy had grown into a man, this kiss torched those doubts and turned them to ash.

He pulled her into his lap, and she straddled him, the tip of her shoe resting against the box that contained her sister's case files. As she toyed with the edge of his T-shirt, she asked, "Do you have a bedroom in this hideaway?"

Without missing a beat, Finn stood up with her legs wrapped around his waist. Bodhi thumped his tail a couple of times as Finn stepped over him on the way to the bedroom.

Finn nudged the door open with his foot and turned slowly in the middle of the room, so she could get the full effect of the large wall of glass facing the dark ripples of the bay.

As he placed her on the bed, she huffed out a breath, curling her legs beneath her. "Anyone could be out there in a boat, peering into your house."

He reached across her and fumbled with a remote. A set of dark drapes automatically slid across the window, casting the room in blackness. He tapped on a small bedside lamp. "Is that better?"

"I'll tell you in a minute." She gathered handfuls of his shirt and tugged.

He raised his arms, and she sat up on her knees to pull the shirt over his head. Running her hands along the hard ridge of muscle on his chest, she planted a kiss on his collarbone. "How does a professor get this hard?"

"I'll tell you in a minute."

Giggling like a tipsy sorority girl, Jessica fell back on the bed and pulled her phone from the pocket of her sweater. She placed it on the nightstand, next to the light highlighting all the bulges and planes of Finn's half-naked torso.

She shrugged out of the sweater. "I need to catch up."

"I can help you with that." Placing his knees on either side of her hips, he peeled her shirt from her body and yanked it over her head. He tossed it over his shoulder as she scrambled out of her bra.

He caught his breath and whispered, "Beautiful."

She arched her back, and he fitted one hand against her spine while he pressed a trail of kisses from her throat to her belly. She squirmed beneath him, heat searing through her veins.

Hooking his finger in the waistband of her jeans, he said, "You're gonna have to stop wriggling around like that. I'm only human."

"Prove it." Her fingers clawed at the button on his fly, but her impatient hands couldn't do the deed.

He unzipped and yanked his jeans and briefs down his muscled thighs. He rolled off the bed to kick them off, and she took the opportunity to shimmy out of her own jeans and the socks still covering her feet.

Bodhi's soft head brushed her foot as he absconded with one of her socks, but the dog was in luck tonight as she had other things on her mind.

When Finn joined her on the bed, he stretched out beside her, and their busy hands explored each other's bodies. They punctuated their exploration with hungry kisses, prolonging the buildup to excruciating heights.

She waited ten years for this; what was five or ten minutes until ecstasy?

Her cell phone buzzed on the nightstand. She laced her fingers through Finn's hair as he imprinted a row of kisses down the inside of her thigh.

"I have to see who it is, in case it's my boss."

Finn growled in the back of his throat, but he rolled to his side as she scooted up and reached over to slide her phone from the nightstand.

Finn's rough voice came from somewhere near her left hip. "Is it your boss?"

She stared at the name and bit the inside of her cheek. "It's Ashley King. It might be important."

Finn grumbled. "It's after ten."

"That's why it might be important." She tapped the incoming call. "What's wrong, Ashley?"

"Sorry to bother you, sweetie, but you wanted me to tell you if I remembered anything else about the time Tiff died."

"I did." Jessica's heart, which had just started to slow down from Finn's attentions, ramped up again and she put her phone on speaker, so Finn could hear. "What did you remember?"

Ashley coughed her smoker's cough. "Something else was stolen from the apartment with that damned doll."

"What was it?" She glanced at Finn, a stack of pillows propping up his head, his gaze sharp.

"Her knitting."

"Knitting? Tiffany didn't knit."

"Crazy, I know, but she was trying to give up smoking and decided to learn how to knit. She was working on something—something for you at the time, and I swear it was taken with the doll because when you came over to collect her stuff, I asked you about it."

"I don't remember that at all."

"You were kinda messed up, sweetie. You hadn't found any knitting needles, so I figured they were taken like the doll. She worked on that damned red scarf every night."

Jessica's fingers curled into the bedspread beneath her. "Tiffany was knitting a red scarf at the time she was murdered?"

"That's right. You can ask Denny. Click, click, click those damned needles. She was working on that red scarf for you…and somebody stole it."

Chapter Eleven

"Sweetie?" Ashley's raspy voice grated across the line, but Jessica seemed incapable of speech, her round eyes glassy in the dim light.

"Ashley, this is Finn Karlsson, a…friend of Jessica's. You might remember me…"

"Oh, I remember you. Found our Tiff's body."

"That's right. I'm helping Jessica." He dragged a blanket up the bed and covered Jessica's shivering body with it. "This scarf Tiffany was knitting, how long was it? I mean how far along was she?"

"Far." She hacked again. "I'm not saying it was any good, but she was almost done with it. She knitted away with that thing curled up at her feet like some kind of red snake ready to strike. I told her one time, Jessie's tall, but hell, that thing could wrap around bigfoot's neck a few times."

Finn winced and squeezed Jessica's thigh beneath the blanket. "You never reported this theft to the police?"

"Like I told Jessie, I didn't think much about it—a doll and a beginner's knitting project. Didn't see the point. Didn't even make a connection with Tiff's murder, but I remembered it tonight when Denny and I were talking about Tiff, you know, good times, and we were joking about her knitting." Ashley sucked in a breath. "Jessie? Is Jessie okay?"

"I-I'm fine, Ashley." Jessica pulled the blanket more tightly around her form. "I really appreciate your call. Anything else you remember, please call me anytime."

"Okay. Didn't mean to interrupt you and Finn. I know you always had a crush on that cop, but at least he's not the po-po anymore."

Finn rolled his eyes at Jessica. "Yeah, thanks for that, Ashley."

Ashley ended the call after more assurances from Jessica that she was okay, even though neither one of them told Ashley the reason for Jessica's shock.

Jessica sat, hunched over, the phone in her lap. "Something old, something dead, something stolen, something red. It's the scarf, isn't it? He stole that scarf from Tiffany at the same time he stole the rag doll, and he's using it to strangle women."

Did he have an answer for her? Did he disagree with her, as fantastic as it all sounded? "But he didn't use that scarf to strangle Tiffany. The investigators are certain Plank—" Jessica shot him a look from beneath her lashes and he held up his hands "—or whoever killed your sister used a tie."

"That's right, even though Plank always used his hands, those big hands." She pulled the blanket up to her chin and pinned it to her chest. "The person who killed Morgan and Missy knows too much about Tiffany—things nobody else would know—not to have been involved in her homicide. That sick poem says it all. Tiffany's murder is old, she's dead, he stole a red scarf from her. It's all there, Finn."

"It's not all there. We have one person of interest. The cops can talk to Deke, and I'm sure they will after the info

I gave them about him, but you of all people know they'll have to find evidence. And why now?" Finn scooped up his jeans and untangled his briefs. "Why did he start up again if he's been living here all this time with access to plenty of young women?"

She pulled a pillow over her face and screamed into it.

That's exactly how he felt right now. Would he ever be able to date this woman without a murder getting in the way?

Peeking over the edge of the pillow, she said, "I'm sorry I took the call."

"No, you're not. We just got another vital piece of information that'll make Detective Morse take that poem in the sympathy card more seriously." He pulled on his jeans as he rose from the bed. "After hearing the phone ring, I doubt you would've been able to concentrate on the business at hand, anyway."

"I wouldn't be so sure about that." She quirked her eyebrows up and down.

"Let's call it a night. I need to let Bodhi outside."

At the sound of his name, Bodhi trotted into the room, a fuzzy black sock hanging from his jaws.

Finn pointed at his pet. "I think Bodhi got your sock. It'll never be the same again."

"He can keep it as a souvenir of the night his dad almost got laid."

"And what does his dad get as a memento?"

"You can have my other sock."

He tried to get her to spend the night at his place, as difficult as that would've been for him to have her sleeping in the next room. They both knew the mood had turned and although he would've given it the old college try, he knew

Tiffany's murder consumed Jessica's thoughts, and he didn't want to compete. Tiffany's ghost already hovered over their relationship. He didn't want her haunting the first time he made love to Jessica.

But she insisted on spending the night at her own place, so Finn followed her outside and checked her car before allowing her to leave with promises she'd text him as soon as she got home and locked the doors.

This killer seemed more interested in taunting and tormenting Jessica than killing her, but you couldn't trust a psychopath. He was moving closer and closer to Jessica. He must have some sort of end game…and that end game just might be Jessica's death.

About thirty minutes later, as he finished up the egg rolls, sharing one with Bodhi, Jessica texted him. She thanked him for dinner, for the files, for the info on Deke, and for listening, couching all those words in a bunch of emojis. But nowhere in the text did she thank him for rocking her world.

Did that mean she regretted it?

Bodhi jumped on the couch next to him with Jessica's sock clenched between his teeth. Finn rubbed the dog's head. "I know you're happy with the spoils of the evening, but I wanted more…so much more."

THE FOLLOWING DAY, Jessica met with Deputy Alvarado regarding the physical evidence for Missy's homicide case. The evidence from Morgan's had already been packaged and shipped to the lab for additional testing, including DNA and possible latent fingerprints.

She'd be packaging the physical evidence from Missy's case and delivering it herself via the sheriff's van. The biological evidence from Missy's autopsy had already been sent to Seattle, including the red fibers, as it had been found beneath Missy's fingernails. Had she tried to remove the red scarf tightening around her throat? Did the killer have this in his hands when he was leading her down the trail to Missy?

She spoke to Alvarado without lifting her head. "Did you see the red fibers before they were sent to Seattle for DNA testing? It could be yarn, couldn't it?"

"Could be." Alvarado smacked the table. "That Deke Macy is bald, shaved head. Might explain why there's no hair left at the scene. Or maybe the killer wore a beanie, tucking his hair in, and this is a fiber from that."

"Or it's the murder weapon. He used it for Morgan, too." She dropped another plastic bag into the pouch. "Have you heard anything more about Macy?"

"I know Detective Morse brought him in for questioning. He may have worked with both murdered women, or at least had contact with them."

Jessica murmured, "And he worked with my sister, Tiffany Hunt, at the time of her murder ten years ago."

Alvarado put down his clipboard where he'd been checking off the items as she put them in the pouch. "I heard about that, Jessica. I'm so sorry. I had a sister who was murdered by her ex-boyfriend—domestic violence case. I know it's tough."

Her gaze flew to his face. "I'm so sorry."

"It's hard to fathom a guy like Macy getting away with one murder and holding off for ten years before committing his next."

"That's true, but maybe he committed crimes while he was on vacation or visiting someone." She dropped the last item into the pouch as Alvarado marked it off on his form.

"I'm just hoping he's our guy and no other young women are in danger."

"I hope so, too. Detective Morse will get to the truth." He scrawled his signature on the form and held it out for her to sign.

They didn't get to the truth of Tiffany's murder.

Jessica added her signature and tucked the form into the pouch. She had already placed the rag doll and the sympathy card in separate bags to bring to the lab, but the sheriff's department wouldn't allow them to be labeled with the official evidence, as she'd already destroyed the chain of custody several times over.

"I'll be phoning in for updates. Can I contact you, Deputy Alvarado?"

"Call me Tomas, and you can." He jerked his thumb at the door. "Wait in the lobby of the station. Deputy Davis is driving the van over."

"Thanks." She slung the pouch over her shoulder and headed for the lobby. She peeked down the corridor, wondering if Morse was grilling Macy behind one of those doors.

After Finn had told her about Deke Macy, she'd looked him up online. Didn't have much of a social media presence. Mostly followed young Instagram models, liking their sexy poses and posting emojis with tongues hanging out. Finn had been right. If he was trying to hide his dirty deeds, he was hiding in plain sight. Of course, that could be a ruse, too—the *do you think I'm that stupid* defense.

Avery Plank had lurked beneath the radar—not exactly a family man, had one divorce and one daughter in his past—but he'd been a respected engineer in his field. He'd escaped his rough childhood, as she had, but the darkness had seeped too far into his soul for him to evade it.

"Ms. Eller?"

She jumped and spun around to come face-to-face with a beefy deputy who looked like he could be a defensive lineman for the Seattle Seahawks. She'd be safe with him.

"Deputy Davis? You can call me Jessica."

"And you can call me Kimani, CSI lady." He patted the pouch. "I'll need to check the form before we get in the van."

She hoisted the bag onto a table in the lobby and slipped out the form. She placed it on the table next to the bag.

He scanned the form and glanced in the bag. "You have two other paper bags coming with us?"

"In my car, not official evidence."

"I'll follow you."

He followed her to her car where she retrieved the two paper bags, and then they got settled in the van for the ninety-minute ride to Marysville, including the ferry across the Sound.

As Jessica adjusted her seat belt, she asked, "You ever play football?"

"Why, yes, ma'am. Washington State Cougars. How could you tell?"

"Ah, because you're as broad as a double-wide trailer, and I mean that in the most complimentary way."

He chuckled. "My wife would take exception. She keeps telling me I don't need to eat like I'm still making those tackles."

She and Kimani chatted easily about football, the King County Sheriff's Department, living on the Sound and his wife's cooking, anything to keep her mind off what was happening to Deke Macy back at the station. Had she ever seen the guy before? If he was the killer, he must know who she was. Knew her car. Had followed her. Had her phone number. The knowledge made her feel slightly nauseous, and she cracked the window.

The hour-and-a-half ride went by fast, and they'd missed most of the traffic, but by the time Kimani pulled the van into the parking lot of the forensic lab, Jessica was ready to stretch her legs.

Kimani parked outside the vehicle inspection center where a few cars perched on hydraulic lifts, ready for a thorough search. She knew several people in that unit, and they'd pull plants from the undercarriage and dig out seeds from the tires in an effort to glean every bit of evidence they could from a suspect's or victim's car. Too bad neither of the crimes on campus involved vehicles.

She hopped from the van and Kimani grabbed the pouch from the back. As he handed it to her, he said, "I'm escorting you to Evidence Receiving, and then I'm going to get some lunch and head back. Are you coming with me or staying?"

"I'll be staying for a while. I can probably hijack one of our vans to go back to Kitsap."

They parted ways at Evidence Receiving when Jessica handed the pouch over to Nicole Meloan, the supervisor. She shook the paper bags at her. "A couple of things in here I'd like tested, but I compromised the chain of evidence because I found them on my own, and in the case of the doll, I carried it around with me."

Nicole clicked her tongue. "Michael know about your little faux pas?"

"I told him. He was…disappointed."

"This evidence won't be in lockup long. I've had lab rats knocking on my door all morning looking for it."

"There's not much to paw over, and the evidence that might contain DNA has been sent to Seattle."

Nicole unzipped the pouch and plucked out the form. "I hear that's on a rush, too."

"Have you heard anything else? The sheriff's department is questioning a person of interest. He may have worked with both women...and he was there ten years ago when my sister was murdered."

Nicole put a gloved hand on her arm. "Do you think these cases are linked to Tiffany's?"

Flicking her finger at the paper bags on the table, Jessica answered. "That's what these are all about—a card that mentions my sister's name and a doll that may be one my sister had in her possession at the time of her murder."

"You're kidding. That's significant...and scary for you. Are you all right?" Nicole's dark brown eyes got huge. "Wait, is that why you found the second victim? This guy told you where she was?"

Jessica told her the story of the text, the meeting that never happened and how the killer lured her to Missy's body. "It was awful. Somehow discovering a body like that was a hundred times worse than coming into a murder scene where dozens of cops and CSIs are already roaming around."

"I can imagine." Nicole waved her arms around the room, shelves stacked with boxes, plastic and paper bags. "It's all so sterile in here. Anyway, I haven't heard anything about a person of interest yet."

"I'm keeping my fingers crossed." Jessica tapped the form on the table. "Initial this, so I can get out of here and go find Michael."

Jessica passed by several of the labs where the techs would soon be analyzing the evidence from Missy's homicide. She made a right turn at the end of the hallway and tapped on Michael's open door.

He glanced up and waved her in, rolling his eyes and pointing at the phone. He'd just dashed her hopes that he'd be in a good mood and this interview would go better than she deserved.

When he ended the call, he dropped the phone on his desk and dragged his hands through his black hair, which made his light blue eyes even more startling when he skewered her with his gaze.

"So, Nancy Drew is back in the lab."

"Yeah, so funny." She plopped in one of the two chairs facing his desk without an invitation. "But Nancy's the one who found Missy Park minutes after her death. The cops could've caught the guy right then and there."

"He must've had some sort of escape plan mapped out in advance, knowing you'd find the body and report it right away." Her boss steepled his long fingers. "I heard Finn Karlsson was on the scene with you."

"He was there. We've been in touch since I've been in Kitsap."

"He's writing a book about Plank. Did he tell you that?"

"Y-yes." Eventually. "But he's going to have to write an addendum when we find out Plank didn't murder my sister."

"Deke Macy is not looking like the guy for these crimes, though."

"Really?" Her head jerked up. "Who says?"

"King County Sheriff's Department. Just got off the phone with one of the deputies. Macy has an alibi for both murders. Have to be checked out, of course, but easy to find out if he's lying." He held up his hands. "Suspects lie about alibis all the time, knowing full well the investigators can figure that out after a few phone calls, interviews or camera footage. Could still be the guy."

"But unlikely." Jessica slumped in her seat. "I knew he was too good to be true. Creepy dude icking on college coeds and following young Instagram models—and not trying to hide it."

Michael narrowed his icy eyes. "Sounds like you did quite a bit of your own research on the creepy Mr. Macy."

"He worked with Tiffany ten years ago."

"If you want to be a cop, Jessica, go to the academy and be one. If you want to be a top-notch forensics investigator, do your job."

"Like you didn't do your own investigating once upon a time."

"Yeah, that was because I was accused of murder."

His office phone rang, and he dropped his gaze to the display. "Sheriff's department again. Maybe Deke Macy did lie. Wilder here."

Jessica studied Michael's impassive face, which gave away nothing.

"I see. Good. Rush job. Yeah." When he ended the call, Jessica was none the wiser.

"Did he lie about his alibis?"

"No, but something almost as encouraging. They found trace DNA on both sets of red fibers…and it doesn't match the victims' DNA reference samples."

Chapter Twelve

"How did they get those results so quickly?" Finn pushed a piece of crinkly yellow wax paper piled with french fries toward Jessica, sitting in his office visitor chair. She'd driven straight to campus from the forensics lab in Marysville once she'd discovered he was working late.

"The lab got the victims' DNA, called a reference sample, right away so they can rule them out when they start processing the evidence. Further tests can then be done if the samples show similarities. They discovered the trace DNA on the red fibers from Morgan's crime scene right away and started processing that. They're still testing and analyzing it to see if there's enough to send through CODIS." She pinched a french fry from his offering and bit off the end. "Did you know that Morgan's family owns the biggest logging enterprise in the state?"

"I thought I heard something like that. Are you telling me Morgan is getting special treatment because of her family?" He clapped a hand over his mouth. "I'm shocked. Just shocked."

"I mean, I'm glad she is, but every victim deserves special treatment and fast-tracked results. Avery Plank's sex worker victims sure didn't get any such consideration. The DNA on those cases took weeks, even months."

"At least Missy benefits from the Flemmings' connections." Finn dusted the salt from his fingers onto the paper bag that had contained his dinner. "Deke Macy is a disappointing suspect. His two alibis look solid—at a karaoke bar one night where several patrons have already attested to his horrible singing and down in Seattle visiting his brother on the other night."

"Family members lie all the time. Hell, his brother could even be involved." She wedged a shoe on the edge of his desk. "Why are you working so late in your office? You can't grade those exams on your laptop at home?"

"I'm giving another exam on Monday, and I promised my students extended office hours. I started grading, got hungry, ordered food and by the time the students' visits trailed off, I was on a roll. Told myself I'd finish here."

"And I interrupted you."

"I was almost done, and I wanted to hear about the DNA tests. You said the lab hasn't run the DNA through CODIS yet."

"Not yet. They had the victims' reference samples, so they were able to test it against those, and there's no match to the victims' samples." She rubbed her hands together. "Let's hope they get enough of the sample to run through CODIS, and that there's a match."

He offered her the rest of the fries, and she declined, so he scrunched up the paper and shoved it into the plastic bag. "There was never any DNA recovered at your sister's crime scene, so it's not going to help there."

"No, but I'm certain there will be a connection. I could've gone along with the theory that someone was playing stupid games with my tires and even the doll, but that speculation ended when he led me to Missy's body. The person leaving me clues is the same person who murdered Morgan and Missy."

"You're right, but it doesn't necessarily mean he killed Tiffany. Could be a copycat." Finn pushed back from his desk and grabbed the plastic bag by the handle. "I'm going to drop this in the trash can in the hallway, so the smell doesn't linger in my office."

He squeezed past her chair and pushed open the door, which he'd left ajar. As he stepped out of his office, a shadow flashed at the end of the darkened corridor. He called out. "Hello? It's Professor Karlsson. Did you need to see me?"

A flurry of footsteps echoed from around the corner, and Finn's cop instincts spurred him on to give chase. "Hey!"

He took off running down the smooth hallway in his loafers, slipping every few feet until he reached the end of the corridor. Finn skidded around the corner, and the side door at the bottom of the stairs slammed shut.

He loped downstairs, hanging on to the banister, taking two steps at a time. When he hit the bottom, he scrambled for the door and heaved his body against it to shove it open, stumbling into the small quad.

Panting, Finn stopped and scanned the trees that bordered the quad, his gaze darting back and forth between the two walkways—one leading into the main quad in the front of the building and the other skirting another lecture hall.

He crept silently to the corner of the building and peered around the edge. When the door burst open behind him, he spun around.

Jessica careened around the corner and almost bumped into him standing still in the front quad. She drew herself up and grabbed his sleeve. "What's going on? Why did you take off like that?"

"There was someone lurking in the hallway outside my office. I thought it might be a student thinking I was busy, but when I called to him, he took off."

"Him? Are you sure it was a man?"

"Yeah. I just saw his shadow, but he moved like a guy." Finn wiped the back of his hand across his brow. "Why would he take off like that?"

"Is there anything to steal up there? Any reason to be there other than to see a professor?"

"Shouldn't be anything to steal. All the offices are locked up. There are classrooms on the first floor, but the second floor is the humanities office and the professors' officers. The humanities office is locked, too."

"Were there any other professors holding office hours?" She glanced up at the building sporting a few lights in the windows. "Maybe he was there to see someone else."

"Professor Godwin was working late, but he left about thirty minutes before you arrived." He pushed his hair back from his forehead, his adrenaline rush seeping from his system. "Why would any student of Godwin's take off running from another professor in the building? The doors are locked, but it's not like students aren't allowed in the halls. They are. You can even go into a lecture hall after hours and sit down if you want. The university holds some night classes, some extension classes."

Jessica settled her back against the rough stone of the building and crossed her arms. "What do you think he was doing there, and why do you think he ran?"

"Did you notice anyone following you here when you got to town?"

She licked her lips and her gaze flickered over his shoulder to the empty quad. "I drove here straight from the forensics lab. Someone would've had to have been following me for a long time."

"I think the person was trying to spy on us. Listen to our conversation. I never completely close my office door unless I'm alone. I'd left it ajar, and anyone in the corridor could've heard our conversation. Voices carry down that hall, so the person wouldn't have even had to have been that close. He heard me announce that I was going to throw the trash into the can and started moving toward the stairs."

"Why would someone be spying on us?"

"I don't know. We've been asking a lot of questions of a lot of people. I questioned Macy and the cops knock on his door the next day. He must know I put them onto him."

She rubbed her arms. "Do you think that was Deke?"

"Wish I had caught up with this guy." He glanced at his useless shoes. "Should've worn some running shoes to class."

"I think I left your door wide open when I followed you out here." She pushed off the wall. "Maybe he came back and stole something."

"To do that, he would've had to run out here to the main quad, and then circle back into the building from the front. I think he was more concerned with getting away. He couldn't have known you'd follow me, anyway."

"Unless he was hoping to find me alone in your office."

Grabbing her hand, he tugged her. "Let's take a look."

He led her to the main entrance to Waverly Hall, one of the four lecture halls that fronted the quad. Head down, he studied the steps to the front door. "If he came this way, he would've left footprints from the wet grass we went through to get here. I don't see anything, do you?"

Jessica lifted her own foot, leaving a damp imprint on the step. "None but ours, but his could've dried by now. We stepped in some dewy grass, not the Sound."

One of the double doors to Waverly stood open and yellow light spilled onto the steps. Finn asked, "Is this how you came into the building earlier?"

"It's the only way I knew how before you went charging out of that side door. Didn't see anyone, and nobody followed me." She ascended the remaining steps and stepped into the building. "Maybe someone was after you this time."

THE FOLLOWING EVENING, Jessica got ready for the university's candlelight vigil in honor of both Morgan and Missy. The gathering had several functions—to pay respect to the women, of course, but also as an informational safety meeting for the students and although not advertised, law enforcement would use it to scan the crowd for unusual activity or people.

Jessica knew she'd be keeping a sharp eye out for the latter. The spy at Waverly Hall last night had scared her more than she'd let on to Finn. If the person had been an innocent student, why not stop when Finn spotted him?

Would the killer really be so bold as to try to eavesdrop in an empty college building? What would've happened if Finn had caught this person? The killer didn't use a knife or gun on his victims, but that didn't mean he didn't carry a weapon. She knew Finn had a conceal-carry permit from his days as a cop, but the university didn't allow guns on campus—and that rule extended to the professors.

She tucked her own weapon in her purse. It might extend

to visitors, too, but she was a member of the Washington State Patrol. She could make a strong case for carrying.

Finn had come to campus today for a department meeting and had stayed in his office marking papers and entering midterm grades. Was he hoping to catch the spy again? She planned to meet him at his office and attend the vigil with him. It wouldn't take them long to get there as the main quad right outside his building was hosting the gathering.

She grabbed a jacket on her way out of the hotel room and waved to the clerk as she stepped outside. She texted Finn before starting the drive to the university. She didn't want him thinking she was the spy creeping up on his office.

When she reached the campus, traffic came to a stop. The regular lots were already full, a couple of TV news vans taking up more than their share of spaces.

Jessica turned onto the side street where she usually parked and took the back way to the campus. She used the newly discovered side door to Waverly Hall and tripped up the steps, making sure her low-heeled boots made plenty of noise.

She nodded to another professor heading down the hallway on her way to Finn's office. His door stood wide open, but she tapped anyway as he hunched over his laptop completely absorbed.

"Hey, Professor Karlsson, what can I do to get an A on my test." She batted her lashes when he glanced up. "I'll do *anything*."

He rubbed his eyes with the heels of his hands. "Damn, I thought that was a legitimate offer coming my way."

She made a face at him. "You've been hanging around Deke Macy too long. His ick is rubbing off on you."

"Speaking of old Deke. I heard from my buddy at the

sheriff's department, and that karaoke alibi for Morgan's murder is rock solid. They found security cam footage of him at the bar well before and after her time of death."

"I thought it might be too good to be true." She wedged a shoulder against his doorjamb. "Are you ready? It's getting crowded out there."

"I got halfway through the grading." He closed his laptop and packed up his bag. "I'm going to keep my stuff here. I don't want to take it down with me, and I don't want to leave it in the car."

"The campus police are out in force tonight. I'm sure Detective Morse is going to be looking at all the male attendees very closely."

"I know he's going to have a few deputies in plain clothes, too." Finn stood up and stretched, and Jessica wondered, not for the first time, how all his female students managed to concentrate in class.

He swiveled around to a filing cabinet and swung back, holding out two small votive candles in jars. "One for you. Someone from the Women Against Violence Against Women came through the offices today handing these out for the vigil."

"Someone will have lighters down there?"

"I'm sure of it." He emerged from behind the desk and lifted his jacket from the hook on the back of the door. "Let's do this."

When they exited the front of Waverly Hall, they joined a surge of people carrying candles and signs. Some of the girls were already crying. Jessica gritted her teeth, preparing for a rough night.

People were walking around with lighters and Jessica and Finn held out their candles to join the sea of lights bobbing on the quad. The sheriff's department took the stage first, and Detective Morse's distinct red hair blazed from the center of the group.

As she and Finn staked out a place at the edge of the crowd, a deputy approached Finn.

"Professor Karlsson, can we please have you join us on stage again? You don't have to speak this time, but you're a popular professor and the students will feel comfortable seeing you up there with all us cops."

Finn opened his mouth and turned to Jessica, but she nudged him. "Go ahead. You'll probably have a better view of all the attendees up there. If I spot someone suspicious, I'll text you."

"Meet me back at my office when this is all over."

She watched Finn's back as he and the deputy made their way to the stage. Then she cupped the candle in her hand and scanned the crowd. Even without high heels, Jessica's height allowed her to see over a lot of heads—not that there was much to see. Many people wore hoodies, the ovals of their faces dimly illuminated by the candles in their hands.

When Detective Morse tapped the microphone, Jessica swiveled her attention to the stage. Finn stood behind Morse along with several other people—both civilian and law enforcement. An Asian couple stood to the side of Morse. Their faces, masks of shock and grief, flagged them as Missy's parents.

Jessica studied the other expressions and found another couple with the same hollowed-out look on their faces. She recognized Matt Flemming from the online articles she'd looked up, but his appearance tonight bore little resemblance to the confident and powerful businessman who smiled in his pictures. Position and money might help speed up an investigation, but they could never bring back his little girl.

Jessica blinked back her own tears and tried to tune in to Morse's speech. He repeated much of what he said the other day about staying vigilant and keeping off the trails by the creek. He advised women to travel in groups and report any suspicious activity. Same stuff women had been hearing for years. When were the cops going to catch this guy?

Apparently, that thought had occurred to other women as well. A few disgruntled voices in the crowd yelled questions as if Morse were conducting a press conference. Shouts rang out asking for accountability. For suspects. Status on Deke Macy.

Jessica actually felt bad for the guy, whose face was turning the same color as his hair. She knew firsthand the deputies didn't have many leads. Their one good suspect had alibis. But the crowd wasn't having it.

People from the back surged forward, nudging Jessica into the person in front of her as someone stepped on her heel and apologized. This could get ugly.

Her cell phone buzzed in her pocket, and she pulled it out. Had Finn had enough? When she glanced at the display, her blood ran cold. An unknown number.

She tapped the text with her shaky thumb, and her breath hitched in her throat when she read the message. Getting rowdy

She didn't need to ask the sender's identity. Are you here?

I was. Took a break from the crowd with a friend

Her heart beat so hard, it rattled the buttons on her jacket. She texted him a flurry of questions. Where was he? Who was he with? Had he hurt anyone?

A throng of people rushed toward the stage, hoisting signs and screaming for answers. Someone bumped her elbow, knocking her phone to the ground. She dropped down to retrieve it, and then crawled away from the mob to the perimeter.

She blew out her candle and rolled onto the damp grass. On her knees, she held her phone close to her face, watching the bubbles on the display, waiting for his answers to her queries.

Art garden fountain maybe u won't be too late this time

Jessica staggered to her feet, jerking her head toward the stage. Finn, his head dipped, was in conversation with Morgan's father. Jessica waved her arms at him to get his attention, but more people and their signs got between her and her view of the stage.

She stabbed at Finn's phone number in her contacts. It rang three times and rolled over to voicemail. She shouted into the phone. "Come to the Art Garden."

She then grabbed the nearest person and yanked his arm. "Come to the Art Garden with me. There's another woman in danger."

The man shook her off and raised his fist at the stage. She tried getting the attention of another man, but if he could even hear her, he didn't seem interested in what she had to say.

As she started running along the side of Waverly Hall, she fumbled with her phone, forwarding the unknown caller's text to Finn. She wound up in the smaller quad where Finn had chased the spy. She headed for the walkway that led to the Art Garden, a garden filled with sculptures that fronted the fine arts building.

Panting, she thumbed 911 into her phone. "Send the police. I'm heading toward the Art Garden on campus. I have reason to believe someone is in danger."

"How do you know this, ma'am?"

"Somebody texted me a threat. The cops are already here on campus. Send a few to the Art Garden."

"Someone texted you?"

"Oh, for God's sake. I see someone in the Art Garden with a gun. Send the police."

Gripping her phone in one hand, Jessica pulled her weapon from her purse with the other. She hadn't been lying to the 911 operator. There was going to be someone in the Art Garden with a gun in a few seconds.

She made it to the path that wound its way through shrubbery and flower beds, a sculpture positioned every few feet. The fountain gurgled in the middle of all this beauty and art, and Jessica made a beeline toward it, holding her gun in front of her.

"Where are you? The police are on the way."

She rushed toward the fountain and almost tripped over a body on the ground at the edge. She cried out, "Not again. Not again."

As she collapsed next to the still form, her gun hanging at her side, someone barreled into her back, driving her over the edge of the fountain. A gloved hand gripped the back of her neck and shoved her head into the water.

She tried to roll to her side, twist her head, but her attacker had his weight against her hips and his hand in her hair, keeping her head submerged. She couldn't move…and she couldn't breathe.

Chapter Thirteen

As he bent his head toward Mr. Flemming, Finn felt his phone buzz in his pocket with a text message. When Mr. Flemming turned to his wife, Finn glanced up at the unruly mob. He understood the students' frustration, but this was not the time or place to vent those frustrations.

His gaze scanned the crowd, trying to pick out Jessica's blond hair. He caught sight of her on the edge of the pressing throng of people, moving away from the quad.

He patted his pocket and pulled out his phone. He had a missed phone call he hadn't even heard due to the shouts and chants. The text message was from Jessica, a forwarded text message.

He squinted at the display as if that could help him make sense of the cryptic message. Art Garden. Fountain. Too late.

Understanding slammed into his chest so hard, he gasped. He jerked his head up, zeroing in on where he'd last seen Jessica. She'd disappeared.

Adrenaline flooded his body and his limbs jerked. He touched Mr. Flemming's arm. "Excuse me."

Finn ducked back from the grouping on the stage and cranked his head back and forth, looking for a cop other than Detective Morse—who was trying to field questions from a horde of angry and agitated people. The majority of the deputies were among the crowd, some at the front of the stage to make sure the irate mourners didn't overrun it.

He'd have to go it alone. He jumped from the stage, grateful he'd swapped his loafers for a pair of running shoes. Maybe he'd had a feeling he'd need to run. So he did.

Finn took off, skirting the perimeter of the crowd, in the direction of the Art Garden. He dashed across the smaller quad behind Waverly Hall and took the walkway toward the art building, Callahan Hall.

As soon as he stepped foot in the Art Garden, he started calling Jessica's name. More than anything, he just wanted her to stop. To turn around and wait for him. Was he too late as the text message had taunted?

He broke onto the pebbled surface that surrounded the fountain and his stomach dropped when he spotted two bodies next to the fountain.

As he ran toward them, a figure appeared behind him, and he swung around, his fist bunched.

"Whoa." A deputy in uniform held up his hands. "Do you have the gun?"

Finn ignored his question. "There are two injured women here."

When Finn dropped to his knees, his worst fear was realized. Jessica was slumped over the fountain, her hair wet and matted to her face. He turned her on her back, and his heart lurched at the sight of her pale face, a bluish tint around her mouth.

Her breath was faint but present, so he hauled her up and wrapped his arms around her to give her the Heimlich. One jerk and water gushed from her mouth. She choked and coughed up more water, but she'd opened her eyes and moved on her own.

The deputy wasn't having the same kind of luck with the other woman. Even in the low lights, Finn could see the red mark around the woman's neck. Unlike Jessica, that woman had been strangled.

Two more deputies ran onto the scene, all of them chattering about a gun.

When Jessica stopped sputtering, Finn curled an arm around her shoulders. "Are you all right? The cops are here, but I don't know why or how they knew to come."

Jessica swiped an arm across her nose and mouth. "I called 911 on my way. Told them someone had a gun in the Art Garden. How's…"

Finn shook his head. "She didn't make it."

Jessica broke down, covering her face with her hands and sobbing, the sound hoarse and broken.

The first deputy on scene, who'd identified himself as Deputy Lorman, took control. "Everyone step back from the body."

Finn shouted, "We need an ambulance. Jessica almost drowned."

Lorman replied, "On it. I called for backup."

Jessica bent forward and Finn caught her before she could pass out on the cement, but she felt the ground with her hands. "My gun. Where's my gun?"

Aiming his phone's flashlight at the ground, Finn said, "He must've taken it. I didn't see a gun."

Jessica, her hand to her throat, said, "Get Detective Morse over here. This woman is another victim of the Kitsap Killer, or whatever you're calling him, and he probably took off toward the woods. He knows them well."

Finn turned toward Lorman. "Jessica's right. He had to have gone toward the woods. I was calling Jessica's name as I was running toward the fountain. I must've scared him off, but he didn't come at me, so he must've headed for the woods...unless he's in Callahan Hall."

Lorman's lips flattened into a grimace. "Do you know for sure it's the same guy who murdered Morgan and Missy, ma'am?"

"The killer texted me before he did it." She squeezed out her wet hair over one shoulder. "Or I don't know. Maybe he'd already killed her before he even texted me."

"Description? What was he wearing?" Lorman snapped his fingers at the two deputies guarding the scene.

"I don't know." Jessica shivered. "Gloves and black pants. That's all I saw. He came up behind me."

The deputies responded to Lorman's frantic finger snapping and stood at attention. The shorter one asked, "What do you need, sir?"

"One of you take the woods and the other, Callahan Hall. Check for wet footsteps, broken branches, open doors in the building. Black pants, black gloves. Go, do your jobs." He turned back to Jessica and Finn. "Do either of you know the dead woman?"

When Finn had come on the scene, he hadn't even looked at the girl's face—just the red marks on her neck. Now he peered over Jessica's shoulder at the figure crumpled on the ground.

As Lorman highlighted her face with his flashlight, Finn's eye twitched. He rose from his place beside Jessica and hunched forward. Then he swore.

Jessica clutched at his arm, too traumatized to turn and look, herself. "You know her?"

"That's one of my students—Gabby Medina."

As Finn sank back down, his head in his hand, sirens wailed through the air. This was going to be a long night.

Jessica sat on the edge of the hospital bed swinging her legs. If Finn asked her one more time how she was feeling, she might just scream at him.

He'd insisted the EMTs take her to the hospital, even though she felt fine. The nurses had checked her vitals several times, listened to her lungs, her heart, and had given her intravenous electrolytes.

She was fine. Gabby Medina was dead.

Why her? Why was this person putting her through this? Could she have saved Gabby's life if she'd been faster? Smarter? Braver? Stronger?

That's exactly what Detective Morse wanted to know and had grilled her at the scene, despite Finn's protests. Morse wasn't done with her, either. He wanted her at the station tomorrow morning for the second interrogation. She didn't know what else she could tell him. She'd spilled her guts about the connections to Tiffany's murder—the card, the doll, the burglary of her sister's place and the stolen red scarf.

Morse had confiscated her phone, but she already knew the killer had used a different burner phone from the one he'd used the first time he texted her. Maybe Morse should start looking into who was buying up all the burner phones on Kitsap Peninsula.

Finn looked up from his phone. "Are you sure you're okay?"

Jessica ground her back teeth together behind a smile. The man had saved her life, after all. "I feel fine. Throat's a little raw from upchucking a gallon of water. Neck's sore from where he grabbed me. But I'm just ready to go back to the hotel."

One of the nurses must've been hovering outside because she chose that moment to push through the door. "Ready to leave, Jessica?"

Jessica hopped off the bed. "More than ready."

Forty-five minutes later, she got her wish as Finn wheeled into the parking lot of the hotel. He wouldn't let her drive her own car home.

He pulled into a parking space and cut the engine. "I'm coming up with you, and I'm staying the night. The nurse warned you might have some complications."

"She also mentioned that would be very rare, as you Heimliched all that water out of my lungs." His insistence had put her at ease, though. She didn't want to go to her room alone. Didn't want to spend the night alone. Didn't want to be alone ever again. "What about Bodhi?"

"I already called my neighbor. He probably had a game of fetch in the water, shared some dog food with the golden retriever next door and now they're both curled up in front of a crackling fire."

As they stepped into the lobby, the usually friendly desk clerk didn't even look up from his computer screen when she walked past him. She'd probably become the town pariah. Would Missy and Gabby even be dead if this guy hadn't wanted to somehow show off for her? That's all she could imagine he was doing. Why give her, of all people, a heads-up?

Once inside her room, Finn took charge. He pointed to the bathroom. "Wet clothes off. Take a warm shower. I'll make you some tea."

She followed his orders and grabbed her pajamas on her way to the bathroom. She shrugged off her damp jacket and peeled her sodden shirt from her body. Her jeans were just dirty, and she kicked those off, too.

The warm spray of the shower hit her face, and she jumped. The memory of her face in the fountain, the strong force pinning her down, had her doubling over. After everything, she hadn't actually feared the killer as he never seemed interested in harming her...until now.

She washed her hair and hurried through the rest of her shower. She slipped into her pajamas, a practical two-piece set, and ran a dryer over her hair, scrunching up her curls. True to his word, Finn had a cup of hot tea waiting for her on the nightstand.

He patted the bed. "Come over here and relax."

She appreciated his solicitousness, but she knew he had an ulterior motive—and it wasn't sex. He hadn't been present for most of her conversation with Detective Morse, and he wanted the rest of the details. She didn't blame him. She had questions of her own about Gabby Medina.

She crawled onto the bed, fluffed pillows behind her and sat cross-legged as she slid her hand around the paper cup of steaming tea. "Fire away."

"If you're not up to..."

She sliced a hand through the air. "We both know we need to debrief here."

Finn didn't waste any more time. "He texted you from a different number during the vigil. The text you forwarded to me—was that the first one?"

"No. The first text was that it was getting rowdy *here*. So I knew he was in the quad or had been in the quad. When I asked him, he answered that he had left with a friend.

And I knew then he was going to do something bad or had already done it. I fired off a million questions and he answered with the one I forwarded to you." She slurped the tea. "I really did try to get your attention before I went to the Art Garden."

"I believe you. The scene was crazy. I didn't even hear my phone ring. I did notice you leaving, though, and when I got that text, I figured it out."

"I had my weapon with me, which I no longer have. I should've gone in more aggressively, but when I saw that woman…when I saw Gabby, I lost it. He took advantage of that and attacked me." She tapped a fingernail against the paper cup and stared into her tea.

"What's wrong?"

"He attacked me. He's never done that before—the tires, the doll, even the discovery of Missy's body—he never tried to physically harm me."

"I hope you weren't sitting around thinking you were safe from this guy just because he spared your life a few times." He dropped onto the bed beside her, making her tea slosh in the cup. "He's a psychopath. Now he's a serial killer. He's not rational."

"I know, but why now? And why is he leading me to his fresh kills? It's sick. I hate it." She dropped her chin to her chest, and a tear rolled down her face.

"It has something to do with your sister's murder. Maybe he's a Plank fan. I know, I know. Maybe Plank didn't kill Tiffany, but most people believe he did. This guy believes Plank was responsible for Tiffany's murder, so he's involving you."

"I wish he'd stop." She dashed her wet cheek with the

back of her hand. "What about Gabby? Her name doesn't start with an *M*, but did she work on campus?"

Finn's eyes darkened and a muscle twitched at the corner of his mouth. "She worked at the ice cream shop. I saw her the day I talked to Deke. She popped her head into his office."

Jessica clapped a hand over her mouth. "Does Morse know this?"

"I told him everything."

"Those alibis. I hope the sheriff's department is going to recheck those alibis. Deke has a brother, right? Maybe it was his brother in that bar at karaoke night while Deke was murdering Morgan. Maybe they look alike. Tiffany and I didn't, but we had different fathers."

"I'm sure Morse is on it." He gave her a glance out of the corner of his eye. "He's on you, too. He's not happy the killer led you to two bodies."

"*He's* not happy?" She thumped her chest. "How does he think *I* feel? I didn't ask for this."

"You didn't see anything in the Art Garden?"

She drew her knees up to her chest, wrapping one arm around her legs. "I was so focused on Gabby's body, I didn't even hear him come up behind me until it was too late. I was right at the edge of the fountain, giving him a perfect opportunity. He rammed into me, pushing me into the water face-first. Before I got over my shock, he was holding my head down. I saw black jeans, felt a gloved hand on my neck. He was probably wearing a mask just in case he didn't successfully kill me."

"Didn't see any red scarf, hair color? Smells?"

"No, he wasn't wearing cologne or aftershave. Hadn't eaten any garlic or kimchi, either." She inhaled her tea before taking a sip. "I just don't understand why he tried to kill me."

"Uh, because he's a killer."

"You know what I mean." She yawned, the adrenaline of the evening finally dissipating. "I'm okay now. You can go home."

"There's no way I'm leaving you in this hotel room alone tonight." He got off the bed. "I can sleep on the sofa in the corner."

"With your legs draped over the edge?" She smoothed the covers beside her and then patted the bed. "If you're staying as my protector, you can sleep in the bed. It's not like we haven't shared a bed before."

"Yeah, and I remember how that ended." He toed off his sneakers. "I'll swish some of your toothpaste around in my mouth, and then I'll join you *on* the bed."

The terror of the night had buried any lustful inclinations she might have had about Finn for the moment, but his presence made her feel warm and safe—and sometimes warm and safe beat out lust by a mile.

As Finn took a step toward the bathroom, his cell phone rang on the nightstand. He pivoted. "This time it's my phone."

While handing it to him, she looked down at the display and swallowed hard. "Unknown number."

"Then I'd better take it." He plopped on the bed next to her and put the phone on speaker before answering it. "Who is this?"

A low voice hissed over the line. "It's your subject, Avery."

Jessica hugged herself. His voice sounded even more sinister over the phone.

"How'd you get your hands on a cell phone, Plank?"

"Come now, Professor. You know by now a con can get anything inside—for the right price. I call you after midnight and you're wondering how I got the phone?" Plank clicked his tongue. "You never stopped being a cop."

Finn met Jessica's eyes and rolled his own. "What do you want?"

"I heard all about the hijinks at Kitsap College tonight, Professor, and how Jessica Eller was involved...again."

Jessica scooted closer to Finn and twined her arm through his. She didn't like hearing her name on Avery Plank's lips, even over the telephone.

Finn's voice grew rough. "A woman was murdered, and another was almost murdered. I'd call it more than hijinks."

"Of course *you* would. To me it's a lark."

Finn growled low in his throat. "What do you want?"

"If you're still in touch with Jessica Eller, and I'm betting you are, you need to warn her."

Finn squeezed her thigh. "About what? She already knows this killer has a target on her back."

Plank chuckled. "I'm sure she does, but you'd better tell her to watch that target on her back very closely because I didn't kill her sister. That guy's still out there—and now it's personal."

Chapter Fourteen

Jessica's heart skipped a beat, and she dug her fingers into Finn's arm.

"How do you know this, Plank? What do you mean by personal? Has this guy been in touch with you? Is he a fanboy?"

"So many questions, Professor. I think I like you better when we're discussing your book about me, and I did just give you a nugget for that book, an exclusive. I did not kill Tiffany Hunt. You can tell her sister that bit of news, not that she ever believed I had killed her."

"You got that right, Plank." Jessica punched the pillow in her lap. "Now, how do you know so much about this guy?"

Plank said, "Oh, she's there."

Finn shook his head. Jessica knew he didn't want her talking to Plank, but she was tired of being afraid. "I'm here and I want answers. Why, other than the obvious, do you think these murders are some sort of personal message to me?"

"The first murder was to get you there, to get your attention. He copied your sister's killing—even if he wasn't responsible for that one. The second and third murders were to bring you glory."

She barked out a bitter laugh. "How did those murders bring me glory? They made me sick."

"The Kitsap Killer, as I believe he's now being called, let you find the bodies."

"*Let* me?"

Plank coughed and lowered his voice. "He was doing you a favor, Jessica. He knows your line of work. He figured giving you a heads-up on the murders would win you points the lab."

She snorted. "He doesn't know how the lab works. We're supposed to be investigating and analyzing evidence, not discovering it on our own."

Finn interrupted. "He didn't do her any favors tonight. He tried to kill her."

"Hmm." Sounded like Plank was tapping on the phone. "He didn't plan that. You must've done something to upset him. Did you call him a name? Try to humiliate him?"

"No." Jessica squeezed her eyes closed, replaying the moments when she approached the fountain with the gun pulled. "I had a gun, and I told him I'd called the cops. I *had* called the cops."

"Ahh." Plank released a noisy breath. "That's it. You betrayed him. He was sharing his kill with you, and you came with a gun intending to harm him, and you called the police. He reacted to that."

They could hear another voice in the background. "My turn."

"So sorry, Jessica, Professor. My time is up, but I'll be following the case of the Kitsap Killer—not as colorful as the Creekside Killer, though." Plank cleared his throat. "Now that you know I didn't kill Tiffany, maybe we can be friends, Jessica."

Jessica almost gagged. As she opened her mouth to return a nasty retort, Finn tapped her hand. He shook his head and ran a finger across his neck.

She gulped back her bile. "I don't know about being friends, but I do appreciate your input, and I'm glad to finally get confirmation that Tiffany's killer is still out there. So…thanks for that."

"Of course. If I have any more insight, I'll call you."

"Jessica doesn't have a phone. You can call me."

"Yes, Professor. You'll need to protect her."

Plank ended the call abruptly, and she and Finn stared at the phone on the bed.

She asked, "Is that what you do when you interview him for the book? You pretend to be his friend?"

"Avery Scott Plank is a psychopath. He doesn't understand the concept of friendship, so that's not necessary. It's a game to him. He's a smart guy. Don't underestimate him because he also happens to be evil." Finn drummed his fingers against the headboard. "What he said on the phone about the Kitsap Killer and you makes sense. You were just wondering why KK hadn't tried to harm you before last night."

"Why would he want to do me any favors? He doesn't owe me anything…unless he did kill Tiffany. I don't believe for a second he feels bad about that murder, but maybe in his warped mind he thinks he can make up for my loss by giving me the heads-up on his current crimes. Like you said, it's a game."

"Or he's taunting you."

"Taunting me?"

Finn jumped from the bed and paced to the window. "You couldn't save Tiffany. You were away at college, but you still blamed yourself. KK is giving you a chance to redeem yourself, but not really. It's just an illusion."

"Okay, Professor, you're losing me. Don't forget. I almost drowned tonight." She hit the side of her head with the heel of her hand. "My brain is probably waterlogged."

"Think about it." He raised one finger and took another hike across the room, as if on the stage in a lecture hall. "KK is providing you with an opportunity to save his victims. He contacts you minutes before he kills them, or so he says, giving you the false belief that if you got there quickly enough you could prevent their deaths. He's dangling that carrot. Holding out the possibility that you can right history. You couldn't save Tiffany, but you just might be able to save Missy or Gabby."

"Th-that's sick." Jessica folded her arms across her stomach. "He must be zeroing in on me because he killed Tiffany himself, or because, like you mentioned to Plank, he's captivated by my sister's case. Maybe he grew up here and knows the story. How does he know so much about me, though? That's what makes me think he's actually Tiffany's killer."

Clasping the back of his neck with one hand, Finn stopped his pacing. "Anyone fixated on Tiffany's case would know all about her ardent younger sister. You talked to the press frequently. You gave interviews. You made sure the world knew Tiffany Hunt had a sister and that sister was adamant about getting justice for Tiffany."

"Got me." Jessica rubbed her chin. "I also visited quite a few of those true crime chat rooms."

"You're kidding me." Finn plowed a hand through his hair, making it stand on end like a mad professor's.

"I'm afraid not." Jessica tried to make her voice small,

but the damning statement was out in the open. "I know that was ill-advised, but it seemed like a good idea at the time."

"When was the last time you logged on to one of those sites?"

She knew exactly when, but she rolled her eyes to the ceiling as if she had to think about it. "A few months ago."

"KK could've been in the chat rooms with you. I do a whole unit in one of my classes on these true crime discussion boards, blogs, podcasts. It might be worth checking back with the website to see if we can find any clues now that there's a copycat."

"Or the original." Jessica yawned.

Finn dropped to the edge of the bed and reached for her ankle, wrapping his fingers around it. "I was supposed to be staying here to watch over you and make sure you got some rest. Instead, you're over here talking to Plank and mulling over theories as to why a serial killer is harassing you."

Reclining against the pillows, she said, "Once I heard Plank's voice on the line, there was no way I *wasn't* going to speak with him, and talking to him is what engendered the theories." She picked up her paper cup and drained the remnants of her tea. "You brought me tea, though. You did good."

Finn turned off all the lights except for the lamp on his side of the bed. "I'm going to take a quick shower. Make sure you let me know at any time tonight if you're not feeling well. You're not out of the woods yet."

Finn closed the bathroom door behind him and as the shower started, Jessica crawled beneath the covers and flipped them back on Finn's side. He didn't have to sleep on the tiny sofa or the floor or the foot of the bed.

After the terror of the night, she wanted that man right

next to her. Although sex was the last thing on her mind, she trusted Finn. She trusted him with her life. She could trust him with her heart.

By the time he came back to bed, Jessica's lids drooped heavily over her eyes. He slid into bed beside her, his back toward her. She rolled to her side and wrapped one arm around his waist, burying her nose in the warm, slightly damp skin of his back.

She whispered, "Was Gabby a good student?"

"Bright, inquisitive, the best." Finn's voice was hoarse.

Tucking her hand in Finn's, she said, "Tell me we're going to catch this guy before he can destroy any more lives."

If Finn answered her, she didn't hear him. Instead, she pressed her face against his shoulder as a tear slid down her cheek.

THE FOLLOWING MORNING, Finn woke up with Jessica wrapped around his body—one arm flung over his chest and one long, smooth leg entwined with his.

He closed his eyes as he ran a hand over her wavy wheat-colored hair, and then rolled out of the bed, planting his feet on the floor. Jessica didn't need that sort of comfort right now.

He stalked off toward the bathroom to have a dip in a cold—or at least cool—shower. He squeezed some of Jessica's toothpaste onto his finger and ran it over his teeth—the next best thing to a toothbrush.

"Coffee?" Jessica tapped on the door. "I can either make a cup of instant in the room or order some room service."

"It's Sunday. Go ahead and order some breakfast from room service, unless you have someplace to be. I'd like to take a look at those true crime chat rooms. Been thinking about them all night." He swung open the door and kissed her on the mouth, showing off his new, minty breath. A man could only show so much restraint.

"So, not a good night's sleep for you?" Her gaze did a hungry inventory of his bare chest that weakened his restraint even more.

"Not great." *In so many ways.* "Why don't you get ready, and I'll order the breakfast."

"You got a deal." She slid open the closet and grabbed some clothes, and then they did an awkward dance in the doorway of the bathroom as they switched places.

"Are you an eggs and bacon kind of girl?"

"At this place, I'm a cinnamon swirl French toast kinda girl."

She retreated to the bathroom, and Finn got on the phone to order room service. Then he checked on Bodhi and pulled out his laptop.

The vigil last night had ended in chaos as word of another murder leaked. He'd had doubts that his female students would even make it to class next week. The president was making noise about switching classes online until the police could get things under control.

When the shower stopped, Finn tapped on the bathroom door. "Breakfast is on the way. What's the name of the most recent true crime site you visited?"

Jessica's muffled voice came through the door. "Cold Case dot com. We can access it on my laptop. I have an account with them, and the log-in is saved on my computer. Just give me a few more minutes."

Finn backed away from the door, trying not to picture Jessica stepping out of the shower, rubbing a towel across her body. "Take all the time you need."

He went back to his computer and logged in to the teacher portal for Kitsap College and started entering the midterm grades. He'd done a good job of distracting himself, as he hadn't even noticed Jessica had entered the room until she came up behind him, touching his shoulder.

"Have you looked at any of the news about Gabby's murder?"

"Not this morning." A knock on the door interrupted them. "You can switch over to a news site while I get our breakfast."

He opened the door to a young guy gripping the handles of a cart laden with silver-domed dishes and a pot of coffee. "Good morning... Professor Karlsson."

"Morning." Finn cocked his head. His classes tended to be big, and he didn't always get to know his students.

"Uh, Jamie... Martin." He wheeled the cart into the room and said over his shoulder, "Had you for Criminal Investigations. Good class. I'm planning on law school."

Jessica glanced up and smiled.

As he parked the cart next to the table where Jessica pored over the laptop, Jamie's speculative gaze flickered from Jessica back to Finn.

At least Jessica was fully dressed, even down to her white sneakers. "Glad you got something out of the class."

Jamie started transferring the dishes from the cart to the table. "Did you really find Gabby's body last night?"

"I was on the scene, yeah." Finn shoved his hand in his pocket for some cash. "Did you know Gabby?"

"Not really. Saw her around." Jamie placed some cloth napkins and silverware on the table. "The women on campus are terrified. My girlfriend said she's not leaving her apartment. Are we going to online classes?"

"Maybe." Finn held out a generous tip, folded between his fingers. "Keep that girl of yours safe—and yourself, too."

Finn walked Jamie to the door and locked the top lock behind him.

Jessica picked up the coffee pot and poured two cups. "There isn't much online, but there might be a witness this time."

"That's good news. Did someone see something before or after the crime?"

"A woman thinks she saw Gabby walking away from the quad last night with a guy—dressed in black with a black hoodie."

"These kids wear hoodies like armor. Everyone walks around with their hoods up, hiding their faces. Was that the case with this man? Or woman, who knows?"

"Yes. She can't give any kind of description, other than the clothing, but that would match what I saw. Also, if she was calmly walking away from the vigil with this guy, she must've known him."

"After Deke Macy, the sheriff's deputies are questioning all the people who work on campus."

"That's a tall order." She tapped one cup of coffee with a spoon. "Cream? Sugar?"

"Thanks, I'll dump some cream in there." He lifted the lid from one of the plates and inhaled the sweet cinnamon aroma. "Now, that smells good."

Jessica rearranged the table, moving his laptop to the credenza and pulling out her own, which she set down next to the food. "I'll bring up the cold case website."

"Eat something first." He shoved her plate toward her. "How are you feeling this morning?"

"Physically, I'm fine. Emotionally?" She whipped the

napkin into her lap and sliced a corner off the end of her French toast. "I'm a wreck. Sad, confused, still in shock. I can't believe what I witnessed last night. Can't believe we talked to Avery Plank."

"I hate to admit it, but he made a lot of sense." Finn dived into his bacon and eggs and helped himself to another cup of coffee.

Jessica picked at her French toast, plucked off some candied pecans and then shoved the plate toward him. "Try it."

As he plunged his fork into the cinnamon swirls, Jessica licked her lips and pulled her laptop in front of her. Her fingers tapped the keyboard and she whistled. "Celine, my PI, thinks she located my brother. I had ignored an email she sent a few days ago, so she sent me another."

"That's good." He waved a fork encrusted with sticky crumbs in her direction. "Any news about the case?"

"Nothing." She clicked the keys again and moved the laptop to share the screen with him. "Here's the website, Cold Case dot com."

"Why is your sister's case on here? It's not officially a cold case."

"There are a lot of cases like that—ones where there's doubt."

He raised an eyebrow at her. "You're not the only one with doubts?"

"No, I'm not." She signed into the website and selected a chat room from her saved favorites. She sucked in a breath. "Great minds think alike. There's been a lot of activity here the past few weeks. Those of us who doubted now see the connection between Tiffany's murder and the current homicides—and these people don't even know half of what I know."

Finn placed a hand over hers, hovering over the keyboard, fingers ready to type. "And they're not going to know what you know, right? Keep the card, the doll, the red fibers to yourself. You could compromise this investigation."

She flicked his hand from hers. "I know that."

Peering over her shoulder as she typed, he said, "Your profile name is jessiejames? He was an outlaw."

"Yeah, well, it's not easy thinking up original profile names." She skimmed through the messages. "Yep, yep. These online sleuths noticed the similarities between Tiffany's murder and Morgan's right away. Wow, they've even read about the witness who saw Gabby with someone last night. They're on top of things."

"Any of them ever solve a real crime?" Finn jabbed his finger at an envelope icon with red numbers on it in the upper-right corner of the window. "What's that?"

"Private messages. Members can message each other privately if they want to keep something out of the public chat room."

"Looks like you have messages."

"A lot of time it's personal requests, sometimes appeals for money that the moderators don't allow." The cursor skittered toward the envelope and Jessica clicked on it.

A string of messages appeared, all from the same user. Finn asked, "Do you know who TheHunter is?"

"Doesn't ring a bell." She double-clicked on one of the messages and gasped. "It's him, Finn. TheHunter is the killer."

Chapter Fifteen

A chill rippled down her spine as Jessica double-clicked the next message and the next and the next, all sent by TheHunter, all implicating him as the Kitsap Killer, all pointing to him as Tiffany's killer.

"Slow down." Finn encircled her wrist with his fingers. "What is he saying here?"

Jessica took a big breath and clicked on the first message, sent four days earlier. "This one asks what I thought about the card. The next one asks about the doll."

"Is there any information on the message board about the card or the doll?"

"I-I'm not sure." She clicked away from TheHunter's personal messages back to the board. "I think the easiest way to find out is through a search. I can search the different threads."

She entered the word *doll* in the find field and clicked on the magnifying glass. Her stomach knotted when several threads popped up. "Oh my God. That information is being bandied about here. I swear I haven't even been on this website since the current murders."

Finn, trying to be the voice of reason, said, "TheHunter just might be referring to the rumors on this message board."

"But why is he private messaging me? He calls himself TheHunter. Tiffany's last name was Hunt."

"Are you a frequent visitor to this board? Maybe he...or she sent private messages to other posters. TheHunter is just asking about those items, not claiming he left them. TheHunter could be referring to hunting clues or the truth." He nudged her fingers off the keypad. "Can we see who first mentioned these items?"

What Finn said made sense, but how would anyone on this website know about the card and the doll? As Finn searched, Jessica wrapped her hand around her cup and took a sip of lukewarm coffee.

"Here we go." Finn tapped on the screen. "A user by the name of Queenie posted something four days ago about a sympathy card mentioning Tiffany and a rag doll that you recognized as Tiffany's left at Morgan's memorial site. TheHunter probably just got the info from the boards, but what about this Queenie person?"

Jessica smacked her hand on the table, rattling all the leftover breakfast dishes. "Queenie is Ashley King. Because of her last name, Tiffany used to call her Queenie. I told her and Denny about the card and the doll, and she turned around and blabbed about it on here."

Finn forked the last piece of French toast into his mouth. "There you go. Not optimal but not the killer."

"I'm not that easily convinced. I'm going to go comb through these message boards and find out what else Queenie and TheHunter have had to say in the past. Maybe Denny is the TheHunter."

"Before you do that, maybe you should read your boss's emails." He circled a finger around a message at the bottom of her screen. "That's about the third email notification from your boss that's popped up since we've been sitting here."

She sighed. "Why doesn't he just call me?"

"The sheriff's department has your phone, remember?"

She clicked on the three emails from Michael in succession, each plea for her to call him more demanding than the previous one.

"It sounds like he really, really wants you to call him." Finn slid his phone toward her. "Knock yourself out."

"I don't even have his number memorized." She hunched over the phone and tapped in the personal cell phone number at the bottom of Michael's email. "Voicemail. Hey, Michael, it's Jessica. I'm calling from a friend's phone, as you know very well mine was confiscated last night. You can call me back on this number."

She placed Finn's phone on the table and turned her attention back to the message board. "I'm going to go out and see Ashley again and ask her what the hell she's playing at. I'm pretty sure I told her not to tell anyone about what I'd found."

Finn's phone rang. "That was fast."

Stepping away from the computer to stretch, Finn said, "Help yourself, but you're going to need to get yourself a temporary phone."

"Hello, Michael. Before you rip into me about last night, I did call 911 on my way to the Art Garden, and the sheriff's department grilled me thoroughly. I gave them everything I had—including my phone."

"It's not about that, Jessica. Detective Morse relayed all that to me." He cleared his throat. "It's about that DNA sample, from the red fiber."

She waved one arm in the air to get Finn's attention, and

then tapped the speaker icon on his phone. "Is there a match? I thought we weren't sending it through CODIS yet."

"We're not, but there's an internal match."

Jessica's mouth dropped open. "Internal? You mean like someone in law enforcement?"

"The sample was a partial match to your sister's DNA—Tiffany Hunt."

"What?" Jessica put her hand on top of her head just in case it exploded. "The DNA is a match to Tiffany's? How can that be?"

Michael groaned. "I said *partial* match, which means it's yours, Jessica. You contaminated the evidence. You're off this assignment. You've been too distracted by this whole thing. You've insinuated yourself into this investigation, and now you've compromised it."

"That's not possible, Michael. I handled all the evidence with care."

"Really? Like the card and that doll? Those could've been important to this case, but no attorney worth his or her salt would ever allow that in a court of law." Michael's voice softened. "I know this has been hard on you, Jessica, but you need to take a step back for the integrity of this case and…your own safety. Take a few days off."

Michael wouldn't listen to her weak denials or excuses, so she ended the call with a half-hearted apology. She rapped on her forehead with her knuckles. "I can't believe I did that. Michael's right. I've been treating these cases like my own private investigation. I'm doing a disservice to those young women."

Finn rubbed a circle on her back. "Don't beat yourself up. Your boss is wrong. You didn't insinuate yourself into these crimes, the killer dragged you into them. Like you told Plank last night, you didn't ask for this. Anyone would be rattled."

"Ugh, I can't believe I left my DNA on crime evidence. That's Forensics 101."

"That's also why your DNA, and that of other CSIs and some law enforcement personnel's, is in a local database outside of CODIS. Those checks have to be run first to rule out the people who may have handled the evidence."

"It was so promising."

"But not surprising. The Kitsap Killer hasn't left his DNA yet, but he'll mess up at some point. He'll make a mistake. They all do."

"Yeah, remind me again how long the Green River Killer was at large?" Jessica fell across the bed, her legs hanging over the edge.

"More than twenty years, but you just visited his current domicile." Finn put away his laptop and stacked up the dishes on the tray. "I'll leave this out in the hallway on my way out. If you're okay, I need to get home and collect Bodhi and finish my grading."

"I'll be fine. Didn't you hear Michael? I'm on vacation." She propped herself up on her elbows. "Thanks for staying with me last night, even though…"

"There was nowhere else I wanted to be, even though…." He hitched his bag over his shoulder and strode toward the bed. Leaning over, he kissed her, just like he did this morning.

And just like this morning, the touch of his lips sent butterflies swirling in her stomach.

As he stopped at the door with the tray in hand, he turned and said, "Get yourself a temporary phone and call me later."

When the door slammed behind him, Jessica scrambled

from the bed. She may be on forced vacation, but that didn't mean she had to stop working on this case. She'd been doing her best work on her own, anyway, and as far as she could tell—she was the closest person to catching the killer.

WHEN FINN HAD been gone almost an hour, Jessica pulled on a sweatshirt and grabbed her purse. She didn't have a phone to call Ashley and alert her to her visit, but maybe that was a good thing. Ashley acted as if she wanted Jessica to accept Plank's guilt in Tiffany's murder, but she hadn't moved on herself. *Queenie.*

Luckily, she remembered the way to Ashley's mobile home park. Did Denny have a username on the website, too? Were they both poking their noses into the investigations—past and present? She'd handed them two clues. Why didn't they tell her they were looking, too? Ashley pretended it was a done deal.

Michael hadn't mentioned any other DNA but hers on the red fiber, but maybe they couldn't separate anything else from hers. She'd messed up. Jessica sent a silent apology to Morgan, Missy and Gabby. And then she let out a not-so-silent scream in her car.

She hadn't been on the CSI team collecting evidence in the Art Garden. Detective Morse didn't want her there. Once the detective found out that she'd compromised the evidence in the other two cases, he would probably congratulate himself on the decision to keep her away. That was going to be a bitter pill to swallow in front of her colleagues at the forensics lab.

Jessica wheeled into the mobile home park and waved at a child on a tricycle. Pots of flowers and decorative trees brightened the yards of many of the mobile homes, which made Ashley's drab homestead stand out at the end of the row.

The inside of Ashley's place may be as chaotic as the place she'd shared with Tiffany, but Tiffany loved bright colors and beauty. If she lived with Ashley now, she would've turned the place into a charming, bohemian hideaway.

Jessica sniffed and parked the car in the same place as last time—behind a small white Toyota that had seen better days. At least she'd find Ashley at home this Sunday afternoon, unless she'd gone out with Denny. Jessica hadn't noticed Denny's car when she was here before.

She clomped up the two steps to the door. The mesh on the screen seemed to gape even wider than it had a few days ago. Ashley wasn't going to keep out many bugs, or even critters, with that thing.

The screen door protested when Jessica cracked it open to knock on the door. She stepped back and waited, listening for Ashley's heavy footfall on the floor inside. Instead, the tinny sound of the cheap TV chirped behind the door.

Jessica knocked again, harder. "Ashley? It's Jessica, Jessie, again. I need to talk to you."

She cocked her head, trying to filter out the background noise of the voices on the TV. "Ashley?"

Icy fingers trailed across her cheek, and she spun around. The kid on the trike had vanished, leaving her tricycle overturned in front of a mobile home with a swing set in front, one wheel spinning. A curtain twitched at the window of a home across the way, as a breeze rustled the crunchy leaves in Ashley's messy front yard and gave a silent push to the empty swing.

Jessica smacked her dry lips and knocked for a third time. "Ashley, are you home? We need to talk about your posts on Cold Case dot com. I know you're Queenie on there. I'm not even mad. Please open the door."

Her last words came out on a desperate whine as her fingertips started to go numb. The hair on the back of her neck quivered as she crept down the porch steps and shuffled through the dead leaves to the front window.

"Ashley!" Jessica banged on the window, causing it to quiver. One half of the curtains were pulled too far to the middle, leaving a gap on the side.

Jessica sidled toward the edge of the window, cupped her hands over the glass and peered inside. She could see the end of Ashley's drab sofa. As her gaze focused, she could just make out Ashley lying on the floor of her living room, her head in a pool of blood. So. Much. Blood.

Chapter Sixteen

Finn careened toward the Fairwood Flats Mobile Home Park and slammed on his brakes outside the gates as he met a phalanx of emergency vehicles and a huge crowd of people. He'd never get through all of that, would never get to Jessica.

He spied the red hair of Detective Morse and threw his Jeep into Park as he scrambled out of his car. He'd been elbow-deep in grading all afternoon, but his buddy Zach had given him the heads-up about another dead body—once again discovered by Jessica Eller.

She was supposed to be on vacation.

He elbowed through the lookie-loos until he got to the crime scene tape, keeping the hordes at bay. He edged toward the deputy, one he didn't know, manning the perimeter.

"Hey, man. The woman who discovered the body is my... girlfriend. Can I duck under to make sure she's okay?"

"Sorry, Professor Karlsson. Nobody's going in or out except authorized personnel. I think Detective Morse is almost done questioning Ms. Eller. You shouldn't have to wait long to see her. She's fine." The deputy grimaced. "The other one, not so much."

At least the deputy knew who he was. That might not gain him entrée into the magic crime circle, but it might get him something else. He dipped his head to the deputy's ear. "The other woman, Ashley King, right?"

The deputy nodded once, his gaze darting around to make sure nobody saw him talking to Finn.

Finn whispered, "Strangled like the others?"

"That's the thing." Quick glance over Finn's shoulder. "She was beaten to death with a blunt object."

Finn's gut knotted. The Kitsap Killer had wanted to distinguish this murder from his others. He had to know that killing Ashley King would connect him to Tiffany Hunt's murder, especially with Plank disavowing his previous confession. Maybe he didn't care. Maybe he was ready to take credit for that ten-year-old murder.

Had he called Jessica to the scene again? There's no way she would've come here on her own this time—not after what happened last night and her boss reading her the riot act about mishandling evidence. Besides, Jessica didn't have her phone. How would he have contacted her?

When Morse shifted positions, Finn caught a glimpse of Jessica, her blond hair hanging around her pale face, her arms crossed over her chest, shoulders hunched. It took every ounce of control and reason he had to stay behind the yellow tape and not go charging over there and take her in his arms.

He shuffled out of the crowd and sank down on an upright log that functioned as a barrier to the mobile home park. From his perch, he kept an eye on Jessica as she answered Morse's questions.

After almost thirty minutes, he sprang up from his log when a deputy led Jessica to a waiting patrol car. They weren't done with her. They were taking her to the station for questioning.

Even better. He could wait for her there.

He followed the deputy's patrol car to the station, joining a caravan of other vehicles, including a few news vans. By the time he parked at the station and exited his Jeep, the deputies had already hustled Jessica inside the station.

Finn walked inside and leaned over the front desk. "I'm here to pick up Jessica Eller when she's done."

The deputy on duty answered, "Noted."

While he waited for Jessica, Finn scanned through the news of the murder on his phone. Jessica's name hadn't been reported yet, so some stories were not linking Ashley's death to the current homicides. None of the outlets had mentioned the cause of death yet. Would the beating throw them off the scent of the Kitsap Killer? Fairwood hadn't had a murder in over five years. How coincidental would it be for a couple of killers to snap at the same time—unless Ashley's murder was personal.

How long before some enterprising journalist discovered that the Creekside Killer murdered Ashley's roommate ten years ago? How long before someone other than law enforcement would start piecing together the links between the murders? Everyone still believed Avery Plank had murdered Tiffany Hunt, but he could blow that truth right out of the water. Finn hadn't even told the police what Plank had admitted to him and Jessica. Would Plank backtrack from that admission?

He jerked his head up at the sound of footsteps in the back and half rose to his feet when he heard Jessica's voice.

"That's okay. I can get a ride back to Fairwood Flats."

Finn strode toward the front desk to meet her. "You don't need to do that."

Raising her chin, her eyes widened. "Finn."

A deputy, not Morse, stuck out his hand to Jessica. "Thank you again for your time, Jessica. If we have anything else, we'll let you know. Call us with your new number when you get it, if we don't release your phone first."

"Will do, Deputy Harris." Her pace picked up, and as she met Finn, she said, "Let's get out of here."

Harris pointed down the hallway from which they just emerged. "You can go out the back if you like. The press is still out front. By now, they probably know it's you who found the body."

Harris's implied "again" hung in the air as Finn took Jessica's arm. "Thanks, sir, we'll do that."

They did a 180 and made their way to the back door through the station. Before they exited, Finn draped his jacket over her shoulders, tugging the hood over her blond hair, just in case some sharp-eyed newshound noticed them sneaking to his car. They didn't exchange one word until Finn was behind the wheel and driving away from the station.

Shifting his gaze to the side, he said, "Dinner? Glass of wine? Bottle of wine?"

"I could use some food." She slumped in the passenger seat as he cruised past a news van with a reporter in front on a microphone. "This is already a circus, and they don't know the half of it."

"Neither do I."

She shook the hood from her head. "How'd you know where to find me?"

"As soon as I found out about Ashley's death and that you were the one who found her, I raced to the mobile home park. The deputy on guard wouldn't let me past the tape, but I saw Morse talking to you. Then I saw him lead you to a patrol car and followed you to the station." He clasped her hand. "What happened? The Kitsap Killer didn't lure you out there again, did he?"

"No, although I'm not sure Morse or my boss Michael believe that." She tapped on the window with her knuckle. "They're probably not going to allow me to get my car just yet. Can we go to that restaurant near my hotel? Dockside Fish Grill?"

"Patio should be a private place to talk."

"He did it. I know he killed Ashley." She set her jaw. "I just don't know why."

"What brought you back to Ashley's?" He hit the steering wheel with the heel of his hand. "You were going to confront her about posting as Queenie."

"Of course. I wanted to know why she'd been pretending with me that she believed Tiffany's case was closed while posting clues on a discussion board."

"Maybe it was the stolen scarf. She could've heard about red fibers found at the crime scenes and started putting things together." Finn swung a U-turn and parked a block down from the restaurant.

There were a few more diners outside this time, but they still nabbed a table on the edge of the patio overlooking the water.

As Finn sat across from Jessica, he asked, "Do you want to tell me what you saw? Don't if it's going to upset you."

"I honestly didn't see that much." She downed half a glass of water before continuing. "I knocked on her door a few times. Heard the TV and got an uneasy feeling. I went around to the front window and saw her lying on the floor in a pool of blood. I must've screamed because a couple of neighbors rushed outside. One of them called 911. I didn't even know what had happened to her until Morse told me someone hit her on the head with a heavy object. They haven't identified the murder weapon yet. Nothing left there with blood or hair on it. I didn't even know if she was dead, although it sure looked like it." She punched a fist into her palm. "Why? Why target Ashley at this late date? She couldn't tell the cops anything last time, and she knows nothing about the current murders."

"Where was Denny?"

The waitress interrupted them, and they ordered their food and drinks.

"I don't know where Denny is. Thank God I didn't find his body, too." She chewed her bottom lip. "I hope he's okay."

"They might be looking at him for Ashley's murder." Finn held up a finger as Jessica opened her mouth. "Think about it. This is his second murdered girlfriend. What are the odds? The police don't have anything to tie Ashley to the Kitsap Killer slayings. She's not a student, doesn't work on campus, didn't know the victims."

"She was Tiffany's roommate."

"And Denny was her boyfriend. I'm just throwing him out there as a suspect. You know they'll be looking at him." He thanked the waitress for his beer and waved off the icy mug. "How are you doing? Take a sip of your wine. Maybe it'll put some color back in your cheeks."

She pressed a hand to her face. "Do I look that bad?"

"You look tired and frazzled and a little green around the gills. Did Morse and Deputy Harris grill you?"

She followed his advice and took more than a dainty sip from her glass. "What do you think? They suspected that the Kitsap Killer had given me another exclusive, like I'm a freakin' reporter instead of a forensics analyst. Michael, my boss, got in on the fun, too, calling the station while I was there for further questioning."

"Did you tell them about the Cold Case website and Ashley's posts? TheHunter's private chats?"

"I told them all of that." She swept her glass over the table, and her white wine sloshed inside dangerously. "I think I lost them at Queenie."

"I'm sorry, Jessica. I think you need to back away for a while."

"You're probably right, and Michael just extended my involuntary vacation, but I can't help thinking I'm the only one who can crack this. The Kitsap Killer is reaching out to me for some reason—whether or not he killed Tiffany. He's taking risks by contacting me. He left his comfort zone by murdering Ashley. He's going to make a mistake."

"If he does, Detective Morse will catch it. Let the police handle this. If you had shown up at Ashley's while he was there—" Finn shook his head "—he's already shown he's willing to hurt you to protect himself."

"I know you're right. You're all right. I'm going to give it a rest tonight and email the PI about my brother instead. She must've thought I lost interest."

The food arrived, and Jessica busied herself with tossing dressing into her crab salad and asking for another glass of wine. At least her appetite had returned, and she'd lost the haunted look around her eyes.

She even stole some fries from his plate, and he pretended to object.

As they finished their meal, Finn checked his phone. He still had grading to finish and online classes to plan.

Holding up his phone, he said, "We should've stopped

before dinner to pick up a new phone for you. Everything will be closed now."

"I think I'm good." She drained the dregs of her second wineglass. "Deputy Harris indicated I could have mine back as early as tomorrow."

"Did they find out anything about the phone that texted you?"

"They were able to track the texts to one temp phone purchased in Los Angeles and another purchased in St. Louis, but they haven't gotten any further than that. The text messages I received were from two different phones, and he probably has another."

"And he most likely didn't buy them himself." Finn tossed his napkin on the table.

"Anyway, they have all the info from my phone that they need, so I'll probably get mine back tomorrow."

"Are you going to be okay at the hotel on your own tonight?" He crossed his arms and leaned on the table. "I hate to abandon you, but I have to finish my grading and set up my classes for the week, which are all online now. The president of Kitsap College sent out the message today."

"I'll be fine. I'm going to email Celine, my PI, and watch some TV. I'm officially on vacation."

"Yeah, you were officially on vacation today, too." He tipped his head at the waitress to get her attention. "And you probably shouldn't pick up your car tonight after those two glasses of wine."

"I was just thinking the same thing, not that I could pick it up anyway. Who knows how much longer the sheriff's deputies are going to be at Ashley's."

"How are they supposed to contact you if they need to?"

He pulled a credit card from his wallet and handed it to the waitress as she approached with the bill.

"I'm not in the middle of the wilderness. I do have a telephone in my room. I gave them my hotel. If they want to find me, they will. They're cops."

Once Finn settled the bill, he drove Jessica to her hotel and walked her all the way up to her room. He even stood outside her door until he heard the lock.

It's not that he didn't trust her to stay put. He didn't trust the Kitsap Killer. For whatever reason, this maniac had put a target on Jessica's back—and he was ready to hit the bull's-eye.

THOSE TWO GLASSES of wine had hit the spot. Jessica's neck and jaw didn't feel so tight, and her mind had stopped clicking. She pulled off her boots, gathered her hair in a ponytail, brushed her teeth and splashed some water on her face.

She studied her face in the mirror. Finn had been diplomatic. She looked a lot worse than tired and frazzled. She'd become Fairwood's pariah. She just couldn't shake the stench of death surrounding her.

She unplugged her laptop and carried it with her to the bed. She ran her hand over the smooth pillow beside her. Housekeeping had changed her bedding today and with that, swept away any traces of Finn's scent from the pillow.

Her attraction to him remained strong, despite all the turmoil in their lives—her life. He'd been there for her through every disaster—and it had required no manipulation from her. He wanted to be with her, to protect her.

That had been a hard concept for her, and Tiffany, to understand. Mom had used every tool of manipulation in the book to ensnare men, but they never stuck around. Jessica had never even met her father. He'd wanted nothing to do with Mom—or her. Tiffany's father had died before Tiffany tracked him down.

Her father might not want any contact with her, but apparently her brother had shown some interest. She flipped open her laptop and accessed her email. She vowed to stay off the cold case crimes website...for now.

She double-clicked on Celine's email. Seems her brother was skittish after hearing bad things about his family but might be interested in meeting her—and his other sister. Celine explained that she hadn't thought it was her place to tell him his other sister was dead. What a way to start off a new family relationship.

She dragged the hotel phone onto the bed and called Celine's number.

"Celine Jerome, private investigations."

"Hi, Celine. This is Jessica Eller. I got your email."

"It's about time, girl. I sent that a few days ago, and I've been trying to call you on your cell phone."

"I know, sorry. I've been busy...with work, and my phone isn't working."

"Understood." Celine shuffled some papers. "Good news is, I found your half brother, and he lives in Seattle, believe it or not. The bad news is, he's not absolutely sure he wants to establish contact. He's happy, he's settled."

"Wow, Seattle. I may have already met him in some capacity. I get that he might be leery." Jessica twisted her ponytail around her hand. "And I haven't even gotten to the part where his other half sister was murdered. Once I tell him that, he may just go running for the hills."

"He might. I know you've been anxious to meet him, but

I wanted to check with you before giving him your contact info. He wants to be the one to make the first move."

"That's fine. I do want to meet him. In fact, I'd welcome the distraction about now. I'm not going to have my cell phone back and working until sometime tomorrow, but you can give him my cell number and my email address. Give him my work email, too. He might feel more comfortable if he sees I work for the Washington State Patrol. H-how does he sound?"

"Haven't spoken to him, and he doesn't want me to tell you his name, but our text exchanges have been good—no anger or outrage that you hired a PI to track him down. Seems cool."

"Great. I could use some cool right now. Go ahead and give him my details and tell him to reach out any time. And thank you so much, Celine. Send me your final bill."

"Don't thank me yet. He might decide to forgo the relationship. Like I said…jumpy."

"That wouldn't be your fault. I'm sure you told him what a spectacular person I am."

Celine chuckled. "I didn't, but you are. Take care."

When Jessica ended the call, she placed the receiver in the cradle. Celine's tone had changed at the end. Had Celine already read about her issues here in Fairwood? Once her half brother knew about those, he really wouldn't want to have a relationship with her.

As she put the phone back on the nightstand, a fire alarm in the form of unremitting beeps filled the room. Jessica jumped from the bed and poked her head into the hallway. One door opened at the end, and Jessica shouted "Is this for real?"

The woman yelled back, "Not taking any chances."

Sighing, Jessica shoved her feet into her boots and zipped them up. She sniffed the air. She didn't smell any smoke, so she left her laptop, grabbed her purse and a jacket, and left her room.

She passed the elevator and pushed open the door to the stairs. As the woman down the hall had said, why take any chances. Luckily, no high-rise buildings were allowed in Fairwood, including hotels, so she had just three flights of stairs to navigate.

At the bottom, she shoved open the fire door that opened onto a side parking lot and sucked in the cool air. She ambled around to the front of the building. Other hotel guests and employees were scattered around the front of the building.

She spied the front desk clerk and made a beeline toward him. She didn't even have to ask her question, as he addressed a small clutch of people vying for his attention.

Raising his hands, he said, "I don't know if there's actually a fire in the hotel or not, but when the fire alarm goes off, everyone needs to evacuate and stay outside until the fire department comes, checks things out and gives us the all-clear signal. I'm sorry for the inconvenience. There are a few restaurants down the road still open, and you're welcome to enjoy our beautiful dock on the bay while you wait."

The sun had already set, but Jessica had grabbed her jacket on the way out, so she hugged it around her body and crossed the road to the water. She didn't want to clomp all the way out to the dock, and she didn't want to dangle her feet in the water again, so she clambered onto a pile of rocks that stood sentry on either side of the dock.

She brushed a layer of sand from the flat of one of the boulders and sat down. Closing her eyes, she focused on the sound of the water lapping against the wooden pilings of the dock.

Sand scuffled behind her, and she whipped her head around, almost colliding with a man's leg. When she opened her mouth to scream, he fell against her back and clamped a rough hand over her mouth.

Chapter Seventeen

She wasn't going down without a fight this time. She drove her elbow back, connecting with a kneecap.

The man grunted and his hand loosened on her mouth. She bit into the fleshy part of one finger, gritty with sand.

He yelped. "Ow! Jessica, let go. It's me, Denny."

She unclenched her teeth and spit into the sand. Then she jumped up from the rock and spun around, her fists raised.

Denny flinched and flapped his hand. "That hurt like hell. I think you broke the skin."

She snarled. "Good! What the hell are you doing sneaking up on me and covering my mouth? You're lucky my gun was stolen." Glancing over his shoulder at the hotel parking lot, Denny tucked his scruffy hair behind his ear. "I didn't want you screaming."

"You could've called my name first."

"Like I said, I didn't want you screaming." He flipped up his hood. "People think I killed Ashley. Do you think I killed her?"

"You're not a suspect, Denny. You're a person of interest. As far as I know, the police don't have any evidence against you, but you are…were her boyfriend and lived there with her. They need to talk to you."

"Yeah, they're gonna talk to me, all right. 'Your girlfriend was murdered ten years ago, Denny, and now you have another murdered girlfriend. Explain that while we lock you up.'"

Her breath returning to normal, she wedged her hands on her hips. "Did you pull the fire alarm in the hotel?"

"That was me." He patted his scrawny chest. "I knew you were staying at this hotel. Saw you go out with that cop."

"He's not a cop."

"Whatever. I knew that desk guy wasn't going to give me your room number, and I didn't want to give him my name." He hunched his shoulders. "I figured the fire alarm would get you outside where I could talk to you."

Narrowing her eyes, she asked, "Where were you when Ashley was murdered?"

"See? You think I did it."

"It's a simple question, Denny."

"I was in my rig on the outskirts of town. Me and Ashley had a spat." He sniffed and rubbed his nose. "She told me to take a hike, so I slept in my rig and I was still there."

She had to admit, his story was weak. "What was the fight about?"

"Other women. Always about other women."

Her gaze wandered from his bleary eyes to his stubbled chin down to his dirty jeans and scuffed boots. Real ladykiller. "Did she threaten to kick you out?"

"Nothing like that, but it's what she said before, Jessie. She was scared—not of me."

"Scared of what?" Jessica watched a couple of fire engines pull into the hotel parking lot, their sirens wailing. She could always make a run for it if Denny turned violent…or she could probably take him out herself.

"Some guy." Denny picked up a rock and skipped it into the bay. "She told me she'd seen the same guy in town who'd met with Tiffany years ago. She saw him for the first time yesterday. They met eyes, and she recognized him and realized that he knew she'd recognized him."

"What guy is this?" She snapped her fingers. "Ashley did mention someone she thought might've stolen the doll and scarf, but she said he left town before Tiffany was murdered."

"That's right. She told the cops about him at the time, but she didn't know his name or where he lived. He just showed up one day, hung out with Tiffany a few times and left. Tiff never introduced him to us. I never even saw him, but Ashley saw them together drinking coffee one day. She never saw him again—until yesterday, the day she was murdered."

"You think he killed Ashley because she recognized him."

"Yeah. I put two and two together. That's the only thing that makes sense to me." Denny covered his face with his hands, and his shoulders shook.

"I'm so sorry, Denny." Jessica rubbed his back. "Ashley was the sweetest person. I hope I didn't... I mean I hope my visit didn't draw the killer's attention to her."

He dragged his arm across his face. "That's not it, Jessie. It was that man. I'm telling you, Ashley was terrified."

"You need to go to the police, Denny. Tell Detective Morse everything you told me."

"What if this guy comes after me? What if he thinks Ashley told me or that I remember him? I don't. I don't."

"The police can protect you, Denny. This is important information they need to know."

"Like they protected Morgan, Missy and Gabby?" He

took a cigarette from his pocket, which trembled as he held it between two fingers. "I don't think so. Just stay safe, Jessie. You don't even live in Fairwood. If you're done with your work, go back to Seattle." He squeezed her hand and turned away.

She watched Denny's dark figure climb over the rocks, the glowing light of his cigarette bobbing with each move.

Was she done with her work? She was done with her official work, but the unofficial work had consumed her and now Denny had handed her another clue. She owed it to Tiffany to follow up. She owed it to Morgan, Missy, Gabby and Ashley, too.

FORTY-FIVE MINUTES LATER, the fire department had given the all-clear signal, and Jessica shuffled back inside the hotel with the other guests, quite a few a little tipsy from their forced evacuation. The effects of her two glasses of wine had completely evaporated, and her nerve endings tingled anew after her encounter with Denny.

When she got to her room, she reached for the phone to call Finn and tell him all about this new piece of information. As soon as she picked up the receiver, she dropped it—and not because she hadn't memorized Finn's number, which she hadn't. If she ran to Finn with Denny's theory about the mystery man, Finn would only remind her to step back and leave it to the police.

And he wouldn't be wrong.

Instead, she got ready for bed and slipped between the covers, the TV remote on one side of her and her laptop on the other. She selected a reality TV show from the menu and pulled the computer into her lap. Without her phone, her email had become her only connection to the outside world.

Several new emails loaded, and she started with the oldest, a message from Celine with her final invoice and the news that she'd sent Jessica's contact info to her brother.

Jessica switched to her bank's website and sent Celine the money. Back to her email, she skimmed through a message from Michael reminding her to fill in her time sheet with her *vacation days*, as he still insisted on calling them. She had a different name for it—a forced leave of absence.

She clicked on the newest message from armybrat, an unknown email address. Excitement fizzed through her veins when she read the message. It was from her brother, and he'd signed the email with his name—David.

An image invaded her mind, and she squeezed her eyes closed to focus on a scene with a baby, almost a toddler, in a bouncy seat and a little girl with blond curls waving at him and giggling and chanting. "Wavy Davy, Wavy Davy."

Her lids flew open. Is it possible David had kept the same name Mom had given him? She'd remembered his name was David or maybe Tiffany told her that, but this was the first time she remembered the nickname she'd given him—Wavy Davy.

A tear trembled on the edge of her eyelash as she smiled. He wanted to meet her, but he had reservations, and he only wanted to meet one sister at a time. The tear dropped to her cheek and rolled down to her chin where it quivered before splashing onto the laptop. He'd never have that pleasure.

Her fingers hovered over the keyboard as she composed an email to the brother she hadn't seen in over twenty-five years.

THE NEXT MORNING all through breakfast, Jessica could hardly eat due to the butterflies in her stomach, but for a change these butterflies signaled excitement instead of fear. After exchanging several emails with David last night, they'd agreed to meet for dinner down in Kingston, as he'd be in Edmonds today and could take the ferry over. She felt giddy that she could complete one of Tiffany's dreams for her.

The hotel phone startled her, and she crossed the room to answer it, the butterflies turning into knots. "Hello?"

"It's Finn. How are you this morning? I regretted leaving you after dinner, but I figured you'd fall asleep right away."

"Not quite." She proceeded to tell him about the fire alarm and Denny's warning.

Finn swore. "Did Denny tell the police?"

"He's trying to avoid the police, but I'm going to mention it to them when I drop by the station today to get my phone."

"My first class starts in about an hour, but I called to see if you need a ride to pick up your car."

"No, I'm good. I can get there on my own. Then I'm going to see if I can get my phone." She paused. "I made contact with my brother last night."

Finn asked, "How'd that go?"

"Better than I expected. He's kind of guarded, and I still have to tell him about Tiffany."

"What's his name?" Finn had an edge to his voice.

"David, and he lives in Seattle. We're meeting for dinner tonight in Kingston."

"What's his last name?"

She cleared her throat. "H-he didn't reveal that to me. Like I said, skittish."

"Or weird. Why doesn't he want to tell you his last name?"

"Calm down. Celine vetted him. Remember, I reached out to him, not the other way around."

"Where's the dinner?"

"A restaurant called Salty Girls. He let me pick, and I figured that was appropriate as both Tiffany and I were salty girls." She checked the time on her laptop. "I need to run. I'll give you a call before I leave for Kingston, hopefully from my recovered cell phone. Good luck with those online classes."

She made her next call to the sheriff's station. When the deputy at the front desk answered, Jessica identified herself and asked if she could retrieve her car from in front of the crime scene at Fairwood Flats Mobile Home Park. When he gave her the okay, she traipsed down to the front desk to call a taxi. She couldn't even order a car without her cell phone. She should've asked that deputy if she could get her phone, too.

Fifteen minutes later on the taxi ride to Ashley's mobile home, the driver twisted in his seat as he pulled out of the hotel parking lot. "You heard about that murder out there."

"Yeah, terrible." Jessica clapped her sunglasses on her face and turned her head to stare out the window. She should follow Denny's lead and try to cover up so people wouldn't recognize her. Luckily, this driver just seemed to be sharing gossip with a fare.

When they arrived, she had the driver drop her off at the entrance to the mobile home park. She didn't want him dropping her off in front of a mobile home ringed with crime scene tape.

The deputies hadn't removed the yellow tape yet, but none of it circled her car. She crept up to the driver's-side door, her head turned away from Ashley's place.

As she grabbed the door handle, a woman across the way looked up from her gardening and gave Jessica a hard stare.

Jessica yanked open her door, dropped onto the seat and cranked on the engine. Denny had been right—she needed to leave this town. As soon as Deputy Morse gave her the go-ahead, she was out of here.

She'd lost her sister, but she had a brother. She needed to let Tiffany go and concentrate on forging a new relationship with David. Tiffany would've approved. Being the oldest sister, Tiffany had missed Wavy Davy more than Jessica had. Jessica had just been about three years old when child services took David away from Mom. Tiffany had been twelve, already too old for her years—a childhood lost.

Jessica drove straight to the sheriff's station from the mobile home park. Even though her forensics services were no longer needed or wanted on the case, she still had business to conduct.

She sailed through the front doors of the station like the frequent flyer she'd become. The deputy at the front desk, asking if she needed help, sounded like the same one who'd answered the phone earlier.

"I'm Jessica Eller. Detective Morse confiscated my cell phone for evidence, and he indicated yesterday that I might be able to pick it up today. Do you know if it's ready?"

The deputy picked up the phone. "Let me check with Deputy Lorman. He's in charge of that evidence from that case."

Lorman must've picked up because the front desk deputy started explaining the who, what, when to someone on the other line. He eyed Jessica as he nodded. "I see. Uh-huh. Yeah, I'll let her know."

Jessica raised her eyebrows when the deputy ended the call.

"I'm sorry, Ms. Eller. He's not ready to release your phone yet. Maybe later this afternoon or tomorrow."

"Ugh." She sawed her bottom lip with her teeth. Should she go through the trouble of getting a pay-as-you-go phone or not? She could touch base with David via email before she left, just to confirm. And she could always call Finn from the hotel phone. Her car had a GPS for the drive down to Kingston, not that she didn't know the way to Kingston, and she could plug the restaurant into her GPS.

"I'll get it tomorrow." She pointed to the phone. "Is Deputy Lorman available or Detective Morse? I have some information about the King homicide."

"They're both busy right now, out in the field. Unless you know who did it, you can probably give them a call and leave a voicemail. They both check in regularly."

"I'll do that." Denny was right. The investigation team probably wouldn't put much stock in anything Denny had to say—until they could get their hands on him to question him.

She spent the rest of the afternoon on errands and finishing up her work on Morgan's case, if Michael would accept it. Before she got ready for her dinner with David, she left Detective Morse a voicemail, left another message for Finn, who hadn't picked up, and sent an email to David to confirm.

When she emerged from the shower, the only one who had bothered to respond was her brother. All set.

She dressed casually in a pair of jeans, a green blouse, a caramel-colored blazer and low-heeled boots to match. She'd discovered a spot of ketchup on the green sweater she told David she'd be wearing, but she didn't bother to update him. He said he'd be wearing glasses and a gray jacket. She'd find him. Would she know him anywhere?

She set the GPS in her car for Kingston and took off, her

palms a little sweaty on the wheel. Was David as nervous as she was? The thirty-five-minute drive took her away from the coast and through a long stretch of greenery. When she passed the casino, she knew she was close.

Once she reached the town of Kingston, she spotted the red clapboard in front of the Salty Girls restaurant. Jessica pulled into the small parking lot on the side of the building and flipped down the visor to freshen her lipstick.

She walked into the restaurant and craned her neck to scan for any single guys sitting at a table. A man in glasses with brown hair half rose from his chair and lifted his hand.

A grin stretched Jessica's mouth as she approached her brother's table. When she reached it, he stood up fully and extended his hand and then dropped it when she moved in for a hug.

They gave each other one of those awkward one-armed clasps, and she laughed self-consciously. "David, finally. It's good to finally meet you."

"You, too. It's been a long time." He gestured to the seat across from him.

As Jessica sat down, she tilted her head. "Have we met before?"

FINN TRIED JESSICA'S hotel number one more time, a kernel of unease lodged in his throat. He didn't like the idea of her meeting a stranger, for all intents and purposes, a stranger in another town with no cell phone.

Kingston wasn't that far, and she'd told him the name of the restaurant. He could always do a reconnaissance mission to spy on her and her brother. She'd be angry if she spotted him, though.

He blew out a long breath. He'd finished all his grading

yesterday, and the online classes had gone better than expected. The young women in his class were relieved to be able to stay at home.

He'd get some dinner, do some research for his book and wait for Jessica to give him the report on her brother. He wanted her to leave Fairwood for now, but this time he didn't plan to let her disappear from his life. He hoped she felt the same way. He thought she did.

As he opened his fridge door to investigate what he could make for dinner, his cell phone rang. Spinning the phone around on the counter, he saw a number from the Washington State Patrol on the display. He grabbed it and tapped to answer. "Hello?

"Is this Finn Karlsson?"

"Who wants to know?"

"Sorry. This is Michael Wilder from the Washington State Patrol Forensics Division. I'm Jessica Eller's boss."

"Yeah, I know who you are. Are you trying to reach Jessica?"

"I am, yeah. It's important. When Deputy Lorman took her phone, she gave me your number."

"She went out to dinner."

Wilder swore under his breath. "I really need to talk to her. It's...well, it's her safety at stake here."

Finn had been hunched over the counter, but Wilder's words had him snapping to attention. "I know where she is. I can get to her. What's going on?"

"She probably told you how she contaminated the DNA evidence on that red fiber, right?"

"Yeah, yeah. She told me all about it. Felt incredibly stupid, too."

"Well, it wasn't her fault. She *didn't* contaminate the sample."

Finn's heart pounded in his chest. "What do you mean? That wasn't her DNA from the sample?"

"The forensics techs jumped the gun. It was just a trace, a sample, and it partially matched right away to Tiffany Hunt's sample on file. The techs made an assumption before running additional tests on the sample. Once they ran further tests, they discovered it couldn't be Jessica's DNA."

Finn tried to swallow, his throat sandpaper. "Why couldn't it be a match?"

"Oh, it's still a partial match, but the DNA can't belong to Jessica because it belongs to a male. The trace DNA from the red fiber belongs to a male relative of Jessica's—like a brother."

Chapter Eighteen

Her brother smiled, and her heart skipped a beat at how similar it was to Tiffany's smile. He said, "It's funny. I feel the same way—like I've seen you before."

"It's more than that." She shook her head. "It's your voice...and your smile is so much like Tiffany's."

"I'm glad you see the resemblance." He put his hand over his heart. "You can tell her you found me, but I'm not ready to meet everyone yet."

Jessica swallowed and smiled too brightly. "I can understand that.

"So, tell me all about yourself." She planted her elbows on top of the table, ignoring the menus, and sank her chin in her palm. "What does your email name, armybrat, mean? Was your adoptive father in the army? Did you move around a lot?"

"Whoa! Slow down." Chuckling, he held up his hands and crossed one finger over the other. "My father was in the army, retired now, so I followed in his footsteps like a dutiful son. Spent some years in the army myself. Honorable discharge, got my teaching credential, thanks to the GI Bill, and found a job in Seattle. The Pacific Northwest always called to me."

"That's good. I'm glad life worked out well for you. Our sister—" Jessica chewed on the side of her thumb, not ready to spill the beans about Tiffany yet "—she had some issues as an adult. Chaotic childhood."

He dipped his head. "That's sad, but you turned out okay."

Jutting out her chin, she said, "Tiffany turned out okay, too."

"Of course, I'm sure. Looking forward to meeting her." He waved to the waitress. "Are you ready to order?"

"Oops, you go ahead. I haven't even looked." She scooped up one of the menus and ran her finger down the fish specials while David ordered.

When the waitress turned her attention toward Jessica, she ordered a platter with the fish of the day and a glass of pinot grigio.

The waitress asked David, "Something to drink, sir?"

"Water is fine." He gave Jessica a tight smile when the waitress left. "I don't drink alcohol."

"Oh, that's…good." Now she felt guilty about her glass of wine. Did he not drink because he had a problem with it? Alcoholism ran in families, and both Mom and Tiffany had suffered from the disease. As far as she could remember, David's biological father was a hard-drinking navy seaman. Maybe that's why David was dry.

When her wine came, she took tiny sips to make it last so she wouldn't need to order another. She still had to drive home, anyway.

They exchanged life stories over dinner, and Jessica couldn't shake the feeling that David's recitation was memorized and rather sterile. Was he trying to present a picture of perfection? She didn't need perfection from her brother, just a human connection, which she hadn't felt yet.

When David finished another story about the lessons he taught, not the kids, just the lessons, Jessica excused herself to use the ladies' room. She dismissed her disappointment. They were strangers, hadn't seen each other in over twenty-five years. The last time she'd seen David, he was barely a toddler. How would he even remember anything about her?

Maybe they wouldn't be best buds, but she had a sibling and she'd try to forge a relationship with him.

By the time she returned to the table, David had paid their bill. "I think we should get out of here while it's still light outside. I have a great idea."

"Oh?" Jessica sat down and finished her wine. She'd need it to spend any more time with David. "What do you have in mind?"

"A surprise." He clapped his hands together like a child.

"Maybe another time, David, and I hope there is another time, but you need to catch the ferry back to Edmonds and I need to drive back up the peninsula."

"You should probably wait to drive, anyway, Jessica, after drinking that wine." He tapped her glass. "I have something in mind that I think will bring us a little closer. You feel it, too, right? That bond between us is missing, but I think this little road trip will give it a boost. What do you think?"

So, he'd felt it, too. Maybe it was her fault. And when she looked into his brown eyes, so similar to Tiffany's, she decided she couldn't refuse her little brother anything.

She grabbed her purse and said, "Why not? Let's go make some new memories."

FRANTIC, HIS FINGERS SHAKING, Finn searched his computer for Celine Jerome's information. This couldn't be happening. It was all some weird mistake.

He'd questioned Wilder, and Jessica's boss admitted the DNA could be from any close male relative, even her father. Finn dug his fingers into his hair. That wouldn't work. Jessica and Tiffany had different fathers. The sample DNA from the red fiber wouldn't have matched Tiffany's DNA if it belonged to Jessica's father.

He finally found Celine's phone number and called her. "Celine Jerome, private investigations."

"Celine, you don't know me, but I'm friends with Jessica Eller. She told me all about how you located her half brother for her."

"Whatever you say. Can't discuss my work."

Finn rubbed his eyes. "I understand that, I do, but this is a matter of life and death—Jessica's. She could be in danger from her brother."

Celine sucked in a breath. "What are you talking about? He's a nice, normal guy. An army veteran, an accountant, a student."

"Would a nice, normal guy have his DNA at a murder scene? Please, Celine. I need to know his name. Jessica called him David, but I need to know his last name. Jessica is with him now and is in danger."

"Wait a minute. Who said his name was David?"

"Jessica. She told me he didn't want to give her his last name, but he said his name was David, same as it was when he was a baby."

"That may have been his name as a baby and maybe he decided to give that name to Jessica, but that's not his legal name."

"What is his legal name?"

Celine hissed on the other end of the line.

"I'll turn this over to the police, anyway, Celine, and

they'll make you give up this information—only it might be too late for Jessica."

"Oh, all right, but you didn't hear it from me. His legal name is Dermott Webb."

After the call, Finn sat stunned, the phone still held to his ear. His student Dermott Webb was the Kitsap Killer? Jessica's half brother. Of course, it made sense. He was on campus. He worked in that accounting office where those women had taken the register money. Wasn't the sheriff's department supposed to be questioning and investigating anyone who'd worked with the women?

He'd call the police, but he wasn't going to waste any more time. At least he knew that Jessica and Dermott were at a restaurant in Kingston. What was the name of it? Salty Ladies? Salty Girls?

If they were meeting for dinner, they could still be there. At least it was a public place. He grabbed his keys and ran from his house. As he sped down the 104, he got Detective Morse's voicemail. He told him about the DNA, advised that he call Wilder for a better explanation, and let the detective know that he was on his way to Kingston to interrupt Jessica's dinner with her brother—the Kitsap Killer.

He made it down to Kingston in record time and asked his phone for directions to the Salty Girls restaurant. Turns out he was just two blocks away, and he swung an illegal U-turn in the middle of the street to find it.

As he passed the full parking lot, he released a sigh of relief when he spotted Jessica's car. Thank God they were still here. He'd decided not to rush in with guns blazing, accusing Dermott of being the Kitsap Killer. He'd make up some other excuse for being there...and then what? It was going to be awkward that his student, Dermott Webb, was sitting with Jessica, his sister. The sister he'd never contacted while in Fairwood. Hell, Dermott had even met Jessica once. The first time she sought him out, Dermott had been in the lecture hall.

He parked in the red zone two doors down from the restaurant and burst inside. He must've looked like a madman, as several diners turned to stare at him. His gaze darted around the room, but he didn't see them.

A hostess approached him. "Are you looking for your party, sir?"

"Yes, yeah. A couple, a tall blond woman and a man—average height, short, brown hair, maybe wearing glasses." He put out his hand about chin height. "Tall woman, wavy blond hair."

A waitress passing with two empty wineglasses slowed her gait. "I remember them. They sat at my station. The dude paid the check when the woman went to the ladies' and he stiffed me on the tip—not even ten percent. It's like he just rounded up, and I'm like, dude, this isn't Europe. He gave me a dirty look."

"Where are they?" Finn turned in a circle, hoping he'd just missed them the first time.

She shrugged. "They got out of here after he left me that crappy tip."

"Left? Her car's still here."

"Yeah, I don't know. They walked out together." She swept past him to the bar while Finn felt like screaming.

Where did they go? Why would she go anywhere with him in a place not home to either of them? Maybe something happened to her car, and he offered to drive her back to Fairwood. It wasn't that far.

He rushed from the restaurant and jogged to Jessica's

car in the parking lot. He checked the tires, tried the door, peered into the windows. Everything looked normal—but nothing was normal.

He went back to his own car and sat in the front seat, gripping his steering wheel. Where could they be? How did he get her out of that restaurant? Dessert? Ice cream somewhere? Murder?

His fingers closed around his phone in his jacket pocket. He had to do it. He'd grovel, if necessary. He cupped his phone in one hand and tapped the number for the Washington State Penitentiary.

"I need to speak to prisoner 562334, Avery Plank."

Fifteen minutes later after some explanations and name-dropping, Plank came on the line. "My biographer. What can I do for you, Professor?"

"I need your…criminal mind."

Plank responded. "It's all yours. Did Miss Jessica figure out why the Kitsap Killer wants to reward her?"

"We've moved way beyond that. The Kitsap Killer is Jessica's half brother. He took her somewhere, and I don't know where. Where would he take her? Where would he want to kill her?"

Plank gave a low hum. "Really, Professor. Perhaps you're not the one to write my story. This is an obvious one. He'd want to take her to where their story began. Where he was forged in hate and resentment and envy. Where he still lives every day of his life."

Finn ended the call, cutting off Plank without a thank-you. Of course. How could he be so dense? Dermott was taking Jessica to the family home, and it wasn't far from here. He could be there within a half an hour—but would he find Jessica dead or alive?

Jessica clenched her hands in her lap as David drove them toward the Bangor Trident Submarine Base on the other side of the peninsula. The drive took about twenty minutes, but as the miles passed, Jessica felt as if she was going back in time—to a very bad place.

A navy buddy of Jessica's grandfather had allowed Mom to live in his house north of the base with her children almost for free. The man had never checked on the property—or Mom. He'd moved to Hawaii when he retired from the service and had owed Tammy's father a big favor from their time in the navy. The house was his payback.

She'd taken Finn there once after Tiffany's murder. The place gave her the creeps, and she'd never been back. But it had been hard to refuse David.

He wanted to see the last place he'd been with his sisters and bio mom. He knew where it was. Maybe that's why he had suggested Kingston in the first place. He already had this plan in mind when he agreed to meet her.

"We're getting close, aren't we?" David flexed his fingers on the steering wheel.

"I hope you're not expecting too much, David. The last time I was there, the house was a ramshackle mess. It's probably even worse now, or maybe the owner sold it, and a new family is living there."

He lifted his shoulders. "That doesn't matter. I just want to see it. Maybe if you tell me about our family while we're there, it will mean more, give us that bond."

She lifted one side of her mouth in a weak smile. Maybe over time, she and David could form some sort of sibling connection, but that immediate spark between them hadn't materialized.

She didn't blame him. She and Tiffany had been so close,

she'd expected the same from a brother, but she and David had never even met before today, despite that first impression. When he first spoke, his voice struck a chord of familiarity in her psyche.

"This is the way, correct?" He'd slowed down where a smaller road branched off the main one on the way to Lofall.

"That's it." Jessica tugged her jacket closer around her body. Once David saw the place, he'd understand that it didn't hold good memories for her—not the kind of memories she'd want to share with a long-lost brother.

As they headed down the road, darkness closed in on them from the looming trees. His headlights picked out a few other properties on the edge of town, tucked away from the bay and the sparkling homes that inhabited its shores. This area was definitely the bad side of town, the "waterfront" a dirty creek, the people here recluses or meth heads or both.

She gave a nervous laugh. "Not much to look at."

"That doesn't matter to me. A person has to see his roots, don't you think?"

"I suppose." She jabbed a finger at the windshield as a dark, hulking structure came into view. "That's it. The old homestead."

He wheeled the car into the dirt driveway in front of the house, the headlights shining a glaring spotlight on all its misery. The front windows, both broken, stared balefully at anyone who approached. The porch sagged, a booby trap for anyone who dared to darken the door. The screen door hung from one hinge, and in the wind, must emit a fearsome squeal further warning off strangers.

"Looks like he never sold it—or did anything to repair it." She turned to him, suddenly afraid to get out of the car.

"It's a mess. No place to reminisce. Let's head into town here and get some dessert. I'll tell you all about Mom and Tiffany there."

But he'd already cut the engine and had his fingers on the door handle. "Humor me, Jessica. I remember a creek out back."

Before she could continue to reason with him, he scrambled from the car, leaving the door open in his haste. As she watched him slog through the weeds in the front to reach the dirty trickle of water that ran behind the property, Jessica unclicked her seat belt.

How could he possibly remember the creek? He'd been younger than two when he left. Had he been out here by himself before?

As she twisted in her seat, the dome light illuminated a gray backpack tossed onto the back seat. The corner of what looked like a knit cap was caught in the zipper. Was it red?

"C'mon, Jessica. I found the creek and the picnic table."

The picnic table. A sour taste flooded her mouth as she remembered hiding beneath the rotting wood of the picnic table as Tiffany told one of the enraged stepdaddies that Jessica had run into the woods to avoid the strap. She gagged recalling the sound of that strap as it connected with Tiffany's bare legs.

"Jessssica!"

David's singsong voice brought her back to reality, and she staggered out of the car and followed his trail through the tall weeds.

She rounded the house and found him standing next to the creek, which had widened since she'd last seen it. "This is it, David. Not much of anything to see, and…honestly, this place doesn't hold very fond memories for me."

"Really?" He cocked his head. "You grew up with your mother and your sister."

This place had animated her brother. Even his posture seemed different—more erect, more vital, more...aggressive.

"My mother, who had issues, my sister and a series of nasty, abusive men."

"Was my father one of those nasty, abusive men?"

"I-I don't really remember him. Navy man, didn't stick around long. None of them did." She didn't want to tell David she'd remembered his father as a violent drunk.

"I didn't stick around long. Somebody ratted out Tammy."

Her head jerked up. "Ratted out? I mean, I guess so. She couldn't care for you. It was for the best."

"Best for whom? You and Tiffany? You got all Tammy's attention, and she sent me away."

Jessica's fingertips began to buzz. This felt off. Why had David's demeanor changed? He couldn't possibly believe the things he was saying.

"Believe me, David. You were the lucky one. You got a loving, adoptive family while Tiffany and I had to deal with all of Mom's problems."

Then he laughed, a high-pitched cackle that she'd heard before, and the blood in her veins turned ice cold.

Chapter Nineteen

Finn tore down the road toward Lofall. The house sat in the forest, down a small lane that wound off the main road. There weren't that many of those. If he started seeing signs for the base, he'd gone too far.

Unless someone had bought the property and torn down the house and rebuilt, he'd remember it. Most of the houses out this way had seen better days, but Jessica's childhood home was the most dilapidated of the lot. He remembered a creek running behind it and a crumbling picnic table.

He cut his lights first. He couldn't go revving up to them, showing his hand. Also, as soon as he and Webb saw each other, the jig would be up. Maybe Webb didn't intend to harm Jessica. Finn had to make sure she got out alive. Tiffany had made that happen the first time, and he was here to finish Tiffany's work.

He rolled past one house, a glow of lights in the windows and shadows of people in the kitchen. Jessica's house had sat farther back from the road.

Then he saw it up ahead—Dermott Webb's white car. He'd seen it before on campus. Dermott had been leaving one day, getting into his car, when he spotted Finn and waved him over to ask him more questions about class.

Finn had been annoyed at the time, but now that moment had served its purpose.

Finn turned off his engine and let his car roll downhill for several feet on silent as he steered it off the road. He clicked his door closed and crept toward Dermott's car. He'd left the driver's-side door open. What did that mean? Had Jessica jumped from the car, and he'd exited in a hurry to go after her? Did Jessica even know what she was dealing with here?

She must know. She'd met Dermott in the lecture hall. She must've been shocked to see him and worried when she realized he'd given her a different name.

Then he remembered—she hadn't met Dermott. She'd been on the stage. The lights in the hall had already been dimmed. Finn knew from experience you couldn't really make out faces from the stage when the lights were low. That bit of knowledge made his breath come a little easier as he veered into the woods before he got to the decrepit house. He couldn't go charging into the middle of their meeting.

He drew his piece from his pocket. But he could end that meeting if need be.

JESSICA CLUTCHED HER throat as David pointed her own gun at her.

"Oh, it's the laugh, isn't it?" He shrugged but the gun never wavered. "You were going to find out one way or the other, weren't you?"

She fought off the fog in her brain. She had to stay alert, look for a way out. "Is the red scarf in your backpack in the car?"

"Oh, you saw that, too?" He clicked his tongue. "Now *that* was a mistake, but you should've run then, Jessica. While you had the chance."

"I-I wasn't sure what it was, and then you mentioned that damned picnic table. You have no idea what you escaped, David. No idea what the *rat* saved you from."

"That rat was Tiffany." His dark eyes narrowed, and they looked nothing like Tiffany's beautiful, soft doe eyes. "I found out a lot from my stupid adoptive mother. She told me it was the older girl who had reported Tammy to child protective services. *She* was the one who wanted me gone."

Jessica swallowed. How could he get it all wrong? "If Tiffany reported our living conditions, she was trying to save you, just like she saved me. Tiffany loved you. She tried to find you."

"She found me." His flat, cold voice chilled her to the bone.

"You met Tiffany?"

"Of course I met Tiffany. I killed Tiffany. She'd turned out just like Tammy. Sex worker." He spit into the dirt. "She was a whore, just like dear old mommy dearest."

Jessica had known the truth even before he told her, but hearing the words made her double over and sob into her hands. Lifting her head, she wiped her eyes. "I hate you."

"Yeah, yeah, I'm sure you do. You disappointed me, Jessica. You turned out normal. I was trying to get you brownie points at work, and then you betrayed me at the Gabby murder. You called the cops on me."

She dashed the tears from her cheeks. "Why here? Why now? Why those young women? Why did you pick them?"

"That's easy. My first kill was here. Tiffany was my first…and Morgan was not my second. Why those girls? Because I knew all of them from my work in the accounting office. They worked on campus. Every one of them had brought the cash bags down to the accounting office at some point. They knew me. They didn't fear me. Would you fear a guy named Dermott?"

"How did you get away with the other murders between Tiffany and Morgan? Unless—you didn't commit them in the Pacific Northwest?"

"Europe and Asia. I was stationed at various bases over the years in the army. I'm an accountant. I'm meticulous. Never got caught. Nobody ever suspected."

Jessica pressed her hands to her stomach, her gaze flickering over David's shoulder. She caught her breath when she saw a light in the woods that bordered the creek. She looked away quickly, not wanting David to notice her attention. Was someone out there? Was some stranger listening to this madman, ready to jump in and help her?

"*You* didn't suspect me. All the time wondering who killed Tiffany while seeking that killer, inviting him into your life." His grip on the gun had grown slack as he recounted his feats, but now he held it more firmly and trained it on her once again.

She wanted to give him the opportunity to brag—prolonging her life. "What about Ashley? Why did you kill her?"

He sighed, as if Ashley's murder was a huge inconvenience. "She recognized me from before. Of course, I always knew I was taking that chance by returning to the scene of my first kill, but nobody had met me here. She saw me and Tiffany together once or twice, peeked out the window when I came to get Tiffany. Nosy cow. Then we locked eyes in a coffee house yesterday, and I knew. She knew, too."

Kicking at the rotting wood on the picnic table, he said, "She ruined my aesthetic. I didn't want to kill her as the

Kitsap Killer, so I beat her with the butt of your gun. Kind of poetic, don't you think?"

"Kind of sick," Jessica growled, more angry than sad now. "Why did you start? Why did you kill our sister? She would've done anything for you."

"I told you that already." He rolled his eyes, clearly tired of explaining himself. "She's the one who ripped me away from my mother."

"You said it yourself. Tammy was no mother of the year."

"That doesn't matter," he shouted. "You and Tiffany had a family. I had adoptive strangers who never treated me like they treated their own."

A branch at the edge of the clearing shook, and Jessica marshaled all her strength not to react when she saw Finn in the bushes, his finger to his lips. How had he known she was here? In danger?

"What now, Wavy Davy?"

David's mouth dropped open, and the whites of his eyes gleamed in the dark. "What is that? Why'd you call me that?"

She spread her hands in front of her. "It's what I used to call you when you were a baby, both Tiffany and I, but I think I came up with it. I called you Davy, and when you learned how to wave, I called you Wavy Davy. You loved it. It sent you into a fit of giggles."

He choked. "You're lying."

"You know I'm not, Davy." She took a step forward, holding out her hand. "We loved you, Tiffany and I. She was the best big sister anyone could wish for. She protected me by taking on the abuse herself, and she protected you by sending you away. Mom couldn't care for a toddler. You'd barely survived your infancy and only because of Tiffany."

"She was bad. She turned out bad." The gun wavered in his hand.

"You met her. She wasn't bad. She made bad choices, but she'd changed. She loved you, and she loved me. She would've done anything to help you…and so will I. I'll do what I can to help you, Davy. Drop that gun. We can walk away from this together."

His head sank and a sob escaped his lips. That's when Finn made a move, waving his arm over his head. She didn't need him to spell it out for her.

As Finn shouted Dermott's name, Jessica lunged behind the picnic table, rolling beneath it, just as she used to do when she was a child.

A shot rang out, and her nostrils twitched at the smell of gunpowder. On her knees beneath the table, she peered through the legs. Both men were grappling on the ground, so she scrambled from her hiding place. She didn't want anyone to die.

By the time she was on her feet, Finn had taken her weapon from David and tossed it toward the water's edge. He had one knee on David's chest and the other on his wrist.

"Grab my phone from my pocket, Jessica, and call 911. I alerted the sheriff's department on my way out here, so someone should be close."

She leaned over the bodies and slipped Finn's phone from his pocket, meeting David's red-rimmed eyes.

As she called in the emergency, Finn leveled his gun at David's head. "Stay on the ground where you are. It's over, Dermott."

"It was over a long time ago, Professor Karlsson. It was over the day my mother gave me away."

Epilogue

Jessica stretched her wiggling toes toward the bay as she reclined on a chaise longue on Finn's deck, scratching Bodhi behind the ear. "I'm just glad I didn't put my career in jeopardy by tainting the DNA sample."

Finn walked barefoot onto the deck and handed her a glass of wine before nudging Bodhi out of the chair next to Jessica. "I don't understand why the initial test didn't show that the DNA on the red fiber was male DNA. That would've ruled you out immediately."

"Remember, it was just a trace, and they didn't know if they had enough of it to run a full test. There are different types of DNA tests, and that initial one they ran wasn't the mtDNA test for mitochondrial. That showed up in the subsequent test."

"I'm glad they didn't stop the testing. When I knew that DNA belonged to your brother and that you had just gone out to meet him that day, I went into panic mode." He reached over and ran his hand down her arm, giving her goose bumps. "I didn't want to lose you so soon after rediscovering you."

"If that's your panic mode, your focused mode must be intense. You had it together enough to contact Celine and to remember the name of the restaurant where I was meeting David... Dermott." She slid her hand in his, lacing her fingers with his. "How did you know where to find us? You never told me that. I know I took you there once, but how did you figure out we'd be at the house?"

"I have a confession to make." He swirled the beer in his bottle and took a sip as he squinted at the sun dipping into the bay. "I contacted an expert."

"An expert?" She hung her leg over the side of the chaise and ran her foot over the soft fur on Bodhi's back.

"I called Avery Plank." He squeezed her hand. "And I don't regret it. He pointed out the obvious, but I wasn't thinking straight. When he said Dermott would go back to the beginning, where it all started for him, I knew he'd take you to the house. And why not? Nobody suspected your brother yet. Why would anyone think the Kitsap Killer would take you to your childhood home?"

She wrinkled her nose. "Ugh, Plank must've reveled in that."

"I didn't give him a chance, but I'm sure he'll remind me at our next meeting."

Finn asked, "Are you going to visit Dermott in prison? At least he confessed to all the slayings, and he's working with the authorities in Europe and Asia to solve some of those cases."

Disentangling her fingers from his, Jessica put her feet on the deck and stroked Bodhi's back. There was a reason people used dogs for therapy. Petting Bodhi calmed her nerves enough to answer. "I don't know if I can ever forgive him for taking Tiffany from me and killing all those other women. It makes me ill to think we have the same mother."

"But different fathers. Sounds like Dermott's bio dad was a piece of work. Sometimes nature is stronger than nurture."

She rubbed her tingling nose. "I'm not sure his adoptive family was all that nurturing."

Finn snorted. "If you believe Dermott. He's just like Plank, blaming everything on his upbringing for sympathy and understanding."

She glanced up, her hand still on Bodhi's back. "You're still writing the book, even though your link to Plank, finding Tiffany's body, has been blown out of the water?"

"That was an important hook, for sure. That's how I got my agent interested in the book, but I've got an even better hook now—how I saved Tiffany's sister from the Kitsap Killer who let Plank confess to his crime." He laced his fingers together. "The stories are linked. My agent is happy—if you can be happy about murder."

She drilled a knuckle into his biceps. "Oh, is *that* why you're dating me?

"Dating?" He placed his bottle on the deck and shifted his chair to face her. "Is that all we're doing?"

A smile played over her lips. "Well, we keep getting interrupted. I think we're destined to circle the flame."

"Come over here." Leaning forward, he lightly clasped her wrists and tugged her toward him. "I think I'm ready to jump into the fire."

She stepped over Bodhi, who barely lifted his head, and sat in Finn's lap, her legs swinging over the side of his chair. As he pulled her close and kissed her mouth, she felt that spark she'd always felt for him. But this time there was nothing between them.

She murmured against his lips. "Let the inferno begin."

* * * * *

COLTON'S VOW

CHARLENE PARRIS

To my mom, who thought my writing was just a hobby until I showed her my first Mills & Boon book. The huge smile on her face was priceless!

Love you always

Chapter One

Dani Colton, who had arrived at Mariposa Resort for her sister Laura's wedding, and a well-deserved vacation, sat in front of her siblings, shock reverberating through her tired body after a long flight and very unsteady helicopter ride. "So, let me repeat what you've just told me, so that I'm clear," she said. "You're asking me to *spy* on Matt Bennett while I'm here? Matt Bennett, Glenna's nephew?"

She watched their expressions. Adam's looked determined, but then he always looked that way. Laura seemed irritated, so Dani hoped her older half sister wasn't on board with this idea. As for Josh, his smirk and the bright twinkle in those baby blue eyes told her he was all for it.

Adam sighed. "I admit I'm not wild about this idea, but desperate times call for desperate measures."

"Just for the record, I'm against it," Laura chimed in. "I don't believe Matt has anything to do with what's going on here. He was on his best behavior during his last visit in April."

"Which could have been a cover-up for all the shit that's happened," Josh retorted.

Laura gave him a pointed look. "You don't like him anyways."

"I never said that. I said I didn't *trust* him. He seems like a nice guy, but we don't know what he's capable of."

Dani glanced at Josh. "So, you're all in for the spying. I can see it on your face."

The youngest Colton shrugged. "I think it's the best plan we could throw together on short notice, Dani."

She mirrored Adam's actions and blew out a loud sigh herself. She had called Josh a couple of weeks ago to find out what the hell had been going on at Mariposa, and discovered it was worse than what the media had portrayed. With Laura's upcoming wedding, Dani hadn't hesitated in negotiating with her new employer to delay her starting date at her new job and managed to catch the next earliest possible flight from London to Phoenix.

Dani wanted to be there to support her brothers and sister, especially Laura. Between the wedding and all the other awful stuff happening at the resort, the poor thing would be a bundle of stress. But Dani hadn't expected this.

"You could pretend you're like that English spy dude in the movies, James what's-his-name," Josh said. Was that a hint of excitement in his voice? Seriously?

"Oh, sure," she quipped. "Walk around Mariposa all nonchalant with a small caliber pistol strapped to my thigh. Are you bloody daft?"

"Don't listen to him, Dani." Adam sat forward in his chair. "We have a serious problem, and I don't know what else to do."

Hearing Adam say he couldn't figure out a solution to a problem made Dani's ears perk up. She saw the weariness in his eyes, the way his mouth sort of drooped—he looked depressed.

And knew she would do everything possible to help her family. "Damn it. All right, let's give it a shot."

Laura's eyes widened with surprise. "You're joking."

"Nope." Dani shook her head. "If Matt has anything—anything—to do with the crap going on at Mariposa, you'd better believe I'm going to wring it out of him." Her body was tense, and as she observed, she noticed how Josh glanced at Adam and opened his mouth, then closed it. Something wasn't right. "There's something else, isn't there?" she asked.

Adam jerked in his seat, but it was Laura's face, her eyes bright with tears, that put Dani on high alert. "What's going on?" she demanded.

Josh cleared his throat. "Remember what I told you about Clive and Colton Textiles owning the land under Mariposa?"

"Yes." Fear wrapped around her stomach, threatening to squeeze up into her throat.

"We had negotiated a partnership with Sharpe Enterprises." Adam picked up where Josh left off. "They would purchase half of the resort, and that would give us enough cash to buy out our father's ownership of the land. We're not enthusiastic about only half owning Mariposa, but it's better than losing it all to him."

"I agree." When no one continued, Dani prompted them. "But?"

"Sharpe pulled out," Laura told her. "They wouldn't tell us why, and they paid the early termination fee without any fuss."

Dani pressed her lips together, knowing she was making her "scrunched-up, thinking face" as Josh affectionately called it. "You'd made this deal after finding out Clive owned the land but before the murder and other accidents?"

"Actually, they agreed even after Allison's death and Josh's leaked photos to the media. They were impressed with how we handled everything and know that Mariposa is a stellar business."

"Which means someone must have told Sharpe something so horrible that their only option was to pull out. And you think that someone is Glenna."

"Maybe. We don't have any proof."

Dani's mind whirled with possibilities, but she would stick to her siblings' original plan. "I'm here for all of you, you know that. I'll keep an eye on Matt Bennett." She looked at her sister. "But you're going to need me when we get close to the wedding. Don't worry, we'll work it out."

Laura rubbed her forehead. "Speaking of Glenna…"

If Dani wasn't on full alert before, she certainly was now. "What is it?" she said slowly.

Laura bit her lip. "I extended a wedding invitation to her and Clive."

A storm of emotions whirled through Dani's mind. She was already distraught that her older sister would start a new journey of life in a few days. But to invite the two people they couldn't tolerate… "What did they say?" she whispered, scared to hear the answer.

"They said yes."

Dani couldn't keep her frustration inside anymore. "Son of a bitch! I'm sorry Laura, it's your wedding and you have every right to invite whoever you want, but…" She took a deep breath. Arguing with her sister wasn't going to solve anything. Somehow, they'd have to keep Clive and Glenna away from Laura and the wedding party.

"Dani, I said they changed their minds."

Her gaze snapped to Laura's relieved face. Dani's brain

had been so engrossed on how to keep them away that she hadn't heard her. "What?"

"They're not coming."

A world of anxiety lifted from Dani's shoulders. Finally, some good news for a change. However... "Did they say why?"

"We think Clive and Glenna knew they wouldn't be welcomed," Adam told her. His angry expression made her wonder if he had something to do with it. "Don't worry, they won't make an appearance."

She nodded. "Thank God for small miracles."

She walked out of the office, her mind on overdrive. Josh had updated her before she arrived at Mariposa, which she appreciated—she didn't want to walk into a ticking time bomb. He hadn't mentioned Clive and Glenna, though he didn't need to since they had turned down Laura's wedding invitation. But to actually spy on the enemy during the week that Laura was to be married? This was crazier than one of James Spy-Name movies.

Dani smiled. Josh knew she would be up for the challenge, and in all honesty, a thrill of excitement coursed through her. Usually, she kept herself far away from the Colton problems, but she loved her brothers and sister. If they needed help, she would do her damned best.

She got into one of the several golf carts parked outside the office and drove to her bungalow, located at the rear of the property. Normally, she could walk the distance with no problem, but Arizona was known for its heat at this time of year, and it didn't disappoint. Despite the breeze blowing around her, she was sweating all over by the time she got to her front door.

Dani walked through her bungalow's spacious living

room, wiping her face with both hands. First, a cool shower, then she'd give Laura a call to see if there was anything that needed to be done. The wedding was this coming Saturday, and Adam would be closing Mariposa for the big day. Unless Matt Bennett was invited to the wedding, which she was sure he wasn't, she only had a few days to get close and personal with him and try to discover his secrets.

Sure, no big deal.

After a refreshing shower, she changed into a pair of linen shorts and tank top and pulled her hair back into a ponytail. As she walked back into her living space, Dani stopped and looked around her. Her bungalow was more than three times the size of her London flat, which she shared with two roommates. It was luxurious, with no expense spared in its renovation. Exclusive guests stayed here—she knew because she had seen A-list actors, some walking no more than a few feet away from her. All because of her siblings' hard work and perseverance.

And now the old man was trying to take that away from them.

Impulsively, Dani screamed at the top of her lungs. "Damn you, Clive Colton!"

He would not leave his kids alone, even when they had moved away from California. The old man was a manipulative piece of work, and she worried that even if Adam paid him off, the old fart would ask for more.

Now that she got some of her frustrations out, she checked the time. It was an eight-hour gap between here and London, and she would need to go to bed as late as possible so that her body could adjust to the time difference.

Adam had shown her a picture of Matt before she left his office. He was actually very good-looking, with brown hair, dark expressive eyes and a smile that caught her attention and made her stare at his picture a little longer than necessary.

She grabbed her phone and pulled it up again, as she had asked Adam to forward it to her. "At least he's decent to look at," she mumbled to herself. "Should make the spying job easier."

But her first priority was Laura and the wedding. She would need to talk to her about any final details before the big day, which was barreling toward them at a fast clip. Her sister would be Mrs. Steele before she knew it.

Dani had arranged her maid-of-honor wedding attire carefully in the large walk-in closet, placing her dress, shoes and accessories at the back, with her summer clothing near the front. During her first visit to Mariposa, she'd been overwhelmed by the heat and dry air that was a natural feature of the region. She'd almost fainted and would have hit the hard ground if Josh hadn't caught her. He'd given her some tips on how to handle the heat, and now she believed she was prepared. It would be embarrassing to faint when Laura said, "I do."

Dani chuckled, imagining that scene. Everyone would freak out, but it wouldn't happen. She'd be okay.

Now to call her sister and see what needed to be done.

MATTHEW BENNETT FINALLY saw Mariposa's buildings, almost blending with the surrounding landscape, as he trudged the last mile of his difficult hike. There was something about the land here that called to him, to test his survival skills against the beautiful harshness of the Arizona desert and its elusive creatures. But he also loved the solitude, to get away from anything and anyone related to work and family life. He stood on top of a boulder and looked down at the resort—serene, quiet. A bird chirped somewhere behind him, and a little farther away, the soft gurgling of the nearby river.

The last time he visited had been in April. He really enjoyed the activities Mariposa offered, and its exclusive privacy was what he needed. But he hadn't been able to avoid the subtle animosity he felt from the Colton siblings.

He couldn't blame them, although he wished they'd direct their suspicion at the guilty person who'd been spreading bad rumors about Mariposa to the media. Matt was sure Aunt Glenna was behind some of the extra problems the siblings had gone through—shit, she had even been arrested for interfering with the police investigation surrounding the murder of Allison Brewer at the resort, but she wasn't charged before being released. He was sure Clive Colton had something to do with getting his aunt out of jail.

Without solid proof Aunt Glenna leaked news to the press it had been hard to convict her. In the meantime, Matt did his best to show the Coltons that he was no threat to them. In all honesty, if there was a way to help them out, he'd do it in a heartbeat.

As he headed for his bungalow for a much-needed shower and break, Matt thought about the wedding invitation he'd received from Laura. Seeing it in his mail had been a shock. But he had accepted gladly, hoping it was a step in the right direction toward an amicable relationship with the family. He had been on his best behavior, which wasn't hard at all. He had chatted with Laura and thanked her for having him here on her special day.

The hot water eased his sore muscles as he cleaned up. Feeling ten times better, he grabbed a plush robe and shrugged into it as he sat down. Although he had promised himself not to look at his work phone, the habit was almost impossible to break. Being a solo entrepreneur meant being on-call 24-7, even though he had informed his clients about his vacation. Still…

"Damn it." Matt took his chances and turned it on, then waited as it booted up. When he finally looked at his inbox, he was pleasantly surprised. No more than eight new messages awaited him.

One of them was from Aunt Glenna. Well, that was one way to ruin a good day.

He went through his client emails, answered three of them, and told the others he would call back on his return to the office. Now he sat and stared at his aunt's email, whose subject line read: WHERE THE HELL ARE YOU???!!!

It was just like her to type all in caps, practically screaming her anger at him. She yelled at him in person too—this was no different.

His finger skimmed over her email as he hesitated. Aunt Glenna had made him do things he wasn't proud of, all for her sake. It was always about her. But Matt had done what she asked because he'd been grateful that she had taken him in after his mother couldn't raise him anymore. How could he ignore a family member who had looked after his well-being?

After graduating college, Aunt Glenna's demands had gotten worse, to the point where Matt had started questioning her motives and his involvement. She had tried to verbally inflate the value of Colton Textiles to new vendors several months ago and asked for his help. He had no idea she'd been lying about the business and had approached some of his own clients to see if they would be interested.

When he had been scoffed at for even suggesting the company, Matt had confronted Aunt Glenna, who admitted to the lie. That had been the catalyst that made him put distance between them. She was willing to sacrifice Matt's stellar reputation in order to improve her own.

Her email stared back at him, as if daring him to ignore it.

He turned off his phone and tossed it into his briefcase. It felt like an emotional rope between them had finally snapped. She was still Aunt Glenna, but Matt was his own person. He had graduated with high honors and now owned a successful business. He had to get his priorities straight and, as he got dressed, mentally moved his aunt close to the bottom of the list.

THE L BAR was quiet when Matt walked in later that evening. It wasn't an extensive room with lots of tables. In keeping with the private exclusivity of Mariposa, it was smaller, with about a dozen round marble tables. Matt actually liked these—they were heavy three-foot high white columns with streaks of bronze throughout, imitating the colors of the Arizona landscape. The chairs imitated the tables—white legs with dark bronze material covering the seats. The full-length bar continued the color scheme, giving the room a light and luxurious atmosphere.

The wall behind the bar was fully stocked, but the newest addition was a huge glass door which he noticed as light bounced off the surface. As he sat down at the bar, Matt looked for and saw the security lock touchpad mounted beside the display. The Coltons weren't taking any chances of having their booze poisoned again.

"Hi, Matt." Kelli Iona, the hospitality director, appeared.

"Hey." He was surprised to see her behind the bar. "I thought you'd be finished with work."

"I am." She shrugged. "Just a little nervous about the bridal shower."

He picked up on what she didn't say—that if she could keep the bar from being vandalized, she wouldn't be here. "You could close the bar early, right? There's only a few guests here. And the wedding is still a few days from now. I'm sure Adam and Erica have everything covered. Try and get some rest."

Kelli smiled. "Thanks. What can I get you?"

"Tequila Sunrise, please." Normally, he wouldn't have alcohol, but he needed something to relax him. Sooner or later, he'd have to read Aunt Glenna's email.

"Anything to eat?"

His stomach immediately growled. "I'll take a Sonoran hot dog."

"Good choice. Coming right up."

"Oh, Kelli. Would you mind turning on the television? I'd like to see if an international soccer match is playing."

"Sure." She pulled a remote out from someplace beneath the bar and switched the TV on, then handed it to him. "I'll be back in a few with your drink."

"Thanks." Matt flipped through the channels until he found the soccer match he wanted between France and Cameroon. The teams had finished their halftime break and were getting ready on the pitch. The score was even at 1–1, and he had high hopes for the African nation. As the second half started, he was impressed with Cameroon's strategy of trying to break through France's defense—divide and conquer. It was a classic maneuver, and with some tough offense, Cameroon managed to squeeze through and score a goal to make it 2–1.

"Yes!" He pumped his fist.

"Here you go, Matt." Kelli placed the drink in front of him. "Your meal should be here in a minute. And I think I'm going to take your advice."

He sipped his drink. Thankfully, it wasn't loaded with too much booze. "My advice?"

"About leaving early. I can barely keep my eyes open." She glanced down to the other end of the bar. "Denise will be here, but I'll tell her to close in an hour or two. No one's here anyways. She'll bring your food over."

"Good move, Kelli. I'll see you tomorrow."

He knew everyone was on pins and needles, and with Laura's wedding coming up, the atmosphere would grow tenser until the nuptials were over.

Damn Aunt Glenna. To think he was even remotely related to her gave him the creeps.

He dug into his favorite meal. The hot dog was loaded with pinto beans, onions and tomatoes, so he was careful not to get the condiments on his clothes.

As he continued watching the game, Matt groaned out loud when France's top player pulled a fancy trick and managed to even the score at 2–2.

"How's the game coming along?"

The woman's voice startled him, but Matt kept his gaze locked on a Cameroon player who was moving the ball into France's territory. "They're tied right now."

"I know. If that player keeps his cool though, Cameroon should get a goal."

She knew soccer—interesting. He hadn't turned around yet and felt his excitement rise as the player, with unerring accuracy, got the ball around the last French defender and scored a goal high in the net. It was now 3–2 for Cameroon.

"Damn, that was amazing!" He turned around to see who had joined him and stopped.

The woman was beautiful. Slim with a light brown complexion that looked almost luminous beneath the lights. Her brown eyes twinkled at him as she winked. "Told you so."

Her voice held a British accent, which only added to her allure. She wore a white tank top and beige shorts, which didn't hide her feminine curves.

"My name's Dani." She held out her hand.

He hastily wiped his hands clean and shook. "Matt. Nice to meet you."

She had a firm, warm grip. As she sat down beside him, Dani tilted her head. "Looks like France is pissed off."

"What?" Matt turned back to the television screen. The French players were ganging up around a couple of Cameroon's best players, trying to prevent them from joining in the defense. "Son of a bitch," he murmured.

"I'm fairly confident Cameroon won't let the goal through."

He looked at her. "How can you be so sure?"

Her smile was bright. "Would you like to place a bet?"

Wow. Matt turned to face her. "What did you have in mind?"

She pointed at the television. "If France gets that goal, I'll treat you to a great meal in Sedona. Whatever you want."

Did she just arrange a dinner date? Matt's interest in the soccer game started to die away as his attention was captivated by his female sport acquaintance. "And if France doesn't make the goal?" he asked.

She smiled. "I would love to eat at the fanciest restaurant I know."

He nodded. "Deal." They shook hands.

Matt's nerves tingled, knowing that Dani was only inches behind him as they watched the game. France had managed to move closer to Cameroon's goalie, and the team hastily arranged a wall of players, with several others running the outskirts.

"Shit, I don't think that's going to work." Matt's gaze moved from the French defense to the Cameroon players protecting their territory. "They're too scattered."

"Cameroon is known for their speed and thinking on their feet. Also, watch their goalie, he's giving them directions."

Dani was right—the Cameroon goalie was pointing and yelling. "Don't know how they can hear him over the crowd, though," he said.

"Watch his hands."

Curious, Matt kept his gaze on the goalie, and yeah, it looked like he was using hand signals. "How did you know...?" he asked, then stopped, fascinated at what happened next.

Matt held his breath as the French players kicked the ball in a precise, organized manner, inching closer toward the Cameroon goalie. The goalie's teammates kept up their erratic movements, creating a blocking pattern, and systematically harassing the French team just enough not to be penalized.

And then suddenly, he saw it—somehow, the African team were herding the French away from the Cameroon net. Matt couldn't believe it. "That is the weirdest and most brilliant tactic I've ever seen," he said.

The French must have realized it at the same time, and

that's what got them into trouble. A French player, clearly frustrated, charged at a Cameroon opponent and deliberately tackled him. The whistle immediately blew, and now Cameroon had the ball.

The French team was furious, and made errors that should have been easily avoided until Cameroon scored another goal. The African team was now ahead by a score of 4–2.

"I'll be damned." He turned to Dani, who had a big grin on her face. "How did you—"

"I became a soccer fan while living in England. I also studied business strategies. When Cameroon came onto the scene, I saw they had a knack for maneuvering around the field in a particular way. When I researched it, I found out it's a similar method to herding cattle."

"Cattle?" Matt was incredulous.

"Farmers herd cattle to where they want them to go, right?"

He sat in shock for a moment before bursting into laughter. "I can't believe it! It sounds both ridiculous and sensible at the same time."

"Told you." She sat back in her seat. "There's a new authentic Mexican restaurant in Sedona I'd love to try."

That's right—Dani had won the bet. "Congratulations," he said, and meant it. "How long are you staying in Mariposa?"

"About a week."

"Same here. Would you like to meet up for lunch tomorrow?"

"Make it dinner, and it's a deal."

"Dinner it is." Matt was intrigued with her bold personality. "Is there anything else you're good at?" he asked. An innocent question, but it could be taken the wrong way.

"As if I'd tell you everything after one drink." She wagged her finger at him. "You're just going to have to wait."

He smiled, fully enjoying their chat. "I might be a little impatient."

Her eyes widened at that before her expression changed. With an impish smile, she stood and whispered in his ear, "Good things come to those who wait. Pleasant dreams."

Chapter Two

Dani stood at the edge of the pool, admiring the clear blue water that sparkled beneath the Arizona sun. It was late morning, and already the temperature was hot enough for beads of sweat to glisten on her arms.

Looking up, the sky was as blue as the water, and just beyond Mariposa Resort's rooftops, the iconic and familiar red sandstone cliffs stood like ancient sentinels.

Taking a breath, she dove into the water, relishing the cool feeling against her skin. When she broke the surface, she turned onto her back and stroked her arms slowly over her head, letting her body drift.

She thought about the meeting yesterday with her siblings. Adam was in a tight spot. It was bad enough Clive was trying to extort money from them, but not surprising. His textile business was slowly falling apart, and without funds to keep it above water, he would go bankrupt.

But to discover that he held ownership of the lands that Mariposa stood on was devastating. Josh had believed his father was lying to make them pay up, but nope—good old Clive had emailed a photocopy of the will, showing that he'd been given the property. She believed he had manipulated

Annabeth into giving him the land, but Dani didn't want to say that. What a load of crap they found themselves in.

Her hand brushed the side of the pool. She did a somersault in the water and pushed off with her feet. This time she swam a slow breaststroke to the other end. She caught a glimpse of someone out of the corner of her eye but ignored them as her brain sorted through the mess.

Adam would need to find another business partner, and fast, in order to raise money to buy the land beneath Mariposa. Their father was more than callous enough to sell the property from underneath their noses if he wanted.

With university finally finished, Dani might be able to help with the marketing side of the business before starting her new job in London, but she didn't have much time. She still needed to discover if Matt had anything to do with the recent problems at the resort, Laura was getting married in less than a week and the bridal shower was in a few days' time.

Talk about stress. But Dani had learned to handle stress most of her life. She'd power through.

She pulled herself out of the pool in one smooth move, courtesy of the consistent workouts she'd stuck to while attending school. She stood, stretched and then grabbed her towel, loving the thick plushness of the material as she rubbed it over herself.

That's when she noticed Matt sitting on the lounge chair about twenty feet away looking at her.

Wow. He had been gorgeous in person last night, and seeing him now in only his swim trunks only cemented his hotness. Sculpted muscular body, dark tousled hair and a face Dani didn't mind staring at. He smiled when he noticed her staring at him.

Damn it, this was supposed to be a spy mission, not a flirtation session. But it could work to her advantage.

She grinned back. "Are you just going to sit over there or are you going to join me?" she called out.

That caught him by surprise—she could see it in his expression. But in another moment, he had collected his things and started walking toward her.

Perfect. She laid another towel on her lounge chair before reclining and watched behind her sunglasses as Matt approached.

"Hey there."

"Hey yourself." She patted the lounge chair beside her.

With a smile that seemed almost shy, he placed his towel on it, then dumped his duffle bag beside it. "How are you?"

"Glorious. I love this weather. England can get hot during the summer too, but it's more humid. This—" she inhaled the sharp dry air "—I don't know how to describe it, but it feels cleansing."

"The heat will tear a strip off your skin if you're not careful." He tilted his head. "Are you wearing sunscreen?"

"Bugger." She knew she forgot something when she left the bungalow this morning.

"I've got some if you want to use it." Matt grabbed his bag and rummaged through it before pulling out the large plastic bottle and holding it out to her.

"Thank you." It was an unscented brand, which was perfect. She squeezed out a good amount and rubbed the lotion onto her legs, arms and stomach, then dabbed a little on her face. She sensed him watching, which was fine by her. She handed it back to him. "You're a lifesaver."

"You're welcome."

Dani was treated to the sight of Matt suddenly turning

and diving into the pool in a single movement. She watched him glide through the water, strong arms flashing as they cut through the surface. They were the only two people at the pool, and basking beneath the sun, she closed her eyes, hearing birdsong and feeling the occasional stir of a breeze as it rustled the tall hedge behind her.

Between last night and now, Dani picked up that she and Matt had hit it off. She knew she had to keep her mind on one thing—to discover if he had anything to do with Mariposa's problems. That was the priority. If they continued to like each other, she might be able to find out a snippet of information, hear an unexpected admission of guilt that she could use against him.

Suddenly, cold water splashed her legs. "Hey!" she yelled as her eyes flew open.

Laughing, he climbed out of the pool, and Dani had a glorious moment of watching the water run down his taut abdomen before he grabbed a nearby towel and dried off. She caught his gaze as it quickly traveled over her body and the skimpy dark orange string bikini she had decided to wear.

He was taking the initiative and she appreciated that. She had spent most of her time studying through boarding school and university, and very little with the opposite sex. Her roommates had entertained her with stories that sent delicious chills down her spine, but Dani refused to be persuaded. However, there was that one time when her best friend had set her up on a double date…

She smiled to herself. Now that she'd graduated, with a prestigious job waiting for her, Dani could finally indulge in flirting, even if it was with a possible enemy. "You know, I'm not sure if I should be even talking to you. Resort regulations, remember? No conversations with other guests."

His expression held a tinge of disappointment before turning to look out over the pool. "Yeah, I forgot about that." He looked back and winked at her. "But you're to blame. You started talking with me first last night."

She burst out laughing. "I did, didn't I?" *If you only knew why.* "I haven't met anyone else at the resort who was interested in soccer, so when I saw you watching the game, I couldn't help myself."

His brown eyes widened in surprise for a moment, before a huge grin lit up his face. He actually looked more handsome. "So, what do you think? Should we be obedient guests and follow the rules?"

Dani shifted onto her side. "Well," she said, letting out a loud dramatic sigh. "If that's how you feel about it…"

"However, there are exceptions to any rule if you can find a loophole." He laid down as well and faced her.

"You like to break the rules. A man after my own heart."

He laughed. "A rule isn't broken if you're not caught breaking it."

Dani took his comment in stride, but it made her think hard on what exactly he meant by that. "Very true."

"I love your accent by the way," Matt told her. "Are you from England?"

"No, I was born in the States but moved to Europe as a teenager." She had a flashback of how that happened and tried not to shudder. "I wanted to broaden my education."

"That must have been fun." He raked his hair back with a hand. "Sometimes, I wish I had been given an opportunity like that."

He didn't elaborate. Matt being at Mariposa meant he had money, so lack of funds wasn't the reason. "Just didn't work out?"

He glanced at her, his face sad. "Something like that."

She couldn't figure out why his expression bothered her, and quickly changed the subject. "May I ask what you do for a living?"

He swung his legs around and sat up. "Mergers and Acquisitions. I have my own company. It's small but going a lot better than I expected."

Dani's ears perked up, hoping she could tease out more information. "Really? I received my MBA from Cambridge. I've been offered a job as a business manager for a prestigious marketing firm. I plan to start in about two weeks, hence my long-awaited vacation at Mariposa."

"Congratulations."

She sighed. "I'd love to own my business someday. It must be lovely having your own schedule."

Matt laughed. "It is until your client demands your time."

"But then you can charge extra." She winked. "Always got to get that next dollar!"

The thought did occur to her that he could be the one responsible for canceling the merger between Mariposa and Sharpe. "Mergers and acquisitions must be challenging work."

He nodded. "It can be. I'm the middleman between two companies and two sets of board of directors who each want the best for themselves. It's a delicate compromise."

Dani thought back to her conversation with Adam yesterday. "So, a merger doesn't always work?"

Matt clasped his hands and rested his arms on his knees. "There's a lot of detail involved and a lot of posturing. Who's the better company? Who should be the major shareholder? That kind of thing. I'm in between all of that, but I help by offering suggestions, trying to negotiate a deal that's best for both parties." He shrugged. "So, yeah, sometimes it doesn't work out."

She wondered how much she could press on the subject, then decided to ask another question. "Have you seen any weird stuff happen during merger negotiations? I'm sure you've had your share."

"Not personally, no." He gave her a weird look. "Are you thinking of what happened between Mariposa and Sharpe Enterprises?"

Dani fought to keep a straight face. "I don't watch the news very much." Which was true. "But a roommate watches the American business news, and the story about Mariposa came up." Which was a lie, but he didn't have to know that.

He shook his head. "I feel bad for Adam. The partnership was a great idea. Sharpe is a growing company, and their president is smart as a whip. With the extra cash, Adam and his siblings could have really upgraded the resort."

"I heard Sharpe pulled out of the merger. Can they do that?"

"Of course, but they were stuck paying a termination fee, which is a hefty chunk of change." He frowned. "I wonder what made them rescind their offer. From what I've read and heard, they were pretty excited about being partners with Mariposa."

Matt's observations were going in a direction Dani hadn't expected—he talked as if he were surprised about the failure of the merger. "Maybe we'll never know, unless the media digs up some gossip on it."

"I don't think Adam would let that happen, do you?"

Dani knew her eldest brother very well. "I doubt it."

"I'm sure it was something like a renegotiation of pricing." He shrugged.

So, Matt had provided some ideas without implicating himself. Or was it possible he wasn't involved? Dani wasn't sure.

"Dani, I wanted to ask about dinner tonight."

She sat up, wondering if he was going to cancel.

"Do you mind if we go into Sedona a little earlier? I'd like to do some shopping first."

"Shopping?" That threw her off. "Um, sure. What are you getting?"

Matt's smile was adorable. "A present."

As HE GOT ready to head into Sedona with Dani, Matt couldn't believe how comfortable he felt while hanging out with her.

In the days before he arrived at Mariposa, stress had been his constant companion. Work was piling up, which was a good thing, but not when he was preparing to go to a wedding and adding on a much-needed vacation. It took a lot of negotiating, persuasion and a bit of luck to get his clients to wait until his return. He'd have to start thinking of hiring a second employee for his solo enterprise.

His aunt was another matter. Bossy, demanding and critical, Matt sometimes imagined Glenna sitting on his shoulder, whispering manipulative suggestions into his ear. In some way he'd been correct in that assumption. Since she took over from his mother in raising him, she had managed to turn his life around to her advantage. He had gone from a child that needed love and support, to a young man who resented his own family.

And then Aunt Glenna married Clive Colton.

Matt suspected she didn't love her new husband. Their union had been for convenience. He was sure his aunt thought she would inherit something substantial when Mr. Colton died, and he wouldn't be surprised to find Aunt Glenna plotting an "accident." But that was the kind of person she was, and despite being related, he had never been fully comfortable around her.

When Matt had received the unexpected invitation to Laura's wedding, he felt like he had made a huge step in the right direction with the Colton siblings. Back in April, when he had taken his first vacation of the year at Mariposa, the brothers and sister were cool toward him. Matt was sure they didn't like Aunt Glenna either, and their wariness of her had spilled over to him. He couldn't blame them—he would have felt the same way. All he could do was show them he was not on his aunt's side.

His arrival a few days ago was met with warm greetings from Adam and Laura, and a stern look from Josh. The youngest Colton was still skittish around him, and Matt respected that. He hoped he could change the young man's mind eventually.

He had used the time to decompress by enjoying the extracurricular activities around the resort and visiting nearby Sedona. He hadn't told Aunt Glenna of his vacation plans or the wedding invite, and her angry email subject line said she wasn't impressed with his actions. But he refused to let that ruin his holiday. Matt knew he would have to acknowledge her email, possibly call her too, but he would do that when he was ready.

Meeting Dani at the L Bar last night felt like someone had been listening in the universe. She was beautiful and had a fun attitude that he'd been immediately attracted to.

Matt was glad that she'd spoken to him first, or he might have sat there admiring her from afar, which could have amounted to being creepy.

But at the pool, he couldn't help himself. When he'd seen her climb out of the water, his eyes were locked on a beautiful sight. Her light brown skin was framed by a dark orange string bikini that made him break out into a cold sweat. Her hair was dark and sleek against her back, and as she dried herself off, he could see the toned definition in her legs.

Thank God she had noticed him and called him over to sit with her, or he would have continued to sit in his chair, looking like a grinning fool.

As they chatted, he realized they had made an almost instant connection. He enjoyed her company and witty remarks, and her questions were about him, which made him feel good.

However, her sexy body in that little two-piece string bikini was distracting him big-time, and in a moment, he dove into the pool to give himself space. The cold water helped to clear his mind too. When he surfaced, he floated on his back for a moment to admire a sky so blue and clear it hurt his eyes. Matt could get used to living this kind of life.

He turned over and started swimming, using fast powerful strokes to get his muscles fired up. He traveled several times across the length of the pool until his body screamed at him to stop. Every part of him was exhausted, sore and trembling, but he loved it.

When Matt finally came up for air, Dani was lying back in the lounge chair, arms above her head and eyes closed.

He started to get out, but at the last minute, cupped some of the water in his hand and splashed it on her. It was a risk—she could get pissed off—but she took it in stride.

He even caught her staring at him from behind those sunglasses as he dried off, a hopeful hint that she was just as interested in getting to know him better.

Her questions about his profession were intelligent, as if she wanted to better understand the world of mergers and acquisitions. However, he also heard the note of concern in her voice as she asked about Mariposa, and what it might mean for its future. It was obvious she loved the place—he did as well—and the Colton siblings were a friendly, tight-knit family.

Matt had planned to buy Laura and Noah a wedding gift, but he would have to purchase it today in order to get it to Erica in time. He would let her know when he got back to his bungalow.

But then another idea popped into his head, and the next thing, Matt had invited Dani to come with him. When she said yes, he thought his world had become just a little bit brighter today.

However, Matt felt the invisible weight of resentment hanging over him when he remembered Aunt Glenna's email. The debate of whether to deal with it now or wait until he returned only lasted a few seconds.

He retrieved his cell phone and turned it on. Just as he opened her email, the phone rang.

It was Aunt Glenna.

Matt bit his lip as guilt, anger and remorse swarmed him until he felt like he couldn't breathe. He shouldn't feel like this—no one should. Yet his aunt had a way of making him feel so insignificant that sometimes it took all his strength to resist.

When he finally found the courage to answer, the call

had ended. He was about to look at her email when it rang for a second time.

It was her. Again.

Sucking in a deep breath, he pressed the green button. "Hi, Aunt Glenna."

"Why haven't you called me back or answered by emails?"

Here we go. No greeting, as usual. "I was busy."

"Doing what?"

Matt almost gave her one of his automatic answers—checking emails, working, just got in, on the other line. But something made him hesitate until, with a shock of clarity, he figured out what it was. Anger.

He was angry with her. He knew she took advantage of his business skills, but he'd never said anything because... well, Aunt Glenna had taken him in when his mother refused to care for him. Matt had been grateful that he remained with family instead of being pushed into a child welfare system. But as Glenna's treatment of him got worse, he had fought and succeeded in attending a prestigious college in California and lived on campus. Those had been the best four years of his life.

However, before his studies were over, Aunt Glenna had married Mr. Colton. After their wedding, Matt was tricked into providing strategic advice that sometimes bordered on the illegal. He didn't want to tarnish the reputation he had built for himself, but Aunt Glenna had been ruthless, threatening and cajoling him into giving her information that made him fear he would lose his start-up business.

And now she was spreading rumors about Mariposa, threatening the siblings' livelihood. Why?

He answered his own question. *To ruin other people's lives.*

"That's none of your business." The words came out before Matt thought about how to say it tactfully.

Silence on the other end for several seconds. "What did you just say to me, young man?" she demanded.

"I know you heard me the first time." There was something…liberating about the way he was talking to her now. It wasn't just a pent-up release of emotion. It felt like that heavy weight was finally sliding off his shoulders. He was standing up for himself against his aunt because of her inhumane behavior toward him, the Colton siblings and countless others. "Did you want something?"

"I want you to stop talking so disrespectfully to me!" she shouted.

The familiar urge to apologize was strong. Matt stood firm against it, keeping quiet.

Aunt Glenna made a rude sound. "Fine, since you're going to be that way. How long are you staying at Mariposa?"

How did she find out about his plans? Shit, he must have said something. "About a week."

"So, you'll be there when Laura marries that cop this weekend." Her tone of voice told him of her disgust at the thought.

"I was invited to the wedding." Matt hadn't felt the need to tell her when he had left California. It was a vacation, but with the added bonus of seeing Laura getting married.

"You were what? And you didn't have the brain cells to tell me this?"

"I assumed you would know, since you and Clive would have been invited as well." Matt refused to get into a shouting match with her. He never won, and with his newfound decision to treat Aunt Glenna as a distant acquaintance, he wanted to maintain his aloofness—no more falling for her bait.

"Laura didn't mention you. Anyhow Clive and I changed our minds. We're not coming."

Wow. Now that *was* news. Again, he almost provided an automatic answer—an apology—but bit his tongue. "I wonder why."

"Don't get sarcastic with me, Matt!"

It was obvious she was upset. "It's a valid question. I'll bet you don't want to hear the guests gossiping behind your back. You're lucky Clive made bail when you were arrested."

She grumbled something incomprehensible. "Since you're going, I'd like you to do something for me."

Matt felt himself tense. "I could relay your best wishes to Laura, but it might be better if you—"

"I have no plans on telling her congratulations."

He frowned, not liking how this conversation was going. "I don't know why you can't be happy for Laura."

"She could have done a lot better than marrying some orphaned no-name detective. But never mind, she's going through with it. I need your help."

He was afraid to ask what and decided to stay quiet.

"I take it your silence means yes. Good. I want you to—"

"I haven't agreed to anything," he interrupted.

Aunt Glenna kept talking as if he hadn't spoken. "I want you mess up Laura's wedding."

He was stunned into shocked silence. "What did you just say?"

"You heard me. Figure out a way to ruin the wedding. Something so bad it gets reported to the news."

Matt couldn't believe what he was hearing. "You have the nerve to ask me to screw up Laura's happiest moment?"

His aunt chuckled.

He held the phone away from him. How in God's name was he related to this person? His stomach churned with fear, and Matt worried he would throw up right there in the front hall.

"Make sure to call me back and let me know what happened," she said.

No. No, this had to stop now. There was no way he would do something like that. And hearing the sinister plan from Aunt Glenna's own mouth, Matt realized that she must have something to do with all of the horrible events that occurred at Mariposa.

He was going to put a stop to it. "No."

There was a gasp. "What the hell do you mean, no?"

Matt hardened his resolve. "I mean no, I won't ruin Laura's wedding. In fact, I'm not doing anything else for you."

"You ungrateful little bastard! I ask for your help and this is how you treat me!"

He knew what was coming next and braced himself for the sob story—her sacrifices, wasting her time raising him, his useless mother. He should have just hung up the phone, but when he had realized earlier how he truly felt about Aunt Glenna, it was like a switch had been flipped. What he now felt was a quiet detachment from a woman who became less of a family member and transformed into a stranger.

And he wasn't upset at all.

When she finally stopped, Matt said, "Don't call me again unless it's an emergency," and hung up before she could reply. He then deleted her email, switched the phone off and shoved it back into his briefcase.

He felt like a light had gone off in his head. Aunt Glenna had been there for him when he had been abandoned by his mother, and he'd been grateful that she adopted him. But it was time to cut the family strings. Of course, he'd always be there for her, but under his conditions. If his aunt tried any more of her stunts, he would walk away.

His hands were shaking. That had been the toughest ten-minute call he had ever taken. Dealings with big corporate CEOs were easy compared to talking to Aunt Glenna. But he'd managed to get through it. And the best thing? He didn't feel bad or guilty.

It was a great start.

Chapter Three

Sedona was a touristy city, catering to the many whose different languages blended into one huge melting pot. Dani thought it would be busier, but the crowds resembled London on a Sunday evening—it was quiet by her standards.

"So, what store did you want to visit to buy this gift?" she asked as Matt parked the car at a downtown city lot.

"I looked up a few places on the internet," he said. "The store I liked the best is a few minutes from here."

As they headed down the street, Matt held out his elbow. It was a small gesture, but for Dani, it meant something more.

And it started to worry her. Was it a genuine step in an unexpected, budding relationship? Or was he doing this to throw her off course?

Dani had no idea, but she couldn't ignore it. She took his arm, and they strolled down the busy street, dodging the crowds of people. She'd been here before but didn't remember this area. It was filled with all types of shops, small restaurants and cafes.

"We're heading over there." Matt pointed to a store called For Your Eyes Only, painted in bright, cheery colors. Inside, large windows allowed plenty of light to come in, but the sun's strength was muted with blinds that held back the heat. It was refreshingly cool in here.

Dani looked around the large space, interested in what she saw. The room was split into two sections, men's and women's. She saw beautifully patterned silk pajamas, lingerie that ranged from demure to downright racy, plush robes that rivaled Mariposa's. Another area of the store was dedicated to both men and women, and she noticed things like champagne gift boxes, towels and fun sex toys. "Wow, this is awesome."

"It's a great store, isn't it?" Matt started looking through the men's sleeping garments.

"Are you looking for anything in particular? Maybe I can help." She saw a silk tank top and boxer short set, in swirls of deep blue, emerald green and bright yellow, and grabbed a set in her size.

"Well... I'm actually buying a wedding gift for Laura and Noah."

Dani froze, wondering if she heard correctly. "A wedding gift?"

"Yeah." He turned around, holding a men's navy silk two-piece shirt and bottom set. The color was so deep it looked like it held its own inner glow. "Laura sent me a wedding invitation and I accepted." His smile seemed almost wistful. "I'm honored that she would even ask me to attend, since..."

He stopped, and she moved a little closer to him. "What?" she asked. It sounded like Matt might admit something to her.

He looked at her, and Dani became mesmerized by his eyes. Not just because of their lovely brown-gold color but by what they revealed.

She had a strange feeling that Matt was not the person they were looking for.

He blinked, and the moment was gone. "Nothing," he replied. "I'm just surprised that's all."

"Why? Laura wouldn't have invited you unless she liked you a lot." Which was true. Laura must have seen something in him that her brothers did not, and Dani would need to chat with her sister about her reason behind this.

"I hope she does. I wouldn't do anything to…" he paused. "Never mind. Let's find the rest of the stuff and have dinner. I'm starving."

Dani was shocked. Laura hadn't mentioned anything about inviting Matt. It now meant she had to find out if Matt had been involved with any of the accidents at Mariposa before the wedding. As soon as he discovered she was a Colton, all bets would be off. "That's fantastic news. You must be excited."

"I am, yeah." He strolled past her, glancing at the outfit she had picked for herself. "I love those colors," he said in a quiet voice, but his expression said something very different.

Dani felt a little embarrassed at being caught with the skimpy outfit clasped in her hands. She hastily deflected the subject. "Do you have an idea of what you'd like to get for Laura and Noah?"

"I'm not sure. I admit that's one of the reasons I asked you to come with me."

"Oh, how sweet." And in a way, it was. Matt needed help with a special gift and came to her for advice. "Let me see what I can dig up."

Dani hunted through the selection of high-quality clothing until she picked a woman's pajama set similar to what Matt had found for Noah. It was a short-sleeved buttoned top and lounge pants in a similar dark blue color, but the piping along the hem was bright pink. "Get this one for Laura," she told Matt, handing the pajama set to him. "She and Noah could be twinsies."

He laughed, giving the outfit a once-over. "I like this."

"Glad to be of service." Dani had brought a couple of bridal gifts from England, but now that she looked around the store, she wanted to get a few more things. A naughty idea came to mind—Laura should really have an outfit to rock Noel's socks off. "I'm going to take a look around," she told him. "If that's okay?"

"Sure." He pointed toward the register. "I see a couple of extra things I'd like to grab. I'll meet you there?"

"You bet." Dani went toward the back of the store, where the really sexy lingerie was displayed. After a bit of browsing, she found the perfect item for her sister—a baby-doll set. The top had thin straps with a cute bow tie at the shoulder, with two more tied straps conveniently located at the bust and waistline. It flowed outwards from the gathered bust, and if she judged its length correctly, it ended at hip level. The high-cut thong panties were very suggestive, and the whole outfit was lacy, white and covered with pale pink hearts. "This should do nicely," she murmured. If Matt made a comment, she would tell him it was a gift for herself. Dani grinned, wondering how he would react to the outfit, which had less material than the one she was currently holding.

She headed toward the cashier, where Matt was looking at a large display. "Have you found anything else that caught your interest?" she asked him, then noticed what he had piled up on the counter. "Whoa."

He had picked out a bottle of very nice champagne with two fluted glasses, each engraved with *His* and *Hers*. Two pairs of cute fuzzy slippers, a large photo album, a French Press coffee maker and a gourmet coffee basket completed his haul.

"Smashing job on the choices," Dani observed.

"Thanks. Laura deserves it. She's stood up for me a couple of times."

"Oh? Why would she do that?" Matt had been letting certain things slip, and she'd been trying to capitalize on them to see if he would implicate himself. But it hadn't quite worked out that way. "Did someone blame you for something at the resort?"

He paused in front of a table with essential oil diffusers. "Not directly, but it was implied." He picked up a cylinder-shaped diffuser in a matte black color.

"How horrible." Glenna had already been arrested once, and Dani was sure the woman didn't want to go through that humiliation again. Was it possible that by just being the nephew and visiting the resort, her siblings—hell, maybe even the staff—automatically assumed Matt would cause trouble?

That wasn't fair to him, but Dani still didn't know the truth. She would have to try harder during their dinner date.

MATT SLOWED TO a halt, letting his gaze take in the large restaurant, a perfect integration of stone, wood, metal and glass.

"Welcome to Dahl's Mexican Fusion Grill—the place to be." Dani posed before the front gates and spread her arms wide. "And the view from the back! It could rival Mariposa."

He had made the reservation when she told him where she'd like to go for her congratulatory meal, and he was glad he took Dani's advice in booking early. Even now, several couples and a large group of people had filed past them into the beautiful building. "It's amazing," he said. "Look at these torches—they're like firepits, except they're seven feet tall."

"Did you notice the design surrounding it? Butterflies. It's so pretty." She grabbed his hand. "Come on. Wait until you see the inside."

They had lined up behind a boisterous group, waiting to confirm their reservation, and Matt took the time to look around. Beyond the host stand, a wide area at the rear of the restaurant had enough space to seat almost one hundred guests. And there was another area to the right, an open patio, that looked like it could seat another fifty. That would be a perfect spot to watch the Arizona sun setting on the red cliffs.

A wide set of stairs to his left led upstairs.

"That's the fancy part of the restaurant. The bar's up there too." Dani linked her arm through his.

"I managed to get us a table toward the back." He enjoyed Dani's closeness. She didn't hesitate in grabbing his hand or standing close enough that their bodies touched. Being under Aunt Glenna's constant overbearing shadow had almost transformed him into a recluse, avoiding people and not becoming intimate with a woman. Going to college and living at the dorm had been his first real taste of freedom, and those four years allowed him to discover who he truly was as a person. Aunt Glenna had still been her bossy self when he graduated, but this time, he had put up a mental boundary, refusing to be pushed around.

The hostess led them to their table, where the full view of the red cliffs stood out in stunning display against the backdrop of a darkening sky.

"Wait a minute. No windows?" Matt asked, then carefully stretched his arm out until it hovered past the four-foot stone wall. "My God, this is amazing!"

"One of the best views in the restaurant. This area's covered by the roof." She pointed to the patio next to them. "That has a 360-degree view and is fully open, but it's hard to get a table even when it's a quiet night."

"That's okay, I love this spot." A three-foot-high elaborate water fountain took center stage in the large space. He also noticed the seats he had chosen offered an intimate setting away from the larger tables. He couldn't have done better with the reservation. He escorted Dani to the cushioned bench.

Her smile was gorgeous. "Thank you."

He sat across from her but then started to look around again. "Sorry," he apologized. "I just can't get over how great this place is."

Every window and open space offered an unparalleled view of the Arizona landscape—the green of the forest below offering the sharp contrast to the oranges and reds of the butte cliffs that towered over them. And above, the blue sky slowly transforming into the multihued scenery of a perfect sunset. The tables were arranged to offer the best opportunity to admire nature.

"It's something, isn't it?" She propped her chin on her hand. "I could sit here for hours looking at this and not get bored."

Matt could sit right where he was and not get bored admiring Dani—she looked amazing. The dark green dress with wide straps flowed around her shapely legs, which he had immediately noticed when she had arrived at the Mariposa parking lot, where he had waited for her. Thick brown hair framed her face in loose waves, brushing against her shoulders. She pushed a section of it behind her ear, but it kept floating back to brush against her cheek. Damn, he wanted to touch it, to feel its softness.

Matt swallowed—time to think of something else.

"A penny for your thoughts?" she said quietly.

He bit his tongue, worried that she caught him staring, then shrugged to give him a moment to collect himself. "Just admiring the scenery."

She grinned. "I noticed."

Damn it. He chuckled. "Guess I'm guilty as charged."

"Doesn't mean it's an actual crime." She watched him.

Matt knew she was flirting, and he enjoyed the attention. He was just worried about how to reciprocate without coming across as stalky, pushy or creepy. He hadn't been on a real date for some time—work always seemed to get in the way, along with Aunt Glenna. She had chased off his ex-girlfriend, who he had met during his studies. When he finally confronted his aunt, her only response was that no one was good enough for him. He'd been absolutely pissed off.

"You're drifting again." Dani waved her hand in front of his face.

"I'm sorry." Man, he had to stop thinking of the negative shit.

"Don't be sorry. Talk to me, what's wrong?"

At first, he didn't want to say anything—just thinking of Aunt Glenna upset him. But when Dani reached out and placed her hand over his, something opened within him. He felt a connection with her that he'd never experienced with his aunt or mother. Dani had made him feel comfortable with himself when they had first met. She had accepted him unconditionally, and though they had only known each other for a couple of days, their chemistry was real.

"Have you..." He paused. "I guess it's always hard to understand a family member's intentions."

Dani's eyes widened, but she didn't react. In fact, her expression changed to one of sympathy. "All families have their secrets," she replied. "Mine for instance...well, let's just say it's pretty messed up."

"Seems to be a common theme, then."

The server arrived to take their order for drinks. Matt kept his simple, while Dani ordered a fancy cocktail. Matt noticed she hadn't moved her hand away from his, and on an impulse, he turned his hand over so that he could link his fingers with hers.

She squeezed his hand. "My dad is the worst. Honestly, I don't understand what women saw in him. As soon as I was old enough, I moved out and traveled halfway across the world to get away from him."

"I wish I could have done that." Aunt Glenna had verbally abused him when he said he wanted to live in the college's dormitory. *Those living quarters are disgusting*, she had said. *Only kids with poor backgrounds live in assisted housing.* But he put his foot down, knowing that being away from her would help him mature into the man he wanted to become. Despite her warnings, he had enjoyed the best four years of his life there. "But I managed the next best thing, which was living at my college's dorm. Really learned a lot from my friends."

"You must have done well in school too. Owning your own business in your twenties and making it successful takes a lot of work."

"I loved every second of it." Making his own mark in

the world had given Matt a sense of purpose. He wanted to build something with his own hands, because he worried that taking money from his aunt would create a bond he refused to have between them. Unfortunately, that didn't stop Aunt Glenna from taking advantage of him whenever she could, and he would mentally kick himself each time her manipulations fooled him into doing something stupid.

"But?"

He blinked, realizing his thoughts made him drift away again. "Hmm?"

"I sense a *but* in there."

Matt glanced down at their linked hands. He really didn't want to talk about Aunt Glenna, not when he wanted to enjoy this evening with a beautiful woman sitting across from him. And yet…it felt good to get some of his frustrations off his chest. "I don't want to bore you."

"You're not. And maybe if you talk a bit about it, you'll finally relax and enjoy the rest of the evening."

Startled, he glanced at her amused expression, then began laughing. "Do I seem tense?"

"You *are* tense. You're squeezing my hand a little too hard."

"Shit." He let go, feeling embarrassed and angry with himself. "Did I hurt you?"

Dani shook her head.

Before he pulled his hand away, she grabbed it. "Oh, no you don't," she told him. "Stay right here. Don't worry, I'm fine." She patted his hand. "Do you feel like talking a bit more about it, or are you okay?"

Matt shook his head, feeling confused. "You really want me to vent about my aunt?"

"Your aunt? Is she the one driving you daft?"

"Daft? Oh, you mean up the wall. Yeah, you could say that."

"Then why don't you cut ties with her? Just get away and live your own life?"

Matt was saved from answering when their drinks arrived. Dani's question touched on a sensitive spot, and the distraction provided him with time to think of an appropriate answer.

"Your drink looks very colorful," he said, admiring it. It was bright orange, with slices of red chili pepper floating on top.

"It's a Juniperita," she said, turning the martini glass around. "It's gin with juniper berries—there's plenty of those around here—and it has agave syrup, lemon juice and elderflower liqueur." She stared at his. "What did you get?"

"A Bourbon Calle." Whiskey wasn't his top drink, but flavored with Agwa de Bolivia coca liqueur, simple syrup and orange, he thought it would give the drink a more robust taste.

"I love the color, very orange, like the sunsets here." She raised her glass. "To new beginnings, friends and experiences."

They clinked glasses. Matt's drink was smooth, and the flavors added a nice transition between the whiskey and orange. "Man, this is really good."

"And I'm loving this drink. Lemony and sweet."

They sat in silence for a few minutes. Matt started to relax, listening to the constant buzz of conversation around them.

"Look!" Dani exclaimed. "The sun's about to disappear behind the red cliffs."

He looked up in time to see the huge fireball sink slowly behind the mountains, inflaming the stone with an unworldly hue of reds and oranges before slipping out of view. "Now that was something," he said.

"Wait until it gets dark. The stars are beautiful."

As the sky deepened into shades of blue and black, the restaurant's lights came on. "What shall we order for dinner?" he asked.

Dani picked up the menu. "I was thinking we should try the tapas so that we could try a little bit of everything."

"Excellent." He placed the order and took another sip of his delicious drink.

"So, about your aunt…"

He almost spat out the liquid. "You're not giving up on the question, are you?"

She smiled. "Just offering a friendly ear."

He cleared his throat. "I haven't abandoned my aunt because…she saved me."

Dani's eyebrows rose but remained quiet.

"My mother wasn't a good parent. I don't know the details because Aunt Glenna refuses to tell me, but…" Man, after all this time, it was still painful to talk about what had happened in his young life. "My aunt took me in and raised me. Maybe she wasn't that much better than my mother, but she did her best, I guess."

"So, you feel like you owe her." It wasn't a question.

"She got me into good schools, let me live a normal kid's life." Matt remembered some of the fun times he had as a boy. But once he hit his teenage years, his aunt's attitude started to change. "But when I was older, she had me do things that I wasn't proud of." He didn't want to say anymore. Some of the schemes she had concocted over the years should have thrown her into jail.

Dani nodded. "I know that feeling too well."

They sat in a comfortable silence, watching the sky turn black and slowly transform as stars sprinkled across it.

"I heard Arizona is one of the best states to stargaze," she told him. "I think Mariposa has a constellation tour or something like that?"

"They have a strict no-lights policy on certain nights to allow guests to admire the night sky." He hadn't participated in it either, but maybe he could get Dani to hang out with him on one of the evenings.

Their food arrived, and his mouth salivated at the delicious combinations, their scent hitting him until his stomach growled in glee. "Dig in."

They had asked for the empanadas, yuca fries and a gaucho plate filled with sliced chorizo sausage, butter beans and focaccia bread.

"My God, this is delicious!" Dani popped a slice of sausage into her mouth. "I gotta say, I chose an excellent spot."

"Yes you did. A beautiful ending to a beautiful day." He was glad Dani had turned the conversation away from their families. It sounded like both of them had led hard lives and tried their best to make themselves happy.

"If you need help wrapping the wedding gifts, let me know." She winked. "I love doing that kind of stuff."

He laughed. "Thank God you offered. I suck at that kind of thing."

She asked if it was okay to have another drink. "Go for it," he told her. "I'll have a soda to keep you company."

They talked about other things—their love of sports, movies, TV shows. They touched on politics, but mutually agreed to leave that hot-button topic alone. Their musical tastes varied wildly until they found themselves in a friendly argument as to which band and singer were the best during the last ten years.

Matt glanced at his watch. "Damn it, look at the time. We should be getting back."

"Do we have to?" Dani gulped the rest of her drink. "Alright, let me freshen up and I'll be right back."

He watched her as she headed for the ladies' room, her hips swaying. Being the first date, there had been no mention of relationships or significant others. Dani's silence on the subject hopefully meant that she wasn't involved with anyone. Why did it matter, though? In a week, Dani would head back to England and he'd never see her again.

The thought bothered him more than he wanted to admit.

He finished paying for the bill when she returned. "All set?" he asked.

"Yeah." When he got up from his seat, she moved close and slipped her arm through his. It felt natural, and as he looked at her bright smile and felt her warmth, he wished he could think of a way to make the night last a little longer.

DANI LOOKED OUT the picture window of her bungalow. It was nighttime, the sky a black velvet and filled with stars that twinkled like diamonds. The Arizona weather, though incredibly hot during the day, had become chilly as she hurried inside. As soon as the sun went down, it could get as cold as an English winter.

What she loved most about Mariposa was how it blended with the desert landscape. All the buildings were made of the same red sandstone as the cliffs surrounding them. And the resort's remote location gave the guests the utmost in privacy. The resort had exclusive bungalows, offering the best in understated luxury for the wealthy and well-known A-list guests who vacationed here.

During her previous visits, she'd never met anyone on a personal level. It was a strict Mariposa rule that all guests were to be left alone unless they participated in a tour or took lessons from the various activities offered. But Adam had asked her to ignore the rules, to get close to Matt Bennett and try to discover if he'd been responsible for any of the accidents that had occurred at the resort.

She turned back toward the living room, running her hand over the smooth glossy wood that decorated one wall. What perplexed her though was that she didn't believe Matt had anything to do with the mishaps. In her opinion, it all stank of Glenna.

In fact, she hoped she was right. Because Matt was getting under her skin in a very good way.

Dani stopped and rubbed her face with both hands. "Bollocks."

She hadn't quite seen this coming. Sure, they got along, but Matt's brooding handsomeness caught her unawares, and next thing she knew, her deliberate plan of flirting with him and taken a turn for the real thing. She liked the guy—a lot.

Glenna might be married to Clive, but Dani and Matt were not related, which was a big plus in her view. Nevertheless, she would be leaving Mariposa at the end of the week. When Matt found out at Laura's wedding that she was related to the Coltons, she had no idea how he would react. She would have to spend the last couple of days of her vacation hiding from him until her return flight.

All she could do now was roll with the punches until Matt gave her the cold shoulder. Dani had no choice but to be ready for that sad bit of news.

Chapter Four

Matt held the reins tight as his stallion galloped across the flat Arizona desert. The thrill of the speed, feeling the animal beneath him and mimicking the steed's movements had been an unexpected joy he had discovered during his previous visits to Mariposa.

He had originally viewed riding as nothing more than a pleasant pastime. His first love lay in analyzing businesses and the details of mergers and acquisitions. He loved taking a company apart, discover what made it tick and putting it back together. His advice to CEOs had been taken seriously, a testament to his hard work and dedication to his company. Matt made a substantial salary as a consultant because of his expertise, but he refused to let it get to his head. He loved his job.

During his first visit to Mariposa though, his views changed. California and Arizona were two very different environments, and he eventually found enjoyment in the dry air and intense heat. But his other love lay in the excited horses that had pranced before him in the corral. He had paused in front of the fence, mesmerized by their fluid movements.

He had decided to take a riding lesson and never looked back.

"Hey, Matt, you're doing great!" Josh yelled out. "I'll

have you riding like a cowboy in no time!" The youngest Colton caught up to him. "You're a natural in that saddle."

"Thanks." He patted the horse's sweaty neck as they slowed to a stop. "Never thought I would like riding so much. I've always been a surfing guy."

"That's something I want to try one day."

Matt dismounted and slung his mount's water bag from the saddle. He opened it, placed the wide strap over its neck, then adjusted it properly. Ares slurped greedy gulps of the liquid as Matt retrieved his own large flask of water.

"We should be heading back." Josh had just finished watering his horse and held the reins loosely with one hand. "Let's walk and give the horses a breather."

"Sure." Matt could just see the outline of Mariposa's buildings in the distance.

"So, Matt," Josh started, "looks like you're one of the few regulars still coming to the resort."

Matt took a minute to think on the statement, but he understood Josh's thinly veiled implication. Despite Allison's death, several accidents and alcohol poisoning at Laura's bachelorette party, Matt was here for another vacation and Laura's wedding, and the young Colton was suspicious.

"I love it here." Matt meant it. "I try to come down every chance I get."

"Hmm." Josh kept walking, his horse obediently following behind. "So, all the crap that's happened hasn't scared you off?"

Matt stopped walking. "It hasn't scared you or the others off either."

"We're not running from cowards or threats." Josh stood across from him. "Mariposa's our home."

"I know. Your sister's getting married here in a few days.

Adam wouldn't have agreed to that unless he knew he could keep her safe from...whatever the hell is going on around here."

"Laura must think highly of you."

"I hope she does." Matt had to play things careful so as not to upset Josh.

"Unlike my father and your aunt."

Matt noticed Josh didn't say stepmother. "I heard they changed their minds about coming to the wedding."

"Which is fine by me. Bad enough that Glenna had been spreading rumors to the media about Mariposa. Too bad she didn't stay locked behind bars when Noah arrested her too."

Matt had the feeling Josh was baiting him to react. Well, it wasn't going to happen. "I agree with you."

Josh's eyes widened in surprise. "What?"

Matt squinted up at the sun as it beat down on them. "Let's keep moving so the horses don't get heatstroke." He headed for the nearest stretch of juniper trees, which would provide some shade. "Look, I know where you're going with the questions," he said as they continued walking, "but I honestly don't know what Aunt Glenna's scheming is supposed to accomplish."

"Scheming? The alcohol at Laura's bachelorette party was poisoned, Matt. That could be construed as attempted murder!"

Josh was going to lose his cool if Matt didn't calm him down. "There's no proof that Aunt Glenna was involved with that. She isn't stupid. She's devious, bitchy and manipulative, but not a murderer. She loves her life too much to risk that."

Josh glanced at him. "I'd like to know if she has anything else up her sleeve."

There it was—the accusation. "Are you assuming I would know anything about my aunt's ideas?" Matt demanded.

"You are her business manager after all. Maybe you're managing her stunts."

There. Josh said it, and despite half expecting the comment, Matt had still been caught off guard. He stopped walking and faced Josh. "I have nothing to do with Aunt Glenna's stunts." He enunciated each word slowly and clearly.

Josh stood several inches away, and Matt could see that his body was trembling. "Really? Prove it."

This was looking bad. Matt didn't want to fight—Josh had a few inches and several muscular pounds on him. "Look, I found out about everything the same way the public did. I tried to confront her about it, but she wouldn't admit to anything and brushed me off."

Josh raised a brow.

"My aunt is not someone I care about." Matt felt the familiar feelings of hatred and scorn rising every time he thought of Aunt Glenna. His aunt and mother both made him feel inadequate, dumb, worthless. Despite his aunt's odd decision to make him her business manager, Matt quickly realized it was her way to manipulate his every move, to isolate him.

Not anymore. "I'll be honest. I was shocked when I received a wedding invite from Laura, but I accepted because I wanted to be here and wish her the best. Nothing else."

Matt knew Josh didn't believe him, and it hurt. But he also knew living within Aunt Glenna's tainted shadow meant that the Coltons' distrust of him had been part of the bargain. "I wondered why you wanted to go riding," he quipped. "I thought maybe you would leave me out here to rot."

Josh stared at him, shock written all over his face before cursing, the words burning the hot air surrounding them. "I'm impulsive, not calculating," he yelled. "And to even say something like that…"

Matt bit the inside of his cheek—maybe he'd gone too far, but Josh's hatred for Aunt Glenna was obvious. "I'm not stupid, I see how this looks," he retorted, and started walking again. Man, the heat was intense today. "But being related to Aunt Glenna doesn't mean I'm like her." He glanced at Josh. "Maybe you should start with that first before judging me without evidence."

A few minutes went by with no comeback from Josh, and Matt was fine with that. Things had gotten a little heated between them, and he wanted the peace and quiet to calm down. Also, he really liked the Colton siblings.

"Hey man, I'm sorry."

It took a second for Matt to realize Josh had just apologized. He stopped walking. "Excuse me?"

Josh scuffed the ground with the toe of his boot. "I jumped the gun, chewing you out like that."

Whoa. He remained quiet.

"It just seemed weird that you were here when shit hit the fan." Josh shrugged and pushed his cowboy hat back on his head.

"The last time I was at Mariposa was in April—you know that." Matt thought a moment. "You're thinking of those photos that got leaked to the media, aren't you? I understand why you thought it was me, but I didn't do it. You'll have to take my word on it. Also, stalking? That's gross."

Josh took off his hat and rubbed his hand over his hair but didn't say anything.

Aunt Glenna had been caught spreading rumors—that much Matt knew. When she'd been arrested for obstruction, he had half hoped she'd stay in jail. But it seemed Clive Colton still had connections and had her released. One evening at the house where she and Clive lived, Matt had overheard Aunt Glenna screaming she would get her revenge. Matt hadn't been sure what to do with that information—he knew his aunt would instantly deny even saying that if confronted. But now, after listening to Josh's concerns, he decided that a talk with Adam would be in everyone's best interests. Matt wanted to reassure them that he was on their side.

The rest of their walk back to the stable had been silent, except for a few comments about Laura's upcoming nuptials. "Listen, Josh, if you all need any help picking up stuff or getting things arranged, let me know, okay? I'd like to lend a hand if I could."

Josh gave him a weird look. "Yeah, sure. Thanks, man."

Matt helped to put away the saddle and reins. "Say, is it okay if I rub down Ares? He's been a great horse."

Again, that weird look, but Josh handed off his stallion to Knox Burnett, his assistant. "I'll show you how it's done."

Matt watched as Ares was bridled inside his stable. "We like to hose down the horses to help cool them off. Then we towel dry and the last step is brushing."

Matt followed Josh's directions until he was satisfied. "Thanks Matt, that's great. I'll work on Ares's legs. He can get unpredictable, and I don't want you to get kicked."

"Fair enough." He stood back as Josh quickly worked on the stallion.

"Hey, Matt, I was curious about something."

Matt watched him carefully as he rubbed down the horse's back leg. What was on this Colton's mind now? "Yeah?"

Josh looked up. "I noticed how you and Dani are getting along pretty well."

Answering questions about Aunt Glenna was one thing—Josh sticking his nose into Matt's personal business was another. "Is there a problem with that? I know the resort rules, but we started talking and realized we had a lot in common." He crossed his arms. "Including enjoying each other's company."

Josh shrugged and continued working. "That's cool."

Wait, was Josh jealous? Matt bit his lip, then decided to keep quiet—all's fair and all that. "Did you need help with anything else?"

"I'm good." Josh hadn't raised his head.

"Thanks for riding with me today." Matt left the stables, wondering if he now found himself between a rock and a hard place. If there was something between him and Dani, he'd immediately back off, but Josh hadn't provided any clues.

Returning to his bungalow, Matt couldn't stop thinking about his conversation with Josh as he showered and pulled on a casual light blue shirt and beige shorts. Thankfully, their chat had helped to resolve some of the tension between them.

He rubbed his chest as a small tendril of anxiety set in. Aunt Glenna was a devious woman. Manipulative, a liar and a schemer—all of them her middle names. She could pull these stunts in her sleep. He should know.

Josh's accusations against her were true. Matt knew she

was capable of bringing down Mariposa if she had a half-good reason.

He stuck his wallet and bungalow card key into his pockets, intent on heading to the restaurant to grab breakfast, but he felt restless, edgy. The horse ride was supposed to be fun and relaxing, but it ended up being anything but.

"Shit." He started walking. Maybe he'd see Dani, but she'd mentioned earlier she would be busy, although he couldn't think what she'd be doing this early in the morning. His mind was so focused on Josh's cryptic remarks about Dani that he didn't sense someone beside him until an arm slipped beneath his.

"Hello, stranger."

Dani's sexy voice caught Matt's full attention. "Hey yourself."

She moved closer to him. "So, what's a dark, handsome bloke doing out here by himself?"

He loved how Dani made him feel—like he was special, someone who deserved kindness. But her flirty comment immediately had him thinking about Josh's wariness of how close they were getting.

"Something's bothering you."

He nodded. "Do you have time for breakfast with me?"

She smiled. "Of course I do, there's always time to enjoy food."

He chuckled as they headed into the restaurant. "What have you been up to?" he asked.

"Well, Erica asked me to help with some last-minute items for the wedding."

"She did? That's nice of you. Oh, by the way, are you still up for the offer in helping me wrap my gifts?"

"You bet. Any chance to spend some extra time with you."

At any other time, Matt would have done a mental fist pump, but he needed some answers first.

After they placed their order, Dani leaned forward, resting her chin on folded hands. "Spill. Is your aunt ticking you off again?"

He gulped down the orange juice, figuring out how to broach what was on his mind, then decided to just go for it. "I went for a horse ride with Josh earlier."

"Oh, I didn't know you rode. You and I will have to hit the trail at some point."

There she goes again. "When we were rubbing down the horses, he asked me specifically if you and I had some kind of relationship."

Dani frowned. "What kind of relationship?"

Matt wasn't happy with her vague answer. "You know what I mean. Is he interested in you? Are you two...?" He waved his hand in a helpless gesture.

She sat back in her chair. For a moment, he thought she was going to admit to something, but Dani did something completely unexpected—she laughed, the sound intensifying until a couple of the servers looked at them. "Are you seriously taking the piss?" she demanded, the words coming out in between gasps.

He knew what she meant—Dani believed he was joking. "Josh acted weird when he asked the question, so I thought—"

"Trust me, Matt, you have nothing to worry about. Josh and I are not an item." She continued laughing, the sound gleeful. "There's no way in this world that would happen."

He sat there, feeling a little foolish against Dani's obvious disbelief in his question, but glad there was no claim behind the suspicion. "Thanks for being honest with me," he told her, trying to regain his composure.

She wiped her face with one hand, still chortling. "I haven't laughed that hard in a long time. Thank you."

He twisted the fork between his fingers. "I didn't think it was that funny," he stated, his ego bruised.

"Oh, trust me, Matt—it is." Dani finally calmed down, but occasionally, little snorts burst from her which she tried to smother with her hand.

Well, that hadn't gone the way he expected, but he was happy with the outcome, nonetheless. He dug into the brioche French toast. "So, now that we've cleared that up…"

"We? You were the one who was worried."

He shrugged, hoping to move past the subject. "This is delicious. I haven't tried this breakfast before." The French toast was an inch thick, crusty on the outside, soft on the inside. It was dusted with sugar, and strawberries decorated the top in a small pyramid. On the side was a small glass bottle of whipped cream, accompanied by a little jug of Canadian maple syrup. He also had three slices of bacon.

"I wonder…" Dani waved her fork at him. "Were you a little bit jealous yourself?"

Matt paused, the fork almost to his mouth. Was he? He didn't think so. He chewed slowly, wondering if Dani was teasing him again.

She glanced at him, her gaze curious as she ate her omelet. "If I had said that Josh and I were in a relationship, would you react differently, I wonder?"

"I would have backed off," he replied quickly. The last thing he wanted was a pissed-off Josh picking a fight. But the other more important reason was that he would have retreated to avoid any backlash that could be perceived as one of Aunt Glenna's schemes. He could see it in his mind—Josh accusing him of backstabbing and being part of his aunt's machinations to undermine the Coltons' tight family bond. He shuddered inwardly.

She looked at him as she sipped her coffee. "You know, I believe you would."

They ate in silence. He wondered what she was thinking, then decided not to ask. The air felt tense between them, and he didn't want to aggravate it any further.

"Dani! Oh, thank God you're here!"

Erica had just entered the restaurant and hurried toward them. "Laura is missing something blue for her wedding attire."

"Seriously?" She glanced at him. "Well, no time like the present to get it. Did she have something in mind?"

Erica shook her head. "Just as long as she can wear it during the wedding, that's good enough. Maybe a simple bracelet or necklace…"

"I have a couple of ideas. Matt, would you like to accompany me to Sedona?"

He grinned. "I thought you'd never ask."

Erica gave Dani a weird look, but it disappeared so quickly, Matt hadn't been sure he'd seen it.

"Thanks, Dani, I owe you one." Erica kissed her cheek. "See you later! Still need to do some last-minute stuff."

And just like that, she was gone, her dark hair swinging.

"I didn't realize the staff knew you so well," he said as he finished eating.

Her expression confused him—she seemed, he wasn't sure, nervous? "Oh! Well, I make friends easily, I guess. And I did say I would offer to help." She finished her coffee and stood. "Shall we get going?"

He watched her, wondering why she was in a hurry all of a sudden. "Would you like anything else?" he asked, while remaining seated. "We don't have to go now, do we?"

"Well…" Dani made a face. "I guess not. But if we go now, we can spend more time together." Her smile was mischievous.

Matt chuckled. "I like the way you think. Okay, let's head out. But I'm holding you to that promise of spending quality time with you."

"Don't worry, I won't forget."

As Dani and Matt drove into the city, she texted Laura.

Erica said you needed something blue. How about a garter belt?

She waited as Laura replied, the three dots flashing across her phone screen.

Excellent idea! I can't believe I forgot something blue. Tallulah mentioned it when she looked over my wedding ensemble.

Trust Mariposa's Head of Housekeeping to spot that missing item. Tallulah was like a mother to the siblings, and Dani appreciated everything the older woman had done for them.

At the entrance to For Your Eyes Only, Matt grabbed her arm. "What exactly are you buying for Laura?"

Dani noticed he looked nervous. "Don't be a baby. You had no problem coming here yesterday."

"My plan was to buy…conservative presents."

She practically dragged him into the store. "And you did, lovely ones. But now I have to get her something blue."

"How about a necklace? I think Erica's suggestion is great."

She made a rude sound. "Are you going to react like this when you meet the woman of your dreams?"

He leaned down and whispered in her ear. "Certainly not."

His breath and deep, sexy voice tickled her skin. Dani bit her lip, feeling her body clench in interesting places.

A warm hand stroked her arm. "Maybe you'd like to find out."

Damn. Dani knew she'd like that very much. How was she supposed to stay in spy mode when the so-called *enemy* came onto her with such a delicious counterattack?

But she was finding it harder to believe that Matt was the nemesis behind Mariposa's problems. Their first meeting hadn't revealed anything, but as she got to know him, her gut instinct was telling her something completely different—Matt was a decent guy and wanted to do the right thing. Also, his hints about Glenna during dinner had forced her to truly rethink Adam's suspicions that Matt had a motive to bring Mariposa down. She just wasn't sensing it.

But it didn't mean Dani should let her guard down either. She could play on both sides of the fence—enjoy his company while still trying to get him to admit some kind of guilt—if there was anything to admit at all.

"Maybe I would." She placed her hand over his, then turned to look at him. This close, his eyes gleamed golden, and she smelled a hint of cologne that swirled around her senses. Yeah, this could get bad really quick—in a good way.

But everything was heading in the right direction, and she had just the idea to make it happen tonight. But first...

Matt's gaze narrowed. "Do you mean that?"

"Of course I do. I would have thought you'd gotten the hint while we were at the pool."

He stood straight, his expression now a mixture of confusion and happiness. "The pool? I didn't think..."

She blew out a loud sigh. "Men. I swear, hints are lost on you. Let me get Laura's blue wedding piece, then maybe we could have a coffee before heading back? And I can let you know exactly what hint I gave you earlier." She raised a brow. "Unless you figure it out."

One of the staff pointed toward a section of the store where the garters were. Dani sifted through the items, feeling the material and looking at the different patterns until one set caught her eye, a pale blue lacy pair adorned with flowers of different sizes. A pearl sat in the center of each flower. "Now this..." she held it up for Matt to get a full view, "...is gorgeous."

As a backup, she also found a simple dark blue silk wrap bracelet with a sterling silver ornament shaped like a butterfly. This would be perfect.

Thrilled with her find, she grabbed Matt's hand and headed out. "Now, let's see if we can find a nice coffee shop," she said, then stopped, staring at him.

Matt was blushing so deeply that Dani actually felt sorry for him. "I can't believe you had me come with you to buy..." he pointed at the small pink-and-white paper bag she carried.

"You said you wanted to come with me." Honestly, why did he look so innocent now? Only a few minutes ago, he had made a bold move to become more intimately acquainted. Maybe he wasn't entirely confident in himself, and that was possible, from what he had told her about Glenna during dinner. Dani would let him know that he deserved better than how his aunt had treated him. "I had no idea you'd be embarrassed. You handled yourself well in the store, I wouldn't have guessed."

He smiled. "Thanks." He pointed down the street. "There's a great donut shop in the strip mall over there. I stopped in once because I was starving, and their donuts and coffee are…" He kissed his fingers.

She snorted. "There's no donut I know of that could taste so good."

"Prepare to be amazed." He tucked her arm around his and they headed off.

Matt was comfortable having her close to him, which ticked off another box in Dani's arsenal of getting close and personal. And while she hadn't forgotten the ultimate goal—to discover if Matt was responsible for any of her siblings' concerns with Mariposa—Dani knew that she was falling a bit more for Matt every time she was with him.

She'd have to be extra careful, keep her mind focused. It was becoming more difficult though. Matt's charming personality was winning her over, and if she wasn't on top of her game, Dani worried he might try to manipulate her thoughts to defend him instead of her siblings.

Dani had seen this happen with one girl and her boyfriend at university. Over the course of several weeks, he had effectively turned the young woman against her friends. Dani hadn't found out what happened to her and could only hope she was all right.

She had to keep her mind sharp. Any slipups could

mean potential disaster for Adam and the others, and possibly herself.

Shit, she hated this conspiracy stuff. Maybe Josh had a point—act like that famous James The-Spy, pretend to like someone while gathering their secrets. It went so much against her moral code, but she had to do it for her family.

The biggest problem she faced right now was she didn't have to pretend to like Matt—she really liked him, to the point that instigating her plan to seduce him tonight thrilled her. She wanted to enjoy their time together without thinking about the other stuff.

Dani stopped in the middle of the sidewalk. She'd been so caught up agonizing how to get Matt to talk, she hadn't allowed herself to just work on this in simple terms. Why shouldn't she enjoy herself with Matt? She could flirt—and more—to her heart's content, be at the wedding, where Matt would unfortunately discover who she really was, but by that time, she'd be on a plane back home. Simple, right?

She immediately shook her head. What a shitty situation.

"Hey, you okay?"

Startled, she looked at Matt, who was staring at her, his brows raised in curiosity. "Yeah, sorry. I was just thinking of something."

"Want to talk about it?"

No way! "I'm all right, I think I figured it out."

The large building mirrored the same rusty red color of the butte cliffs surrounding the small city. As they crossed the parking lot, a man caught Dani's attention. She didn't know why she noticed him. He seemed to walk with a purposeful stride toward the donut shop. Probably needed his caffeine fix.

But there was something about his face that looked eerily familiar…

Inside, there were more customers than she expected. "Is it always this busy?" she asked as they lined up.

"Yeah. They only stay open for six hours." He glanced at his watch. "It's twenty minutes before closing. Makes sense it's packed."

She nodded, looking around. It was a small store, with their selection of donuts the biggest display. T-shirts hung on the walls, while at the back, she could hear shouting as the staff was probably getting ready to close. "How about we get a box of goodies for later?"

"Later?" He glanced at her. "Do you have plans?"

"Yeah, for tonight, if you're agreeable." She squeezed his arm.

The look on his face… Dani swallowed and glanced away. She felt sure he got the hint.

"The pool."

They had inched closer to the counter. "Hmm?"

"You said you gave me a hint at the pool that you were flirting with me." Suddenly, he clasped her hand with his. "I would have said that it was the amazing bikini you had on, but you couldn't have known I'd be there."

"That's true." His fingers were warm, and she held her breath as he stroked his thumb slowly over her skin.

"But the way you were lying on the lounge chair…" He raised her hand to his lips and kissed it, his gaze focused on her.

"Got it in one." Her voice trembled, and Dani took a breath to steady herself. If flirting like this meant being knocked off her feet every time Matt touched her or gave her a smoldering look, she didn't know how she would keep her head on straight.

"What would you like to order?"

She jumped, startled.

"Do you know what you want, Dani?" Matt asked.

Flustered, she picked out a dozen donuts. "It's nice to have a few around in case we don't get back to Sedona," she explained when seeing the incredulous look on his face. "I'm not eating them all at once!"

Matt offered to pay, and she wandered outside, glad to be away from the small interior and the claustrophobic crowd. She raised her face to the sun, enjoying its heat.

"Excuse me."

Today was full of surprises. Controlling her urge to utter a squeak of fright, she managed to cough instead and turn to the person addressing her. "Yes?"

She recognized the man who had entered the donut shop in front of them. Up close, he looked to be in his fifties, about six feet with a stocky build. His dark brown skin gleamed with sweat, despite just leaving the cold confines of the donut shop. His head was shaved, but he wore a full black beard streaked with gray. Black-rimmed glasses perched in front of a pair of dark eyes.

Dani caught all of this in a glance, but what made her take a step back was his proud, almost arrogant expression. She wasn't afraid, just cautious.

He leaned forward, squinting. "You really do look like her."

Okay, she wasn't expecting that. "What?"

The stranger took off his glasses, and she felt a sudden moment of déjà vu, as if she should know him somehow. He looked less stern. "You look just like your mother, Dani."

She sucked in a breath and took a couple of steps back. Her vision narrowed until it was focused only on his face. This guy knew her name. "Who are you?"

"Hey!"

She jumped, grasping her chest. Matt had come out of the shop, one hand carrying a box filled with donuts, the other holding a coffee tray. He strode toward them until he stood in front of her like a wall. "Unless you want this coffee all over you," Matt threatened in a loud commanding voice, "you stay the hell away."

Dani placed her hands on Matt's back and peeked around him. The stranger hadn't moved, and he didn't look happy that he'd been interrupted. His gaze came back to her.

"Guess you didn't hear me the first time." Matt raised his hand that held the coffee tray.

"No!" She grabbed him. "It's not worth it." She gave the stranger her best glare. "And don't waste the coffee."

The man slipped his glasses back on. "Maybe I have the wrong person. Sorry." He turned on his heel and quickly walked off.

Dani had seen his face though. It was the look of someone who knew her.

Chapter Five

"Oh my gosh, those donuts were so good."

Matt laughed. "I saw you reaching for a third one before changing your mind."

They had spent the past hour outside in the meditation space shaded with large umbrellas. It was peaceful here, with no sound except birdsong and the silhouette of a large bird as it slowly circled above them. At one point, she heard an animal call she didn't recognize.

"That's an elk," Matt told her. "I've seen them when I go on hikes back home."

The sound was musical as it echoed off the buttes. "I've never seen one when I've been here."

"They tend to stay away from people. I'm not worried about them, it's the rattlesnakes and scorpions I want to avoid."

She shuddered. "I saw a snake in the pool once. Thank God I noticed it and started screaming. If I had jumped in without looking…" She couldn't finish. That incident had made her more cautious. "Now I check under the furniture for anything, even though the staff are excellent at keeping the bungalows spotless."

"It's a good habit to have." He stood up and stretched.

The resort had been quiet when they returned. No one was at the pool, and as they passed the L Bar, Dani noticed CJ Knight sitting at one of the tables talking to Kelli. The current guests were people who'd been invited to Laura's wedding, along with a few others whose vacations would end on Friday. On Saturday, Mariposa would be closed for the special day.

She didn't mind the quiet and tranquility, but she wondered if it was hurting the resort's bottom dollar. She decided that when Laura and Noah left for their honeymoon, she would talk to Adam to see how she could help in drumming up new business.

In the meantime...well, her thoughts about Matt's involvement in Mariposa's accidents were growing more doubtful.

"Hey, do you feel like going for a walk around the resort? I'd like to stretch my legs."

"Sure." She dusted crumbs off her shirt. "I'd like to freshen up first."

He turned to look at her. "You don't need to."

Now feeling self-conscious, Dani jumped to her feet and checked her clothing. "I thought a bit of jam landed somewhere..."

"I don't see anything." He approached her until they stood so close their bodies almost touched. "Except a gorgeous woman standing in front of me."

Dani smiled and tried to duck her head, but Matt's finger on her chin stopped her. He tilted her head up so that she had no choice but to look at him. He didn't move, only stared at her with his brown-gold eyes.

She knew he wanted to kiss her. And Lord help her, she

wanted to do the same thing. It meant crossing into new territory that she'd been aching to explore. Her plans for tonight—to spend intimate time with him under the stars—had just gotten easier to implement.

She stood on her toes and placed a soft kiss on his mouth, gentle, unhurried. Dani felt his lips move beneath hers, and she teased him with a flick of her tongue before regretfully backing away. "So, about tonight…" She paused.

Matt hadn't moved, hadn't taken his gaze off her. "What about it?" he asked, his voice deep with a rough edge to it.

This might work out better than she expected. "I wanted to ask if you'd like to do some stargazing with me. I'm pretty sure this is one of the nights that Mariposa turns all the lights off around ten."

Dani felt his arm slide around her waist. "I can't think of a better way to end the evening," he whispered.

"Especially…" She held up a finger, "…when you have one of Sedona's famous donuts in your hand!"

He groaned and she laughed, knowing she caught him unawares. "That's why I ordered extra," she continued. "But I don't think they'd go well with a bottle of champagne."

He pulled her close. "I think they'll do just fine." He leaned down and kissed her again.

This time, she molded herself to him, her arms coming around his neck. He felt good, smelled better and she was impatient for the night to arrive.

The sudden clang of metal brought her back to the present and she ended the kiss. Dani knew the staff had been told to treat her as a regular guest, without giving away her true identity, but it was a constant worry that if someone saw her get too intimate with Matt, it could be taken the wrong way. Not that it was anyone's business—except Adam's. She would need to talk to him about her thoughts, that she didn't believe Matt had anything to do with the problems at the resort.

"Let's leave the donuts at your bungalow," Dani told him. "Then we can go for our walk."

THEIR HIKE AROUND the resort had been more exciting than Matt would have wanted. The heat was intense, despite staying beneath the abundant juniper pines that grew in dense patches. At one point, they heard a growl coming from behind a thick stand of trees.

Dani swore and practically crushed herself against him.

It could have been a bobcat or mountain lion. Both animals were usually elusive and stayed away from people. But there were black bears too, and they were more curious. He grabbed her hand and moved quickly, whispering in her ear not to run or scream. She held on to him as if her life depended on it, and they quickly made it back to the safety of the resort, slipping through the front entrance and shutting the gate behind them.

"What the hell was that?" she exclaimed. She refused to let go of him.

On impulse, Matt pushed a lock of her hair away from her face. It was damp with sweat, no doubt a combination of the heat and her fright. "Are you sure you want to know?"

Her frightened gaze tugged at something deep within his chest, and he pulled her a little closer as they headed toward the main part of the resort. "I bloody well do not!"

All right then. "Did you want to get a drink at the bar?"

She shook her head. "I'm still freaked out. I'm going to hide in my bungalow for the rest of the afternoon."

Dani was trembling. "Hey." He rubbed her arm. "It's okay. We made it back, right?"

She nodded but remained quiet.

"What time would you like to meet?" Now that they were at the stage of possibly spending the night together, he wanted to respect boundaries. "I could come to your bungalow if that makes you feel more comfortable."

"No!"

He frowned. She seemed a bit jumpy. "All right, then how about meeting in the main lobby? I'll bring the presents with me for wrapping…"

"No, I meant…" She blew out a breath. "Sorry. I guess I'm still a bit shaken." She wrapped her arm around his. "How about I text you later? I'll come over and we can wrap the wedding presents."

"Yeah, sure." He knew Dani had been spooked by the growl, but Matt couldn't help thinking there was something else bothering her, almost like she was hiding a secret. An image of Josh immediately came to mind, but just as fast, he shut that down. She'd been adamant that they weren't an item.

He watched as she headed into the lobby, then disappeared around a corner. Maybe the encounter with the stranger outside the donut shop was bugging her, but unless she opened up, all he could do was guess.

As Matt headed toward the L Bar, he noticed Adam in the wide hallway talking to someone—it looked like his executive assistant, Erica.

He hesitated at the bar's entrance. He had wanted to talk to one of the Colton siblings about Aunt Glenna's wedding scheme, and Adam was the best person to mention it to.

When Adam glanced in his direction, Matt waved his hand to get his attention.

Adam wrapped up his chat and headed his way. "Hey, Matt."

"How's it going?" Matt knew that Mariposa was Adam's baby despite equal ownership between his brother and sister. His worried expressions had only grown more pronounced as the unflattering news media added up. Matt knew there were fewer guests staying in Mariposa, and if the Coltons couldn't turn it around, it would spell serious trouble for the future of the resort. "All set for your sister's wedding?"

"I don't think I could ever be ready to see Laura get married." Adam's smile held a tinge of sadness. "But she's old enough to do her own thing. All I ask is that the wedding be smooth sailing."

Damn. Knowing that Aunt Glenna wanted to destroy Laura's happiest moment burned Matt even more. "I'm sure it'll be fine. Speaking of which, do you have a minute to talk? In private?"

Adam frowned. "Sure, let's go to my office."

The room was spacious, with an amazing view of the Arizona cliffs overlooking the bright green golf course.

"Have a seat." Adam sat behind his large cedar desk. "Anything wrong?"

Matt thought of how to tell the eldest Colton about Glenna's subterfuge, then decided to keep it to the simple truth. "Aunt Glenna called me."

"Oh." Adam steepled his hands beneath his chin. "Did she tell you Laura invited her and Clive to the wedding?"

"Yeah, but now they're not coming, which is honestly

the best decision Aunt Glenna could have made. But there's more. She demanded that I sabotage the festivities somehow."

Adam's eyes widened, but he showed no other reaction.

Matt took a breath. "She told me to figure out a way to ruin Laura's wedding day."

"And what did you say?"

"I said no." He knew it was entirely possible Adam wouldn't believe him.

"You did?"

"Yep. It was the best damn feeling too. I wish I could have seen her face."

Adam hadn't moved, his expression now neutral. "Why are you telling me this?"

He had a feeling Adam would ask. "I don't know what she's up to, but asking me to ruin a wedding was the last straw. I wouldn't be surprised if Aunt Glenna had something to do with all the other stuff happening around here."

"You know Glenna had been arrested for obstruction when she was at Mariposa the last time?"

"Yeah, I heard about that." Aunt Glenna hadn't stopped screaming about her humiliation at the hands of Noah and the Arizona police. "Served her right, too."

Adam nodded slowly. "Matt, could I pick your brain on something? For business."

"Of course." Adam seemed calm, but this question came out of the blue.

"Laura, Josh and I had decided to merge with another company because we needed the cash. Sharpe Enterprises had been on board until a couple of weeks ago when the news of the poisoned alcohol unfortunately got to the media."

"I saw that on the news before coming here. That sucks. Sharpe is a top-notch company."

"They were going ahead with the merger even with the other problems we had, but now they've changed their minds. I wanted to ask…" He stopped, and Matt could see the strain of worry creasing Adam's brow.

"You're wondering what happened." He had been thinking of several answers. "Sharpe may not have wanted to pay the asking price, but then they should have arranged a meeting with you and the lawyers to discuss that. It's also entirely possible they got spooked by all the bad press Mariposa was getting and pulled out."

"Anything else? Could Glenna have something to do with it?"

"Aunt Glenna?" Matt shook his head. "She'd have no say with Sharpe. She wouldn't be able to meet the directors involved. They run a very tight ship."

Adam nodded. "Thank you. So, it looks like Mariposa's declining reputation scared them off." He held his head in his hands.

Matt pressed his lips together. The reasons behind corporations combining their forces were many, but the most important was to increase their bottom line and keep their shareholders happy. Buying into Mariposa was a no-brainer—it was a stellar luxury resort. Yet, despite the Colton siblings being on top of and solving each bad event, and reassuring their wealthy guests that everything was okay, this latest problem of the poison in the alcohol had obviously been too much for Sharpe. Dealing with the liability claims if a guest had been harmed would have been a colossal nightmare.

But Adam said something that caught his attention. He said Sharpe had been scared off. And that didn't make complete sense to him. Corporations such as Sharpe Enterprises were used to problems ranging from mild hiccups to dangerous dips in the stock market. The siblings had handled themselves well and kept Mariposa viable. So either Aunt Glenna managed to get her devious fingernails into the merger, or there was another reason the Coltons hadn't figured out yet.

It was a project Matt would look into. "Adam, would it be okay if I do some sleuthing? I've done work with Sharpe before, so I know a couple of their senior execs."

"You'd really do that?" Adam asked, surprised.

"Of course." He said it without hesitating. "If Aunt Glenna has anything to do with the failed merger, I'll find out and let you know." He'd had enough of her antics. It was time to turn the tables around.

"Thanks, Matt." Adam came around the desk and shook his hand. "It could be that Sharpe just backed off, but…"

"I know, it seems fishy. Leave it to me."

LAURA CROSSED HER LEGS. "So you don't think Matt is involved?"

"No, I don't." Dani needed to talk to someone about her observations. The more time she had spent with Matt, the more convinced she became that he was innocent.

"I don't believe it either." Laura sat in her office chair, and swung her crossed leg in a slow tempo. "But offering Adam only our gut instincts won't be enough."

"He hasn't said much, but Matt talked about Glenna when we went out for dinner. None of what he had to say was good. He wants nothing more to do with her. If we could have him talk to us, maybe we can find out more."

Laura rose and looked out the picture window that faced the meditation circle. "Do you think so?"

"Yeah. I sense there's not a lot of love between them." Dani's memory of Matt's confession during their first dinner together had really struck her. He had hit on points that reflected her own hatred of Clive and a mother who had abandoned her. "Matt does feel like he owes Glenna for adopting and raising him. He said he knows almost nothing about his mother."

Laura hadn't moved. "I don't know how we could get him to talk to us unless we approach him directly." She turned around. "And personally, I think you should stop your covert operation. Once he finds out you're a Colton at the wedding..."

"I know, but you and the boys are my priority. And it's not as if I'll see him again." The thought sent an unexpected pang of regret through her chest. "I'm going to meet him tonight. If the opportunity arises, let me make the suggestion to Matt that he should talk to all of you, and we'll see what he does."

"All right." Laura smiled. "I admit I'm glad you see things my way. I find it hard to believe Matt is caught up in this crap. He's a really nice guy."

Dani nodded, afraid she might say something that would put her sister on alert. She didn't want anyone to know just *how* much she liked Matthew Bennett.

"I'm glad you remembered to grab a couple of gift bags," Matt said as he placed the last item in one. "I completely forgot."

"Much easier than wrapping everything up in fancy paper." Dani had carefully encased the gifts in gold and silver tissue paper, then placed them in the bags. She then grabbed some precut ribbons, looped them around the handles and tied them into a bow. "What do you think?"

"It looks great." He spent a moment admiring Dani's handiwork.

"Did you get a card?"

"A card?" He let out a groan. "Damn it, why are there so many pieces to a simple gift?" He looked at his watch. "If I go now, I could get to a card shop before they close."

"No need, handsome." She waved a small card that flashed beneath the lights. "I bought one for you, just in case."

He grinned. "You are sneaky."

Did Matt just imagine it, or did he see a flash of concern cross her face? "I meant that in a good way," he said quickly. "I'd never have remembered to grab one."

Dani blinked at him, as if refocusing, before her expression returned to its usual cheerful self. "No, it's my fault. Some of the Americanisms mean something else in merry old England. I had to take a moment to figure out you meant it as a compliment."

"Bloody hell, that's got to be a pain in the arse." He grinned.

Dani's shocked expression was priceless. "Matt, you said that almost perfectly, and with an English accent too. Bravo!" She clapped her hands.

Laughing, he stood and swept a low bow. "'Tis a pleasure, my lady."

She giggled, then gathered up the remnants from their gift wrapping and stuffed everything into a small box. "I'm pretty sure Erica's already left for the day," Dani said.

"I'll find her tomorrow and ask where to leave the presents." He placed the two bags on a table by the front door so that he wouldn't forget them, then turned and slid his arms around Dani's waist. "Tonight, I'd rather spend my time admiring the scenery, if you know what I mean."

She slapped his arm. "Oho! You'd rather stare at the stars then?" She sniffed, but he didn't miss the smirk that flashed for an instant on her face.

"Those too." He planted a soft kiss on her full lips.

He felt her arms go around his neck as she pulled his head down. The flick of her tongue across his mouth dared him to delve deeper into her sweetness until her soft delighted murmur had Matt almost crushing her body against him.

He could have kissed her for hours, but her hands pushed against his chest. "I need to breathe," she laughed.

"Sorry about that." He didn't want to release her, but if they were going to stargaze, he needed to let her go to get things set up outside. Then, he could get his hands on her again. "I ordered some snacks for us—buttered popcorn, personal pizzas, fruit and nuts, cheese and crackers. And a bottle of sparkling wine."

"Wow, you think of everything. Are we sitting out front or the back?"

"Back. Even though it's supposed to be lights out by ten, I think mandatory security lights need to stay on." He led the way through the bedroom to the wide patio out back. It held two large lounge chairs and a table in between.

"I'll get the blankets from the storage closet while you wait for our snacks to arrive." She sauntered off, her butt swaying and grabbing his attention in a breath-stopping moment.

Fighting the urge to follow her, Matt headed for the front door, checking his watch along the way. Kelli had advised that Catrina would drop off the food about now.

As if on cue, the doorbell rang. When he opened it, the restaurant server held a large wooden circular platter in both hands. "Awesome," he told her. "Thanks."

"My pleasure. The cleaning staff will bring it back to the restaurant. Have a good night."

"Thanks, Catrina." He closed the door with his foot, then headed to the back patio. He put the food down just inside the sliding door. "Snacks are here," he called out.

"Great." Her voice was muffled behind two large duvets.

"Let me grab that." He took one from her. "We'll need pillows too. I can get those."

Several minutes later, they were settled in. The night air was chilly, and Matt couldn't see anything beyond the glow of the small lamp that sat on the table. "What would you like, Dani?" he asked as he grabbed a plate and a set of tongs.

"A bit of everything."

"A healthy appetite. I like that in a woman." He did as she asked, and passed the plate to her, then poured a glass of wine. He served himself, then sat on the edge of the chair. The food, though simple, was delicious. "This pizza is great," he mumbled between bites.

"The food is always top-notch at Mariposa," she agreed. "Look at that, I've cleaned my plate off already." She laughed. "I hadn't realized how hungry I was."

"How often do you come to the resort?" he asked.

"Once a year, if it works out. I'd like to do it more often."

So, Dani had enough funds to afford a luxury retreat. But she mentioned that she had just finished school, so...

"I guess your parents treat you to a vacation every year?"

Her hand paused in the middle of sipping the bubbly drink. "No."

That was all she said. He couldn't see her expression—the lamplight didn't illuminate her fully—but her tone told him volumes. "I'm sorry," he started. "I hadn't meant—"

"It's okay, Matt. You couldn't know." She sighed. "I'd rather not talk about it, if that's okay? I'd like to enjoy our time together."

"Yeah, sure." It was a touchy subject with her.

His watch beeped—five minutes before showtime. "Did you want anything else, Dani, before I turned off the lights?"

"Yeah." Her expression and soft smile sent chills through him. "Come sit with me."

He didn't need to be asked twice. The lounge chair was wide enough for two, and he squeezed in beside her. "This is comfy," he whispered in her ear.

Dani turned and kissed him softly, just a touch that zinged through his nerves.

He wrapped his arm over her shoulders and felt her snuggle closer. He reached for the lamp to switch it off, and suddenly, everything was bathed in darkness. The setting sun was just a faint touch on the horizon before it slowly disappeared.

It was quiet, hushed. Matt didn't want to break the peaceful silence, just absorb the nighttime sounds of nocturnal animals as they slowly stirred to life.

"Please tell me no wild animals will come up here," Dani whispered.

"I'm sure they're more scared of us than we are of them." He kissed her forehead. "Now, let's see what Mother Nature has in store for us tonight."

The sky didn't disappoint. Matt found the Big and Little Dipper and pointed them out to Dani. "There's the Big Dipper. When you line up one of its stars to the Little Dipper—"

"You locate the North Star," she finished. "I learned that in school."

Slowly, other constellations made their appearance, but there was one that Matt thought he'd never see with the naked eye. "Dani, over there," he whispered, pointing.

She gasped. "Is that the Milky Way?"

"It sure is." He stared at this wonder, an illuminating band of white light surrounded by the blanket of stars that now covered the sky.

"There's no way I could see this in London," Dani breathed. "Maybe in the northern parts of England."

"There are some parks in California where it's visible, but I never had the opportunity. This is a sight to behold." Matt sat still, staring at this celestial wonder he knew nothing about.

"I feel really small right now," Dani whispered.

"It's a very big place out there. In my opinion, it would take several lifetimes before even scratching the surface of the cosmos."

"Well, instead of thinking how long it would take to explore that beauty, maybe we could think about getting to know each other a lot better."

Matt looked down at her, but in the blackness of night, he barely saw her face. "It sounds like you have something in mind."

He felt her hand brush against his chest. "I do, and it's quite daring, but I think you're up for the challenge."

He wasn't sure what Dani meant, until she pushed the duvet to one side, then straddled him. Damn, he felt himself quickly harden with desire as she moved against him. "Wait, are you saying you want to…outside?" Matt asked.

"Why not? There's no one out here." She kissed him, using her tongue to probe his mouth.

He couldn't believe his luck. He hadn't thought Dani would want to make love this soon after meeting, but he couldn't deny they got along really well. And he sure wasn't going to tell her no. He opened his mouth under her insistence, and tasted the sweetness that was all her. Matt caressed her waist, letting his hands travel lower until they reached the hem of her sweatshirt. Slowly, he lifted it up, relishing the warm soft skin beneath his fingers.

"Your hands are cold," she complained.

"Not for long." He reached for her bra and caressed her breasts through the material, enjoying the startled sound of pleasure escaping Dani's lips.

Suddenly, a faint beam of light washed over them. "I want the lamp on," she whispered. "I want to see everything."

Her honest admission surprised and delighted him. Encouraged, Matt pulled Dani's hoodie off in one swift movement. Her sheer, lacy bra did not hide her dark nipples. He brushed his thumbs against them, enjoying Dani's reaction as she squirmed against him. If she kept this up, he was going to lose control fast, but he couldn't resist. He held her still as he flicked his tongue across a swollen nub, then kissed as much sensitive skin as he could reach.

Dani sat up, her hands braced on his shoulders. Her skin glowed under the soft light, her hair a dark halo surrounding her beautiful features.

"Damn it, Matt, you're a little too good at this." Her lips were parted, and her breathing heavy.

He smiled. "I'm just getting started."

"So am I." Dani started rubbing her body against him.

He groaned, feeling himself grow more erect with her movements. "You're not helping," he managed to say.

"Which means I'm doing something right." Dani reached down and started unbuttoning his shirt, then massaged her hands over his skin. "I like the way you feel," she purred. She glanced down at his crotch. "There too."

He had thought they would do some heavy petting, maybe some exploring with their hands. But Dani wanted more.

And he was ready and willing. "It sounds like you want the full tour," he said, his voice rough with desire.

"Mmm." Dani hadn't stopped brushing her body against him, and the delicious friction was driving him wild. He reached for her again and grabbed the waistband of her sweatpants, pushing them down, then squeezed her firm butt.

She lowered herself to him, mouth parted, and Matt caught her lower lip in his teeth, sucking gently until she moaned. She tasted so good. "You're amazing," he rasped.

Suddenly, Dani stood up and kicked her sweatpants off. Within the dim light, her body looked perfect—taut flesh and smooth, soft skin. Her bra and panties barely covered the treasure he wanted to explore.

Matt couldn't take it anymore. He jumped up as well, but needed to do something first. "Let me grab a condom," he managed to say while hurrying to the bathroom. He stripped out of his clothing along the way, leaving his boxers on as he found the box, grabbed one and hurried back.

Dani was stretched across the lounge chair, the duvet half covering her. It was getting colder, but he didn't notice it as he watched her unhook her bra and toss it to one side. "How do you happen to have condoms?" she asked, her brow arched.

He grinned. "Let's just say I like to be prepared for anything. The on-site clinic sells them."

"Then let's put it to good use."

In moments, they were lying beside each other, fully naked with the duvet keeping out the worst of the chill. Matt kept Dani warm by caressing her, his hands discovering secret areas he wanted to explore further, but didn't have the patience. In one smooth move, he lifted her, holding her as he sat up.

"Matt, I know I said I wanted to do this, but..." her voice faded away.

"What's wrong?" He could see how nervous she suddenly became, twisting her fingers and now looking everywhere but at him.

"I'm not very experienced with..." She waved her hand around.

"We'll take it slow, I promise." He kissed her, gentle this time, hoping that she believed him.

Matt maneuvered their bodies until she straddled him, then as he held on to her, slowly guided her down until the tip of his erection brushed against her. Dani's fingers dug into his shoulders, the nails biting into his skin. Her eyes were squeezed shut.

"Hey," he whispered, then kissed her. "It's all right, open your eyes. Don't be afraid of me."

She looked at him, her gaze dark, but he felt her body start to relax. He hadn't done anything, waiting for her to signal that she was ready for him.

Finally, she nodded, then eased down, his hands holding her tightly, guiding. She gasped and he immediately stopped, worried he hurt her. "You okay?"

"Yeah. It's been a long while." Suddenly her face lit up

in a smile. "You're a trooper though, putting up with me like this."

"Are you kidding? Good things come to those who wait." Matt's body disagreed—it wanted to get on with business, but he held himself in check.

Slowly, agonizingly, Dani eased down until he was fully inside her. She was tight, and he clenched his teeth against the desire to drive into her. He held on to her ass and started to slowly move against her, letting her feel his rhythm.

Dani wrapped her arms around his neck and locked her knees against his hips, trying to match his pace. Matt slowed down, not wanting to rush. He wanted Dani to enjoy their lovemaking.

She kissed him hard, then her mouth wandered across his neck, leaving a trail of heat that set his teeth on edge. Her fingers grabbed his hair as she rubbed herself against his chest, making little noises that had him grip her butt even harder.

Then she picked up the pace, slow at first, until she hit her stride, rocking against him, her moans growing louder as she writhed sensuously.

Matt watched in awe as her demeanor changed from a shy woman to a bold, sexy powerhouse. He grasped her neck and pulled her in for a kiss that seared its magic into his consciousness.

Dani tightened her grip on him—she was close. He didn't stop as her body shuddered, moaning into his mouth as her orgasm took hold. He followed right behind her, biting his lip hard as he trembled with the force of his own release.

His energy gone, he gently lifted her off him, then drew her close, snuggling with her under the duvet. He fought to catch his breath.

She traced her fingers over his cheek, then kissed him. "That was one hell of a tour," she said, amusement in her voice.

Matt laughed. "Thanks."

"Maybe we can do that again?"

He looked down at her, surprised and amazed at her honesty. "Really?"

"Mmm-hmm." She wrapped an arm around his waist and rested her head against his chest. "That's a tour I'd gladly revisit."

Chapter Six

Matt woke up, hearing birds singing outside. Sunlight managed to slide around the edges of the blackout curtains, streaking the bedroom with golden rays.

He took a moment to just lie there, remembering his evening with Dani in vivid detail. There had been no awkwardness, no hesitation in what she wanted from him, and his skin still tingled with heat from where she caressed him.

He didn't want to move, just lie here and replay the whole thing in his mind. Predictably, his body reacted all on its own. He wondered if she was still asleep. Maybe a persuasion of kisses and a caressing hands would wake her so they could enjoy their lovemaking again.

Smiling, he turned over, a word of endearment on his lips, then paused.

Dani wasn't there.

He frowned. Where had she gone?

Oh, she was probably in the bathroom. He relaxed back on the bed, chiding himself for thinking she might have left.

He stretched and yawned, thinking of what he'd like to do today and hoping Dani might join him. He had never been to the spa center and decided that would be a great way for them to bond even more.

He sighed. Who was he kidding? It seemed ironic to put so much effort into this when Dani would be leaving in a few days. He had never experienced a long-distance relationship and immediately realized it wasn't for him. Being away from her for weeks, even months at a time, would be out of the question.

Matt felt sure they could maintain a friendship, but did he want that? Dani was fun, had a great sense of humor and was direct—traits he now realized he enjoyed the most about her.

"Damn." His emotions wouldn't stop whirling. He wasn't sure what to do or how to handle that final day when they would go their separate ways.

"I'll cross that bridge when I come to it," he mumbled.

He sat up, thinking Dani was taking a long time. Wrapping the bedsheet around him, he approached the bathroom door. It was closed, and as he leaned forward to listen, he realized he couldn't hear anything.

"Dani?" He knocked a couple of times. "Is everything okay?"

Silence.

He knocked again, louder. "Dani?"

Still nothing.

Nervous, worried that something happened to her, he tried the doorknob. It was unlocked, and he slowly swung the door open. "Dani, why aren't you..."

He stood still, staring into an empty space.

It was then he turned and hurried into the living area. It, too, was empty.

Dani had left without saying anything.

Confused, he automatically got himself ready for the day, taking a shower and getting dressed to head to the Annabeth Restaurant for breakfast. It was difficult not to think the worst—that she had only wanted a one-night stand. But Matt had to be realistic too. Dani knew as much as he that they only had a limited amount of time before never seeing each other again. In some way, she had taken the more practical approach in her view of their relationship, which, he realized, made sense. It didn't mean he wasn't disappointed though.

That's when he spotted the folded sheet of paper beside the wedding gifts by the front door.

He unfolded it and read the short note.

Good morning. I'm sorry I didn't stay, but in all honesty, I didn't think it was the right thing to do. I sound awful, don't I?

I hope you don't think badly of me. I do have things to get done today for Laura's wedding, but I'd like to see you later if you're not mad at me.
D.

Matt stuffed the note in his pants pocket, feeling conflicted. She had apologized, which he appreciated, but to just leave like that...

He drew in a deep breath. He had no right to judge her. Everything they had experienced was mutual. She had wanted to be with him last night, he knew that. And Dani wanted to see him again. Another plus.

Satisfied in his decision to leave well enough alone, he grabbed the gifts, hopped into the golf cart and headed out. He would find Erica first to drop off the wedding present before using the morning to exercise and get a massage.

So why did it feel like his chest hurt every time he thought of Dani's eventual departure?

Dani felt miserable.

The absolute last thing she'd ever thought she would do is leave Matt before he woke up. That hadn't been in her plans.

Last night seemed surreal. His attentiveness, the way his hands stroked her skin, his lips...

She squeezed her eyes shut. She wanted more of those caresses, wanted more of him.

Yet, sometime in the middle of the night, guilt crept its way into her gut. Despite knowing how much she really liked this guy, the thought at the back of her mind reminded her she'd been doing this all along to discover if he was Mariposa's culprit. No matter how much she mentally argued with herself—that falling for Matt had been natural—she still couldn't shake the feeling that if her siblings hadn't asked her to spy on Matt, she may not have noticed him at all during her visit.

It took her almost an hour to finally decide it was best to leave while he slept. Getting dressed in the dark, collecting her things and finally standing outside, Dani thought of herself as a thief, gaining Matt's trust, then sneaking away when he least expected it. However, she couldn't do it—she didn't want to leave him wondering what had happened. She managed to scribble a quick note and left it on the table beside the wedding gifts so that he'd see it.

"Shit!" she swore to herself. Morning had dawned, the sun bright in her living room. She hadn't slept, instead taking a shower and getting changed before sitting in a large comfy chair, dwelling on what she'd done.

Her note wasn't a lie—she had planned on helping with

any other last-minute wedding details, if there were any. And if not, she'd do her best to not bump into him during the day. Ha, fat chance of that.

Her cell pinged with a text. Glancing over, Dani saw Matt's number flash on the screen. The urge to call back was strong, but she had to fight it. She needed to be sure how to approach Matt from now on. Once he discovered she was a Colton...

She shook her head as anger, sadness and frustration warred with each other. She had to get herself together before seeing him. The couple of times he had caught her off guard showed how observant he was. Dani couldn't afford to let the cat out of the bag—not now. She had to keep the charade going until the wedding, then hide from him until it was time to fly back to England.

And that's where her confusion tried to win out. She didn't want to hide from him. She wanted to spend every waking minute with him, in his arms, until it was time to go.

But that would all depend on how he felt about her when she stood beside Laura as her older sister said her wedding vows.

Suddenly, she laughed, she couldn't help it. Never in a thousand years had she thought she'd ever find herself in such a situation! Playing a spy, falling for the enemy and now wondering how to handle the fallout. This was better than a movie. Her roommates would get a kick out of it.

Dani quickly sobered up, realizing the consequence would be Matt's feelings. She had never meant to hurt him. It was supposed to be an easy in-and-out scenario, but now her feelings were tangled, and poor Matt...

"No," she told herself. She wouldn't deliberately hurt him, and she needed to work out a plan so that he didn't hate her, because she had to face that real possibility. She'd tell him the truth of course, but it had to be timed right.

Making her decision, she walked the short route to Laura's bungalow. She had no idea if her sister was awake or already out, but she wanted to spend some time with her. Once Laura got married, Dani wouldn't see her again for a while. The thought hit her hard. Why did it feel like everything was going to pot?

Laura didn't answer when she knocked. Instead of wandering the resort, Dani would take her chances, have breakfast and then spend the morning at the pool hiding beneath an umbrella and reading her long-neglected book.

ON A HUNCH, Matt parked his golf cart across from the pool. After leaving his wedding gift with Erica, he had ventured out on a difficult hike. That had been invigorating, and the massage he experienced under the skillful hands of the masseur left him feeling so relaxed he had temporarily forgotten his problems.

It had felt good to just enjoy.

The glint of water had caught his attention, and before he knew what he was doing, Matt had started to cross the path toward the pool area. When he noticed someone lounging at the opposite end, he stopped, hoping he hadn't given himself away.

Even with the large sun hat and dark glasses, he immediately recognized Dani's sleek figure. She was reading a book and had angled her chair so that she faced partially away from the busy path. It was obvious she wanted to be left alone.

His texts and couple of phone calls to her earlier had also gone unanswered. Matt had no idea what could be bothering her. That much had been clear. Despite her note saying she had to leave to help with the wedding, he sensed that something else was going on, and he couldn't put his finger on it.

Matt had no choice but to wait and see if Dani would open up to him.

Regretfully, he turned and headed back to his golf cart. It was going to be quiet without Dani's laughter and sexy voice. But he had something to keep him busy—discovering the truth behind the terminated merger between Sharpe Enterprises and Mariposa.

Yesterday, before Dani arrived at his bungalow for gift wrapping, he had texted a college buddy who worked at Sharpe. Pete Schmidt had a senior level position at the company, and Matt hoped he could get some information on what had happened. Pete got back to him, saying to give him a call at three o'clock this afternoon so that they could talk privately.

Matt thought he should have Adam on the call. He hadn't lied to the eldest Colton—he would help as much as possible to find out the true course of events. But Matt had to think like Adam too, and he felt sure there were still lingering doubts about his willingness to assist.

He had left a text with Adam after contacting Pete, so when he got back to his bungalow, Matt should have his answer.

After showering and changing into a pair of light cargo pants and white golf shirt, he grabbed his cell and turned it on. Adam had replied, instructing him to come to the office. So, that idea had worked out.

But there was an email Matt hadn't expected.

Aunt Glenna.

Suddenly, his body tightened with tension. Damn it, he

had spent the time here to relax and feel better. Just seeing the email seemed to throw all his hard work out the window.

Her subject line—Need to Talk to You about the Wedding—gave him goose bumps. Aunt Glenna hadn't typed anything within the email—that meant she wanted him to call, despite already giving her his answer. If she was going to try and threaten or beg him again to reconsider...

Matt's head jerked up as an idea flashed in his mind like a light bulb. Why not double his conviction that he was telling the truth? He would call his aunt in Adam's office so that both of them could listen. This would prove to Adam that Matt wasn't lying. Brilliant.

He texted Adam about the change in plans, and if he could arrive an hour before the Zoom call with his friend.

Matt used the extra time to read and, despite promising himself not to check business emails, fired up his laptop and answered the simplest questions from clients. Then he climbed into the golf cart and drove to Mariposa's main building.

Matt was almost bouncing on his toes when he arrived and knocked on Adam's office door. Having proof of Aunt Glenna's plan to destroy the wedding made him feel vindicated.

"Come in."

He walked in and shook hands with the eldest Colton. "Thanks for changing plans to see me earlier."

"No problem." Adam stuck his hands in his pockets. "Glenna emailed you again, even after you told her not to?"

Matt shrugged. "That's the kind of person she is." He put his laptop on a small work table that sat beside a client chair, then got out his cell phone, his finger hovering over his aunt's number. "Ready? I'll put it on speaker phone."

"Do you mind if I record the conversation?" Adam held up his own phone. "I'd like to keep evidence on hand. We know she'll deny it."

"Yeah, great idea."

Adam placed his phone on the desk. Matt pressed the Dial button, put it on speaker and then sat the phone close to Adam's.

He heard a click. "Well, I see you've gotten back to me faster than the last time. You're learning."

Adam cocked a brow.

"Aunt Glenna." Matt paused. "I thought I had asked that you didn't call me again during my vacation."

A snort on the other end. "As if I'd listen to you. Don't tell me what to do, young man."

Matt felt the hairs rise on his neck. "I wasn't."

"And don't argue with me either!" Her voice rose on the last word.

He bit his tongue, so close to telling her to either shove it or to hang up in her ear.

Adam came to the rescue, holding his hands out in a *Calm down* gesture. Matt took a couple of deep breaths, remembering why he was putting up with his aunt's bullshit.

"Fine," he grumbled. "Why did you ask me to call?"

"Humph, your manners. I'm waiting to see if you changed your mind about helping me."

He needed her to be specific for the recording. "Helping you with what?"

"Sabotaging Laura's wedding, you idiot! Are you forgetful as well as stupid?"

Adam was frowning—Matt knew he wasn't pleased with Aunt Glenna's choice of words.

"I already told you I wasn't going to do it."

"Yes, you said that the first time. Now I'm insisting."

"You can insist all you want, I'm not going to—"

"Shut up. This is what I want you to do."

She started to outline a plan, one that made Matt so angry he almost picked up the phone to throw it against the wall. But Adam stepped in, grabbing his arm and placing a finger to his lips. Matt nodded, his body shaking with fury.

"Do you think you can manage that, dumbass?" she demanded.

Adam looked at the phone, then back at him. Matt saw his sympathetic expression but refused to acknowledge it—he knew how to handle Aunt Glenna now.

"A kid could do that," he said toward the phone. "But I won't."

Silence from the phone.

Matt knew Aunt Glenna was fuming. "Did you hear me, Aunt Glenna? I'm telling you no."

She started swearing curse words that made both of them raise their brows in shock. "I don't know why I took you in if all you're going to do is defy me!" she shouted.

"You're telling me to ruin a wedding," Matt yelled back. "How does that even compute in your brain? I never thought you could stoop so low to contemplate doing such a thing."

"I do what I have to in order to better my chances."

That didn't make sense. "Your chances at what?"

Aunt Glenna started to answer, then coughed. "None of your damn business," she told him. "So, you're not going to help me?"

"No. I'm not ruining Laura's wedding. Or anything else."

"Then I guess I can't rely on you anymore." The phone clicked off.

Matt took in a deep breath. He felt like he'd been running a marathon with a make-believe monster on his heels.

"Are you okay?" Adam asked.

"Yeah." Matt's voice was hoarse with anxiety. He rubbed his chest, trying to calm himself down.

"I'm sorry." Adam grabbed his shoulder. "We had picked up on her manipulation pretty quick after she married Clive. We couldn't get away from them fast enough. But you…"

"Don't worry about me." Matt knew without a doubt that he couldn't be around his aunt anymore, and it stung. But not as much as how she'd just treated him during that tense phone conversation. "You have your evidence and confirmation I'm innocent."

Adam smiled. "I'm sorry I doubted you. I'm sure Josh will be too."

Matt brushed it off. "I get it. I'm just glad I could prove I wasn't involved in anything."

"I can tell you Laura had your back."

Matt really appreciated her at this moment. "I figured as much when she invited me to her wedding."

Adam grabbed his phone and stuck it in a pocket. "I promise I'll only use the recording as a last resort if we can't find direct evidence." Adam moved to sit in his chair. "How do you want to set up your Zoom call with your friend?"

Matt grabbed his laptop and moved it to Adam's desk. "Like this is fine." Matt got the machine running and clicked on the link to join the call.

"I just thought of something." Adam leaned forward. "Would your friend mind if your call was recorded?"

Matt paused, thinking of the implications. "I hadn't planned on recording this originally, and I don't want him to get into trouble. He's spilling a company secret to me. If he was ever found out, he'd lose his job."

"I understand." Adam leaned back. "I have a suspicion of who it might be, but having confirmation would certainly help. Let's hear what your friend has to say, then I'll think of something."

"Thanks, Adam." That had been close. Whether or not this conversation was admissible in court wasn't what bothered him—he would have betrayed his friend's trust.

The call was scheduled for three o'clock, and Pete's face appeared right on time.

"Just letting you know, I have thirty minutes for you before my date."

Pete was the senior vice president of business development at Sharpe. They had become fast friends during college, and Pete had convinced his boss to implement Matt's consulting expertise to assist with potential mergers.

"Pete, you're dating again? What happened to the girlfriend who was so into you?"

"She was *too* into me. Started talking about wedding dates and kids! Shit, I'd only dated her for seven months."

"Sorry to hear that. Look, I won't take up too much of your time."

"You won't, trust me. I've been planning this date for the past two weeks. What's going on?"

Matt glanced at Adam, who stayed out of sight of the laptop's camera. "Adam Colton asked me for advice on what I thought happened between Sharpe and Mariposa."

"Wait, you know Adam Colton? How?" Pete's surprised expression filled the screen.

"Long story, I'll tell you about it sometime. Can you give

me the lowdown on what happened? Why did Sharpe pull out of the merger?"

His friend was picking at his fingernails, a habit Matt recognized—he was nervous about something. "So, Adam Colton didn't tell you anything?"

"He doesn't *know* anything. That's why I'm talking to you."

"I get that, but have you asked yourself *why* he doesn't know?"

That made Matt pause.

"Isn't it obvious?"

The idea flashed in his brain. "Whoever's doing this doesn't want the Coltons to partner with a successful company."

Pete nodded. "Bingo. Up until that meeting, the board was in unanimous agreement to join forces with Mariposa. They said it was an excellent investment despite the recent problems they had, because the Colton family resolved their difficulties in such a way that it didn't damage their reputation."

Well, that was good news at least. "So, what the hell happened?"

Pete remained silent, obviously worried about divulging company information.

"I only need a name." Matt fought against glancing at Adam, who hadn't moved. "I plan on helping Adam Colton find another partner, so I want to avoid whoever is spreading false information about Mariposa."

Pete nodded. "Makes sense."

The tension within Adam's office was so thick, Matt thought he'd choke on it. But he didn't want to rush Pete either. It had to be his friend's decision to speak up. "Unless you think Sharpe might reconsider?" Matt didn't look at Adam when he said that. It was a possibility.

Pete's expression told him what he needed to know. "I don't think that's going to happen."

"Then you need to tell me why. Sharpe had reached the agreement stage before pulling out suddenly like that, and paying that termination fee had enough zeros in it to set someone up for luxury retirement for the rest of their life." Matt decided to push his argument. "Mariposa needed that merger."

Pete looked away from the camera, but Matt knew his friend's mind was working through the pros and cons of providing the information. When his gaze returned, Matt knew he had decided.

"All right, I'll tell you, because you're not just a friend but an excellent and discreet consultant." He took a breath. "When he appeared on our floor, my colleagues and I were in shock. But we found out our CEO has known him for a long time."

"Who?" Matt pressed.

Pete frowned. "Clive Colton."

Matt heard Adam suck in a breath. "Are you sure?"

"Dude, I know what Clive Colton looks like. He's been to Sharpe before."

Shit, this was big. "How do you know Clive and your CEO talked about the merger?"

"The CEO asked me to draw up the draft paperwork to rescind the offer. I admit I was surprised—I didn't think Mr. Colton could do that without a unanimous vote from his family."

"You're right, he can't. Adam and his siblings own Mariposa Resort." Matt suddenly realized he was missing a critical piece to this puzzle. "So, you're saying Clive Colton walked into Sharpe Enterprises and calmly told the CEO to cancel the merger?"

"It seems that way. I understand they're old friends too, and Colton has a lot of pull, being of old money, yada, yada." Pete glanced away again. "I know the CEO didn't have the right to initiate the termination, but when I questioned him on it, he threatened to fire me if I didn't follow his orders." He shrugged. "It pissed me off, but I couldn't do anything."

"You're doing something now. Thanks for letting me know what's going on. And, dude, when I'm back in California, we're having a beer so you can tell me about your latest girlfriend," Matt teased.

Pete laughed. "You bet. Talk to you soon." He signed off.

He and Adam had a lot to talk about.

Matt shut off the laptop and closed it so he could look at Adam eye to eye. "So, there's our answer. Your father shut down the merger."

Adam's face had a weird expression. If Matt didn't know better, the eldest Colton looked almost ready to give up.

"Hey, I said I'd look into alternative companies who would be a great match for a merger with you."

"I know, and I appreciate it." Adam rubbed his face with both hands.

Something wasn't adding up. "Pete said Mr. Colton canceled the merger. Do you care to tell me how he could do that? That could only happen if the old man owned Mariposa or owned majority shares."

When Adam looked at him, Matt suddenly felt a chill run over his skin. "What?"

Adam's sigh was loud and filled with grief. "We found out Clive owns half of the land Mariposa sits on."

"What?" He hadn't meant to shout, but Matt was shocked by the news. "How's that even possible?"

"Because he's Clive Colton." Adam smashed his fist on the table, making the items on it jump. "He showed us our mom's will. There's a provision in it that states Colton Textiles is holding the Mariposa land in trust. Which means…"

"Colton Textiles controls the land and essentially Mariposa. Does Mr. Colton own all the stock of the company?"

Adam shook his head. "No, thank God. But he has fifty percent. The rest was split amongst myself, Josh and Laura."

Matt couldn't believe what he was hearing. "So, the merger was to get a big enough infusion of cash to buy out Mr. Colton."

"I'd rather be in a partnership than be under Clive's thumb," Adam said through clenched teeth.

This situation took on a whole new level of desperation. "Pete mentioned paperwork from Sharpe. Has that come through yet?"

Adam shook his head. "My family lawyer told me about it, but I haven't seen anything."

"Okay, that's good news. I would strongly suggest not signing it until we get to the bottom of this mess." Not signing it meant Adam and the others had a chance of changing Sharpe's decision if they were inclined to do so. "I admit I'm surprised Sharpe hadn't discussed any of this with you."

"We received a call from the CEO a few days ago. Their reason for canceling the merger didn't make sense, since they already knew what had happened at the resort the past few months. They were still on board. Even Allison's murder didn't faze them that much after the murderer was caught."

"This means you'll need potential candidates in case you agree with and sign the termination agreement." Matt was ready to take on the challenge. "Give me a day," he said, standing. "I'll have a list of successful companies I've worked with lined up for you, and if you need another assessment of Mariposa, I can do that too, show that it's still a viable business. Keep that information only between your siblings. If your dad gets wind that you're trying again…"

Adam stood as well. "You'd help us out?"

"Damn right."

Adam remained still for several moments before finally nodding. "Let me know when you'd like to get started, and I'll have Erica break out all of Mariposa's financials." He smiled. "You're supposed to be on vacation."

Matt laughed. "Don't worry about me, I can always come back. We'll get the resort ready for its debut with potential partners after the wedding."

Clive and Aunt Glenna had gone too far with their schemes. It was time for some serious payback.

Chapter Seven

Dani climbed out of her golf cart as Matt drove up the path toward his bungalow. Her stomach waged a war within her, filled with tension, anxiety and a healthy dose of guilt. She didn't think she could go on much longer with the spying. The more time she spent with Matt, the less she was convinced he had anything to do with the problems that had occurred at Mariposa the past few months.

With Laura's bridal shower and wedding imminent, Dani felt herself being squeezed between finally confessing to Matt or waiting for his eventual discovery of her true identity when she walked down the aisle as maid of honor. Unless she convinced Adam that Matt was innocent, she would be spending the rest of her vacation after the wedding hiding in her bungalow until it was time to return to England.

However, Adam had been busy this morning, leaving Dani with no time to talk to him. So she found herself here in front of Matt's door, frantically worried about what to say to him.

"Hey," she called out as he approached her.

"Hey."

Matt's white golf shirt fitted him like a glove, outlining the sculpted abdomen she had the pleasure of caressing last night. He had also developed a tan, skin bronzed and shiny in the hot afternoon sun. His cargo pants fit him in all the right places, and she had to close her eyes a moment to calm down her rapidly beating heart. "Had a good day so far?"

He nodded, watching her. Matt wasn't going to make this easy.

Dani finally noticed the laptop clutched under his arm. She pointed at it. "I guess you had to get some work done," she said. Bloody hell, where was the wit she was famous for?

He glanced down at his computer. "I had business to take care of."

"And was that successful?"

His expression... "I got the answers I needed."

She nodded, trying not to shuffle her feet against the ground. Matt hadn't given her any clues. Well, the best way to deal with it was to jump in with both feet. "Matt, I want to apologize for this morning, leaving like that without a proper explanation."

She caught him chewing his bottom lip as he turned around. "Did you want to come in?"

Dani released a quiet sigh—thank goodness, he was being civil. "Thank you."

Dani shivered as she walked into the air-conditioned living room. Matt had one of the larger bungalows at Mariposa, sitting on the east side of the property. She watched him as he put his stuff away, then turned around.

"I'm sorry," she started, knowing what she wanted to say. "I think I freaked out last night." She twisted her hands together. "I haven't spent the night with a man before." Which was the truth. She'd been on an occasional date, but school was too important to develop relationships.

He frowned. "Never?"

She shook her head. "I like what we have, and I loved spending the evening with you." Which was also true. She dreaded the moment when the wedding day arrived and all would be exposed. "But I think the idea of staying overnight was too much for me." She shrugged. "I panicked."

He took a couple of steps closer. "Are you all right?"

"Yeah, just embarrassed."

Matt reached out and touched her arm. "There's nothing to be embarrassed about."

Dani squeezed her eyes shut. He was being so nice about it.

His warm body brushed against her as his arms wrapped around her waist. "I thought...well, I thought I did something wrong."

"What? No, you were amazing. I thought I'd be terrified, but you made me feel so comfortable."

"I'm glad I managed that."

"Of course you did." She grabbed his head and pulled him down to sear a kiss on his lips. "You were very attentive," she whispered against his mouth. "My body ached in places I didn't know could ache."

He laughed and squeezed her tighter. "I didn't hurt you?"

"No, not at all."

He kissed her, molding his mouth and body to her own until her doubts were chased away.

KNOX BURNETT WAS one of the most handsome cowboys Dani had ever seen, and that was saying a lot. In his midtwenties, with shoulder-length dirty-blond hair and killer smile, all the female guests gravitated toward him like moths to a flame. She knew he was also a very loyal employee to her siblings and would never cause drama with any woman on the resort.

"Afternoon, Dani, Matt." He touched the edge of his hat. "All set for your ride?"

"Of course." She stroked Penny's nose. The spirited mare loved to run and terrified anyone who wasn't comfortable in the saddle. However, years of riding lessons in Switzerland and England had honed Dani's skills to equestrian level. She wasn't afraid of Penny, and when she swung herself into the saddle, the mare immediately calmed down.

"So, Dani, are you looking forward to the bridal shower this evening?"

Shit. Thank goodness her back was turned to Matt because her face screwed up into a frown.

Knox realized his mistake at the same time. His moment of shock turned into a coughing fit as he huddled against Ares, the stallion Matt was going to ride.

"Dani, you never said you were attending," Matt inquired.

"I, um, Laura invited me last minute." Confident that her face wouldn't betray her, she faced him. "She said it was a thank-you for helping out."

He smiled. "That's sweet of her. I'll bet you ladies will have fun."

"I think so." That covered Knox's slip up.

Knox shaded his eyes against the sun. "If you all don't mind, could you make this a shorter ride? I found a couple of rattlesnakes near the trail, which usually means there might be more. I'll have to deal with that. Just be careful, you hear?"

"Damn it." Dani loved wild animals, but at a distance. "We'll just go around the resort, Knox. We know the route."

As soon as Matt climbed onto the stallion, Dani encouraged her mare into a fast walk. The heat was intense, so she stayed within the shade of the junipers that lined the trail.

Matt swore, and she turned in her seat to see him fight with the reins as Ares pranced and tried to rear up. "What's gotten into him?" he demanded.

She laughed. "I guess he doesn't want to go for a walk. I didn't know Ares could be so stubborn."

"Neither did I. I'm glad you and Penny are getting along, though," Matt retorted.

"Seriously, Matt, you're doing a smashing job. There are few people who can keep a horse like Ares under control."

Their ride took them up a gentle slope to the nearest red cliffs that overlooked Mariposa. On either side of the trail, juniper trees and short shrubbery sheltered them from some of the worst heat. Beyond, she could hear birdsong, and the rustling of trees as a warm breeze blew over them. Their horses' hoofbeats were the only steady rhythm of sound around them.

Matt finally caught up to her and they rode side by side. "Have you been riding long?" he asked.

"Since I was fifteen." Dani had wanted to be part of her friends' circles, and riding was a priority. Luckily, she took to riding like a duck to water and built her experience. "I even participated in a horse show. It was a lot of fun." She glanced over at him, noticing his riding style. "You seem comfortable in the saddle yourself."

He chuckled. "I haven't been riding as long. I learned at the resort during my first trip and loved it so much I took lessons when I got back home."

They were silent for a while as they rode up to the crest of the red buttes. Reining in her horse on the large circular plateau, she dismounted and stretched her arms over her head. The sun had started its arc toward the west, but it was still hot.

"There's a creek just below here," she told Matt as he got off Ares. "Let's walk the horses down for a drink."

She led the way, being careful across the uneven dirt trail until they reached the creek's edge. The heat of the day dropped sharply beneath the dense shelter of the trees, and when she inhaled, the fresh cool scent of water buoyed her spirits.

The horses didn't need to be prompted—they headed straight for the bank and dipped their heads down to drink.

Matt strolled over to her. "I should have remembered this spot. Knox and I rode through here once because that day had been brutally hot." He looked at the creek. "There must be an underground source around here if this creek still runs during the hottest part of the season."

"I understand there's a few around the area." Dani only knew that because it had been important when Mariposa was built to have several permanent water sources around them in case of emergencies. "But I like this spot because it's pretty. See the flowers there on the bushes across the way?"

As he glanced to where she pointed, Dani couldn't help but admire how good-looking Matt was. His hair was messy from the ride, and she clenched her hands to keep from running her fingers through it.

She had to stop that. Dani really liked the guy, and spying for her siblings did not seem as important, especially as she had already decided that Matt wasn't responsible for the problems Mariposa had faced. She hoped Laura had told Adam her observations, but Dani knew she needed to talk to her brother as well.

"Looks like Ares made sure you looked as dusty as he does." Dani reached up and brushed at his hair. When he turned, she couldn't help but stare at his golden-brown eyes.

"Are you flirting with me?"

She bit her lip, but thought of a witty remark. "What else did you think I was doing?" she quipped.

His hand rested on her shoulder, then slowly caressed the length of her arm until he grasped her fingers, which were still in his hair. "Just making sure."

His other arm came around her waist, and Dani closed her eyes as he leaned down and brushed his lips against hers. Such a gentle caress, but she felt her knees wobble with the force of it. "Blimey," she breathed against his mouth.

He squeezed her tight against him. "Yeah." He looked around. "I guess we'd better head back so you have time to get ready for tonight's festivities."

"You had to remind me, huh?" She smacked his chest.

As she gathered Penny's reins, Dani heard a faint hiss nearby. "What was that?" she asked. The mare nickered, stomping a hoof into the muddy bank.

"Whoa, easy." Matt held on to Ares's halter. "It could be one of those rattlers Knox mentioned."

"Shit." She hung onto Penny as the horse shook her head and started to pull away. "Do you see it? I want to make sure we're not riding toward it—"

Suddenly, the mare reared, knocking Dani off-balance, and galloped to the trail leading back up to the cliff.

"Dani!" Matt shouted.

"I'm okay, just tripped." She sat up, flexing her limbs carefully. Nothing was broken.

Matt hunched down beside her, his expression filled with worry. "You sure?"

"Yeah. Just give me a second to catch my breath."

Another hiss drifted toward them, and it sounded closer. "Can we get out of here?" she asked, forcing herself upright, and held still, her gaze riveted on something that moved beneath the bushes to her right. "Did you see that?" she whispered, inching closer to Matt.

"Yeah, that looks like a big rattlesnake. Come on."

She followed his movements, walking slowly back toward Ares, who thankfully had remained calm. Matt pushed Dani to get into the saddle, and he climbed on behind her as she gathered the reins. As they headed toward the trail, Ares snorted and skittered beneath them.

Dani refused to look over her shoulder, concentrating on keeping the stallion under control as they headed back to the trail. When they reached the cliff, they finally saw Penny calmly munching on a plant.

"Damn you, Penny, taking off like that," Dani scolded as she reined in Ares beside the mare. She slid off the stallion and handed the reins to Matt as he shifted forward. Penny tried to back away, but she grabbed the reins before the mare took off and then got into the saddle. After a few moments of encouraging words and getting a tight hold on the reins again, Dani managed to get Penny under control and started down the trail back the way they came.

"Wow!" Matt shouted. "I don't know how you did that. I would have messed up big-time."

"I told you, riding was like my second life in England."

When the trail widened, Matt moved up beside her. "Are you sure you weren't hurt back there? When Penny reared up like that..." He didn't finish, but she saw the concern on his face. She had scared him.

"Totally fine. I knew I didn't stand a chance holding on

to her, but I dropped the reins too late. It's okay, I didn't get kicked or anything," she said quickly. She patted the mare's neck fondly. "Penny just pulled me off balance."

The ride back to Mariposa was thankfully uneventful, but Dani had to be more careful. As the wedding day approached, there could be more innocent comments like the one Knox had made from other staff members. The excitement of Laura's impending nuptials had been building, and she would need to dodge around Matt and the final preparations until…

Her chest tightened with worry. Matt would never forgive her for the part she played in the Coltons' suspicions. And he'd certainly never forgive her for not telling him her true identity. Dani had planned on staying at Mariposa for a few extra days to make sure the resort was running smoothly before she left, but now she wasn't sure if it would be better to just catch an earlier flight to London—maybe find a flight in the evening after Laura and Noah left for their honeymoon. She wouldn't have to face her guilt every time she saw Matt's face.

Knox was waiting for them by the corral. "Everything go all right?" he asked as he grabbed Penny's reins and Dani slid off the saddle.

"Well, we saw a huge rattlesnake down by the creek," Matt told him. "Penny got spooked and ran off, but Dani wasn't hurt."

"Jeez, I thought I had trained this mare enough that she wouldn't get scared off so easily." Knox wasn't happy with the news.

"It's not her fault," she said. "It looked big." Dani used her hands to show the rattler's size. "I didn't see how long it was, but the body was wide."

"I'll bet it's the hombre that's been eating the wildlife in the area." He took up Ares's reins as Matt climbed down. "I'll take care of them. Where did you see the rattler?"

Dani described the area.

"I know where that is. I'll get a couple of the boys to help me out. I haven't been able to find that rattler recently. I'm glad nothing happened to either of you." He led the horses to the stables.

She linked her arm with Matt's as they headed toward the main building. "Well, that was more excitement than I cared for," she said. "Thanks for keeping me calm when all I wanted to do was run."

He chuckled. "Happy to save a damsel in distress."

At the front lobby, Dani suddenly realized she couldn't have Matt see which direction she would drive to get to her bungalow. "I'm going to look for Laura and see if she needs anything," she lied. She was getting tired of the ruse. "I'll talk to you later?"

"I hope so." Before she could react, he planted a firm, thorough kiss on her mouth.

Dani closed her eyes, losing herself to the wonderful sensation until he backed away. Smiling, he waved as he hopped into a golf cart and drove off.

She sighed, knowing she'd have to enjoy Matt's company as much as possible before the wedding.

THE MARIPOSA FEMALE staff laughed, sang and cheered during the various bridal shower games Erica concocted, followed by an amazing lunch Kelli and her staff put together. The karaoke sing-off was the funniest with a final showdown between Kelli and Laura. The bride-to-be won by two votes.

Dani hadn't laughed this much since…damn, she couldn't remember. She had spent every waking moment studying her ass off, with only occasional nights out with her roommates. They had fun, but this felt different, another level of intimacy with people she admired and loved.

"Laura, that was absolutely brilliant!" She gave her sister a tight hug. "I had no idea you could sing."

Laura giggled. "I do not call that singing. More like yodeling."

"Hey, don't insult yourself." Kelli had come over and placed her arm across Laura's shoulders. "The ladies liked your singing. So did I. It was really good. You could serenade Noah with that voice of yours."

Dani snorted. "She was good, but I don't know…"

Laura took a playful swipe at her. "Come on!"

"All right, ladies." Erica climbed onstage and waved her arms to get everyone's attention. "Let's open Laura's gifts. I'm dying to know what she got!"

The bridal gifts were stacked on a large table beside the stage. Dani and Kelli grabbed a chair, placed it on the stage and had Laura sit down.

"Everyone grab a seat!" Erica was beaming as she handed the first present to Laura.

"This one is from Tallulah," Laura announced as she opened it. The first part of the present was a baby monitor system followed by two baby blankets, one pink, the other blue. Then she pulled out the coziest looking pair of pink and blue onesies.

Dani and the others laughed as Laura blushed a deep pink. "You're being a little too optimistic, don't you think?" she accused.

Tallulah gave her an impish grin. "Hey, you gotta start

sometime." She came up to the stage and placed a kiss on Laura's cheek. "I expect to hear good news soon."

Laura shook her head but smiled as she was given the next present.

Dani admired the variety and creativity of the gifts chosen. What caught her eye the most were the silk bedsheets, a cashmere travel set with blanket, socks and eye cover, and a luxurious skincare selection that made her think she'd buy one for herself when she returned home. When Laura opened Dani's gift and held up the sexy babydoll outfit, the excited screams echoed through the room.

As Laura was given the last gift, her eyes widened. "This is from Matt?"

Dani smiled and wiggled in her seat.

Erica nodded. "I know, right? Surprised me too. He brought it to me earlier and said he hoped it was okay."

"'The Essential Stay-At-Home Kit.' Now I'm curious."

When she opened the first gift bag, Laura gasped, then pulled out each item. The his-and-her set of silk pj's and fuzzy slippers, a small bottle of champagne and two champagne glasses, and a beautiful photo album. The second gift bag contained the French press coffee maker and gourmet coffee basket. The last item was the gorgeous essential oil diffuser.

"Holy crap." Laura carefully placed everything back into the bags.

Dani leaned toward Kelli. "That's one hell of a gift, isn't it?"

Kelli nodded. "He wouldn't do that unless he really liked Laura."

"I know." Matt was really something.

"Speaking of Matt." Her expression became serious. "Dani, have you gotten any info out of him?"

Dani remained quiet, not sure how much to tell the bartender. "I'm working on it," was the best she could say. "I have to update Adam."

Kelli nodded. "I understand Laura doesn't believe Matt is guilty, but anything could happen, I guess."

Dani looked up when Tallulah stood, clapping her hands. "With that gift from Matt, you won't need to leave the bedroom," she called out. "Which means my baby gift will come in handy after all."

The room echoed with everyone's laughter—Tallulah was such a joker, but Dani knew she loved the Colton siblings as if they were her own kids.

"Thank you, everyone." Laura wiped her face with a hand—she was crying. "Each one of you mean so much to me." Her voice broke on the last word, and she covered her face with both hands as Erica hugged and whispered into her ear.

Dani started crying too, but they were tears of joy for her half sister. The bridal shower was a success. Laura was about to embark on the greatest and scariest journey of her life with the man she loved. It was about time something good happened for the Colton siblings.

THE MESSAGE ON Dani's bungalow guest phone sent chills down her spine.

She had noticed the red flash after she walked in from the bridal shower. Turning on the lights, she decided to start her nighttime routine of winding down first—today had been emotional.

Wearing her comfortable pajamas and carefully holding

a mug of hot herbal tea, she sat down in front of the room phone. There was only one message on it. She thought it could have been one of her roommates, but nixed that idea. They would have texted her.

"Probably a wrong number or crank call," she said to herself as she hit the button.

A weird sound echoed through the ear piece. It sounded like wind.

"Hello, Dani? I know you're wondering whose voice this is, but please don't hang up. My name is Ken Curtis. I'm your mother's brother from California."

What the hell? Dani almost pressed the Delete button, but what the stranger said next froze her movements.

"I'm the guy who approached you at the donut shop, the man with the black-rimmed glasses. I wanted to talk to you, but your boyfriend threatened me before I could explain.

"I know you'll want to hang up, but please, let me prove who I am. Your mom was Malia, and she gave you to your father, Clive Colton, when you were seven or eight. I met you a few times before that happened, but you would have been too young to remember. I know you're thinking I could be a scammer, so let me tell you your mom's middle name. It's Helen."

Dani's chest constricted in a panic attack. An uncle she never knew about appeared out of the blue, knew her mother's middle name and said Dani had another family in California. Clive never said a word to her about this while Dani lived under his roof—typical selfish bastard.

"Maybe you'll believe me, or maybe you think I'm a jerk. I've wanted to get in touch with you, but I couldn't find any information on your whereabouts. I only found out about you after I read about Laura Colton's wedding in the newspaper. Mariposa confirmed you were a guest there, but didn't give me any more details. I had to play private investigator until I saw you a couple of days ago. Gosh, you look just like your mother."

Was this real? Dani was torn between deleting the message and a strange fascination to hear more.

"I hope you believe me. I want to talk to you about your mother, our family, everything. I'll leave my number. If you don't call, I won't bother you again, I promise. Thanks."

The phone clicked off.

Once upon a time, Dani would have punched the Delete button before the first sentence was finished. However, listening to Ken's message had stirred a dormant memory of her mother, a woman she used to think looked like a fairy princess.

Before Mom's light was snuffed out by the monster that was her father.

She'd made up her mind and decided to leave the message on the phone. She would call this elusive uncle and discover why he wanted to meet her.

Chapter Eight

Dani hurried across toward Adam's private bungalow. His text message had been brief and to the point.

We might have a problem. Need to discuss privately. Only the four of us.

"What the hell is going on now?" she mused.

She wondered if Adam might have discovered information about Matt she knew nothing about. Had he done his own sleuthing? It was possible, but up until now, it had been left in her hands to find out if Matt was implicated in Mariposa's difficulties.

There had been nothing to convince her that he was. Matt had been nothing but supportive ever since they had met. Spending the large amount of money for Laura's wedding gift had also been a plus, but who's to say he did that in order to better infiltrate and get under their skin?

But Dani's personal experiences with Matt were the deciding factor. She had kept her head in the game despite the caring, attentive way he treated her. Yes, that could have been Matt's plan to make Dani drop her guard, and she admitted to herself that had happened a few times. But in the end, she still believed Matt to be genuine.

Now she had to convince her siblings of her findings.

The hot sun beat down on her as she parked her golf cart in front of Adam's bungalow and knocked on the door.

"Come in, Dani."

She rushed in. "I got your text. What's wrong—"

She stopped dead in her tracks.

Adam, Laura and Josh stood next to a clothes rack. "Hey, Dani," Josh called out as his hands pushed clothing around.

"Um, what's going on? Adam, your text sounded urgent."

"It is." He gestured at the clothes. "I need help selecting a different suit for the wedding."

"What?" she exclaimed. When she looked at Laura, her sister rolled her eyes. "Is he serious?"

"Of course I'm serious." Adam frowned. "Why would I be joking about the most important day in my sister's life?"

"Because you had already chosen a suit. Hell's bells, Adam, you're going to freak Laura out. I'm freaking out. You know the wedding is tomorrow, right?"

"I know. But I didn't like the suit Laura picked. It makes me look old."

"Blimey! The wedding day isn't about you!" Dani watched her sister. "Laura, why aren't you saying something?"

Laura sighed. "I did, but he won't listen."

"Ugh." Dani knew Adam could be stubborn, but this was taking things too far. "Fine. Laura, if it's okay with you, I'll help Adam choose a new suit. I don't want you to worry about anything. I'll make sure he looks great."

"Thanks, Dani." Laura shot an irritated look at her older brother before leaving.

"Laura." Dani had second thoughts about talking to everyone about the mysterious message, then decided to keep it simple so as not to concern everyone. "Can you wait until I'm done? I need to talk to all of you about something."

Laura frowned. "Yeah, sure." She sat on the couch.

Dani now turned her full attention back to Adam. "Seriously, what's the matter with you?" Dani strode to the clothes rack and looked through Adam's custom suits. "Everything had been agreed to down to the last detail of the flowers and your mom's portrait."

"I want to look perfect when I walk Laura down the aisle," Adam retorted.

"And you did. That black suit was made for you." Dani picked out a suit that caught her eye and laid it on the chair behind her.

"It's boring. Noah and his groomsmen are wearing designer black suits that put the one Laura chose to shame. I want to wear something…different, interesting."

"Okay." She eyed Josh. "What about you? Having second thoughts on your suit?"

"No way, mine is sweet. I love the dark green three-piece you picked."

She smiled. Josh was such a relaxed, happy-go-lucky kind of guy, and Dani had chosen an outfit that reflected him. The color also looked stunning against his tanned skin and dirty-blond hair. "Thank goodness for that." She turned to Adam. "Do you have something in mind? What are you thinking?"

"I'd like for you to think of a suit that reflects me as well," Adam told her.

"We got it right the first time," Josh quipped. "Old man clothes."

"Shut up," Adam growled, but she heard the teasing tone

in his voice. Despite what these guys and Laura had gone through, their love for each other was tight.

"Well..." She spotted another suit and put it aside, "...since you're giving Laura away, you need to look your best of course. But it doesn't mean we can't add a touch of color." One suit in particular made Dani stand at attention. "Now this..." She held up the dark brown three-piece suit, "...with a snow-white shirt, dark gold tie and a white flower bud pinned to the lapel? You would look very dashing."

Adam cocked a brow.

"Yeah, Dani's right. The color goes with your hair and makes those baby blues pop," Josh added.

"All right, let me try it on and get your opinion." Adam disappeared toward the back.

When Dani heard a door close, she whispered, "What happened? Yesterday, he was calm, all the arrangements had been made, and Clive and Glenna aren't coming." She glanced down the hallway. "What's gotten into him all of a sudden?"

Josh shrugged. "The pressure, maybe? He's giving our sister away, so my guess is, he needs to look top-notch."

"But he did in the black suit."

"He said Noah and his posse are wearing black, remember? Adam must have found that out recently, so I guess he wants to look just a little different and stand out. Makes sense."

"I just wish he'd said something sooner," Laura grumbled.

Dani nodded. Adam took his responsibilities seriously, sometimes a little too seriously. But as part owner of Mariposa, the strange tragedies over the past few months had slashed their reputation down to a point where only a few of their regular customers were coming. A significant chunk of change wasn't coming through the front doors. The siblings had enough money to tide them over for several months, but if they didn't get back on track soon, they'd be in serious financial difficulty. Then add the astonishing news that Clive actually owned the land Mariposa sat on, and then the failed merger with Sharpe Enterprises…

Dani sighed and rubbed her forehead. If Adam was feeling extra tense and snarky, he had every right to be.

She felt a warm hand on her shoulder. "Hey. Don't worry, we'll get through this."

She looked up, surprised at the serious expression on Josh's face. "The wedding will be a piece of cake compared to the shit we're going through." Dani knew Mariposa needed a miracle.

"So? What do you think?"

She turned to see Adam, all dressed up in the suit that made her blink twice, then rubbed her eyes. "Adam, is that you?"

He chuckled. "It certainly is. Dani, your second choice of suit for me is the bomb. Thank you." He did a turn. "I can't believe how well it fits too."

"It doesn't need any adjusting?" She walked toward him.

"Everything works. The pants are a little long." He slipped on a pair of black shoes.

Dani glanced down. The pants just creased the top of his shoe. "Stand up straight."

Adam complied, and looking again, she wasn't worried. "You're all set. Just don't change your mind again, okay?"

"I promise."

She turned to Laura, who got up. "So?"

Her sister smiled and nodded. "I don't know why you didn't choose that one in the first place."

"Whew! So it's settled." If only all their problems were this easy to fix.

"What did you want to talk about, Dani?"

Right, the more serious business. She took a deep breath. "I have a couple of things. The first one is about Matt."

"Ah. Let me get out of the suit and we'll have a chat. I have some updates as well," Adam told her.

They sat in the kitchen, where she got everyone up to speed. "You don't seem mad or anything," Dani said, holding a mug of coffee in both hands.

"I'm not. Matt's proven to me that he's on our side."

"What? And when did you plan on telling me this? I've spent all this time acting like a bloody spy!"

"I only found out yesterday afternoon. I was going to send a text, but I kept getting distracted with work."

"Damn it." She might have been able to end the charade and hopefully not have Matt angry with her.

"What's the problem? We had to be sure. Matt came to me yesterday and called Glenna, putting her on speakerphone so I can hear and record the conversation. She confirmed she was the one who came up with the idea to ruin Laura's wedding."

"What?" Laura and Josh yelled at the same time.

"At least that proves Matt is innocent," Dani said. She was thrilled her own instincts had been proven right, but there was still the problem of telling Matt that she was a Colton.

"Matt also helped out with the merger problem," Adam stated. "Seems that dear old Clive managed to convince the Sharpe CEO to rescind their offer."

"Clive has nothing to do with our damn business!" Josh said, balling his hands into fists.

"It's the land," Dani chimed in. "He owns half of it. I'll bet he showed the CEO the will too."

Adam frowned. "Matt also discovered that Clive and the CEO are long-time friends."

"There's that too." She sighed. "My concern is every time we find a viable partner, if Clive gets wind of it, he'll pull out the will and show proof he owns half of the land. Who's going to partner with us when there's the possibility he could sell his half from underneath Mariposa? We'd be up shit creek without a paddle if that happened."

"Then we make sure he doesn't find out," Josh said through gritted teeth.

"So, Matt's on our side." Laura rubbed her hands together. "I never had any doubt."

Adam stared at Dani, one brow raised. "How do you think he'll take the news when he discovers you're a Colton?"

She wasn't sure whether to laugh, cry or scream with rage. "What do you think?" she demanded.

Her siblings gave her various expressions of confusion.

"What's the matter?" Josh asked.

Ah, the million-dollar question. Dani felt sure Laura knew, but she may as well confirm it. "The problem is I like Matt. A lot."

"We like him too." Adam said. "I'm just glad he's not a part of—"

"That's not what Dani meant," Laura interrupted.

The room remained silent as Dani worried about how to tell them her feelings about Glenna's nephew.

"Ohhh," Josh crooned. "You like Matt *that* way."

"Shut up," she grumbled.

Adam's eyes widened, finally understanding. "Jeez, Dani, we asked you to spy on him, not fall for him."

"Bloody hell, did you think I planned on it happening?"

"What are you going to do?" Laura asked in a quiet voice.

She shrugged. "I don't know. I've played the charade this long, so I figured I would stay quiet until after the wedding. If he's willing to talk about it afterward, fine. But if he's pissed…" She closed her eyes, trying to keep her anxiety under control. "Well, I'll be back in England soon enough."

"You mentioned two problems," Josh said. He was actually listening.

Dealing with Matt was going to be easier compared to this bombshell if it was true. "There's a message on my room phone." She paused. "From my mom's brother."

The only sound was a gasp from Laura.

"Are you sure?" Adam asked.

"Yes, of course I'm sure." She recited most of the message. "There's no way he could know what had happened to me or Mom's middle name unless Mom told him. I've never talked about my mother to any of you."

"Jesus," Adam breathed. "What do you want to do about that?"

"Not a damn thing until after the wedding and figuring out how to get Clive off our backs. I haven't known about this side of the family at all, what's another few days?" she quipped. But in her heart, Dani knew she wouldn't have any peace until she solved this latest problem.

The ping of a text made her jump in her seat.

Laura glanced at her phone. "It's Erica. She needs to go over some last-minute things before tomorrow." Her face took on a mild look of panic. "How the hell is my wedding tomorrow?"

"It's okay. Erica's done a stellar job pulling everything together." Dani pulled her sister to the door. "Let's see what she needs." Just as she crossed the threshold, Dani gave her brothers a hard stare.

Adam held up his hands. "Scout's honor, I won't change my mind."

Josh made a show of tapping his chin.

"Don't you dare, or you can walk down the aisle in your bloody underwear!" she shouted before slamming the door shut.

Laura giggled. "Wouldn't that be a sight?"

She groaned. "Not you too."

"Don't worry, Josh will want to look his best." Another ping on her phone. "Erica's in the meditation area."

As they came around the corner of the building, they saw Erica standing under a patio umbrella, checking her phone, but she looked up when she heard them. "Hey," she called out, approaching them. "How's everything?"

"Oh, you mean other than Adam changing his mind about his suit?" Dani said, still annoyed with her brother.

Erica's expression made Dani regret her words. "Oh my God!" Erica grabbed her shoulders. "Please tell me Adam hasn't screwed anything up!"

Her green eyes were filled with worry. With everything going on, one misstep in the wedding could send her over the edge. Erica had planned everything out, down to the cutlery, and being super organized was her specialty.

Dani knew the executive assistant could handle almost anything thrown at her, but this *was* an extra special event, after all. She patted Erica's hand. "Everything's good. He put on his second-choice suit, and it looks smashing on him. Crisis averted."

"I swear, that man makes me want to pull my hair out

sometimes." Erica's eyes widened, and she turned to Laura. "No offense," she murmured.

"None taken. Sometimes I want to scream, he's so maddening."

Dani snorted behind her hand. "That good, huh?"

"I just want to make sure the wedding goes off without a hitch." Erica raised her face to the sky. "Lord, please. No more misfortunes."

"Amen to that." Dani hadn't been here for the bachelorette party, but finding out the alcohol had been poisoned had added another level of *What fresh hell is this?* to the mix. If the probable culprit was Glenna, she had more than enough to answer for. This was going too far. "How are you all feeling, by the way? No weird symptoms?"

"The medical team at the hospital gave everyone the all-clear." Laura closed her eyes. "I'm just glad everyone's okay, and Erica didn't touch any of the booze. After all the shit we've been through…"

Dani grabbed her sister's hand, trying to offer some comfort through her touch. "Hey," she said, "it'll be okay. All of your wedding stuff is locked up tight in your bungalow, and Erica arranged to have the catering staff arrive early tomorrow morning. We also hired additional security…"

"No." Laura shook her head.

"You won't know who they are," Erica chimed in. "They'll be dressed as guests. We want to play it safe. Even though your dad and Glenna aren't coming, I just…" she paused. "I don't want to see anything else happening to you and the guys."

"And remember what Adam found out from Matt," Dani added.

Erica looked at her. "What? What is it?"

Laura gave her a stern look, but it was best for the executive assistant to know. "It seems that Glenna was trying to wreck the wedding through Matt, but he told her no and advised us."

"Sweet Jesus." Poor Erica looked like she was on the verge of tears.

"Let's not worry about that right now. Everything's arranged for the wedding. And Laura's marrying a cop—if anything weird happens, Noah's right there with his buddies to take the asshole down."

Laura's eyes widened in surprise, then she burst out laughing. "Can you imagine? Noah's getting married! Oh, wait, he has to make an arrest! But he can't leave the bride's side. It sounds like some comedy show."

Dani was glad to see Laura's humor—hopefully it meant she could relax before the big day tomorrow.

"Oh, Dani, I almost forgot." Laura hit a few buttons on her phone and a picture with text appeared. "Noah and I would like you to read a poem for us before the final vows."

"Really?" She glanced at the excerpt and immediately smiled—this was perfect. "You bet I'll read this. He's one of my favorite poets."

"Oh, thank goodness. I was worried you might be too nervous to do it. The reverend will have this on his podium—he already knows about it."

Dani gave her a thumbs-up but could see Laura was getting tense. "Darling, you have to stop fretting. Why don't you get a massage or relax at the pool? Erica and I can handle any last-minute items. And, yes, we'll text if we need you."

"A massage sounds like a great idea." Erica grabbed Laura's arm. "And I think your favorite masseuse is here today."

As they walked off, Erica looked over her shoulder at her with a worried expression.

Dani frowned. Damn Glenna and her scheming.

MATT SWAM HIS last lap before pulling himself out the pool, feeling sore but invigorated after his daily workout. The cool water clinging to his skin quickly evaporated in the afternoon heat, so he pulled on his shirt and grabbed his things to head back to his bungalow.

On an impulse, he checked his phone to see if Dani had called or texted. Nothing. It must have been one hell of a bridal shower last night if he hadn't heard from her yet.

Matt had been conscious of how time was slipping away. Laura's wedding was tomorrow, which meant one more day, two if he could stretch it out, until he and Dani went their separate ways. His feelings about their inevitable departure were jumbled between sadness, anxiety and a little bit of fear. Would she want to see him again? Could they really do a long-distance relationship? Or maybe Dani thought of them as a fling, and she'd forget about him when she left Mariposa.

He didn't believe that. What he did believe was they had something special, and he wanted to explore their feelings for each other to see where it would take them. The subject of possibly staying in touch hadn't come up yet, so he decided he'd talk to her about it when the time came.

At the bungalow, Matt had taken a shower and changed into dress shorts and short-sleeve shirt. He then pulled out the clothing he would wear to the wedding tomorrow, making sure everything was clean, pressed and polished. He hung his suit outside the closet, placed his shoes underneath it and then put the accessories on a small table, which he dragged beside his clothing. He didn't want to forget anything.

Suddenly, his phone pinged with a text. As he read Dani's note, Matt's stomach twisted around in knots.

Hey there, handsome. Hope you didn't miss me too much!

Wanted to ask if you'd like to grab an early dinner? I need to talk to you about something personal. Could we meet in the lobby at five?

Matt wondered if she had the same idea to talk about whether to continue the emotional connection they had developed.

He sent a reply that he'd meet her at the appointed time, which was thirty minutes from now. He double-checked everything needed for Laura's wedding, then stuffed his wallet and phone into a pocket before heading out.

In the lobby, Matt watched as several Mariposa staff walked by, carrying items that would appear in the wedding—lots of white flowers, chairs covered in white cloth, vases and several wreaths.

"Exciting, isn't it?" Her arm entwined with his.

He looked down, smiling as he watched Dani take in the final preparations. "It is. I've been to a few weddings but never watched the action this close since..." He stopped, remembering the lavish ceremony Aunt Glenna had organized with her usual pinpoint accuracy and bridezilla tactics.

He felt a small tug on his hand. "You okay?"

"Yeah." Laura's wedding would be the exact opposite—a

ceremony of love shared with close friends and family. He couldn't wait until tomorrow.

"It looks like you're going to tear up," Dani told him, smiling.

"I'm not!" He reached around and pinched her backside, receiving a loud squeal of protest. "I'm happy for her, that's all. Come on, let's find something to eat."

The evening's menu was seafood. "My favorite!" Dani said, looking at the menu.

Matt watched her discreetly as he perused the choices. "How was your day? The bridal shower must have gone on late because I hadn't heard from you all morning."

She frowned, which he didn't expect to see. "I offered to help again this morning," she said, still staring at the menu. "I woke up late, ate breakfast at my bungalow and wandered to the main lobby. The staff were running around like chickens without their heads, so I asked if I could help, and the next thing I knew, I was sucked into the vortex of final bridal preparations."

He snorted. "That's one way of describing it. I can sort of imagine that, judging from what I saw."

"It's ten times more chaotic." Dani put the menu down. "The bridal shower was stupendous, and your gifts were a hit."

Matt shrugged, feeling a little embarrassed. "I just thought about what would be nice for a couple during a weekend away."

"Nice? I was with you at the store, remember? You chose top-line items, you gorgeous bloke. Any woman would be into that."

He felt his cheeks grow hot with Dani's praise. "Thanks."

Dani laughed. "Don't be shy, it was a lovely gift." She

chatted about the party, drawing him in with her description of the games, the ladies' antics, and other gifts.

Splurging on Laura was a no-brainer—she had welcomed him into the family circle despite Adam's and Josh's continued wariness. With his help, he had managed to swerve Aunt Glenna's plan to destroy the wedding and discovered Clive Colton's involvement in ending Mariposa's potential merger with Sharpe Enterprises. He didn't do that to prove anything though—his moral code couldn't let him stand by and watch a person take advantage of another. His aunt had done this to him for as long as he could remember, but he'd never felt confident enough to tell her to stop until now. It was possible that he destroyed what little affection was left between them, and while that hurt, Matt knew that in the end, it would be for the best.

A server approached, and Dani placed an order for lobster. "I haven't had lobster in ages," she said, releasing a loud sigh of contentment. "I could live on that for the rest of my life."

"And miss out on other food? No thanks." He ordered the Salmon Wellington. "Would you like wine, Dani?"

She shook her head. "I want to keep myself sharp for the wedding."

He frowned. He didn't know she'd been invited—she never said anything. "Did Laura extend an invitation to you in exchange for your help?"

Her brown eyes widened with shock, and she bit her lower lip. She seemed nervous about something. She asked the server for a soda, then turned her gaze back to him. "I'll be attending."

Her answer was short, almost clipped. "That's great. Maybe we could sit together."

Her expression wasn't what he expected. "I don't think we can."

"Why not?" Dani wasn't making any sense.

"We'll see. Anyway, I wanted to ask you something." She changed the subject without missing a beat.

"Sure." Her attitude seemed off this evening. "What is it?"

He watched as she did something even weirder—she hugged herself as if to ward off a chill. "What would you do if a long-lost family member contacted you out of the blue?"

He pursed his lips, the memory of his inattentive mother's face flashing through his conscious. "I guess it would depend on who it is."

"But what if you didn't know them? Say it was a family member you might have met as a kid, but they proved that they were a relative."

She stared at him, and Matt felt the tension around her, as if her next move depended on his answer. He thought carefully. "If I had a relative I knew nothing about, and they approached me with undeniable proof that we were related, I would talk to them."

"What would you ask them?"

"Well, I guess where they've been. Then if the conversation is going well, possibly talk about family members. I'd think it would be difficult to talk about anything with a relative you don't know. There could be hidden stuff you might dig up and wish you'd never knew."

She nodded, as if thinking.

"Has something happened?" he asked quietly.

Dani's gaze refocused on him. "Do you remember the man who approached me at the donut shop? He says he's my uncle."

Matt didn't know what to say, so he was relieved that their dinner arrived.

"Look at this lobster!" She clapped her hands in delight. "I love this dish. It looks huge but it's not, with the wine-based sauce and just enough cheese before it goes under the broiler." She kissed her fingers. "Magnifique!"

"If you say so. I'm salivating over this salmon." The puff pastry that covered the salmon and spinach had been baked to a nice brown crust and was accompanied with a colorful salad.

He ordered a soda, following Dani's lead, then started eating. He didn't consider himself a food connoisseur, but he knew a good meal when he tasted it. "This," he said around a mouthful, "is delicious."

They ate in silence. Matt had questions and sorted through them in his head. "What do you think you'll do?"

"Hmm?" Dani didn't seem to be paying attention. It was obvious her mind was someplace else.

"About your newfound uncle."

Her fork paused halfway to her mouth.

"Will you call him?"

She put the food into her mouth and chewed. "I already have."

He nodded, watching her. When she remained quiet, he pressed, "How was your talk with him?"

"Short. He wanted to meet in person. I told him I'd think on it."

"What's holding you back?" Matt got the solid impression Dani wanted to meet this uncle, so her hesitation confused him.

"I don't want to meet him by myself." Her expression was a mixture of excitement and fear. "I want to talk to him and discover more about my mom's family. I'm pretty sure it's not a scam, but…" She grew silent, as if thinking.

There was one other question on Matt's mind. "Could I ask you something? You don't have to answer if you don't want to."

Dani looked at him, her expression now curious.

He swallowed, nervous. He remembered her reaction the last time he brought it up, during the night they had stargazed. "Could you ask your parents about this guy?"

He tensed as he watched Dani's expression change with her emotions. "No."

That one word explained a lot. "I'm sorry."

She waved her hand as if it didn't matter, then pushed her plate to one side. "Could I ask you to come with me, Matt?"

"Of course." He understood her wariness. Whether or not this uncle was the real deal, Dani wanted to take precautions, and he was more than happy to help her.

"Thank you." Her smile was beautiful, making his breath catch in his throat.

He smiled back. "When do you want to do this?"

"After the wedding. Laura and Noah will leave for their honeymoon tomorrow in the late afternoon. I thought I could meet Ken for coffee afterward."

"Ken's his name?"

She nodded.

Matt was also curious about how she knew of Laura's plans, then decided she must have heard it from Erica or the staff when she was helping out with the preparations. "Okay, sounds like a plan."

"Are you sure? If you're busy tomorrow…"

"I'm good, Dani. Besides, we only have a couple of days together before leaving. Speaking of which, I was wondering if you'd like to keep in touch after we leave Mariposa."

The look on her face... "Do you really mean it, Matt?"

"Why wouldn't I?"

She shrugged. "We're half a world apart. And I wasn't sure how you felt about a long-distance relationship."

"We'll make it work." Before the words were out of his mouth, Matt knew he wanted to continue the special connection he had with her.

She looked ready to cry. "I think I need to leave now."

"Dani," he called out, but she had already risen from the table and hurried out of the restaurant.

Shit. What the hell did he say to make her so upset?

He ran after her, finally catching up to her by the meditation area. "Hey," he called out, and gently grabbed her arm. "What's wrong?"

She wiped her face with her hands, but not before he saw the glint of tears on her cheeks. "Dani, I'm sorry if I said something to hurt you."

She sniffed and turned around. "I'm okay."

She sure didn't sound it. "Are you sure?"

"Yeah." She wiped her face again. "I'm sorry, I don't know what came over me." Dani walked up and put her arms around his waist. "I don't know how you put up with me sometimes."

He wrapped his arms around her and rested his cheek on top of her head. She smelled like roses. "Trust me, it's not hard."

He felt her laugh against his chest. "You haven't seen the worst of me. I've been on my best behavior around here so far."

He kissed her forehead, just wanting to stand here and feel her against him, listening to birdsong and feel the hot Arizona wind brush against their skin. He had meant what he said—they would make the relationship work somehow.

Dani tilted her head up to his. "I guess we'd better get our beauty rest. Tomorrow's going to be a big day."

Matt nodded, not wanting to let her go. "I guess I can't persuade you to come back to my bungalow then."

"Oh, you!" She smacked his chest. "Not this time, I'm afraid. But I'll leave you with something to think about." She grabbed the back of his neck to pull his head down and pressed her full lips to his.

Her kiss was soft and full of promise. He tightened his grip around her as he relaxed, savoring her taste, her scent. He'd definitely be thinking about this all night.

Too soon, she pressed her hands against him and pushed away. "Well now," she breathed heavily. "I might have liked that a lot more than I expected."

"Is that a bad thing?" he whispered.

She shook her head. "No." She frowned and shook her finger at him. "You are a tempting distraction. I must not succumb."

He grinned. "I'm trying my best."

"I've noticed." Dani grabbed his hand and they headed back to the lobby. "I know you can be a naughty boy when the mood hits you."

At the front doors, she paused. "I'm going to do a last check-in with Erica and Laura, just to be sure everything is ready and there's no last-minute panic. I'll see you tomorrow?"

"You bet."

She blew him a kiss and walked in the direction of the Mariposa's offices.

Matt stood there, enjoying the view until she disappeared around a corner.

Dani hadn't said no to a possible relationship. He had to hope that somehow, they could make it work.

Chapter Nine

Dani took a couple of steps back and admired the ethereal vision in front of her. "Laura, there are no words to describe how stunning you look."

Her half sister stood in the middle of her bungalow's living room, her smile bright and happy. The wedding dress was made of creamy white silk, and the elaborate folds of the skirt cascaded like waves down to the elegant sandals.

Sheer, delicate lace encased her arms and sweetheart neckline. Laura's hair was styled into an elegant chignon, sprinkled with pearls, the veil pinned just above the hair knot. And the final piece was her mothers' small but intricate diamond tiara. A bouquet of white peonies sprinkled with sprigs of green and white lily of the valley was tied together with an extravagant bow of green silk.

"You look like a princess!" she exclaimed. Dani couldn't help it—Laura was absolutely beautiful.

"Thank you. I want to twirl around, but I don't dare."

"You can do that after you're married." Laura and Noah had decided to leave for their honeymoon immediately after the wedding party. "I think you have everything, right? Something old, new, borrowed and blue?"

"I'm killing two birds with one stone on the borrowed

and old. The tiara was Mom's and the diamond stud earrings belonged to my grandmother. The dress is new of course, and as for blue—" she winked "—my new garter belt, thanks to you."

Dani laughed. "It seems you have it all covered." After being away for most of the last year to finish school, Dani could finally spend more time with her siblings, but now Laura was getting married and she would see less of her half sister. As the realization sunk in further, she felt sad.

"Hey." Laura wrapped her in a tight hug. "What's wrong?"

"Nothing." Dani didn't want to spoil the special day.

"Something's on your mind. Spill it."

She shrugged. "I guess I was hoping to spend more time with you and the guys when I finished school. I had no idea you were even thinking about getting married until you called to tell me. I guess it caught me off guard."

"You mean predictable, organized, slightly boring Laura wouldn't have done something like this without thinking it through."

She looked at her sister's beaming face. "Yeah, something like that."

Laura kissed her forehead. "Dani, with all the crap we've had to endure, finding this slice of happiness with Noah has been a blessing. You know me—I would have fully checked his credentials before a first date. But he and I, well, we just clicked."

Dani wondered if that had happened between her and Matt. Dating during school had been a no-go on her journey to independence. Meeting Matt that first time had felt so natural—maybe it had been that same pleasurable rush for Laura. "I think I get it."

"Trust me, when you meet your guy, you'll know."

"I never thought I'd hear you say that." Dani gave her a tight squeeze then backed away. "I think it's time to make you a Mrs."

Laura giggled. Being around her sister these past few days, Dani saw a different person. A Colton who was truly in love, and loved in return, according to a surprised Adam and Josh. It was a bright beacon in the murky darkness of despair they had been suffering.

And were still suffering. If the siblings couldn't find a partner to fend off Clive's threat to sell the land, they would lose everything.

"You ready?" Dani asked.

Laura nodded. "Let's get the show on the road."

In the living room, Laura's bridesmaids chatted as they sat in various chairs, wearing various styles of their dresses, in a beautiful color of that was a mixture of red and brown similar to the Arizona buttes that surrounded Mariposa.

Erica, Alexis, Kelli and Tallulah were more than thrilled to be a part of Laura's special day. What Dani didn't know about was Laura's best friend from university. Willow Sanderson had flown in earlier, but she and Dani hadn't spent much time together at the bridal shower.

Everyone immediately stood up and surrounded the bride, gushing over how beautiful she looked. In the background, the official photographer waited, camera in hand and smiling.

Dani approached her. "I'm sorry you couldn't get photos while Laura was getting ready, but I think she was too jittery."

"Totally fine." She held up the instrument. "We can certainly get some intimate photos here first before driving to the wedding site."

Dani managed to get everyone's attention. "Ladies, let's get some pictures, please. We're running a little late."

The photographer obviously had an idea in mind while taking photos of them in various poses and groups. The last photo, with Dani and Laura sitting on a settee with their arms around each other, brought tears to Dani's eyes.

"That was wonderful, thank you. Now I think we need to head out." Dani glanced at her watch. They were about ten minutes behind schedule, but they could make up for it while driving to the spot where Laura would make her grand entrance.

Four of the resort's luxury SUVs were parked outside, all dolled up with flowers that matched Laura's bouquet, with white, green and terracotta-colored ribbons. Dani, as maid of honor, would sit with Laura, while the other ladies and the photographer led the way in the other vehicles.

They had arranged for Mariposa to be closed for today. Not that it had been hard to do—few guests had booked during the past couple of weeks due to the bad publicity and unflattering media press, despite Adam's attempts to clean that up.

The plan was to have the brothers and the groomsmen arrive first at the staging area, followed by the ladies. Once everyone was in place, their journey would take them across a small section of the golf course covered in white cloth. Behind a hill was the assembled wedding party. Laura had deliberately chosen that spot so Noah wouldn't see her until she stood at the top.

"I can't believe how hot it is this early in the morning," Laura complained. The air-conditioning in the car was on, but the interior thermometer already registered above seventy degrees outside.

"Well, you are getting married in June." Dani sensed that Laura was growing more nervous. "It's all right. The sooner we do this, the sooner you can relax."

The SUVs pulled into a small parking lot reserved for the private guest houses. Adam and Josh immediately came over to open the door and helped Dani and Laura to step out without mishap. "Laura," Adam whispered, staring at her with wide eyes. "You look…" He stopped.

"Breathtaking? Gorgeous? Out of this world?" Dani quipped, hoping to ease the sudden tension.

Adam's expression was one of awe for his little sister. Josh on the other hand, looked like he wanted to hide Laura someplace safe. The brothers were losing their sister to another man, and today it looked like the news finally hit them—they had to be scared.

"Gentlemen, any words of encouragement for your sister? This is a big day for us after all," Dani added, trying to get a response out of her brothers.

"I'm sorry." Adam's eyes were suspiciously shiny with tears. "I guess with all the crap going on around Mariposa, I hadn't focused on the good—no, the best—thing happening right now." He wiped his cheeks with an unsteady hand, then gave Laura a tight hug. "I'm so proud of you. Mom would be as well."

Josh moved toward his brother and sister, and Dani tried to keep her own tears under control as the Colton siblings gathered into a tight intimate circle to share this wondrous moment. The photographer was making the most of it too by snapping plenty of pictures at a discreet distance.

"Dani." Laura held out her hand. "You're part of the family too."

She hadn't expected this. Sure, they had grown closer recently, but at times, Dani still felt like an outsider. She never had a close family, or the kind of support that didn't ask for anything in return. These siblings had been her only true family. And now they fully accepted her as one of them.

Not caring that the tears ruined her makeup, Dani walked into their embrace, kissing each of her family members.

"You're one of us," Josh said, echoing her thoughts. "Don't ever forget that."

Dani nodded, not daring to speak or she'd start bawling.

There was a soft touch on her shoulder. "Dani." It was Tallulah's voice.

Sniffing, Dani took a step back. "Time to go," she announced.

Everyone arranged themselves into place, and at a nod from the photographer, Dani slowly walked toward the path that would take them to the altar.

The procession across the golf course was quiet. Birds sang as they flew amongst the juniper trees bordering the landscape, and a constant breeze rustled the ladies' dresses. Dani led the group as maid of honor, followed by the ten bridesmaids and groomsmen. Laura was at the back, the veil now covering her face, with Adam and Josh on either side of her. What Laura did not know about was the security detail that was hidden around the wedding area. Erica had assured Dani that Roland Hargreaves, head of security at Mariposa, was excellent at his job. As she glanced around, she couldn't see anyone. Which was good, because if Laura spotted any of them, she would have been upset.

As they reached the base of the hill, she heard soft music

provided by the small string ensemble. Today could not be more perfect—clear blue sky, the lush green of the golf course contrasting with the spectacular red Arizona cliffs, the peacefulness of the air hushed with anticipation.

Dani thought of Matt sitting near the front on Laura's side. She imagined his reaction when he saw her come over the hill, but she couldn't worry about that. All her attention had to be on her sister and making sure everything progressed smoothly.

She stopped and turned around. Everyone halted behind her, calm, many of them smiling. Laura peeked around from behind the group and gave her a thumbs-up.

"Here we go," she breathed.

Dani slowly walked up the hill, taking care on the strip of cloth covering the grass until she stood at the top. She had a few moments to take in the scene below her. All of Mariposa's staff had been invited, almost one hundred people, who sat on Laura's side of the altar. Opposite, Noah's guests consisted of his police colleagues. The reverend stood beside the podium talking to Noah and his best man while the string ensemble concluded the last song. The area was covered by a white canopy to keep out some of the heat. At the altar, an arch made of white flowers graced the front of the wedding aisle, and underneath it, on the left-hand side, a portrait of Laura's mother added the perfect finishing touch.

Matt sat in the first row. It made sense as he was Glenna's nephew and related by marriage. Beside him was Tallulah's nephew Mato and Greg Sumpter, the Coltons' private family attorney.

The conductor was watching her, waiting for her cue to begin. Taking a deep breath, Dani nodded.

As the music changed, the reverend looked up, then

moved to stand behind the podium, which alerted Noah and the guests. Everyone turned to watch the wedding party. Dani caught a brief glimpse of Matt's expression before focusing on the reverend.

She started down the hill, lifting the hem of her dress slightly to avoid tripping, keeping her gaze away from Matt. The bridesmaids and grooms followed, in sync with the chosen music for them.

Dani smiled. Everyone was here to celebrate Laura and Noah's happy-ever-after. She glanced around the crowd, hearing excited murmurs floating around her. When she reached the smiling reverend, she moved to the right to stand in front of Laura's section. She didn't have to look to know that Matt's gaze bore into her, but she refused to acknowledge him. The most important person was about to make an appearance.

When the bridesmaids and grooms took their seats, Dani nodded again to the conductor, who took the cue to begin the wedding song.

Everyone's attention was riveted on the hill until Laura, with Adam and Josh on either side of her, appeared at the top. Beneath the glorious Arizona sun and clear blue sky, she looked like an angel. A gentle wind brushed against her, lifting her veil so that it floated around her head like an aura.

Dani glanced at Noah, whose expression was one of stunned amazement as Laura slowly walked toward him. In front of the altar, Adam and Josh kissed Laura and shook Noah's hand before settling into the front row seats.

Noah never took his eyes off Laura as he reached for her hand and kissed her fingers. The love that flowed between them was electrifying as they approached the podium.

As the reverend began the vows, a coyote howled in the

distance. "Dearly beloved, let us gather here today to join this woman and this man in holy matrimony..."

As Dani listened to the reverend's deep, calm voice, she used the time to look around. On top of the hill, Roland and two of his security detail made an appearance. Roland nodded at her before he and his men turned and disappeared beneath the juniper trees. She saw silhouettes of other guards as they casually walked the perimeter. He had promised to be discreet so as not to upset Laura, and it looked like Roland was doing a fantastic job.

On Laura's side of the altar, Tallulah was crying, dabbing at her face constantly with a handkerchief. Dani fought the urge to look at Matt, knowing that if she did, she would grow upset and ruin the wedding. Instead, she returned her attention to Laura and Noah, who were reciting their handwritten vows to one another.

Laura began. "How lucky am I to call you mine. My husband, I invite you to share my life. Together, I know we can do anything. For all those times that we've been together, there's always been a mutual understanding that's only shared when two people love each other truly. I promise to be your friend and partner every step of the way. In your arms and by your side, I'm proud to call you my husband. I can't wait to work hand in hand to build a beautiful life together."

Damn it, she was going to start crying. Dani hadn't known what Laura wrote as her sister kept her vows a closely guarded secret.

Noah traced his fingers across Laura's cheek, and Dani swore she heard a collective sigh rise from the guests.

In return, he had his vows in hand and started to read. "My life is forever entangled with yours from this day on.

Today I join my life to yours, not simply as your husband, but as your friend, your lover and your biggest supporter. Together, we can weather any storm, no matter the season of our lives. You are the strength I didn't know I needed and the joy that I didn't know I lacked. I'm in awe of you, our bond and our potential. I promise to remain in awe while I cherish you for all the rest of our days."

Dani couldn't stop her tears, and dabbed at her eyes. Those vows meant everything Laura and Noah could ask from each other. She knew her participation was next, and managed to keep calm when the reverend asked her to step forward. "Whenever you're ready."

Damn, this meant more than just reading a piece of paper. "Everyone, I want to thank you for being here to share in Laura's and Noah's joyous occasion, and it means the world to us that you're here. I've been asked to share a poem to symbolize their love." She paused to gather herself, then read.

As you begin your new journey in life hand in hand, remember to keep space. What does this mean? Enjoy each other's company, yet allow yourselves to be alone. Love one another, but do not allow it to become a bond; instead, let love flow between you. Stand side-by-side, but not too close together. You are a married couple, and also two individuals. You are attracted by each other's uniqueness. Do not let that blend into one. Remain as you are, and create a new life both of you will enjoy.

Dani waited a moment as the words traveled over the hushed audience. "This is very much how life with someone you love should be lived. Congratulations."

Poor Laura was fighting to hold back the tears as Noah raised her hand to his lips.

The reverend finished the vows, rings were exchanged, and as soon as Laura and Noah kissed, everyone jumped up, shouting and cheering so loud that Dani could hear the echo bounce back from the sandstone cliffs.

DANI WAS A COLTON.

Matt stood by the entrance to the Annabeth Restaurant and watched as everyone congratulated the happy couple. Amongst them was Dani, looking gorgeous in her full-length halter dress. With her hair pinned up and smiling like that, it bothered him even more that he couldn't go up to her and...

Shit. He needed a drink, and there was plenty of it at the bar manned by Kelli and her staff.

"Hey there. I'll have a beer."

As he chugged the cold liquid down, a chorus of laughter filled the air. Matt walked the perimeter of the room, thinking how to approach the now very awkward situation. He decided instead to sit in a chair just beyond the group and finish his drink.

So, what the hell had happened these past few days? Had Dani always been aware of his relation to Aunt Glenna, and that he and Dani were related by marriage?

The thought bothered him a little, but not enough to put a hard stop to it. There was nothing really tying him and Dani together as relatives. It only happened that his aunt married Clive Colton, but he and Dani never grew up together. There was enough distance that if they decided to continue with a relationship, it wouldn't be a problem. At least not for him.

Dani's thoughts could be something else altogether.

Before he could even think about that though, he needed to know the truth from her. Why had she hidden her identity from him? Did she think he would only care about her family ties? Money?

He huffed out a bitter laugh. Matt supposed that was a viable excuse. What bothered him more was her continued silence about her ties to Adam and the others. She knew the wedding would expose her connections, so why wait until now?

He remembered their last conversation during dinner right here at the Annabeth Restaurant. Dani had been nervous, and with a flash of insight, he understood why. Her being upset when he told her he wanted to continue their connection after they left Mariposa. Not coming back to his bungalow last night. The way she avoided joining him in the golf cart. Never telling him her last name.

Dani had kept her true identity under wraps.

He felt like an idiot. There had been hints, but he never picked up on them. Why should he? He never thought that something more devious was going on.

So, why the deception? There was only one way to find out.

Dani had glanced over at him several times, and while he hadn't turned away, Matt hadn't felt encouraged to approach her. He wanted another drink but squelched the thought. Instead, he rose and wandered over toward Noah's colleagues, who were standing in a group by the bar. After a little while, Matt walked among the other guests and staff, chatting about the wedding and anything else that came to mind. He wasn't sure yet what he wanted to do, and with Dani keeping her distance, it didn't help with his decision.

Just as he made up his mind that he would talk to her after Noah and Laura took off for their honeymoon, she left the restaurant with the bridesmaids.

Matt sighed. Maybe the tension was too much for her. She had a lot to explain to him, and probably needed some air. He hoped she didn't plan on avoiding him until it was time to leave.

Matt didn't want to brood on that thought. He wove through the crowd until he reached the couple. "Congratulations." He shook Noah's hand and kissed Laura's cheek. "You look amazing, Laura."

"Thank you, I feel amazing." She leaned toward Noah and kissed him. "Especially with this guy beside me." Her eyes widened. "Oh! And your wedding gift was perfect. Noah and I will put it to good use during the honeymoon."

Noah frowned. "What did Matt get for you?"

Laura grinned. "Oh, don't you worry, you'll find out."

Matt fought to hold in his laughter as he watched Noah's perplexed expression. "You'll enjoy it, trust me," he confirmed.

They talked for a few minutes before another guest came over to congratulate them. Excusing himself, Matt found himself standing outside on the restaurant patio. The heat was like a living thing, slamming into him with a force that knocked the breath out of his lungs. It also helped to clear his mind.

He wanted to salvage what he and Dani had and not give up because Dani didn't explain who she was. Unless there was something more sinister on her end. But she would have to tell him what that was.

"Hi."

Dani. He turned, keeping his emotions in check. "Hi, yourself."

She stepped out onto the patio but didn't come close to him. It hurt, but he picked up that she needed some space. Also, she didn't know how he was feeling at the moment.

"It was a beautiful wedding," he started.

Her smile looked sad. "It truly was. I've never seen Laura so happy."

God, how he wanted to take Dani in his arms. "You look stunning."

That got a reaction. She looked at him, surprised, her brown eyes wide.

"It's true. You are one hot maid of honor."

Dani snorted. "I'm not sure if that's a thing."

"Doesn't matter, it's true." At least she was talking to him. He looked out over the meditation area to the golf course. "You know, I hadn't even thought to play a round of golf since I've been here." He smiled to himself. "Guess I was too distracted."

He heard Dani come closer. "Matt, I have to apologize, but I don't feel that it's enough."

He stuck his hands in his pockets and remained silent, waiting for her to continue.

"My family was in trouble. Glenna had been spreading awful rumors about the resort. When Noah arrested her for obstruction, it was Clive who bailed her out. Ever since, Josh told me weird things have gone on at Mariposa—accidents, bad ones. The one that scared us the most was the poisoned alcohol. Someone could have died."

He nodded as he started to put the pieces together.

"We felt sure Glenna had something to do with it, but we

had no proof." She sighed. "Adam thought, with you coming here for vacation, well…"

"That I might be helping my aunt with her schemes." It wasn't a question.

"It made sense to us. Glenna wasn't allowed to come back to Mariposa. When we found out you were invited to Laura's wedding, we also needed to keep an eye on you, just in case."

"And you were the lucky one who drew the short straw." Matt could have been angry. Instead, he felt a strange calmness, as if solving the puzzle offered him a sense of relief. He had already proven his innocence, so he had no regrets.

"I'd never met you. I guess when I come to visit, you would already be gone."

He saw her out of the corner of his eye, moving around until she stood in front of him. "My brothers and sister needed my help," she said, raising her chin. "And I would do anything for them. They're my family."

Matt looked over her head at the rugged landscape beyond. The next question was going to be the hardest, and he steeled his nerves. "What about us? Was all your undivided attention toward me part of the plan?"

"No!"

When he glanced down at her, he was surprised she was crying, though Dani made no sound. "My falling for you wasn't part of the package, Matt. That happened on its own."

Matt noticed the more emotional Dani became, the stronger her British accent grew. He swallowed the lump that clogged his throat. "So, you're saying…"

"I'm asking for your forgiveness. If you want to tell me to get lost, go right ahead—I won't bother you again, and I'll head back to England with my tail between my legs."

Her mouth quivered, but she seemed to keep herself under control. He realized that the guests were only feet away from them, and if her crying grew louder, they would hear. "Come on," he said, holding out his arm.

Dani linked her arm with his, and he led them out of everyone's view. "Did Adam tell you about my part in all of this?" he asked.

She nodded, wiping her eyes with a tissue. "Bloody well done."

"So, even though he updated you, you continued playing the spy game."

"I only found out yesterday that you were in the clear." She blew her nose. "Trust Adam to wait until the last minute to tell me. By then, I figured I may as well wait until after the wedding to talk to you." She paused. "If you wanted to talk to me."

Dani had given him space to think, to come to his own conclusions. She was willing to disappear from his life if he told her to leave him alone. She was a proud woman and stubborn as hell.

Damn, Matt loved that about her. "We're talking now," he said quietly, halting in the lobby. Chatter from the wedding guests filtered from the restaurant doorway just beyond.

She pulled away, a move he wasn't expecting. "You haven't said whether you'd forgive me or not," she accused.

He tried not to smile and failed. "Wasn't that obvious?" he teased.

Uh-oh. Dani's face screwed into a frown. "No, it wasn't bloody obvious, you—" she stuttered. "You pain in the ass!"

Crap, she looked ready to beat him up. "I forgive you!" he said loudly to make sure she heard him. "To be honest, there's nothing to forgive. If I was in your place, I would have done the same thing."

She calmed down, taking deep breaths. "Thank you."

Matt also wanted to clarify something else. "So, you really fell for me, huh?"

Dani bit her lip. "I wouldn't have said that if it wasn't true."

He approached her slowly until his chest brushed against hers. "Awesome," he breathed. "That makes two of us."

She huffed out a laugh. "You are impossible, Mr. Bennett."

"But I'm never boring, Ms. Colton." He placed a firm, decisive kiss on her lips. When he backed away though, her worried expression made him frown. "What is it?"

She twisted her hands together. "So, the fact that you and I are, um…"

"What? Oh, you mean family?"

She smacked his arm. "That sure as bloody hell doesn't sound right!"

Matt kept his laughter in check—Dani was serious. "We're not related. At all. Stop worrying. Has Adam or the others said anything?"

She chewed her lip again. "Laura seems to be on board with us."

"Adam? Josh?"

She shrugged. "The boys know I like you. The fact that they haven't said anything more about it…" She paused as if thinking.

"Then I say we have nothing to worry about." He held out his hand. "Shall we return to the party?"

Dani intertwined her fingers with his, her grip warm and secure within his own.

Suddenly, a small bell rung, echoing throughout the restaurant. "Everyone! If you could take your seats please!" Erica stood on a chair and shook the bell again. "Unfortunately we're on a tight schedule. Noah and Laura leave for their honeymoon tonight."

"Hey, Noah, you're not wasting any time, are you?" one of his friends yelled out.

The guests laughed and quickly found their seats. Matt sat at a table with a few of the bridesmaids and groomsmen, and joined in their conversation.

He discovered the reception would only be a few hours, as Laura and Noah hadn't wanted anything extravagant. They had wanted a simple wedding with the people they loved and cared about before starting their new life together.

The food was great and the company even better. Several toasts were offered to the couple. Dani and Noah's best man alternatively roasted and praised with stories that had his stomach hurting, Matt was laughing so hard.

Then Noah led Laura into a cleared area in the center of the restaurant. Surrounded by their friends and family, they danced to a beautiful melody whose lyrics mirrored their wedding vows. And when that was finished, Matt found himself caught in a wave of male bodies as they stood behind Noah, who was unbuttoning his jacket as Laura sat on a lone chair in the middle of the room. It was too late for him to back out, but Matt managed to dodge out of the way as the guys scrambled to snatch for Laura's garter belt that suddenly arced through the air.

He noticed Dani got swallowed in a sea of excited, screaming women as Laura got ready to toss her bouquet. Laura teased them, pretending to throw the wedding flowers several times until she finally released them. He watched in awe as the ladies maneuvered around each other like experienced rugby players, blocking and tackling until with a squeal of triumph. Kelli emerged victorious, the bouquet clutched tightly in both hands.

As Matt looked around, he noticed the Colton brothers, arms across each other's shoulders and fighting back tears while their sister's attention was fully on her new husband. Shit, they must be hurting.

He pursed his lips. Matt hardly knew what it was like to be loved. His mother had shut him out at an early age, and Aunt Glenna was no better after she adopted him. Realizing the Colton siblings had finally accepted him for who he was, despite his connection to his aunt, meant the world to him. And he would do everything in his power to help them and Mariposa get back on their feet.

Chapter Ten

Dani stood with the other guests and waved as Laura and Noah boarded the helicopter that would take them to Flagstaff Airport. Adam had splurged on a private jet as a wedding gift, which would fly the couple to Hawaii for their honeymoon.

As the vehicle whirled away, carrying her married sister off to a new life, Dani experienced a moment of panic. Dani had no idea what to expect next. She hadn't talked to Laura about what would happen when the honeymoon was over. Did she plan on returning to Mariposa to pick up where she left off? Or would Laura start a new journey as a cop's wife and live closer to Noah's work?

As the helicopter circled above them, the realization that Laura would be gone for two full weeks finally hit her, and Dani's chest squeezed painfully. Her siblings, once a tight-knit group, were now minus one. She and Laura had developed a special bond, and Dani knew it would never break, but now it felt like she had to take a step back and reevaluate her feelings. She had to remember she hadn't lost a sister—she had Laura and a new brother-in-law, who was pretty cool according to Josh. But their little family wouldn't be the same.

Dani admitted to herself that she was being selfish. If she was truly honest with herself, she was a little jealous too. She would need to figure out these new feelings.

"Hey."

She turned and saw Matt standing a few feet away, dark hair tousled by the hot Arizona breeze, his jacket slung over one shoulder and sleeves rolled up to expose muscular forearms.

"Hi." Dani wasn't sure what else to say. She wasn't really in the mood to talk.

"How are you holding up? You look sad."

"I do?" Had Matt been watching her? She wiped her face with both hands to get rid of the sweat and the tears. "I guess I am."

Everyone had started walking back to the parked SUVs, and she followed them, her steps slow.

"Dani." His hand brushed her arm.

"I'll be okay." She put on her best face. "Laura's found her forever guy. That's a great thing. We all needed something good to happen to us for a change."

He grasped her fingers, and Dani squeezed his hand, afraid he might disappear too.

"Are you up for meeting this Ken guy tonight?"

"Oh, man." She had told herself to call Ken after confirming with Matt that he would accompany her.

"We don't have to go."

"I want to get this over and done with, then we can spend our remaining time together."

He smiled. "I'm down with that."

Dani jumped when a car horn honked behind them. "Hey!" Josh called out. "You all coming or what?"

"Sorry!" She looked at Matt, making an impulsive decision. "Do you mind being with me when I make the call? I'm feeling pretty nervous."

"Sure. Give me twenty minutes to change out of these fancy clothes first, and I'll meet you in the lobby."

DANI STARED AT the resort phone in her living room as if it were some dangerous animal and realized she was scared. What if this man really was her uncle?

Matt's hand rested on her shoulder. "Easy peasy, just like we talked about. Talk to him a little then arrange a meet at the café we agreed on. Don't worry, I'm here."

She reached up and rubbed his hand. "Thanks."

Taking a deep breath, she dialed in the man's number quickly so she couldn't back out, then waited as it rang once, twice...

It clicked. "Hello, Dani?"

She opened her mouth, but words didn't come out. She cleared her throat and tried again. "Is this Ken? I got your message."

"Oh, thank God." She heard something that sounded suspiciously like crying. "I've been hoping you would call. Your aunt and cousins will be excited to know I finally got through to you!"

Dani glanced over her shoulder at Matt, who nodded. "Mom never told me anything about you."

"She and I never really stayed in contact with each other after she moved to Arizona. She visited a few times when you were a young child, but that was it."

Dani wondered how much information he could provide. "So you're saying you don't know what happened to her after she left me with Clive."

"Actually, I do. She had come to visit us afterward and

told us her plans. But I'd like to discuss that with you in person, not over the phone." A pause.

Glancing at Matt again, Dani felt a warmth of comfort settle over her like a plush blanket. Knowing Matt would accompany her gave her the courage to speak again. "Of course. I want to know everything about Mom."

There was silence on the other end, except for the muffled sound of traffic. "Hello?"

"I'm here." Sniffling. "Sorry, I'm just really happy that you want to meet me. Do you have a date in mind?"

"Actually, I'd like to meet you in about an hour."

"Really? Sure! I know a place in Sedona…"

"We've already decided on a coffee shop I know."

"We?" She heard the surprise in his voice.

"Yes. You didn't think I was going to meet you by myself, did you? I'm bringing a friend along."

"Um, okay. They might get bored with our chat."

"I doubt it. Matt is very attentive." She smiled up at him, and she felt his arm go around her waist. "We'll meet you at the Black Cow Café in an hour."

She hung up the phone, then turned around. "What do you think?"

He shrugged. "We won't know until we meet the guy and hear what he has to say. How are you feeling?"

She shrugged. "Flustered, nervous. But I'm leaning toward believing him. There's no way he could have the information he shared unless he was close to Mom."

"Guess we'll find out. Come on."

With a few minutes to spare, they walked toward the Black Cow Café, an older building of dark wood and stone. It looked like a saloon, which gave it a quirky atmosphere. Two wooden statues shaped like bald eagles stood on either side of the front entrance. As they entered the café however, they noticed the interior was very different.

"Wow, it reminds me of a fifties diner," Dani said as she looked around. It was a long narrow room, with a tiled floor and tables lined up against one side of the wall. On the opposite side, a large display counter held various pastries, along with an industrial size coffee maker and the cash register. The place was almost full, and the air was buzzing with chatter and Mexican instrumental music. Above them, ceiling fans kept the place cool against the evening heat.

"Their specialty is ice cream." Matt pointed at the back of the diner. "It's all homemade and they sell it through the window back there. Sometimes the lineups go around the block."

"I'd love to try it." She looked around and spotted someone sitting at a table, holding his hand up to get her attention. "That's him, from the donut shop." She took a deep breath. "Come on. The sooner I do this, the sooner we can get out of here."

Ken rose as they approached. He was tall, with a stocky build. He used a napkin to wipe his brow and bald head, and she remembered how his skin gleamed with sweat the first time she encountered him.

His dark brown eyes looked her over, and she unconsciously stepped closer to Matt. Now that she was here, uncertainty kept her rooted in place.

"Dani," he said. His voice was deep and commanding. "After all these years, I can't tell you how happy I am to see you." He held out his hand, large with thick fingers.

After a moment's hesitation, she grasped it. His grip was firm, but she sensed the strength behind it as well. "Ken."

She quickly released the handshake and stepped to one side. "This is Matt."

Dani watched with interest as the men sized each other up.

"A pleasure," Matt said, holding out his hand. She didn't think he meant it.

"Likewise." Ken frowned, thick eyebrows scrunched into a single line.

They shook once before Matt broke away first, but she knew it wasn't because he was afraid of the man.

They continued staring at each other. Damn it, she didn't need to deal with a standoff when all she wanted was to gather some information. She cleared her throat loudly. "Ahem. If you two don't mind…"

The men sat down. Dani scooted her chair closer to Matt's so that she could talk to Ken face-to-face.

"Would you all like something?" Ken raised his hand to get the server's attention.

"Cappuccino for me. And please, I'm buying." Matt looked at her. "What would you like, Dani?"

Her stomach felt tied up in knots, but maybe having something hot to drink would ease the tension. "A mocha latte please."

When the server left, Ken anchored both elbows on the table and rested his chin on his linked hands, his gaze fixed on her. "You really do look like your mother. You both have that same determined expression in your eyes."

Dani was trying to figure out how to start the conversation, but Matt beat her to it. "How about we cut the idle chitchat and get to what you want?"

Ken's eyes shifted to look at Matt with a mix of surprise and anger. "I wasn't talking to you."

"Okay, you know what? The both of you need to stop." Bad enough she was already on edge, but watching the two men glare at each other like two bulls propelled her to get the show on the road. "Matt, back down, please."

He made a face but sat back in his chair and stretched his legs out in front of him. Dani knew his relaxed posture was anything but.

"Ken, you too. Ease up. If the two of you start fighting, I'm walking out and not contacting you again."

In response, Ken did the same in sitting back but crossed his arms instead.

Men!

"Matt's right though. I'm not in the mood to talk about the weather." Dani kept her hands in her lap and sat straight up in her chair. "It's been what, almost twenty years, and you've decided to contact me now? I wonder why." She wanted to hear what Ken had to say.

"It's not like you were easy to find, you know," Ken said. "No email, phone number or address. I asked everywhere, including the staff at Colton Textiles. No one had any idea how to reach you."

It was true. When Dani had decided to leave the Colton household to study overseas, she needed to distance herself from her father. The only person who ever really contacted her was Josh, and he wouldn't give up her information that easily. "I wasn't happy with the situation I found myself in," she said quietly. "Mom left me behind with Clive, and I never heard from her again. She was the only one I cared for at the time." Tears perched on her eyelids but she refused to let them fall. "If she had mentioned you, I wouldn't remember, I was too young. As far as I was concerned, I had no relatives on her side." She frowned. "I'm still not convinced about you."

Ken nodded slowly. "I figured you would say that." He put a thin briefcase on the table. "I have some stuff to show you."

Their drinks arrived, and Dani took a healthy sip of her caffeinated drink to fortify her nerves. Anything could be in that case, but she wanted to keep an open mind. Because if everything Ken said so far was true...

He unsnapped the case and swung it open. "I have some family photos, documents, that kind of stuff to show you." He pulled out a large photograph and turned it around so that she could look at it.

Dani gasped. There were eight people in the photo, and they all bore striking resemblances to each other, from the facial structures to body shape. And there, standing in the middle, was her mother, and the little girl whose arms were wrapped around the mother's neck...

"This doesn't prove anything."

Startled, she looked at Matt, who stabbed the photo with a finger. "This could be a photo of friends for all we know."

Ken didn't say anything, but turned over the photo. On the back, names were written to help remember who was in the picture. It was dated and signed by Ken almost twenty years ago.

And there, under her mother's name, was the proof that couldn't be denied.

Danielle Curtis.

She looked at Ken, trying to figure out the new emotions that rampaged through her heart. Disbelief was being trampled by hope and joy. "I'm..." What could she say? "I'm gobsmacked."

Ken laughed. "That's one way of putting it." He put the photo back in his briefcase and pulled out another piece of paper—a birth certificate.

And there was her name, date of birth, and her mother's full name, which included her middle name—Helen. There was no way anyone could know that unless they were related.

"That was all I brought from LA. I didn't want to bring everything on the plane." He tossed the birth certificate back into his briefcase, and snapped it shut. "So, Dani, it's up to you what we should do next."

"I want to know more, of course." She took a deep breath as her nerves were on fire with excitement. Questions swarmed in her head to the point where she closed her eyes to get a mental grip on them. When she felt more composed, she opened them. "Have you heard from Mom?"

Ken's surprised look changed quickly to concern, and she felt her heart tighten with fear. Despite how she had been treated, Dani still held a tenuous tie with her mother. "What is it? Just give it to me straight."

Ken sighed. "Malia passed away almost six years ago."

She stared, processing the news. "What?"

He nodded. "Your mother decided to move to another country after giving you up to Mr. Colton. My wife and I argued with Malia about her decision, but she wouldn't listen. She said it would be best for everyone if she just left.

"All I had was her cell phone number. She would call me every couple of weeks to let me know where she was, until she eventually settled in Thailand. She bought a condo and gave me the address and suite number, and that was it. Never heard from her since, despite trying to reach her on the number she'd given me."

Dani bit the inside of her cheek, realizing how both she and her mother wanted to get away from Clive Colton. There was no way she could condemn Mom for making her decision, although knowing why a mother would abandon her daughter may have helped her come to grips with her mother's actions. "Did Mom say why she left me behind?" she managed to ask.

Ken shook his head. "All she said was that you would have a better life with Mr. Colton than with her."

"Do you believe that?" Matt demanded.

"I don't know what to believe!" she yelled. "I have nothing to go on, other than what I'm hearing from Ken, and right now, he's the only one who knows what happened to Mom." She understood Matt's disbelief, but Dani needed to know. "What else can you tell me? How did she..." She swallowed. "How did my mom pass away?"

Ken lowered his head. "When I had tried to contact her at the condo, her cell kept going to voicemail until it wouldn't take any more messages. I did some research and found the condo's property manager's phone number and called him to do a welfare check. That's when they found her in her suite."

Dani rubbed her chest, trying to ease the pain. Twenty years of not knowing anything about Mom or her extended family. "How did she...?"

"Heart attack. The doctor said she didn't suffer."

"And how did the landlord know you were next of kin?" Matt asked.

Ken's lips compressed into a thin line. "When the police arrived, they found my contact information in Malia's possessions."

Matt grunted but remained silent.

"I had no way to get in touch with you, Dani," Ken said again.

"I know, I know." The guilt wanted to build up inside her, but she refused to let it take over. Dani had also displayed that little bit of selfish desire to run away and hide from everyone. But she had been hurting too. Clive Colton was a manipulative, lying son of a bitch, who had treated her and her siblings like props. No love, no caring words, no comfort.

"Your grandparents passed away too. Last year." Ken rubbed his face with a hand. "I'm sorry, all I seem to have is bad news."

Dani had the urge to get up and walk out. She didn't know why—Ken hadn't offered her any hope, other than telling her she had some relatives living in Los Angeles. All of this talk of death when she had prayed she might see her mother again... Dani let the tears fall, fighting to keep her sobs locked within her. She didn't want to start bawling here, in public.

A strong warm hand covered hers. Matt.

She looked up at him, saw the sympathy in his warm, brown eyes, and almost lost it.

"I think you've told Dani enough," Matt said. "You've upset her and she needs time to process."

"Look, I'm sorry. I wish I had better news, but I thought..."

"It's okay." She swiped at the tears. "I'm glad you were persistent in looking for me. Now that I know about Mom, I can work on finding closure."

"Your grandparents were upset when they found out Malia left you with Mr. Colton. They were ready to march to his front door to get you back." Ken smiled. "They wanted to raise you themselves, but I told them Mr. Colton was your father and he had priority custody. They thought about you constantly."

She breathed out a loud sigh. "You know, if your plan was to make me feel guilty, it's sort of working. But I'm also annoyed because you've spent this whole time being negative. My mom's dead, my grandparents are dead." She stopped worrying she might say something she'd regret. "How about some good news for a change?"

Ken rubbed his bald head. "I guess I have been a bit of downer, huh?"

"That's an understatement," Matt grumbled quietly.

Ken frowned. "I'm not sure I like you."

"Ditto."

"Okay, enough," she said. Matt's demeanor resembled a wolf, all bristly and growling. Under other circumstances, Dani might have considered it a turn-on. "I do want to thank you for finally getting in touch with me and letting me know about Mom." It was a chapter Dani could finally conclude in her life. "Did she have any personal belongings? I'd like to take a few things with me when I head back to England."

Ken shook his head.

"No jewelry or clothing?" She was a bit surprised.

"We decided to sell or donate her things." He tapped the briefcase. "I do have some other photos, but they're all at my house."

"Oh." It wasn't quite the answer she expected. "Well, thank you for looking after her estate." Dani didn't know what else to say, so she got up. Matt followed quickly behind her. "We have each other's numbers, so let's stay in touch."

"There is something else I'd like to talk to you about."

Dani felt the hairs rise on the back of her neck, and

couldn't understand the sudden jolt of wariness that came over her.

"Please." Ken indicated for her to sit down again.

She did, slowly. "Is something wrong?"

He rubbed his face. "My wife—your Aunt Carol—is in the hospital. She has cancer."

Dani pursed her lips. "I'm sorry."

"She's been asking for you since Malia and the grandparents passed away. She wanted to know if you were all right."

"You can tell her I'm fine…"

"She wants you to come and visit. My wife insisted that once I found you, you should come and see us."

Dani didn't know how to take this sudden bit of news. "Maybe after my vacation, I can call you and arrange a short visit before going back."

"I hope you can spend more than a few days with us." Ken leaned forward, smiling. "We really want to get to know you better."

Something felt off about this family request. Dani should have been excited to meet her mom's side of the family. But Ken seemed a little too insistent. "I have a job waiting for me back in England," she replied. "I have to be back by a certain date. I'm not going to mess that up."

"Yeah, sure, I understand. It just seems odd you're working a full-time job when you're a Colton."

She knew her face expressed disbelief. "What's that got to do with anything?"

"Well…" He made a show of smoothing his beard with his fingers, "…the Coltons are old money. I would have thought you wouldn't need to work at all. Just ask your old man for whatever you wanted, and he'd give it to you."

"In case you haven't been listening," Matt interjected, "Dani doesn't operate like that."

"I only heard that she's starting a new job," Ken shot back. "Did Mr. Colton pull some strings for you? I'll bet he did, that's what he's famous for."

Their conversation had changed drastically, and not for the better. She needed to leave. "He didn't help me with anything," she started to say, but Ken interrupted her.

"You probably have a nice, fat bank account to help get you on your feet in your new job," he snarled, "while I had to work two jobs to make ends meet and pay my wife's medical bills."

She closed her eyes as the room started to tilt. "How was I to know?" she whispered.

"You do now. If you want to help, some money would be appreciated to get the proper care my wife needs. Medical bills are awful in the US, but *you* wouldn't know that."

"Enough!" Matt slammed his fist on the table, making the dishes jump. "Was this your game all along? To extort money out of Dani by putting her on a guilt trip? Are you for real?"

"Why the hell should you care?" Ken shouted. "You all are staying at a posh resort while I'm scraping money together to keep my wife alive!"

Dani couldn't take it anymore. Her hopes of getting to know her uncle better had dissolved into a demand for money. "I need to go," she said to Matt. Her body shook with dread.

As she stood, Ken mirrored her movements and loomed over her. His hand shot out and grabbed her arm. "You're not going anywhere until I'm finished."

She wanted to scream in anger, but didn't need to. Matt

had immediately wrapped his fingers around Ken's wrist. "Let her go," he demanded.

"Oh, so you're a tough guy, huh?"

As Dani watched, Matt pried Ken's fingers from her arm until she got free, then stood behind him. He didn't cause a scene but kept his grip on Ken. "Touch her again, and you'll regret it," he warned in a quiet, menacing voice.

Ken jerked on his arm, but Matt's grip was like steel. "You going to let me go, or do I have to get angry?"

"Matt, please." She rested a hand on his back. "It's not worth it."

He looked at her, his gaze warm and concerned. "For you, anything," he whispered.

He suddenly released Ken, which made the older man stumble and fall back into his chair. "This meeting was quite the eye-opener," Matt said. "Let's hope Dani doesn't see you again."

She looked over her shoulder as Matt led her out of the café, his hand on the small of her back. Ken brooded at the table, his dark gaze fixed on her.

"Are you all right?"

She shook her head. Did her mother know Ken was like this? Money hungry, demanding handouts? Is that why Mom left the country? "I had hoped to get to know Ken and his family, but now..." she let the rest of her thought fade away.

"It's just my opinion, but I think you have all the family you need in your siblings," Matt said quietly, kissing her forehead.

KEN CURTIS WAS a man with a plan. And he planned on making Dani Colton pay.

He didn't hate the girl—no, nothing like that. But she

had connections to a lot of money, and his family could use some of it to elevate their living.

So what if he lied about his wife. Sure, she was sick, but Carol didn't have cancer, thank God. He didn't know what he'd do if that were true.

He watched as Dani and her boyfriend left the café. If she had been on her own, Ken felt sure he could have persuaded her to offer some cash for his family's well-being. That man, however—Matt. Ken realized quickly that Dani's boyfriend was a guy not to be messed with. He'd been very protective, but listened when Dani asked him to stop his harassment.

He wasn't sure how to use that information, but he'd think of something.

Ken tossed some bills on the table and headed out, breathing in the clean, cool evening air. He could get used to living here. The heat could be intense, but he loved how dry the air was. It would certainly help with his kids' asthma.

When Malia had told him she had demanded that Mr. Colton marry her, he'd been elated. His little sister was always thinking of ways to better her family situation, and marrying a Colton would have certainly done that. Ken wasn't exactly poor, but he was always on the lookout to find ways of making money.

His hotel was several blocks away, and he decided to walk the distance. Exercise always made him think better.

When Malia had given him the bad news that Mr. Colton wouldn't make her his wife, Ken had been pissed. He hadn't revealed his displeasure, worried that Carol would pick up on it and chew him out. Unlike him, she preferred to earn money the honest way by working hard. Yeah, sure, if a person could find a decent job in Los Angeles that paid six figures, but he did not have that.

The main street was quieter than he expected. Sedona didn't quite have the unique vibe of his California hometown, but it also didn't have the crowds, the homeless and no doubt the homicide rate was a whole lot lower. Yeah, he could live here…

He suddenly stopped, realizing he had already arrived at his hotel. It was a small two-story building, farther away from the downtown core. It was also cheaper, but it was clean and functional.

He went to his room, popped the thin briefcase into the safe and then headed down to the hotel bar. Several tables were occupied when he arrived, and he sat at one closest to the window. He enjoyed watching people and the life that walked by.

He ordered a beer, then went over his unsuccessful conversation with Dani. He had really screwed things up. Her boyfriend was shrewd and arrogant, a dangerous combination if not handled properly. Ken had tried to balance putting enough guilt on the Colton girl to coerce her into providing him with money, versus setting off any alarm bells with this Matt guy.

That hadn't worked out too well.

The other problem he should have controlled? His temper. As he watched his opportunity of ingratiating himself into Dani's life dwindle, he had become more desperate. Her refusal to discuss the matter further had set him off, and he reacted badly. If her boyfriend hadn't stopped him, Ken might have done something really stupid.

So, in a way, Matt had saved him from making a very bad mistake.

"Unreal." He shook his head, then took a long sip of the cold brew. Now he had to figure out how to get in touch with Dani again.

How long would she be at Mariposa? It was sheer luck that, as he researched attempts to contact Dani, he discovered Laura Colton was to be married at the resort. Taking a risk, he had flown down, and after a few discreet inquiries, found out Dani would be there. The wedding had happened this morning, which meant he probably had a day, maybe two, to convince his niece to talk to him again.

Right. He would leave her another voicemail message tonight, asking for forgiveness and another chance. And he had just the incentive waiting patiently in his hotel room safe.

Chapter Eleven

Dani spread a bit of caviar across a cracker, then popped it into her mouth. "It took me awhile to acquire a taste for this," she mumbled between chewing. "Adam used to make fun of me for it."

She and Matt were in his bungalow, sitting at a small table in front of the floor-to-ceiling windows. They were open to let in the cool night air, with the screen doors closed to keep out the multilegged wildlife. Beyond the bungalow's circle of light, the Arizona landscape lay in complete darkness. It was so quiet she heard the low hoot of an owl. Occasionally, a breeze would hit her skin, making her shiver.

"I remember Aunt Glenna buying it for my twenty-first birthday." Matt had just finished his portion. "One of the few things she did that I liked."

She pursed her lips. "Bringing her into the conversation had not been my plan."

"How could you know?" He reached for the glass of champagne and sipped it. "This is excellent. I'm glad you begged the chef to give us what they had left before they closed for the night."

"I was starving, even after eating at the wedding reception." She put some smoked salmon on her plate, then proceeded to smear cream cheese on a few blinis before stacking the fish on top. Dani had wanted to eat in Sedona after her meeting with Ken, but her so-called uncle had put a serious kink in her idea. All she could think of was getting away from him.

"If I were you, I'd stay away from that Uncle Ken of yours."

Dani frowned. She knew Matt meant well, but she wasn't sure how to take the sudden change in his voice.

"I'm not joking, Dani."

"Obviously. You don't think I can look after myself."

"Dani." He blew out a loud sigh. "I didn't mean to sound bossy, but that guy rubbed me the wrong way."

"You think? Couldn't miss that sign." She chewed the salmon, not really tasting it. Ken had provided the proof she needed that he was related to her, something she couldn't ignore no matter what Matt said. Although, as she thought on it, Ken sort of acted the same way as Glenna, judging by her siblings' horror stories. Maybe Matt was reacting to that by being defensive.

It didn't matter. When she had returned to her bungalow to get changed, there had been a message from Ken, apologizing for his behavior and hoping they could meet again. Dani had already decided on the drive back that she wanted to see her uncle, and his voicemail sealed her decision. She needed to know more about Mom, her grandparents, Ken and his family. What was their family background, and were there other relatives? Anything to give her a solid understanding of who Mom was and, by extension, herself. Now that she was older, Dani could maybe sympathize with her mom's behavior. She had no idea what Mom went through. Did she regret giving up her daughter? Did

Clive have something to do with it? She'd never know unless she talked to Ken.

She would call Ken first thing in the morning, which meant leaving Matt to wonder where she'd gone. She hated sneaking around.

"Look, I'm sorry. But he just gave off the wrong vibes."

"I wasn't happy about how he acted at the coffee shop either. But he's my uncle, Matt. If he has any more information on my mom, I want to know about it."

He looked irritated. "I don't know what else he could tell you. All he did today was prove he wanted money from you."

"I think he might have told me more, but you acted like a bloody grizzly bear." Dani appreciated Matt being with her—she had no idea what she could have walked into. But Matt's gruff and cold demeanor had put Ken on alert.

"I had every reason to." He finished his champagne.

Dani suspected there had been more documents in Ken's briefcase—she had seen some papers but couldn't read the writing. Her instinct told her there was more to Ken's initial visit than just reviving family ties, and while understanding Matt's concern, she had to find out the rest.

With her mind made up, Dani changed the subject. She sipped her drink, eyeing him. "Shall I assume that inviting me to your bungalow means you'd like me to stay overnight?"

Matt blushed a deep red. "That wasn't my intention."

He looked so cute when he was embarrassed. "Oh, my apologies." She wanted to tease him a bit. "I'll make sure to leave when we're finished."

"Dani…" he stuttered. "If you want to stay, I'd like that."

"Are you sure I won't interrupt your beauty rest? Or any

nighttime activities you indulge in before bed?" She couldn't hold back her laughter.

He cocked an eyebrow. "Such as?"

Oh, he was trying to catch her off guard. "Video games," she replied while trying to keep an innocent expression fixed on her face.

Matt tried to look insulted, but it wasn't working, and he burst out laughing. "And you call *me* naughty," he said, imitating her by wagging his finger. "What the hell?"

She giggled. "Teasing you is so easy. The look on your face just now was priceless."

"Oh, now I get it. Making fun of me at my cost." He rose from the table, and Dani couldn't figure out the smirk that lit up his features. "Well, Ms. Colton, turnabout is fair play."

"What are you—" She squealed and shrank in her seat as Matt started tickling her. "Oy, quit it!"

His hands were all over her now, and Dani couldn't catch her breath, she was laughing so hard. "All right, all right, I give up! Stop!"

Matt stepped back. "Now you know better than to make fun of me."

She waggled a hand. "Maybe."

He moved as if to tickle her again, but she dodged beneath his outstretched arms and ran for the bathroom.

Strong arms caught her just as she reached for the doorknob and picked her up. "Just where do you think you're going?" he demanded.

Dani tried to get away, but he had a strong grip on her. "How about I show you one of the nighttime indulgences I enjoy the most?" he whispered, his breath hot against her cheek. He started walking toward the bedroom, still carrying her in his arms.

"I'm picky about my games," she threw back at him. Once inside, he put her down, and she turned around.

"I think you'll like this one." He pulled his T-shirt over his head and she watched as it flew across the room.

The lighting in here was brighter, letting Dani ogle the defined muscles of his upper body. She couldn't help herself and reached out, letting her hands travel over his warm skin. She trailed her fingers down toward what caught her interest, but he gently grabbed her wrist.

"Sorry, but if you keep teasing me like this, I'm not sure how much I can hold still."

Dani managed to use her other hand to caress his erection, and he jumped, his eyes widening with surprise. "I'm afraid I can't help myself," she crooned, rising on tiptoe to kiss him.

Matt's arms wrapped around her in a crushing grip, and he tilted his head to deepen their kiss, his tongue lavishing her mouth. He finally backed away, and she inhaled deeply to get air into her lungs. His gaze was intent, dark, mysterious.

She wriggled out of his grasp, her own patience wearing thin, and stripped out of her own shirt and bra. She was surprised by how comfortable she felt in front of him as he gazed at her breasts. Feeling cocky, she placed her hands on her hips. "Well? Do you like what you see?"

"I've always liked looking at you." His voice had lowered to a soft growl. In two steps, he was in front of her, his hands caressing every inch of her exposed skin.

She held her breath when his thumbs grazed across her nipples. "Matt," she said softly, arching her body into his warm hands.

He lowered his head and licked her neck, making her

cry out, before he swept her up and laid her on the bed. He crawled over her, rubbing himself against her until she squirmed with impatience. "What's taking you so long?" she demanded, grabbing his shoulders.

His grin was wicked. "Say please."

Damn him and his teasing. "Come on!"

He rose from the bed. "Try again." He went into the bathroom, hopefully to grab a condom.

When did she become so engrossed with getting her hands on Matt? She had certainly enjoyed the first time they made love, but here she was asking for more, and Matt telling her to be polite about it.

She snickered, enjoying the joke. She heard movement, slipped her panties off, and turned onto her side as Matt revealed his fully naked self, a condom held in one hand. "You like to make a grand entrance, don't you?" she accused.

"Just trying to impress."

Dani giggled. "Why don't you come over here and impress me? Or are you stunned into shock by my beauty?"

She wanted to keep their chatter light and playful, yet she noticed a shift in Matt's expression. He seemed thoughtful, and she noticed the change in his movements as he slipped the condom on and got into bed beside her. "Hey, what's up?" she asked. "Besides your friend down there, I mean."

He burst out laughing. "I love how you put me in a good mood."

She bit her lip. "You weren't before?"

"Of course I was. Having you around always cheers me up."

"Well then, get over here."

Matt hovered above her, trailing hot kisses down her body as she squirmed beneath him, her skin slick with sweat.

He caressed her thighs with firm strokes, making her gasp with anticipation, but when he spread her legs, she suddenly tensed.

"It's okay," he soothed, continuing to stroke her legs until she finally started to relax. Dani wasn't sure what to expect, and when Matt's tongue touched her most sensitive skin, she arched off the bed, her fingers digging into the sheets. Heat gathered in her belly, and Dani's soft moans rose as Matt continued to drive her closer to release. She wrapped her fingers in his hair, writhing beneath his hot mouth until her body suddenly tightened with her orgasm. Dani rode on its glorious wave before relaxing down onto the bed, sweaty and in bliss.

Matt crawled up to lie beside her, propping himself up on one elbow. "That was a nighttime indulgence I'll never grow tired of."

Dani huffed out a laugh. "Good to know." Despite that amazing orgasm, she still wasn't satisfied. She reached for him, giving him a deep kiss that made her think of nothing else.

Matt got the hint, crawling on top of her, then paused.

"No need to wait," she breathed, wrapping her legs around his waist.

He pushed slowly into her, and Dani released her breath in a low hum of desire as she started to move, emptying her mind of everything except Matt, inhaling his scent and tasting his skin. She wanted to make this last, just hang on a little longer, but her body had other ideas. She held on tight as Matt increased their pace, the sounds of their lovemaking so intense she couldn't help herself and cried out as her body spasmed.

Matt held her tighter, his groan loud in her ear as he trembled from the force of his own release.

They didn't move. Dani had thought the first time was amazing, but this… "Bloody hell, Matt, are you a wizard? Magician?"

He chuckled and slowly shifted his weight until he was beside her. His kiss was tender, soft. "Not that I know of."

"Well, I think you've put a spell on me." Dani never thought she would enjoy lovemaking so much.

"Funny, I was sort of thinking the same thing," he said, a slight frown marring his features.

Dani pursed her lips but remained quiet. Instead, she curled up against him. She didn't want to think about anything—their inevitable departure from Mariposa, the possibility she might not see him again. She only wanted to think of what they had right now, in this moment.

She would learn to deal with the heartache. She had a lot of practice with Mom and Clive.

"Where are you going so early?" he asked.

"I need to talk to Adam about something. He's an early riser, and I'd like to catch him before he gets busy." She finished getting dressed. "I'll talk to you later?"

"You'd better."

Seeing Matt lying on the bed still drowsy with sleep, Dani had to fight the urge to jump back in with him. She gave him a quick kiss, grabbed her things, slipped on her sandals and headed out to the golf cart. Seeing Adam *was* part of today's plan, but not until much later.

She was going to invite Ken to the resort for breakfast, and she needed the time and space for them to talk without Matt hovering over her like a hawk. She had lied to Matt again, which riddled her with guilt, but if she had told him her plans, Matt would have voiced his displeasure, and she didn't need that.

However, she didn't want to meet her uncle at her bungalow. Instead, she was going to host him at the Annabeth Restaurant, if he was willing to come on short notice. She wanted him mentally off balance if possible.

She made the call from her room. He actually picked up on the second ring. "Hello, Dani."

"Good morning. I wanted to ask if you'd like to meet for breakfast."

A pause. "I'm pretty sure I can swing it. Where do you want to meet?"

"At the resort."

"Mariposa?" Another pause, and Dani imagined hearing the wheels turning around in his head. "I thought it was guests only."

"I can make exceptions. Are you interested or not?"

"Yeah, yeah, I can come over. Should be there in about an hour?"

"Works for me. Oh, and bring whatever pictures and documents you have of Mom and our family. I'd like to spend time talking to you about them. We won't be bothered."

"You bet. See you soon." The phone clicked off.

Dani stared at the receiver, wondering if she had made a mistake, but tossed the thought aside. She had the impression Ken was just as eager to learn more about her, so they would spend the morning going through as much information as possible.

She got changed, slipping into a pair of linen pants and pulling a golf shirt over her head. Tying her hair back into a ponytail, Dani stared for a moment at the mirror. She had done the best she could with her life, and she didn't regret any of it. Mom could have been more thoughtful and tried to stay in contact with Dani after leaving, but she hadn't bothered. Funny, that still stung after all these years, and she took in a slow breath as her chest constricted with the pain of loss.

Maybe Ken could offer some insight into her mother's decision to leave her only child behind.

She thought about calling Adam. If she told him what she was doing, he'd insist on being there with her, and she didn't want that—not yet anyway. And being in the restaurant meant the staff would be around, so she wouldn't be completely alone. Dani compromised and texted Adam, saying she had an important meeting and would update him when it was finished.

Feeling a bit better that she wasn't being completely secretive around her siblings, Dani headed out, arriving at the main lobby within minutes. Ken would have to come through the front gates and arrive here at the reception area, so she sat to one side of the lobby. It was too early for Alexis to arrive, so she had the area to herself. Dani could hear staff talking in the nearby restaurant, along with the clatter of dishes as they prepared the Annabeth Restaurant for the morning service.

Dani was normally patient, but the tension of seeing Ken again made her get up and pace the length of the lobby, which also made her start thinking about what else he might tell her.

Although she understood Matt's trepidation in seeing Ken again, she couldn't ignore the fact that this man was her mom's brother. He had provided more than enough solid proof that she could no longer doubt him.

She wondered why he wanted to meet again—his cryptic message had been too vague to figure out. Sure, he wanted them to get to know each other—that much was obvious—yet Dani also couldn't ignore the tiny bit of doubt that nibbled at her consciousness. He hadn't made any effort in contacting her since Mom dropped her off with Clive. Though she kept her life private, Ken could have approached her siblings with his evidence that he was indeed her uncle. Mariposa and its owners were public knowledge.

But he hadn't. And his aggressive attitude toward her had been a warning that she should probably give up on this. Matt certainly believed so.

Why had Ken waited so long after her mother died before appearing? That was six years ago, according to him. A very long time to wait. However, Dani thought, would she have wanted to be in contact with her mother's family? Mom left her behind with Clive and never made any attempt to stay in touch—Ken and his family had done the same. Dani shouldn't care.

She halted and wiped her face with her hand. But she did care, probably too much. Dani had no idea she possessed another set of family members, and it didn't seem right to just ignore them. She could at least get to know Ken a bit better, maybe meet his family in the near future. If they turned out to be less than desirable, then she would forget about them and get on with her own life. Maybe Matt was right—that Adam, Laura and Josh were all the family she needed.

God, she wished Matt was here. But his instant animosity toward Ken would prevent her having a decent conversation without judgment. Dani, on the other hand, could keep her emotions in check, since she had plenty of experience while living with an emotionless father and somewhat depressed siblings.

She checked her watch—Ken should be arriving any minute. Dani had insisted on meeting him at Mariposa, as she wanted people she knew surrounding her and he would be on her turf. No way was she going to agree to seeing him in town with no backup. Thankfully, Ken hadn't argued about the arrangements, giving her breathing room and time to think on what they would talk about. If Ken had additional information, she believed he would share it more easily with no other people around.

"Morning, Dani."

Dani had been so engrossed in her thoughts that she hadn't heard him come into the lobby. She turned quickly, spying him just inside the entrance. "Hi," she called out, and glanced at her watch—he was right on time. "Hopefully the drive up here was okay."

"Nothing I can't handle."

As he walked farther inside, she was struck by his stocky build, now that she had a chance to get a closer look at him. Add in his rude personality traits, and Dani knew he would try to intimidate her despite her fighting tooth and nail against it. She had made the right call in having him come here.

"Look, I'd like to apologize again for being rude yesterday." He took a step toward her. "I was feeling a bit anxious in meeting you, and your boyfriend got me riled up. I'm not usually like that."

She nodded, but Ken's behavior at the cafe had raised a red flag she wouldn't easily forget. "I understand. I've ordered breakfast for us." She led the way.

In the Annabeth Restaurant, everything had been set up

for the morning service. Two servers waited near the front entrance. "Morning, Dani." Billy greeted her.

"Morning." She led the way to a table beside the floor-to-ceiling windows that overlooked the pool and sat down.

"Fancy place." Ken sat opposite her and looked around. "Must be nice to stay in accommodations like this for free."

If he was trying to goad her, it wasn't going to work, but she would remain polite. "That's an assumption on your part."

He raised his brows. "Your siblings don't let you have free rein? That's cheap of them."

"No, it's business."

Billy came over and laid out their meal.

When he left, Dani continued. "Speaking of business…"

"Ah, not wasting any time, are you?" Ken started eating without acknowledgment, and she noticed how he took his time, remaining silent as he cleaned off his plate like some starving man. "Got any seconds?" he asked, then burped loudly.

Dani knew her face showed her distaste as she asked Billy to bring over another plate. She started to eat, pointedly ignoring Ken while he watched her.

"The silent treatment. I get it."

"Turnabout is fair play," she replied, using Matt's phrase. She kept eating as a second breakfast was set before her uncle.

"What did you want to talk about?" she finally asked. For some reason, Dani was suspicious that reminiscing about family ties wasn't the only thing on his agenda.

"I wanted to apologize in person for my behavior."

Dani knew her face betrayed her incredulity. "Excuse me?"

He moved the dishes to one side and propped his arms

on the table. "I was an asshole to you yesterday. I honestly wanted to get to know you during our first chat, but your boyfriend…"

"Let's not blame Matt for the argument," she interrupted. "You had something to do with it as well."

Ken had the grace to bow his head. "Let's talk more about your mom and grandparents." He picked up his briefcase. "I brought more pictures like you asked."

The opportunity to see more of her mom and the family she never knew about tugged at her soul. "Yes, please."

With their table cleared of dishes, Ken pulled out a couple of photo albums and a folder. "We'll start with this one," he said, opening it up.

Dani's emotions tangled within her as she gazed upon her mother's smiling face. She was young in this photo.

"That's Malia just before she graduated college," Ken started. "She wanted to work in human resources."

"What happened?" Dani asked.

"She found a job at a start-up tech company. It paid really well too, but after about a year, Malia quit. She didn't tell us why. Then next thing we knew, she decided to take a job as head housekeeper." He looked at her. "At Mariposa."

Dani was stunned. Why would her mother change her mind and accept what some would call a menial job after completing all of that education?

"The only explanation I can think of," Ken said, as if reading her mind, "was that Mr. Colton convinced her to take the job."

"How in bloody hell could Clive have done that? He would have had to get to know her first."

"Maybe she met him through a friend of hers? Bumped

into each other at a coffee shop? Saw the job in a newspaper? I have no idea, and Malia never explained herself to us."

Dani never had the impression her mother was unpredictable. Calculating, yes, but not unpredictable. "I think there's more to it," she said, staring at her mom's photo. What she refused to tell Ken was that she had fragmented memories of her young life. She remembered playing with her doll as a little girl while Mom talked to people, and following her mother around as she went through her workday. She also remembered Clive, who terrified her at the time. But the memory that had stuck with her all these years was the bitter argument Mom had with Clive. Dani had hidden beneath her bed as the yelling intensified, followed by awful noises that still reverberated in her mind even now.

"Maybe, but we'll never know."

He flipped through the rest of the album, giving Dani an emotional tour of her family members. She placed her hand on a photo of a middle-aged couple.

"Your grandparents moved to the States from St. Lucia. Like everyone else, they wanted to make a better life for their kids. They did all right."

She thought of the struggles they must have encountered while establishing themselves in a foreign country. Dani knew, with a bitter taste in her mouth, that she had avoided a lot of the red tape involved when she relocated to England, all because she was related to the Colton dynasty. "Where do you work?" she asked.

He laughed. "I had a variety of jobs. I couldn't stay put in one for long." He ticked his fingers. "Construction, delivery, private investigator, ship's officer. I was in the Navy for a bit in my twenties."

"And now?"

"Property manager. I have a few businesses under my belt, which means there's always something different going on. I like it because I do it on my own time, as long as the buildings are taken care of and serviced. It's not boring." Ken smiled. "Yet."

She nodded. "I'll be working for an advertising firm when I go home. It's exciting, but eventually I'd like to have my own business."

"Nothing wrong with that." He closed the first album. "Maybe your old man will help you with that."

Dani's hands clenched with a will of their own. "I don't know why you think Clive will help me," she gritted out between clenched teeth. "When I left the States, he hadn't offered to provide any support, not that I would take it. And even though I was only a kid at the time, I saw how he treated Mom. He wasn't a nice man."

Ken stared at her. "Did you know your mother wanted to marry Mr. Colton?"

Dani gasped in shock. "You're lying."

He shook his head. "Malia told us she'd been in a long-term relationship with Mr. Colton until his wife passed away. She came to visit us and brought you along. You were just a kid at the time. Malia assumed he would marry her."

"But he didn't."

Dani watched as Ken's face displayed his anger and frustration. "I guess old man Colton didn't think my sister was good enough for him. I wanted to call him out on it, but Malia refused to have me involved. But I also knew she was shrewd. She planned on embarrassing him in public. Seems that Coltons can have affairs, but in secret. She was going to risk her reputation by telling the media she had been Clive Colton's mistress."

Dani bit the inside of her cheek. She didn't know her mother very well like Ken did, but for some reason, that type of retaliation didn't ring true. But what did she know? "What happened?"

"At the time, I hadn't heard from Malia in almost two weeks, which freaked out all of us. By the time she finally called, she said that she was quitting her job and moving overseas."

What a strange sense of déjà vu, how Dani and her mom left the United States because of a Colton. "And that's when I started living with Clive." She smacked the table with a fist. "Damn you, Mom, why didn't you take me with you?" She wanted to cry, but the emotion refused to reveal itself, as if it weren't the right reaction. Instead, Dani turned her head to find Ken watching her.

"Your grandparents fought for custody, but they had no chance of winning against Clive Colton." Ken snorted his disgust. "I told them they were going to bankrupt our family if they didn't stop. Of course, Mr. Colton promised to have you visit us, which didn't happen. And my guess is that he didn't tell you anything about us or what had happened."

"The only thing he told me when I was old enough to understand was that Mom abandoned me, and he took me in." She had learned, though, as she reached her teenage years, that Clive was a lying, scheming son of a bitch.

Ken closed the photo album and put it back in his briefcase. "That's not the full story."

"What?" she yelled, then bit her lip, glancing over her shoulder. If the staff heard her, they didn't acknowledge it, but she knew they'd jump into action if Ken did anything stupid. Their loyalty was what made Mariposa such a unique place. "What are you talking about?"

"Let me show you the rest of the photos first," he replied, opening the second album.

This contained more pictures of her grandparents, mother, Ken, aunts and cousins. She gazed at the celebrations, the birthdays, having fun at the beach, sports events. Dani envied their lives, the fun they obviously had as a family.

"Thank you for showing these to me," she said softly.

"No problem." When he placed the album into his briefcase, Dani spied the lone folder. "What's in there?"

Ken placed a hand over it. "You think your mother abandoned you. That's only half true. Mr. Colton made her a deal for her silence. We pleaded with her not to take it, but…"

The tension was becoming too much for her. "But what?"

He rubbed his hand across his head. "When Malia had called us to say she was leaving, she said that Mr. Colton offered her a substantial sum of money, enough to get away from the States and live life on her terms."

Dani couldn't swallow past the lump in her throat. "Mom abandoned me for a bribe."

"I told you, these Coltons have a lot of power. Malia must have realized she couldn't fight against it, despite us telling her she had to, for your sake." He opened the folder. Inside it were various papers which he shuffled through. "But I think Mr. Colton had been really nervous that my sister would blab to the press, so he offered her these too."

When he turned the two pieces of paper around for her to read them, Dani's body suddenly went cold with dread.

Sitting in front of her were color photocopies of two stock certificates belonging to Colton Textiles. They were certified to Clive Colton with the address of their family home in California, signed by an officer of the company and registered with a unique ID number.

"How the bloody hell did you get your hands on these?" she demanded.

Ken's smile was cold. "I told you Malia was shrewd. She wanted a piece of the man who refused to marry her. Money comes and goes, but Colton stock…she knew they were worth a lot at the time. In her will, she left them to me."

Dani stared at the two pieces of paper, her mind whirling. With these certificates, Adam, Laura and Josh could own the majority of Colton Textiles, and the land that Mariposa stood on. They could finally be free of their conniving father and vindictive Glenna…

Wait a minute. "Ken, did you just say that Mom left these certificates to you in her will?"

"Yeah." He smoothed his fingers over the paper. "Guess my little sister was looking out for us after all."

Something wasn't ringing true with her. "What about me? Was I mentioned at all? Do you have a copy of Mom's will in that folder?" she asked. "I'd like to see it."

Ken made a show of putting the photocopies back in the folder, then fussed with his briefcase. "Well, I didn't think to bring it with me. The lawyer said something about you inheriting some of Malia's possessions, but I'd already sold her stuff before the reading of the will."

He was lying. Dani wasn't sure how she knew, but what Ken just said didn't sound right. "I see," she said quietly. "Nevertheless, I'd like to have the lawyer's name and business information so that I can contact him. Do you have that in your briefcase?"

"I'll have to search for it." Ken did everything to not look directly at her.

So he had the photocopy of the certificates to show her,

but not a copy of her mother's will or the lawyer's business card? Yep, definitely lying.

"What I wanted to talk to you about are these certificates."

Dani held still, suspecting what her uncle was about to ask. "What about them?"

"I did a bit of research on the stock exchange and found the company. I'm wondering if you know how much these stocks are worth?"

"I'm sure you already know the answer to that question," she snapped back, catching onto his game.

He laughed. "You're right, I do. They're not worth very much at all." He linked his hands. "But to the right people, those two pieces of paper are worth their weight in gold."

"You know what? Matt was right. You do like to beat about the bush. Just come out with it." Dani wasn't stupid—she knew Ken wanted money, but she wanted him to admit it to her.

Ken leaned forward. "I want to sell these to you for five million."

She almost choked. "Five million dollars? Are you bloody insane? I don't have that kind of money."

"But your half siblings do." He leaned back in the chair. "If I sell these to you, you and the others will have a say over Colton Textiles. Your father can't do anything to the company without your input."

Technically, what Ken said was true. However, he didn't know the deeper implications these certificates held. If she and Adam could get their hands on them, they would own the majority of Colton Textiles *and* the Mariposa land. "You're absolutely right," she said quietly, while her mind worked out various scenarios.

"But—" he shrugged "—if I decide to approach Mr. Colton…"

"You won't need to," she said hurriedly. "I'll figure something out, but you'll have to give me a couple of days to get that kind of money together."

"Of course. You're my niece after all. And I'd rather you had the stock than Clive Colton. I need to respect Malia's last wishes after all, and in my eyes you're a Curtis, not a Colton." He dropped the folder into his briefcase. "When you're ready to talk, give me a call."

Seems like bribery and greed ran on both sides of her family. "Fine," she said, getting up. There was no need to say anymore. At least Ken had the consideration to show her the family photos before revealing one of the biggest surprises in her life.

In the lobby, Ken grabbed her shoulder. "I'm counting on you, Dani," he said, coming around to face her. "I'd rather sell the stock certificates to you than Mr. Colton, especially after the way he treated Malia, but…" He shrugged.

"I get it." She had no idea how she kept her voice calm. "You want your fair share. Don't worry, I'm on it."

He moved forward, and at the last minute she realized he was going to kiss her cheek. She didn't want him touching her, but if she backed away, there was no telling if he would be offended and call off the deal. So she offered her cheek, trying not to cringe. "It was nice seeing you again."

The kiss was quick, perfunctory. "You too. I hope we see more of each other, and you come to the house for a family visit when this is all over."

Her smile was genuine. "I have a new job I'll be starting soon. We'll see how things turn out."

Ken gave her a look before leaving. As soon as the doors

closed behind him, she dropped into a plush leather chair, trying to catch her breath as if she'd run a marathon.

Her siblings had a once-in-a-lifetime chance of finally owning everything their mother had given them.

And there would be no way in bloody hell Clive would find out about this.

Chapter Twelve

Dani observed the stunned looks from her brothers and the executive staff—Erica, Greg, Tallulah and Roland. It was so quiet in Adam's office that she heard the rumbling of a lawnmower on the golf course.

Wait for it, she thought.

"Are you sure? Absolutely sure?" Adam demanded.

"I'm sure all right. Even though I was young when mom left me behind, he showed me more than enough proof and told me things that only my mother could know. Ken is my uncle."

Josh, who stood beside Adam, turned to his brother. "Adam, you have a picture of your Colton Textile stock certificate, don't you? Show it to Dani."

Adam tapped a few buttons on his phone, then passed it to her.

She carefully looked over the screenshot. "Yeah, they looked just like this, white with orange borders. And Clive's middle initial too."

"The certificates also have the Colton name watermarked diagonally across the paper. I don't believe it." Adam's hands were bunched into tight fists. "If we can buy those two stock certificates, we have a chance to get Clive off our backs for good."

"And where the hell are we going to get five million dollars?" Josh demanded. "I don't think I can scrape that much out of my bank account, just so you know."

"You won't have to." Dani's brain was piecing together a plan. "But we'll need about one million in order to pull this off."

"Wait a minute, Dani, what are you thinking?" Erica asked.

"Some kind of a stalling tactic. I'm having a hard time believing the Textile stock was willed to Ken." She had spent some time thinking about the meeting with her uncle. "Why show me photocopies, bragging they belonged to him, but not show me Mom's will to prove his point? And why wait six years?" Dani shook her head. "Too many questions with no answers."

"You mentioned he was honoring your Mom's last wishes right? To keep the certificates out of the Coltons' hands." Adam shrugged. "It's possible he knows that Colton Textiles isn't worth much now and wants to sell the stock. He approached you because you're part of his family despite having the Colton name.

"We also need to know if your hunch about the certificates not being willed to him is right." Adam propped his arms on the table and rested his chin on his hands. "How do we find proof?"

"Wait a minute, how can we say those certificates weren't willed to him?" Josh interjected. "What if he did inherit them? Otherwise, how could he have shown Dani photocopies?"

"We have to find my mom's lawyer. Ken said he didn't

have the contact info with him, but I think he does. He just doesn't want to give it to me." Dani looked at her brothers. "I'm not sure where to start."

"Maybe I can help."

She and everyone else turned to stare at Roland. "You?" Dani asked. She hadn't expected the head of security to chip in with an idea.

He laughed. "Don't sound so surprised, Dani. My job is to collect information, decipher it then decide what to do with it. If your Uncle Ken knows the lawyer's location, I can flush it out of him."

"I sense Ken is not the kind of man you can just get information out of." She chewed on her lower lip. She received first-hand knowledge of that during their breakfast meeting.

"Dani, you're talking to a guy who can outsmart James The-Spy," Josh quipped. "If Roland wants intel, he'll find a way to get it."

The powerfully built Black man grinned. "Do you have a picture of your uncle?"

She shook her head.

"That's fine, I can pull it from the security feed when he met up with you earlier today. I'm sure Ken's in Sedona—he's waiting on you to call him. It shouldn't take more than half a day to find him and get what we need. I'll keep you all posted."

As Roland left, Dani felt a tendril of hope loop through her chest. She would cross her fingers and toes that the head of security would bring back good news.

But if he didn't... "I wonder if we should cover all our bases," she said to the group. "In case Roland isn't successful."

"You have a point." Josh started pacing the office. "So, how do we find this mysterious lawyer?"

"We can start with Sedona," Adam replied. "Dani's mother worked at Mariposa for several years, and it's the closest major city."

"It's worth a try. I'll pull together a list of family lawyers," Josh offered.

Dani chewed her lip. Though she hardly knew her mother, they seemed to have similar qualities, which included defending their privacy. "I don't know if I would hire a lawyer in the nearest city," she thought out loud. "If it were me, I would worry if Clive had second thoughts about giving me Colton Textile stock."

"What are you thinking Dani?" Erica asked.

"She's thinking of a lawyer as far away from Mariposa as possible but still able to reach by car or bus," Tallulah chipped in.

Everyone looked at the housekeeper.

"I've heard the stories you kids told me about your father." Tallulah looked ready to spit. "If I wanted to hide something from him, I'd make sure it was nowhere nearby."

Adam sighed. "Which means checking out the other Arizona cities. Phoenix, Tucson, Scottsdale and Flagstaff."

"Let's start small," Dani said. "We could be blowing this out of proportion too. I was thinking out loud." She hadn't mentioned California, where Mom originally came from, but it had to be considered as well, if all else failed. "I'll search Sedona and Flagstaff."

"I'll take Phoenix," Greg spoke up. "I have lawyer friends living in the area. It'll be faster for me to check."

Adam nodded. "I'll take Tucson, and Josh, you research Scottsdale. There has to be something on the internet if we look carefully."

"What parameters should we use?" Josh asked. "This could take a long time if we're not careful."

The room was quiet as everyone thought how to initiate this daunting task.

"How about lawyers who hate Clive Colton?" Tallulah suggested.

Dani laughed. "Nice and simple. Plus, I'd love to see how many hits we get with that search!"

"Then I suggest we start looking." Adam stood. "We'll report back to my office in a couple of hours. Maybe Roland will have found something by then as well. Greg, Dani will need that one million to lure Ken." Adam turned to her. "Why one million, Dani?"

"Because it can fit into a large backpack." She held up her phone. "Did some quick research on the internet."

He grinned. "Good thinking."

"And how are you going to stall him if he wants the full amount?" Josh chimed in.

Dani had thought of that scenario. "I'll need to bring him someplace where I have the advantage. I'm going to make him come here. Maybe Roland and his guys could make a citizen's arrest and we have Ken charged with, I don't know, stealing the certificates."

"But we don't have proof that your uncle has stolen anything," Tallulah cautioned. "We need to be very careful with this plan. If your uncle is as devious as he seems, he will disappear if he thinks he's being played, or charge Mariposa with physical assault if Roland and his team manhandles him. That's the last thing all of you need."

Trust Tallulah and her common sense.

"All right, then we stick to handing over the one million,

with the promise of giving him the rest when he hands us the stock," Adam stated. "No certificates, no more money."

"And I'll make sure the bills are traceable," Greg added. "If we're lucky, Dani's uncle won't run off with just the one million. He'll want the rest of it."

"I disagree. I think Ken will grab his family and disappear," Dani countered. She glanced at Josh. "We may have to level up our James The-Spy game and bug the backpack so we can track him."

"Unfortunately, we're just theorizing right now," Adam interrupted. "Let's get on the internet and see if we can find anything first, then reconvene."

IT WAS TWO o'clock before Dani finally tore her gaze from the laptop screen. Her eyes were burning from staring at the results of all the searches she'd performed, going through each one to see if they had the information she sought. A few looked promising, and she wrote those down, then did a meticulous vetting of her possibilities.

So far, nothing.

She leaned back in her chair and sighed, hoping the others had better luck. Tallulah had been right—a lot of people hated Clive. The few articles she had found dated back to when he and Annabeth visited Mariposa on a regular basis. Even while on vacation, he had pulled business stunts that had left potential investors disgruntled. What a jerk.

Dani closed her eyes for a slow count of ten, then opened them. Turning back to her computer, she thought of other ways to find the information they were looking for. Then it hit her.

See if her mother's name would come up in a search.

It was a long shot. She started typing.

Malia Curtis appeared within a high school website in California. Dani's throat constricted with anticipation, and while she debated whether to click on the link, her body beat her to it. The site opened onto a page of students wearing graduation clothing, and her mother was at the top, smiling into the camera.

She took a screenshot and saved the photo to her laptop, intending to print it later and put it within her secret childhood stash when she got home. Dani had very little of her mother's things—anything that she managed to collect as a girl was kept in a memento chest that lay hidden in her flat back in England. Trinkets, letters, little notes, school medals—all of these were memories that gave her the most happiness. The letters and notes were mostly from Mom, praising her as a student, athlete, and for being "Mommy's little princess."

Damn, she was going to start crying. She hadn't thought about Mom in a long time while she had studied her ass off in England. But now everything was coming at her in waves, and it felt like she would drown beneath the emotions that swept across her.

Fighting back tears, Dani continued searching her mother's name. The only other article that appeared was the announcement of a new tech start-up at about the same time Mom would have graduated. That would have been the human resources job Ken had talked about during their meeting. Further research revealed the start-up had gone bankrupt a year later. That would explain why Mom left the company.

There was nothing else, and Dani finally closed her laptop. Mom had certainly kept an almost invisible profile.

Dani glanced at her phone. Matt had texted her a couple

of times, but she hadn't noticed—she'd been too engrossed in her searches. Dani also needed to get back to Adam's office and report what she found, which was nothing, basically.

She called Matt, who picked up almost instantly. "Hey."

"Hi." Hearing his voice, Dani felt calmer.

"I know that tone. What's going on?"

She laughed. "I'm that obvious?" Dani hadn't realized that Matt could already pick up on her moods.

"Oh yeah." She heard the amusement in his voice. "Is everything all right?"

Should she tell him? Adam hadn't invited Matt to the family gathering. "Not really. I had a chat with Uncle Ken this morning."

Matt swore. "Is that why you left my bungalow so early?"

He was upset. "I had to. He gave me news that...well, could mean the difference between keeping or losing Mariposa."

That shut him up. The line was silent for several seconds. "Can you tell me what's going on? Or is that a Colton secret?"

"I don't like keeping secrets from you. I've had enough of that." Leaving Matt this morning without telling him why had bothered her more than she realized. "And I'm sorry about today, but I needed to talk to Ken without a grizzly hanging over my shoulder."

He made a sound. "And what did your uncle talk to you about?"

Dani paced her living room as she got him up to speed on the additional photos of her mom, grandparents and other relatives. "Oh, and he dropped a bombshell about inheriting two Colton Textile stock certificates."

"Say what now?" he demanded.

"Yeah, that's how we reacted."

"Do you believe him?"

Dani stopped. "Ken had photocopies, so it must be true. He didn't have Mom's will to show me that he actually inherited the stock. That didn't stop him from trying to extort me."

"So he offered to sell them to you." She could almost see the wheels turning above Matt's head. "And the cost?"

"Five million."

A low whistle. "What did you tell him?"

Dani prepped herself for Matt's reaction. "We accepted his offer. Before you start shouting in my ear," she said hurriedly, "just hear me out."

He grumbled a bit before finally quieting down. "This had better be good," he told her.

She got about halfway through her plan before he cut her off. "That is a dumbass idea, Dani."

"What the bloody hell do you want us to do? He threatened to sell the stock to my father. We're not letting that happen. Adam has his attorney getting the money together. In the meantime, all of us have been searching for anything on the internet that might provide a clue to Mom's lawyer. I had hoped to see a business card or something in Ken's briefcase during our meeting, but he guarded it like a pit bull."

Another pause. "All right, I understand your logic. I don't like it, but I get it. What's next?"

She blew out a breath. "We're supposed to meet and see if anyone's found anything and keep my fingers crossed."

"Do you mind if I tag along?"

Dani didn't see a problem with it—if Adam said no, then Matt would leave. "Sure, why not? I'll be there in ten minutes."

She powered off the laptop and shut it with enough force to make it snap in protest. Who were they kidding? They weren't going to find this lawyer, at least not in time. The group would have to think of a different plan or give up the one million dollars to Ken with no guarantee of getting the original Colton Textile certificates back. Dani prayed that Roland discovered something.

Dani drove toward the L Building, the heat of the Arizona sun beating down on her. She had thought she would have gotten used to it by now, but it seemed like nature had a surprise for her everyday between the weather and the too-close wildlife. She parked the golf cart, and was so focused on reaching Adam's office, she didn't see Matt coming up alongside her.

"Hey."

She squawked in fright. "Bloody hell, why did you do that to me?"

He frowned. "You didn't hear me calling out to you the last couple of times?"

"You did?" Man, she must have been really out of it. "No." She massaged her temples. "I guess this situation with Ken is really bothering me."

"I'm not surprised." He put his arm across her shoulders and kissed her cheek.

She leaned into him, savoring his strength and warmth. How did Matt know to do the right thing to calm her nerves?

"I'm sorry you're going through this. Aunt Glenna was bad enough, but..." He lapsed into silence.

"Right now, your aunt has the lead. I only met Ken a couple of days ago. Give him a chance to catch up." She laughed, but she wasn't in a humorous mood.

He tightened his grip. "Come on, let's see if your brothers have any news."

Inside, it was only Adam, Josh, Erica and Greg. Roland hadn't returned.

"Hey, Matt," Josh called out.

Matt paused in the doorway. "Is it okay if I join you all? If not, I'll leave."

"Come in, have a seat," Adam told him.

Matt led her to a small couch. She sat beside him, but perched her butt on the edge—she was nervous. "I found a law firm that might be promising, but I need to go through each lawyer," she started.

"I only found a lead between attorneys and your father," Greg told them. "A friend in Phoenix knows a couple of lawyers who worked with potential investors to Mr. Colton some years back when he was trying to breathe new life into Colton Textiles. From what they know, Mr. Colton took the money and blew through it." Greg shook his head. "The investors are still trying to get their money back."

"Good luck with that." Josh sat on the corner of Adam's desk.

"As for the lawyers, none of them have Malia Curtis as a client," Greg added.

"I didn't get any hits in Scottsdale," Josh said. "Plenty of news on Clive, but nothing tying him to angry lawyers or schemes. Like Dani, a few law firms look promising. I wrote those down."

"I got the same thing with Tucson—angry investors, nothing more. The lawyers don't have Dani's mom as a client." Adam leaned back in his chair.

Dani watched as Matt rose and walked the length of the

office. "So you all have been focusing on finding lawyers who would be angry with Mr. Colton?"

"We had the idea that someone who's pissed off at Clive would take Dani's mom as a client. Something like kindred spirits—everyone hates Clive Colton, let's gang up on him," Josh explained.

Matt shook his head. "That's a very convoluted way to find someone."

"We had to start somewhere," Dani told him.

"Sure." He turned around. "But now that hasn't worked. What's your next move?"

"Unless Roland comes back to us with something we can work with, we hand over the one million." Adam watched Matt. "Give him traceable bills so we know where he banks the money. It'll mean involving the police."

"Do you really want to do that? The media backlash would be fierce if you get this wrong." Matt approached the desk. "You don't want that in your life, and when—not if—Aunt Glenna gets wind of that juicy piece of news, she'll never leave any of you alone. What if he doesn't have the certificates when you're ready to do the exchange?"

"We're not giving him a million dollars for photocopies," Adam spat out. "We go back to square one."

Matt nodded. "I know none of you trust Ken. Hell, he ticked me off before I made up my mind about him. However, if he's looking for money and knows he can get it from you? You bet he'll have the original certificates with him."

"You're more optimistic than we are," Josh said.

"You're talking to a guy whose aunt is notorious for getting what she wants. As much as you don't want to believe it, let's work with the idea that Ken has the original stock."

Matt turned to her. "My next question is for you, Dani."

She got up, feeling the hairs rise on the back of her neck. The way he looked at her... "What is it?" she asked.

"I know it's a long shot, but...do you think your mom would have provided you with any clues before she left?"

Everyone turned to look at her, and Dani felt herself shrink beneath their thoughtful gaze. "I don't know what you're talking about," she whispered.

"I think you do." Matt stood before her. His hand came up, and she felt his fingers brush gently against her cheek.

"My mother abandoned me when I was a kid." Against her will, the memories came flooding back to her. She had thought she'd forgotten most of her early childhood, but it seemed her mind refused to let go. "She took me to Clive's house, told me to be a good girl until she came back for me and never returned." A sob broke out of her, and Dani covered her face with one hand, embarrassed to have anyone see how that one moment still affected her.

A pair of strong, warm arms encompassed her, pulling her tight against a muscular chest. "Shh," Matt crooned. "It's okay."

"It's not okay." She fought to slowly control her emotions. "What parent does that to their child?"

"A desperate one maybe?" Adam said gently.

"I bloody well doubt that." Dani wiped her face with her hands. "Mom should have come back for me."

"What if she couldn't?"

She looked up into Matt's serious expression. "What?"

He eased away and put his hands on her shoulders. "Did your Mom really desert you? Or did Mr. Colton tell you that?"

She heard someone gasp, but she continued staring at Matt, letting her mind finally wander back to that fateful day. "I remember Mom telling me to put on my best dress because we were going on a visit." It was a blue dress with big yellow sunflowers—Dani remembered it because when she twirled, the skirt fanned out into a big circle. "I even had my suitcase packed because she said we were staying overnight with relatives."

She remembered the drive, because it was a different direction to her school route. Dani recalled the field of flowers that looked like the ones on her dress. "When we got to the house, I think I asked Mom if she got lost."

"I seem to recall that," Adam told her. "It was the first time we all met."

She nodded, her mind sorting through that day's events. "I think a lady answered the door," she continued. "Mom and I had to stand in the hallway while she walked off."

"That was the housekeeper," Josh said.

"I remember you and your mom coming into the living room," Adam added. "We were all there because Clive told us a new member of the family was joining us."

Dani had a recollection of the siblings when she first walked in. They stood close together, with Adam shielding Josh and Laura. "I don't remember how I felt when I first saw all of you," she said, brushing past Matt and making her way toward Adam and Josh.

"I know I was angry." Josh frowned, but not at her. He looked like he was trying to remember something. "Mom had passed away less than two years before Clive introduced you as our long-lost sister. All I could think about was how he cheated with another woman." His expression turned to pain. "I recall being angry with you and your mom."

"Yeah, I remember that too, but I talked you down,"

Adam replied. "I kept telling you it wasn't Dani's fault, it was Clive's."

Dani felt it was important they talked out their feelings but wasn't sure if this was the time to do it.

"Dani."

She turned back to Matt. His smile hinted at the understanding between her and her brothers. While he may not have gone through the same situation, his adoption by Glenna would certainly have triggered feelings of abandonment by his own mother.

Dear God, they were a bunch of messed-up kids.

"Do you remember anything else?" he asked.

The pain—hell, the pain when her mother said that she was leaving Dani alone with a bunch of strangers until she returned. "Mom told me to be brave," she whispered. "I didn't know why she said that, but I knew she was coming back for me." She paused. "Until she didn't."

"Is that all?" Matt pressed.

"Matt, what are you trying to do?"

"I'm trying to get you to remember if your mom said or did anything different, something unusual. If your mother knew she wouldn't see you again, what would she have done to let you know that she loved you? Did she give you anything special? Did she say anything, like a secret phrase only the two of you would know?"

Dani shook her head, feeling confused, torn. She understood what Matt was getting at, but trying to sort through feelings she had buried for years felt like trying to claw her way out of quicksand. "I need a minute," she whispered, staggering to the nearest seat and dropping into it.

"Dani, I'm sorry." He stood behind her and massaged

her shoulders. She felt her body relax as his fingers pressed deep around her neck. "I pushed you too hard."

"No, it's all right." Matt had been trying to make a point, she knew that now. Somehow, he believed that Mom had provided a clue that only she would know how to decipher or find. "Mom bought me some stuff she knew I'd like. An art book with paints and brushes, a diary, hair clips shaped like birds." All of these were in her pile of treasures back in London.

"Was there anything hidden in the diary?" Matt asked.

"Honestly, Matt, I can't remember." Her body tensed with anxiety.

"Okay, I'm sorry." She felt his lips on her forehead. "I admit I was holding on to the hope that your mom left you something in particular that you cherished. She might have hidden a letter or a note that could have—"

"Wait." Dani listed the items from her memento box in her mind. Amongst the small trinkets and paper cards, her prized possession revealed itself—a little handbag. "Mom gave me a purse before she left. She told me she left some money in it to buy whatever I wanted." She held out her hands and looked down at them as if she was actually holding it. "It was round, and it had all my favorite colors—blues, yellows, oranges, greens. It was made with tiny beads. It would shine when I was outside with it."

"I remember that. You wouldn't let Laura touch it." Adam smiled. "You were very protective of that little purse."

"That could be a clue. Do you still have it?"

"Yeah, along with some other child stuff I collected. It's in a memento box back in London."

"It's worth a shot," Adam said. He moved closer, then

grasped her hand in his. "Is there anyone you trust who could look at it?"

"Um, yeah, Samira. She's my roommate and best friend." Dani had never told Samira about her mother and her early life as a Colton. It looked like some secrets would have to be exposed in order to find any clue about Mom's secret lawyer. She looked at her cell phone. "It's ten o'clock in the evening over there," she said. "Let me call her now."

It felt like the longest ten seconds in her life as she waited for her friend to pick up.

"Dani! Darling, how are you? Are you enjoying your vacation?"

Dani's body relaxed—Samira always had a cheerful voice. "Hi, Sam." They had met during their early days at university and immediately hit it off. "I need to ask a favor."

"Of course, anything."

Dani took a breath, bracing herself for what was coming next. "In my closet, there's a blue wooden box sitting on the top shelf, tucked away in a corner. Could you grab that, please?"

"Give me a minute."

She listened over the line as Samira rummaged through Dani's things. The box would not be immediately visible, as Dani had stacked a couple of bags filled with clothing in front of it.

"Got it. You didn't warn me you had it buried!" Samira was laughing.

"I...need you to look for a little sparkly handbag," she instructed.

Dani heard the slight creak of hinges as Samira opened the box. "Oh, Dani, you have some lovely things in here," she whispered. "Let me see…"

"It should be near the top," Dani interrupted. She didn't think she could handle Samira naming each item without growing emotional.

"Ah, yes, here it is. It's beautiful. I love the colors and the way it glitters."

"I got it as a present." Dani turned on the speakerphone so everyone could hear Samira. "Can you unclasp it and see if there's anything inside?"

"All right."

Dani could hear everything, and imagined the scene—Samira sitting on the bed, the box in front of her with the lid swung back, revealing her most precious heirlooms. Her friend was the first to see what Dani treasured, and in a strange way, she felt relieved, as if a door had finally opened. When she got back home, she would explain to her best friend what each memento meant during her young tumultuous life.

"There's nothing here."

Dani felt her stomach drop. "Nothing at all? No business card?" She thought quickly. "Can you look through the rest of my mementos and see if you find any information about a lawyer?"

It felt like a lifetime while she waited for Samira to thoroughly go through her treasures.

"I can't find anything, Dani."

Adam's office was silent.

"Well, that was a crock of shit," Dani said with a slight tremor in her voice.

Samira sighed over the phone. "Dani, I'm sorry—"

"I'm not. Mom wasn't much better than Clive." Dani couldn't cry now, she had to keep herself together. Once this nightmare was over and she managed to get the stocks in her hands, then she would give herself time to—what? Grieve? Be angry? Scream?

Yeah, she would do all of that in the privacy of her bungalow when the time came. "Thanks, Samira, I'll explain everything when I get back." She clicked the phone off and almost threw it across the room.

"Damn, there was nothing after all." Adam rubbed his face with his hand. "I'm not sure what else to do except keep searching."

"And hope Roland finds something," Josh added.

Roland knew his search for the mysterious uncle in Sedona could take longer than a few hours, but he was hopeful. Dressed in his favorite jeans, white T-shirt and cowboy boots, and carrying Ken's picture, he visited his favorite haunts first to make inquiries. It was his final contact at a popular convenience store who told him Ken had come in a couple of days ago, asking for recommendations of cheap hotels in the area.

There were only a few, and one of them was located on the outskirts of the city. He would start there.

Roland knew of the hotel—a couple of team members had brought him here one night for drinks to celebrate his birthday. The bar wasn't special, but the prices were reasonable and the patrons civil.

He stopped a hotel cleaner who was passing through the lobby. "Good afternoon," he said. "I wanted to ask if this gentleman was staying here?" He showed her Ken's picture.

She nodded. "He went out about an hour ago." She glanced at her watch. "He's usually back by three o'clock for happy hour in the bar."

"Excellent, thank you." He had thirty minutes to wait and to flesh out his plan.

He sat the bar and ordered a beer. His idea, to pretend he was about to get divorced, could backfire. Ken might not believe him—hell, Ken may not come near him. But it was worth a shot if it meant getting the lawyer's information, and giving the Colton kids peace of mind and possibly, the majority ownership of Colton Textiles.

He checked the time—five minutes to go. As he glanced at the entrance, he noticed Ken coming in, heading toward the bar.

Perfect. Roland started chatting to the bartender about mundane things before going into his story. "Hey man, you ever been married?"

The bartender laughed. "I've heard enough stories to make me stay away from marriage."

"Good, keep it that way." Out of the corner of his eye, he saw Ken sit down two bar stools away. "My faith in it has been shattered."

Roland waited as the bartender served Ken before continuing. "Never saw it coming. One minute, everything's great. Then the next thing I know, she wants to hang me out to dry." He finished his beer. "I guess you don't know a good lawyer?"

The bartender shrugged. "Sorry." He walked away to serve another customer.

Roland put on his best *so sad for myself* expression, twirling the bottle on the counter.

"You're having wife problems?" Ken was looking at him, his brows raised. "Sorry, couldn't help but overhear you."

Roland pretended to be defensive. "What's it to you? Are you a lawyer? You don't look like one."

"No, but I know a dude who might be able help you."

He kept his victory in tight control as Ken rummaged through his briefcase before pulling out a business card. He slid it across the bar toward him.

Roland made a show of picking it up and reading it. "You think this guy can help me?" he asked. He couldn't believe his luck at how easy it had been to get what Dani needed.

"He's one of the best in Sedona, according to my research." Ken smiled. "My sister found him. Good luck."

"Thanks." Roland carefully put the business card in his wallet.

He spent a few minutes talking to keep up the charade. Ken mentioned coming to the city to visit a relative, but missed his own wife back home in California. "My niece and I had to talk family business in person," Ken said as he finished his beer.

"I hope that turned out okay." Roland was curious if Ken would answer.

"Not yet, but it will." He put some money on the bar and slid off the stool. "Sorry man, gotta go. That lawyer should be able to help you out."

"I'll call him, thanks again."

Roland waited a few minutes, then paid for his drink and slowly walked outside. He glanced around but didn't see Ken anywhere.

As he headed back to his car, he pulled out his cell phone and sent a text to Adam.

I have the lawyer's business card.

Chapter Thirteen

As soon as Roland walked into Adam's office, Dani threw herself at him. "My God, you are a rock star!" she yelled at the startled man.

Josh approached Roland and clapped him on the back. "Told you he was better than James The-Spy."

"Damn right he is." Adam was beaming. "Did you have any trouble?"

Roland shook his head. "None at all. Did a little sleuthing, made up a convincing story that he would overhear and voilà." He pulled a card out of his wallet. "I'm sure the dude's a sneaky bastard like you described, but he fell for my divorce story hook, line and sinker." He handed the business card to Dani.

"Levi Blumstein, Family Lawyer, 224 West Birch Avenue, Sedona, Arizona," she read out loud. She also recited the number. "I don't think we should wait." She pulled out her phone.

"Dani, maybe we should just take a breath first and get our thoughts organized," Adam said.

"Why? We found the attorney, thanks to Roland. The sooner we get this done, the better it'll be for all of us."

She waited as the phone rang. "Damn it, it's going to

voicemail." She left a message, telling Mr. Blumstein her identity and callback number before hanging up. "Let me send an email to him too." She started typing on her phone, repeating what she had said in her voicemail. "That should get his attention. All we can do now is wait."

"I don't know about you all, but I'm starving," Josh announced. "Can we get something to eat while we wait for the lawyer to call back?"

"Excellent idea, we need a break." Adam turned to Erica. "Could you move any meetings I have for tomorrow, please? If this lawyer wants to talk to us, I'd like to jump on that."

"You bet." Erica hurried out.

"And if you'll excuse me, I need to get back to work." Before Dani could thank him again, Roland had quickly left the office.

"Greg, were you able to withdraw the one million we talked about?" Adam asked.

The lawyer nodded. "It's locked up in the large safe off property. I don't like the idea of Dani giving that kind of money to someone who claims he's her uncle, true or otherwise."

"If it comes down to that, we'll be ready for him."

"Let's hit the restaurant," Matt said. "We could continue talking while we eat."

He grabbed Dani's hand. She squeezed it, appreciating that he had remained close to her. "Thank you."

He frowned. "For what?"

"For being here with me." She couldn't remember if she'd told him how grateful she was for his support.

He looked so adorable when he blushed. "Why wouldn't I be?" he demanded.

She didn't answer, instead just enjoying the moment as they followed the others to the restaurant.

They sat at a corner table farthest away from the doors.

"Dani, did that lawyer come up in your searches?" Josh asked.

"Not him specifically. I found the building he worked in, but I hadn't broken it down yet. That would have been my next move if Roland and Samira hadn't found anything."

"Do you know this Mr. Blumstein, Greg?" Adam inquired.

Greg shook his head. "Never been on my radar."

They placed their order, and Dani sat back in her seat, hugging herself. "I hope the lawyer calls back soon. I can't take the tension much longer."

"I'm sure he will, especially if there's something in your Mom's will that you've inherited." Adam rubbed his chin. "Your mother must have provided instructions to Ken if he knew which lawyer to visit."

"I was thinking about that." Matt leaned his arms onto the table. "Ken could have found the information in Ms. Curtis' condo when he got the call about her death."

"I still don't understand why it took six years for Ken to contact me," she said. "Holding on to the certificates to respect Mom's last wishes could be the right answer, but..." Dani stopped.

"Don't forget, if Ken had been looking for you, it was almost impossible to discover your location. You made sure to keep your life private," Adam told her.

She sat up. "You don't think Ken knows what's going on, do you? About the land?"

"We can't be sure. For all we know, Ken could have approached Clive to tease out information about the stock without revealing he had them." Adam smacked a fist into his palm. "I'm getting sick and tired of being taken advantage of."

"Once we get those certificates back, we won't be." Dani had to stay optimistic.

As if on cue, her phone rang. It was the lawyer. "Mr. Blumstein," she said, relieved. "Thank you for calling me back."

"Ms. Curtis, the words surprise and disbelief don't begin to explain how I feel at this moment." His voice was deep, friendly. "I've been searching for you for the last five-odd years."

"My name is actually Dani Colton." She provided a summary on her family circumstances.

Silence on the other end for several seconds, before… "Ken didn't tell me anything."

"Why am I not surprised?" she mused.

"Ms. Colton, can you meet me? Today if possible?"

"I'd thought you'd never ask." Mr. Blumstein had jumped on her idea first. "We need to get some things straightened out before my uncle discovers that we've visited you."

"We?"

Dani glanced at her brothers. "Adam and Josh Colton. They'll accompany me."

"Of course. If you can get to my office in the next hour, we can…"

"I'd rather not." She thought of Ken and how he had found her. "Ken would still be in Sedona. He's…" she thought fast. "He's waiting for me to make a decision on something. And he's told me he used to work as a PI. I can't afford to have him see me come to your office. Is there someplace else we could meet?"

"Come to my house." He provided an address. "It's a gated community. Arrive two hours from now, I should be home by then, and I'll provide the security team with your names."

"Thank you." As much as Dani wanted Matt to come with them, she thought it best to keep this discussion within the family circle.

"I'll bring the will with me so that you and your family can go over it. See you all this evening." The phone clicked off.

Finally, they were moving in the right direction. Dani should get solid answers before the night was over, then she and her brothers could decide what to do next. She turned to Matt. "I can't thank you enough for pestering me."

Matt's eyebrow arched high. "Um, you're welcome?"

Josh laughed. "Our sister certainly has a way with words!"

She smiled. "Your brilliant idea that Mom might have hidden her lawyer's info amongst my mementos. It didn't work out but thank you just the same."

He grinned back. "My pleasure."

"Sorry we couldn't include you," Adam said. "No offense, but I'd like to keep this particular meeting between the three of us."

"Yeah, no problem." Matt wrapped his arm around her, gave her a tight squeeze and kissed her cheek. "I'll be waiting for your call when you get back," he whispered in her ear.

THEY HAD ARRIVED at the specified time in front of a massive iron gate. Two security personnel approached them from either side. After providing their credentials, the gate swung open, and Josh drove the SUV to Mr. Blumstein's address, located at the end of the cul-de-sac.

He whistled. "The houses get bigger the more you drive within Pine Canyon."

Toward the end of the road, they finally located the lawyer's residence, an expansive two-story home with a long, curved driveway and surrounded by a thick wall of tall juniper trees, providing privacy. The building and large paned windows gleamed beneath the setting sun.

"This is some house," Josh whispered as they parked in front of the four-car garage. "Gotta be at least three million."

"We're not here to sightsee, Josh." Dani strode toward the front door and pressed the doorbell, listening as it echoed through the house. Loud barking ensued, growing louder as it reached the door before the dogs were hushed by someone. "Yes, who is it?" a lady's voice came through an intercom located above the doorbell.

"I have an appointment with Mr. Blumstein. My name is Dani Colton and I'm with my brothers Adam and Josh."

"Oh, yes, he told me you were coming. Let me get him."

The woman's voice faded away, but not before Dani heard her calling out to the lawyer. Moments later, hurried footsteps came to the door, which opened. A slim man stood before them wearing navy pants and a white shirt.

"Hello everyone. Please, come in."

They stepped into a spacious foyer filled with light from the sun as it angled through the second-story windows.

Mr. Blumstein shook her hand. "I'm glad you're here. We have a lot to discuss."

"Thank you for seeing us."

The lawyer shook her brothers' hands. "Come on, we'll sit on the back patio. Would you like anything?"

"I think coffee all around is okay?" She looked at her brothers, who nodded.

Dani heard laughter from one part of the house. "Sounds like someone is having fun."

"My kids invited some of their friends over. Video games." He rolled his eyes. "And the dogs love visitors. Follow me." He walked back out the front door and led them past the garage to a stone path that circled around to the back. A wide elevated porch took up the whole back of the home, with enough room for thirty people. As she climbed the steps, Dani noticed the built-in family barbeque and outdoor fireplace. Beyond the backyard fence was a golf course.

"Sit down." Mr. Blumstein headed for a door behind them. "I'll get the coffee started. Shouldn't take more than a few minutes."

When he went inside, Josh leaned toward her. "What do you think? If we're here, is it possible your mom left something for you in her will?"

Dani had entertained the thought, but the certificates were her main concern. "Honestly Josh, I don't care. I just want to know for sure that Ken inherited the Textile stock. Anything else right now is…" She shrugged.

Adam looked like he was about to say something.

"What is it?" she asked.

"I was wondering if you didn't like your mother at all."

A valid question, and one Dani had pondered on after traveling down memory lane with her brothers in Adam's office. "I thought I did," she said quietly. "But then I realized I don't truly know her. How can I hate someone I know almost nothing about?

"I think I feel disconnected. Mom went through a lot of shit with Clive." She looked at him.

He nodded. "Our mom did too, but at least she was there for us." His eyes were suspiciously shiny. "I'm sorry, maybe I shouldn't have asked."

"It's okay." She shrugged. "It only makes me happier that I have you, Laura and Josh."

"Don't forget Matt," Josh added. "He's sort of family too."

"No, he's not!" she shouted and smacked her fist against his arm. "Why did you say that, you jerk?"

Josh laughed. "Because I knew it would rile you up."

"Sorry I took so long." Mr. Blumstein appeared with a cart loaded with coffee and snacks. "My wife saw I was struggling and helped me." He parked it at the end of the small table and laid everything out.

"Thank you for your hospitality, Mr. Blumstein," Adam started, sipping his coffee. "And for seeing us on short notice."

"Of course, of course." He fussed with his drink and finally sat down. Dani saw how nervous he was.

"Before we start." She reached into her purse, pulled out her passport and showed it to him. "Just to be clear that currently I'm known as Dani Colton. However if you need proof that I'm Malia Curtis' daughter, I can provide that as well."

"Your mother left a copy of your birth certificate with her will. I just need you to verify a few things." The lawyer reached down and pulled something from the bottom of the cart—a small leather satchel. He opened it and took out some papers.

Dani pulled out her phone, tapped a few times, then opened her Personal ID folder. She found her birth certificate and magnified it. "Here." She placed her phone in front of the lawyer.

Mr. Blumstein carefully compared the paper document

he had to Dani's picture. "Yes, they're exactly the same." He breathed a loud sigh of relief. "Thank you. No wonder I couldn't locate you after your mother's death. I was looking for a Danielle Curtis."

She put her phone away, preparing herself for what she would find out in Mom's will.

"I'm surprised you didn't contact me after I met with Ken," Mr. Blumstein told her.

She made a rude sound. "That's because my uncle didn't tell me anything."

His brows rose. "Ken never informed you of our meeting?"

"Actually he did, but he refused to provide your contact information. He admitted to selling all of Mom's possessions." Dani still burned with anger at that piece of news. "He also told me he inherited two stock certificates for Colton Textiles."

The lawyer nodded. "That's correct."

"Son of a bitch," Adam swore. He looked ready to throw his coffee mug.

Mr. Blumstein looked at her, curious. "Is something wrong?"

"We're not sure yet." Dani kept her answer evasive.

So it was true—Mom had given the stock to Ken. Now they'll have no choice but to find the money to pay her uncle off and get the two certificates into their possession.

"Malia was very specific in her will—she wanted the stock to stay within her immediate family."

"I guess Ken didn't lie about that after all," Josh grumbled.

"As to your mother's possessions, Ken only sold what Malia had in her condo."

She looked at the lawyer, her mind carefully piecing together what Mr. Blumstein just said. "So, you're telling me..." She stopped, too scared to continue.

"Your mother has left you an inheritance," he said quietly. The lawyer held up a notarized piece of paper. "This is your mother's will."

Dani's hands shook as she held it. Her mother had made arrangements for her even though Dani had been left alone to live with the Colton family. It was a hard pill to swallow.

"Dani, do you want me to read it?" Adam asked gently.

"No, thank you. I'll read it out loud." In a clear but trembling voice, she recited her mom's wishes. Mr. Blumstein had been right—Mom's will was simple and clear. Ken was given the two Colton Textile certificates. However, when she reached the section concerning her mother's finances, she halted at a particular sentence. "Wait a minute, is this right?"

"What is it?" Josh asked, leaning over to see what surprised her.

"Mom put her money in a trust fund for me." In a moment of clarity, it made sense. It kept Ken's greedy paws off it, and the money belonged solely to her. The amount Mom left behind was... "Bloody hell," she whispered in awe.

"If you keep reading, it states that the money can't be touched by other relatives. Your mother must have believed you would find out about it sooner or later. She invested her money in a very reputable bank in Nevada."

With this trust fund, Dani could do whatever she wanted for the rest of her life and still have money left over. She could help Adam if he needed it—hell, she could help all of her siblings. "Is it hard to take money out of a trust fund?" she asked.

"Not at all. I can go with you to establish that you're the

rightful owner, and you would need proper documents to prove your identity, which you already have. Once that's done, I believe you can set up an online account if you wish. There are some rules, but nothing too arduous."

She placed her hand over her mouth, fighting to hold back the tears and failing miserably. "I never thought Mom would ever do this," she mumbled around her fingers.

"Mr. Blumstein, does Ken know how much money Dani inherited?" Adam asked.

The lawyer shook his head. "Malia left instructions that I read the will. When Ken found out he only inherited the Colton Textile stock, he was very angry." The lawyer frowned. "Usually I would read the entire document, but you weren't at the reading, Ms. Colton, and to be honest, Ken's reaction put me on alert. He insisted I read the rest of the will. I told him you would inherit your mother's possessions. I deliberately kept it vague, and now I'm glad I did."

"So am I." Dani turned to her brothers. "It looks like our original plan is still a go."

"Plan?" The lawyer fixed his gaze on them. "What kind of plan?"

"I don't think we should tell you, Mr. Blumstein." Adam rose from the table and shook the lawyer's hand. "The less you know, the better. Thank you for your time and advising us on Dani's situation. I trust we can call you if anything else arises?"

"Sure, sure." He then shook Josh's hand, but when Dani held hers out, he covered it with both of his. "Ms. Colton, I'm glad you finally reached out to me."

"Thank you for seeing us so quickly. If my uncle hadn't been so secretive…" She let her thought slide away—no use in dwelling what had happened. "I'll be in touch to set up my account."

As they drove back to Mariposa, Dani sorted through the information Mr. Blumstein had provided. The stalling tactic she had thought of earlier was a no-go. Ken legally owned the stock, and they would need to give him the full five million dollars to get them back.

She mentally tweaked the plan on how they would make the exchange. Dani hoped everyone would agree to what she now wanted to do.

"So, YOU'RE GOING ahead with giving Ken the money in exchange for the certificates?" Matt asked.

He wasn't surprised when Dani nodded—nevertheless, his blood pressure rose when she insisted on doing this alone.

"I don't have a choice," she said, her fingers spinning a bar coaster on the smooth surface.

"Let Adam or Josh take your place. Even I—"

"You know that's not going to work." Her smile was faint. "If Ken saw you, he'd disappear in a puff of smoke."

When the family had returned, Matt got a summary of what happened. Dani's swollen red eyes and shaking body were enough to make him wrap her within his embrace and whisk her away. But when they reached his bungalow, she shook her head. "I need a drink."

They now sat in the L Bar, and he watched carefully as Dani downed two hard drinks in less than thirty minutes. When she raised her hand, he gently grabbed it.

"What do you think you're doing?" she demanded.

"If you're meeting Ken tomorrow, don't you want to be one hundred percent sober? You're insisting on going by yourself. You need to bring your A-game." He knew she'd get upset—it had been an emotional day for her, and all the more reason for him to intervene to be sure she was ready for this.

Her body relaxed. "I'm sorry," she whispered.

"Don't be." He rose from his seat and hugged her. "But I will question your decisions if they sound ridiculous."

This time, she trembled with laughter. "Very considerate of you, Mr. Bennett."

He tipped her chin and kissed her, tasting remnants of the rum and cola she had just finished. "Hence why I'm asking about your impulsive idea of meeting Ken alone with a backpack filled with money. Are you sure he'll have the stock certificates with him?"

"He'd better if he wants the money." Her expression confirmed his doubts.

"You know, we could do the same security setup you and Erica planned for Laura's wedding. Have Roland and his team dress as tourists and be in the area if something goes wrong."

"That's an idea. I did want Roland nearby. I'll let him know."

"Ken is meeting you here, right?"

"That's what I'm going to tell him tomorrow morning. I haven't called yet because…" She paused.

"You wanted to be sure this was going to work." If he were in Dani's shoes, he'd think the same thing. One good lesson he'd learned from Aunt Glenna was to cover all the bases. "I think it will. But if you think I'm going to be waiting around while you're in possible danger, forget it. I'll be the guy standing behind a door or the interior foliage, keeping an eye on you."

Her smile tugged at something deep in his chest. "You are something, you know that?"

He kissed her again, not caring if Kelli or the guests were watching. "Just don't do anything stupid, all right?"

Chapter Fourteen

"Hey, Dani, I was wondering when you'd call." Ken's voice sounded too cheerful this morning. "I was getting worried."

"Yeah, I bet you were." She stood in her living room, fully dressed and ready to go. The large backpack filled with one million dollars sat on the chair by the front door. It was just past nine in the morning, and if she was lucky, her nightmare and salvation would be concluded before lunch.

"What the hell does that mean?" he demanded.

"Cut the bullshit, Ken. Matt was right—in the end, you were only in it for the money."

"And what's wrong with that?"

Dani bit the inside of her cheek. The fact that Ken answered in such a cold manner only meant one thing. He had no desire to get to know her, unless funding his family's lifestyle was part of it.

She sighed. "For you, nothing."

So much for getting to know Mom's side of the family. Ken shut the door on that.

"I've got the original certificates in my briefcase. How do you want to do this?" Ken asked.

"I want you to come to Mariposa for the exchange. No

one will be around—I told my family I have to do this on my own."

Ken snorted. "Your family."

Suddenly, Dani was angry. "Yeah, my family. The siblings who supported me with no questions asked, no matter who my mother was. That's what a family does, Ken. Unlike family that looks for any opportunity to demand a handout."

"I told you what my family's been through!" he shouted.

"And you survived. I admired you for that." She could feel her anger starting to rise as well. "Maybe if you treated me as someone who was part of your circle instead of a bloody money tree, we might have even gotten along. I'm glad you didn't waste any time in showing me who you truly are."

Silence on the other end. Damn it, she let her emotions do the talking, but she didn't think Ken would hang up on her. He couldn't risk losing five million dollars.

"You know what? You're right. Let's cut the crap."

Something didn't feel right, and Dani's stomach twisted as she waited for Ken to continue.

"I'm not meeting you at Mariposa. I don't care that you said no one's around, because I don't trust you. You're going to meet me at a neutral location."

She'd been suspicious Ken might pull this stunt, changing the place, and she'd been ready for it. "All right, what do you have in mind? I have a couple of ideas. Maybe the coffee shop where we first met or someplace quiet, like a library."

"Nah, too many people around. We're going to meet at Eagles' Nest."

"The hiking trail?" She'd been there once when she first visited her siblings. Josh had given her a tour of the area. It was a challenging hike that took about two hours to complete, and at this time of year, it was going to be really hot.

If there were no tourists around or no cell phone service at a particular spot, she might not be able to call for help. "That's an odd place to meet."

"It's quiet, and there won't be a lot of hikers when we arrive—it'll be too hot. There's an area off the trail I have in mind where we could have a quiet discussion without being disturbed."

Dani was liking this less and less. "Where exactly are we meeting?"

"At the trail's parking lot. Once I see that you haven't brought anyone with you, we'll head in."

She was losing control of the situation and had to think fast. "Why all the conspiracy?" she asked. *More James The-Spy stuff, as Josh would say,* she thought. "We can easily do the trade in my car, and you drive off."

"We could, but again, I can't trust that no one's tailing you. Make up your mind. I'll give you an hour to get to the Eagles' Nest parking lot, otherwise I'm gone with the certificates."

"Hang on, it's going to take more time than that for me to get there! The drive is a good ninety minutes," she countered. She had to at least text her brothers about this new situation before running outside to grab one of the resort's SUVs. "Cut me some slack. Carrying that kind of money in a large backpack isn't easy."

He was silent for too long.

"Are you still there?"

"Fine, I'll meet you two hours from now, and you'd better be alone, or I'm taking off."

Dani was sure he was bluffing. Ken wanted the money, and knew that he would get his hands on it before the day was over. "If I'm stuck in traffic, I'll call you." She clicked off the phone.

Right, the change in plans meant a change in clothing. The temperature this morning was already in the low eighties and dry. By the time she arrived at the hiking trail, it would be a lot hotter. And there would be less chance of finding shade beneath the juniper trees or dense vegetation the higher they climbed the path. Cell phone connection would also be spotty. There were a few houses located on the opposite side of the parking lot, but they would be too far for her to reach if she had to make a run for it.

She hurried to her bedroom and changed into a light cotton t-shirt, hiking shorts with plenty of pockets, and pulled a baseball cap onto her head. Her purse was now a cross-body pack in which she stuffed a large water bottle and trail snacks, and she perched a pair of sport sunglasses on her head.

Thick socks and hiking sneakers completed the gear. After stuffing her phone into one of her pockets, she hefted the backpack onto a shoulder and hurried to the golf cart. In moments she was speeding to Mariposa's main parking area, where she would grab an SUV.

No one was in sight, which was part of the plan Dani had put together. Roland and his team would only appear when the exchange happened.

Dani had to text someone fast, and pulled her phone out. Matt's was the first number that came up. She sent a quick message.

Hey, change of plans. Meeting Ken at Eagles' Nest 2 hours from now. Won't be in parking lot, not sure where. Josh knows how to get there.

Shit, this was serious spy-level stuff now.

She got the SUV in gear and drove out onto the state highway, being careful not to go over the speed limit. It was a two-lane route which provided a scenic drive through Arizona's landscape. Thankfully there weren't too many cars on the road this early in the day, because getting in the middle of an accident or rush hour would have ramped up her frustration. She drove as fast as she dared, keeping watch for state troopers who would be patrolling.

DANI'S PHONE FINALLY RANG. It was set in a holder beside the steering wheel, and she saw Matt's number appear. She hit the Speaker button. "Good morning."

"Not in my view, it is." There was a tinge of a growl in his voice. At any other time, she would have found that sexy.

"I'm not happy about it either, trust me."

"Where are you now?"

She glanced out the window and saw a sign come into view. "I think I'm about thirty minutes away."

"We're about twenty minutes behind you. Josh said make sure your phone GPS is on. He also mentioned there's a chance of heavy rains in the next hour, so keep an eye out for that. Is there any way you can stall Ken in the parking lot?"

She bit her lip. "I can try, but I don't think it'll work. He just wants to grab the money, then take off."

"Do what you can."

"Hey, do you mind staying on the phone with me until I arrive? My nerves are working overtime."

"Sure."

Dani caught a glimpse of the sign for Eagles' Nest Trail—getting closer.

"Dani, I wanted to ask what you're going to do after this

is over." A pause. "Will you be staying to help out Adam and Josh for a few days before heading back to England?"

It was a logical question. The boys would need some extra help to get Mariposa back to its former reputation, and with her marketing knowledge, she could offer her insight. But Dani didn't think that was what he meant. "I'm pretty sure my employer can give me an extra week," she said. "What about you? Will you stay and help Adam with the business side of things?"

"If he needs me, I can…"

"Oh my God, you two!" Josh's voice came over the speaker. "Could you just finally admit you want to pursue this relationship and work something out?"

She laughed. "Trust my brother to be up front."

"He has a point. We can talk about it later tonight."

"It's a date. I gotta go."

"You had better be careful, or you'll answer to me," Matt warned.

"Aye-aye, sir. I'm going to put the phone on mute when I arrive. I'm worried if Ken hears it, he might try something, and I'll need all my concentration if push comes to shove."

A pause. "You're making me really nervous now," Matt admitted.

"That makes two of us!" Josh confirmed.

"I promise I'll call when I can. I'll talk to you later." She clicked off the phone and turned into the Eagles' Nest Trail parking lot.

Ken was located farthest away from the tourist center. "I hadn't realized how long the drive would be," he said when she stepped out of the vehicle. "I got here five minutes ago."

"Don't lie to me, you knew how long it would take." Dani glanced over his attire. He was dressed similar to her, but he wasn't wearing a hat, and it didn't look like he had a water bottle—in half an hour, he'd be sorry for not having either. "Where are the certificates?"

"In here." He patted the briefcase.

"Let's see them."

"Show me the money first."

She reached into the passenger side and hauled out the backpack, having no idea if Ken would guess that the full amount wasn't with her. She laid it down on the hood of the SUV and unzipped a small section. Bills were bundled into small stacks. "The stocks, if you don't mind." She secured the backpack. The tension was making her angry, and Dani had to keep it under control, or she'd do something she might regret.

Ken pulled a sheet of paper out and held it up for her inspection. She took a step closer, immediately seeing the orange border, and looked for the Colton watermark. Adam had said it would be etched diagonally across the width of the paper—sure enough, she could see it as the sun shone on it from behind. "Show me the other one too."

"Picky, aren't you?" He put the first one down beside the backpack and pulled out the second certificate, which confirmed her inspection. "Satisfied?"

"Yeah." She looked around. "Are you sure you don't want to do the exchange beside our cars? I see maybe five people at the tourist booth. And making the switch here would be much faster too."

"I said I don't trust you." Ken's gaze darted from the booth, to the other end of the parking lot, and to the highway before finally stuffing the stocks back into his briefcase. "Let's do this."

"We need to go over there." She pointed at the booth,

where tourists were lined up at the center, waiting to pay the fee required to hike the trail.

Ken looked in that direction. "There's no way to sneak in? I'd rather not have the hassle of people recognizing me."

"You can't get to the trail from here. If the bush doesn't cut you up, the grounds are hazardous enough to break your ankle. I'm not walking through that." Matt had asked her to stall as long as possible. She locked up the car, hoisted the cross-body pack and large backpack onto her shoulders and started walking toward the center. "You can follow me or stand there looking lost."

Dani moved as slow as possible, but it only took a few minutes to pay the fee and stand at the head of the trail.

"Let's go." Ken led the way, his footing sure as he strode away.

Dani glanced at the sky. Thick clouds were rolling in from the south. If Josh was right, they'd be hit by a thunderstorm soon. She followed her uncle, but not too closely, wanting to keep a bit of distance between them.

For the first ten minutes, they kept a brisk pace, the trail even and flat. It wasn't midmorning yet, and the heat was already growing intense. Dani noticed the sweat dripping off Ken's bald head. If she was lucky, he would pass out from heatstroke.

She grabbed her water bottle and took a few small gulps. "Are we planning to climb?" she asked.

He glanced over his shoulder. "Maybe. I haven't been here before, you can give me a quick tour."

She looked around. "There's a reason why it's called Eagles' Nest, you know that, right? It takes almost three hours to complete, and the hike will get steeper."

He kept walking, but Dani knew that if he didn't hydrate soon, he was going to faint.

"Part of the trail passes Juniper Creek," he announced. "It'll be cooler under the trees."

She was wondering what Ken had in mind. None of this felt right. Why did he pick Eagles' Nest? Sure, it can be remote, as June was one of the worst months to hike the trail because of the scorching heat, but a few brave tourists did come here, which negated the privacy he wanted to achieve. Hell, they could have driven a few more miles south, where no one was around, just empty desert. So, why here?

They reached the bridge, and Ken turned right. This section of trail ran alongside Juniper Creek, so the vegetation was denser and a brilliant green against the clear blue sky. It was also much cooler.

She knew the trail, but it seemed her uncle had knowledge of it as well.

Dani watched Ken carefully, wondering what his next move would be.

KEN FELT DANI'S stare bore into his back as he trudged onward.

The path beside Juniper Creek gave him a chance to cool off as they hiked beneath the dense foliage. The heat in Arizona was different than what he was used to in Southern California. It was a lot hotter and much drier, and the air seared his lungs. He forgot to bring water with him, a stupid mistake on his part. Dani no doubt had her own, but she wouldn't share it, he knew that. He'd have to conduct the exchange as quickly as possible before he got serious heatstroke.

He took a deep breath of the cooler air. "Hey, you don't happen to have any water?"

"Only enough for myself," was her snarky retort.

He grumbled beneath his breath. No matter—once this was over, he wouldn't see her again, no matter how much Carol begged him to introduce Dani to their family.

Ken found a worn path that led down to the water's edge. He knelt and splashed water over his face and head, feeling a bit better after getting out of the brutal heat. He paused, going over in his mind again what he had planned. A part of him rebelled against it, but he'd been furious when Mr. Blumstein advised him that Malia only passed down the two Colton Textile stock certificates to him.

The stock was essentially worthless to most people, as Colton Textiles was about to go bankrupt. The only bit of sheer luck he had was that they could be important to someone who wanted to own Colton Textiles. Remembering how Dani instantly offered to buy them, Ken surmised that she and her siblings would be willing to pay a hefty price to take the company away from their father.

He stood up and turned. Dani remained several feet away, her gaze locked on him, distrustful. He couldn't blame her. "Ready to move on?"

She nodded.

He stepped to one side. "Care to lead the way?"

Dani gave him a look but moved ahead, setting a pace that wouldn't be easy for him to keep up with. "Hey, slow down," he called out.

She did, but remained several feet in front of him. Her lack of trust was so obvious, he almost laughed. "How long is the trail?" he asked to fill in the silence, although he already knew the answer.

"About five kilometers," she said. "The climb to the top is gradual, but still steep." She stopped and looked at him. "Are you sure you want to do the exchange here? You don't have any water, and the heat is going to get worse. Plus…" she pointed to the sky on her left.

Ken was surprised at the thick dark clouds that hung in the sky like a rolling wall. "That doesn't look good."

"It can get here in three hours or thirty minutes."

Damn it. He'd have to do this quick and get back to his car before her family showed up—Ken was sure they were on their way here even now. "Let's go to that spot on the trail," he said, pointing.

They hiked upward for the next ten minutes, but it felt longer than that. His stomach cramped from lack of water, and the top of his head felt as hot as a boiled egg. If he was going to get this done, it would have to be soon so that he had some strength left to make it back down the trail and get water from the tourist center before driving off with the money.

"This is a good spot," she told him, looking out over the Arizona backdrop. The thunderclouds were closer, roiling amongst each other. A flash of lightning lit the clouds with an eerie white light. "But we'll need to leave soon." She turned to him. "How are we doing this?"

Carefully, he thought, but didn't say it out loud. "See the two large rocks there, sitting side by side? I'll put the certificates on one, you put the backpack on the other. We'll do it at the same time, take a step back. We'll count to three, then you grab the shares while I take the backpack. Does that work for you?"

After several moments, she nodded. "I don't know why

we couldn't do this reasonably," she complained. "All this secrecy wasn't necessary."

"I didn't want your family around, butting into our business," he retorted. "Especially that Matt guy."

He saw her smile, which irritated him even more. He took out the two certificates and held both of them up for Dani to see. In response, she took the large backpack off and held it in front of her. "Go."

They placed their items down, then backed away a step. Dani's gaze was glued onto the certificates—he had made a good call in finally locating her whereabouts and selling the stock to her and her siblings. He, on the other hand, had to control his drooling over the huge amount of money that sat a couple of feet away. He and Carol could buy a larger house, give some money to the kids and kick them out. Maybe travel once she was feeling better…

"Hey, we finishing this or what?" Dani demanded.

Ken bit his tongue to stop a furious answer. He'd be rid of her soon. "On three," he said. "One…two…three."

They stepped forward and grabbed their respective prizes. Dani thoroughly looked over the certificates, then stuffed them into a second, smaller bag slung across her shoulder. He crouched down in front of the backpack and opened it. The bundles were in stacks of one-hundred-dollar bills. He started counting them, then quickly realized…

"Ken, I need to tell you, it's not all there."

The little bitch. He surged to his feet, his anger threatening to overtake him. "Are you kidding me?" he shouted.

"The rest of the money is at the resort," she said in a loud voice. "I couldn't physically carry five million—that's 110 pounds! And I wasn't going to carry five million bloody dollars on my back for cripes sake!"

He took a step toward her, but Dani skittered away. "I promise, the rest of the money is at Mariposa. I'll accompany you to the off-site safe, get the rest of the money and put it in your car. You can take off and we won't see each other again."

Dani made it sound so simple, but Ken knew perceptiveness ran on his side of the family, and Malia had a lot of it. Why not her daughter? "It smells like a trap," he growled.

"No tricks, Ken. I told you my siblings want these certificates, and we have the money. I just couldn't carry all of it."

He hunched down and zipped the backpack shut before slinging it over his shoulders. Ken didn't believe her. How could he? He was sure the police or Dani's brothers would be waiting for them back at the resort. Shit, they could be here right now.

Ken thought quickly. He could leave with the one million, tell Dani goodbye and never look back. Or…

He stared at the small pack slung over Dani's shoulder. If he could grab the certificates and escape, he could sell them to Mr. Colton, possibly even get more money than what Dani had promised. It would go against Malia's wishes, but it wouldn't bother her since she was already dead.

Dani glanced at the sky. "We really should get going."

He moved closer, hoping to get within striking range.

Dani must have sensed something, because her body tensed as she stared at him. "What are you doing?"

Ken reached out quickly and grabbed her shoulders.

"Ken, what the bloody hell—" she shouted, as he started pushing her backward. "What are you doing? Get off me!"

At this height, Ken saw Juniper Creek as it curled beneath the thick juniper trees. As he looked over the cliff, its side was covered in loose red rock and scattered pockets of dense brush. It wasn't as steep as he thought, but Dani would never get her balance back before crashing into the forest below.

However, Dani was a lot stronger than he realized, and managed to kick the inside of his thigh, just missing his groin. The backpack was heavy, but the added weight allowed him to push her one step closer to the edge.

Suddenly, she screamed, a piercing sound that reverberated off the red butte cliffs. Someone would definitely hear that. "Shut up," he grunted.

Ken shouted in pain as her finger dug into his eyeball. It hurt so bad that his grip loosened, and he stumbled forward.

"Dani!" A man's voice. Shit! Matt and her brothers were close.

She tried to slip past him, but in a moment of desperation, he grabbed her leg as he found himself off-balance, teetering over the cliff edge. With an anguished yell, he went over, using his free arm to take the full impact. He still held Dani's foot, but a body appeared out of nowhere and started kicking his arm. Ken hung on, fighting to brace his feet against the unstable rock face, but his hand grew numb, and he screamed as his fingers lost hold of Dani.

Ken's breath was knocked out of his lungs as he slid down the rocky surface. He tried to use his feet and hands to break his fall, but it was no use. Gravity had taken over, and all he could do was hold his breath and protect himself as best as he could while he tumbled to the forest below.

Chapter Fifteen

Matt jumped out of the SUV before Josh brought it to a full stop. Dani's GPS displayed her location at Juniper Creek, but as he watched, it started moving.

They were hiking the route.

"Son of a bitch, we need to get moving!" he yelled.

"I called the police," Adam said, joining them.

"By the time they get here, something could have happened to Dani." He refused to wait. Ken was twice her size, and if he tried to hurt her... "I'm going in."

"There's a slim possibility they'll come out at any moment, and everything will be okay."

"Seriously, Adam? Look at the GPS—they're going the wrong way. When Ken finds out Dani doesn't have the five million..." He stopped, determined to ignore everyone and find Dani himself. "You can stand here and wait for the police," he said, anger and fear making his body shake with adrenaline. "I'm going in after your sister."

"I'll go with you," Josh said. "I know the trail. And those thunderclouds don't look good. We could get hit anytime now." He went around the vehicle. "We're going in the back way, I know a shortcut that'll take us to Juniper Creek."

"I'm right behind you."

Matt heard Adam shout something but didn't pay attention as he stayed close behind Josh, running through thick bush and dodging huge juniper trees.

This plan to retrieve the stock certificates from Ken had been faulty from the start. Anything could happen, and Dani being in the middle of it had not done Matt's blood pressure any favors. He'd been sitting on pins and needles since Ken's sudden decision to move the exchange into the middle of a hiking trail.

They had reached the creek. It was wide, about twenty feet across, and slow-moving. A thick stand of trees bordered the other side of the water.

Matt carefully scanned the area—he couldn't see Dani. He pulled out his phone and checked her location, with Josh looking over his shoulder. "They haven't stopped moving. How far ahead are they?" he asked.

Josh looked at the moving GPS dot that was Dani. "It looks like they've reached the base of the first summit. Why the hell are they heading up there?"

"Something must have happened." Matt noticed a few tourists on the trail. "I wonder if Ken got spooked."

"It doesn't make sense. They could go off the trail for fifty feet into the brush and have total privacy. Why head up to the nest?"

"Let's figure that out while we find Dani. Which way?" he asked.

"We'll cross the creek. The trail loops into a wide U-turn. We need to narrow down the distance."

Matt gasped as the cold water hit his legs. He stumbled as his feet slipped on the wet rocks, but he managed to make it across without injury. They raced across the trail, with Josh taking the lead. Soon, the path angled upward, but Matt still couldn't see Dani.

"Where the hell are they?" he yelled. He moved ahead of Josh, being careful to stay away from the cliff's edge. He pulled out his phone. Dani's GPS indicated she should be close by...

Suddenly, a scream cut the air above them, the sound traveling across the trail as it echoed amongst the sandstone cliffs.

"Dani!" Matt shouted, taking off at a run. As he reached the top of the first climb, the trail curved left, and there...

Two people struggled against each other, their arms locked as they fought. Ken had the upper hand, taking one step forward, which pushed Dani closer to the edge of the cliff.

Matt's heart dropped into his stomach as he ran, keeping his entire focus on her. She managed to stab Ken in the eye with her finger, and the large man faltered, loosening his grip.

Matt stretched out his arm, yelling. Dani slipped around Ken as the large man lost his footing and started sliding down the cliff, but at the last second, he grabbed Dani's foot.

"No!" Matt screamed.

Dani's expression was filled with terror as she was dragged over the edge. Without hesitating, Matt dove toward her, reaching for and grabbing her arm. The combined weight of Ken and Dani pulled Matt's body half over the cliff face. With his other hand, he dug his fingers into the ground, straining his muscles to hold on to her and to keep from going over. She didn't make a sound, just stared at him with wide frightened eyes as she tried to kick off Ken's hand. But her movements were making Matt lose his own tenuous grasp on the rock face.

"Dani, don't move. I can't keep a firm grip!"

"Hold on!" Josh yelled. He scrambled down to where Ken hung on to her foot with a crushing grip. Matt gritted his teeth and shifted his body so that he didn't lose his balance as Josh kicked at Ken's arm until the man let go.

Josh grabbed Dani around her waist, and Matt grabbed both of her hands, then slowly crawled backward while Josh pushed her from behind. In moments, all three of them were lying on their backs on the trail, gasping for air.

"Matt!" Dani's body covered his as she wrapped her arms around his neck, sobbing uncontrollably.

He sat up and crushed her to him, kissing her face and murmuring soothing sounds into her ear. He had never been so scared before in his life. "Hey, it's over. He's gone," he said softly.

She looked at him, her face a haunted expression that scared him all over again. "Did we…? Is he…?"

Matt had concentrated so fully on getting Dani to safety that he hadn't noticed what happened to Ken. "Josh, you all right?" he shouted.

"Yeah." He was standing at the edge of the cliff, looking down. "I can just make out Ken's body at the edge of Juniper Creek."

"Oh God." She hid her face in his shirt.

"He's moving, but I'm sure he broke several bones. He's not going anywhere."

"Are you okay?" Matt asked her quietly.

She nodded. "He tried to kill me," she choked out. "Why?"

He remained quiet, just holding her, gently rocking back

and forth. He had seen how greed made Aunt Glenna impossible to live with anymore. She had this certain expression that would warn him she was up to something. Ken didn't have that look—he hadn't been as subtle. He'd been very vocal—and ironically, honest—in his expectations from Dani. Her uncle wanted a lot of money from her because she bore the Colton name. He could have kept that one million and left Dani alone, but the greed was too tempting.

"I'm sorry," was all he could say.

Josh came over. "The police are going to grab Ken," he said, holding up his phone. Matt could hear a very loud voice through the speaker. "They have the coordinates. Adam is screaming bloody murder. He wants to talk to you, Dani."

She wiped her face and grabbed the phone. "I'm all right," she said, but Matt could still hear Adam yelling. "We all agreed to this plan, right? I didn't expect Ken to push me off a bloody cliff!" she yelled.

Matt rose and held out his hand to her. As she got to her feet, he noticed the various cuts and bruises on her body. She was also missing a sneaker—Ken must have pulled it off. But it was the furious expression on her face that made him take a cautious step back.

"If there's a next time, Adam, then you can bloody well be the pawn!" she shouted, and hung up. She glared at Matt. "Are you going to give me grief as well?" she demanded.

Matt held up his hands. "Not saying a word."

She looked at Josh, who stood there with his arms crossed. "Well?"

"You make a great James The-Spy," he said, catching both of them off guard. He hugged Dani to him. "I'm just glad you're safe, little sister." He kissed the top of her head. She hugged him back, burying her face in his chest.

Matt blew out a breath. "Let's start heading back." Movement at the bottom of the cliff caught his attention. Several officers had congregated around Ken, who still couldn't get up. "Dani, can you manage to walk down?"

"I'm not an invalid, Matt." But as she stepped down on her foot, she winced. "Bugger."

"Let me carry you down."

Dani gave him an incredulous stare. "On this trail? Are you daft? Let me put my arm over your shoulder and you can support me."

Matt obeyed, being careful not to move too fast as they hobbled back down the trail, with Josh following behind.

At the visitor center, Adam immediately ran over and picked Dani up in a bear hug. "If you ever scare me like that again…" he told her.

"Trust me, if I want to scare you, I can do a better job than this," she retorted, but she hugged Adam tightly.

Matt smiled—Dani was full of surprises. He loved it.

"Dani can be a handful." Josh mirrored his thought as he stood beside him. "Are you up for that?"

Matt grinned. "I wouldn't have it any other way."

IN ADAM'S OFFICE, Dani—after a hot shower and change of clothes—held up the two Colton Textile stock certificates for everyone to see. The only people there were her brothers, Matt, Greg and Erica. "We finally have them," she announced. Her emotions were mixed though, because Mom's family was now off-limits.

"There's still some legal work involved," Greg announced. "Ken survived the fall and he's recuperating at the hospital in Sedona. He'll be charged with attempted murder and extortion. I'm sure I can expedite the civil court case and witness statements, and the judge will disinherit him. But, yes, the stock technically belongs to you, Dani."

She stared at them in awe. How these certificates could make such a difference…tears threatened to take over. "I'm just happy that I could do something like this for my brothers and sister. You were the only ones who accepted me as a family member. Ken and Mom…" She had to stop and sit down. Knowing now that Ken wanted nothing to do with her, except take whatever money he could grab, hadn't really sunk in until he had accused her of not paying the full amount for the stock. Maybe she should have seen the signs earlier, and it was possible she had, but Dani didn't want to believe it. Now, she had no choice. Her own uncle had tried to kill her.

A strong arm wrapped around her—Matt. The man she had been asked to spy on, who had been a possible threat to her siblings. He turned out to be the best thing that ever happened to them.

If Matt and Josh hadn't reached her in time on the trail…

"I need some air," she whispered.

Matt pulled her up. She glanced at Adam, who looked worried. "I'll be all right," she told him. "It's a lot to take in."

They headed toward the pool. She took a deep breath of the hot, dry air. "Sometimes, I think I can get used to this," she murmured. It had been an idea that touched the back of her consciousness for some time, but she wasn't ready to seriously think on it.

"Including the rattlesnakes and creepy crawlies?" Matt asked, smiling.

"I forgot about that." She leaned against a wall.

He laughed. "It's a valid thought though. Laura won't be

back for another two weeks. Unless your new boss needed you to begin work right away."

Dani would have to call and request another extension, but she wasn't sure how her new employer would take it. "That will be a conversation I'll have to prepare for."

Matt stood beside her, and she glanced at his strong profile, the muscular arms folded against his chest. She wondered what he was thinking.

"What about you?" she asked. She didn't want to voice the question, but it had to be brought out in the open. "Mariposa won't need to have a merger deal with another company. Does that mean you'll head back home?"

"Probably." He shifted and put his hands in his pockets. "I haven't looked at my phone recently, but I'm sure my clients are wondering where I am."

She nodded, staring out over the sparkling pool toward the red cliffs that made Arizona such a special place. She hadn't been joking about staying. As Dani spent more time with her siblings, she realized how much she would miss them when she returned to England. It had been an exciting time for her though while growing into her womanhood—dedicated to her school studies, making new friends, learning a new culture. But now, she needed something more... solid, a foundation on which to stand and spread her wings.

And she believed she could do that right here.

She turned to stare at Matt. "What would you think if I decided to move back to the States?"

His brown eyes widened with surprise, and she thought, with delight. "Do you want to, Dani?"

"I've been thinking about it. I love my friends, but that's all I have in England. Here, I have a family that loves and wants me with them, and a business I'd love to sink my teeth into."

"That's true. Mariposa will need a new facelift, and I'll bet you can find a job in Sedona." He frowned. "I'm worried about Aunt Glenna trying something stupid again."

"We'll be ready for her." She clasped her hands behind her back. "So, what do you think?"

His frown confused her. "Are you still okay with a long-distance relationship? You'll be here in Arizona while I'm in California."

She swallowed, nervous. Was Matt having second thoughts? "If it's with the right person, then yes, of course."

"I'm not."

Disappointment ran ice cold in her veins. "I see."

She didn't, not really. Was Matt as cold-hearted as his aunt? Had he deceived her so thoroughly that she missed the telltale signs? Damn him.

"I can see the wheels turning in your head," he told her.

Dani hid behind a mental wall of frustration so that her vulnerability didn't show. "Oh, can you now? So you're a magician? Tell me what I'm thinking, then."

"How about I tell you what's on my mind?" He approached her, but she wasn't sure what he was up to.

Dani backed away, careful not to fall into the pool. "What's your game, Matt?"

He didn't answer, but he angled his movements in such a way that before she knew it, she was cornered against a wall with no easy way of dashing past him.

"No games, Dani. No tricks. I've had more than enough from Aunt Glenna." He propped his hands on either side of her, which cut off any chance of escape.

"Bloody hell, Matt, what do you want?" she demanded.

"You."

She bit her lip, looking into those brown eyes with flecks of gold. He seemed serious, and yet… "You said you didn't want a long-distance relationship."

"I don't."

Dani wanted to punch him and actually balled her fists. "Matt, I swear if you don't stop this nonsense…"

"It's not nonsense." He leaned down, ready to kiss her.

She should stop him. He didn't want to be with her, and yet here he was, all puckered up and waiting. Well, if he wasn't going to put the effort into staying together, she'd leave him with one last searing kiss that will make him think of her for a week.

She molded her mouth to his, wrapping her arms around his neck. His grip took her breath away as Matt mirrored her intensity with a kiss of his own that would have knocked her off her feet if he wasn't holding her. He groaned when she flicked her tongue over his lips, and delved into a taste that was uniquely his own.

Dani ran her hands through his thick silky hair, remembering its feel. Her hands came around to his face, and with a regretful sigh, she backed away.

Matt was breathing hard—good, that's what she had aimed for. "Why did you stop?" he asked, his voice hoarse.

She rolled her eyes. "We won't be doing this again, will we?"

"What are you talking—"

"You said you didn't want a long-distance relationship, remember? What's the point of…" She stopped, biting her tongue—she had said enough. "Just let me pass."

"I haven't told you what's on my mind," he whispered.

"Matt, don't aggravate me." Seriously, he was acting like

a jerk. She tried to dodge, but he blocked her way. "For cripes sake!"

"Can you just stop for one minute and let me talk to you?"

She crossed her arms. "I'm waiting."

He cocked a brow. "You know, Josh told me you were a handful. I can see his point."

"Bloody hell!" His smile told her he was teasing, but she ignored it. "What do you want to tell me?"

"Humph, with that attitude, I'm not sure I want to move to Arizona now."

It took several seconds for the words to register in her brain. "Wait, what did you just say?"

"You heard me." He stepped back. "I thought about moving to Arizona if you decided to live with your family here."

Okay, that was something she had not expected to hear. "Why would you do that?" she asked quietly.

"You mean other than the obvious? There's several advantages, such as more client opportunities, lower tax bracket." He winked. "No Aunt Glenna."

"That last point makes the best sense." She thought of something. "What about your current clients?"

"It's my business, remember? I can move it to wherever I want, and there's no time difference between the two states, which is a win all around."

Dani nodded. Matt was saying all the right things, yet...

He laughed. "Will you stop trying to put together a conspiracy theory? I think you took your James The-Spy role too seriously."

"James The-Spy always got the girl in the end."

Matt tsked. "He got a lot of girls in the end. I only want one."

Dani was finding it hard to breathe. "Saying lovely things like that might get me to do whatever you want, Mr. Bennett."

"Well, all right, Ms. Colton." He wrapped his arms around her. "Let's start with another kiss and see where it takes us."

* * * * *

COMING SOON!

We really hope you enjoyed reading this book. If you're looking for more romance be sure to head to the shops when new books are available on

Thursday 19th June

To see which titles are coming soon, please visit
millsandboon.co.uk/nextmonth

MILLS & BOON

OUT NOW!

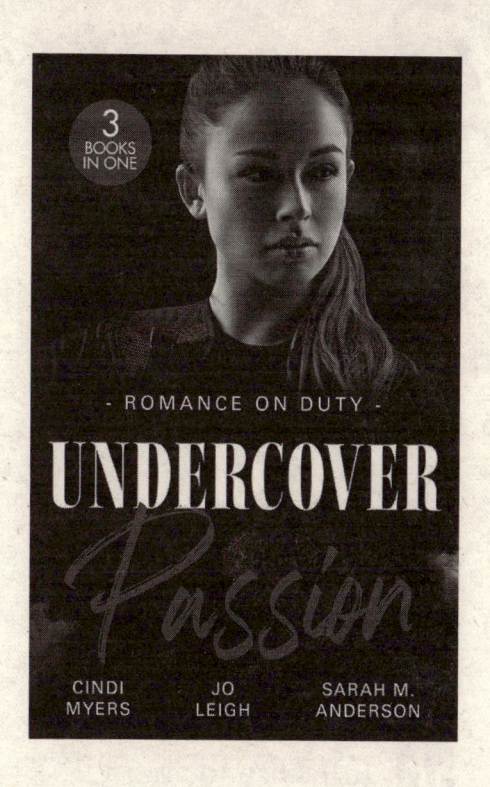

- ROMANCE ON DUTY -

UNDERCOVER
Passion

3 BOOKS IN ONE

CINDI MYERS JO LEIGH SARAH M. ANDERSON

Available at
millsandboon.co.uk

MILLS & BOON

LET'S TALK
Romance

For exclusive extracts, competitions and special offers, find us online:

- **f** MillsandBoon
- **X** @MillsandBoon
- **◉** @MillsandBoonUK
- **♪** @MillsandBoonUK

Get in touch on 01413 063 232

For all the latest titles coming soon, visit millsandboon.co.uk/nextmonth